Michelle Douglas has been writing for Mills & Boon since 2007, and believes she has the best job in the world. She lives in a leafy suburb of Newcastle, on Australia's east coast, with her own romantic hero, a house full of dust and books and an eclectic collection of sixties and seventies vinyl. She loves to hear from readers and can be contacted via her website: michelle-douglas.com

Christine Rimmer came to her profession the long way around. She tried everything from acting to teaching to telephone sales. Now she's finally found work that suits her perfectly. She insists she never had a problem keeping a job—she was merely gaining 'life experience' for her future as a novelist. Christine lives with her family in Oregon. Visit her at christinerimmer.com

Discover more at millsandboon.co.uk

REDEMPTION OF THE MAVERICK MILLIONAIRE

MICHELLE DOUGLAS

THEIR SECRET SUMMER FAMILY

CHRISTINE RIMMER

MILLS & BOON

First Published in Great Britain 2020
by Mills & Boon, an imprint of HarperCollinsPublishers,
1 London Bridge Street, London, SE1 9GF

Redemption Of The Maverick Millionaire © 2020 Michelle Douglas
Their Secret Summer Family © 2020 Christine Rimmer

ISBN: 978-0-263-27879-8

0520

MIX
Paper from
responsible sources
FSC™ C007454

This book is produced from independently certified FSC™
paper to ensure responsible forest management.

For more information visit: www.harpercollins.co.uk/green

Printed and bound in Spain
by CPI, Barcelona

REDEMPTION OF THE MAVERICK MILLIONAIRE

MICHELLE DOUGLAS

To the Lucas crowd, past and present—for the street parties, the chats over the front or back fences , the eggs, and the all-round general neighbourliness.

CHAPTER ONE

THE PHONE IN the top pocket of Damon Macy's pristine white business shirt vibrated. He pulled it out and gave it a cursory glance. A text with an email link and then a message. You need to read this.

What the hell was Clay thinking, sending him anything today? He slipped the phone back into his pocket. *Later*.

His phone vibrated again but he ignored it. Darrell, his driver, as if sensing his employer's impatience, glanced in the rear-view mirror. 'Your flight is on time, Mr Macy. We'll reach Sydney airport in another four minutes. There will be an airline official waiting to escort you to your seat.'

'Thank you, Darrell.'

His damn phone vibrated again. For pity's sake, Clay knew he was off to clinch one of the biggest deals of his career. He'd been working on this deal for a solid eight months. It would cement him and his company—Macy Holdings—in the big league for good. He had no time for distractions.

He pulled his phone out again.

YOU REALLY NEED TO READ THIS!!!!!!

He blinked at the capitals and the line of exclamation marks that followed. Clay wouldn't be contacting him now unless he thought Damon needed to know whatever that website link had to tell him. His best friend was always lecturing him that he needed to stop and smell the flowers, but he'd never undermine Damon's work or aspirations—he knew how important this deal was.

'You have two minutes, Clay,' he murmured, clicking on the link.

A newspaper headline loaded on his screen. He stared at it.

Mirror Glass Bay residents outraged at new development!

Every muscle stiffened.

Mirror Glass Bay?

She lived in Mirror Glass Bay. He leaned forward to read the newsprint more quickly. *She'd* moved there and had built an entirely new life for herself after he'd...

He pressed a hand to his forehead, acid burning in his gut as he pushed that thought away and scanned the article. There was no reference to an Eve Clark. Not that he expected one. She'd worked hard to maintain a low profile.

According to the article, a new luxury beachside resort was being built in Mirror Glass Bay—less than a seven-minute walk from her beachside motel. His knuckles whitened about his phone. A brand-spanking-new resort had the potential to destroy her business.

He tried to still the churning in his gut. He owed that woman. And here was an opportunity to finally make amends—an opportunity for which he'd been waiting four long years.

She said she never wanted to clap eyes on you again.

His heart pounded. Hard. As if it were punishing him for the choices he'd made four years ago. The edges of his vision darkened and it took three breaths before he could ease the vice-like grip that tried to crush his lungs.

He would never hurt her again. *Ever.* But she didn't have

to *clap eyes* on him—he could make sure that didn't happen. Regardless of how his every atom ached to catch the smallest glimpse of her.

'We're here, sir.'

He snapped to at Darrell's words. Owen, his VP, who had preceded him to the airport, had opened the car door and was waiting for his boss to emerge.

'Change of plan, Owen,' he said, exiting in one smooth movement, although internally things burned, rocked and crashed. Damon had learned early on never to reveal internal turmoil—a skill that had held him in good stead in the piranha-infested waters of the corporate world.

'Damon?'

'You're going to Frankfurt without me.'

Owen's mouth worked but no sound came out. With a visible effort, he reined in his shock. 'You are planning to be there, though? I mean—'

'Of course,' he cut in, irritable with his VP's shock, even though it was perfectly justified. 'This is nothing more than a minor delay.'

His second-in-command straightened with a nod, all brisk efficiency again. 'When will you arrive?'

Damon's mind flashed to the newspaper article. Greamsman Industries Pty Ltd was behind the development. His lips twisted. He and Kevin Greamsman had history. 'I'll aim to fly out tomorrow.' He bit back an oath. 'But in all likelihood I won't get away until Wednesday.' The timing couldn't be worse.

'Negotiations are expected to proceed the day we arrive.' Owen's colour came and went. 'Herr Mueller is going to be…disappointed.'

Herr Mueller would take it as a personal affront. They both knew that. 'Thank you for pointing out the obvious.'

His VP had the grace to look shamefaced.

'I'm not expecting you to perform miracles, Owen. Just

concentrate on smoothing things over as well as you can until I get there.'

'Got it,' the other man said with a lamentable lack of enthusiasm.

He forced a weary severity to his voice. 'This is what I pay you the big bucks for. If you're not up for it, there are at least five other candidates who'd snap my arm off for the opportunity, and—'

'I'm definitely up for it,' Owen assured him with what should've been gratifying haste. 'You took me by surprise, that's all.'

Damon had taken himself by surprise; he was risking eight months' worth of hard work.

You owe her.

'I'll take care of Herr Mueller. You have my word.'

He clapped his VP on the shoulder. 'Good man.'

Damon turned to the airline executive who stood waiting nearby. Until this moment, he'd never particularly regretted not owning his own private jet. It had always seemed such an unnecessary indulgence.

Until today.

He consoled himself with the thought that, if he closed this deal with Herr Mueller, he could buy a whole fleet of jets if he wanted.

'I need to get to Byron Bay. Can you organise a charter for me?'

The airline executive gave a nod, pulled a phone from her pocket and began making the arrangements.

'Is there anything I need to know?' Owen hesitated. 'About Byron Bay?'

Damon shook his head. 'This is personal, I'm afraid. Not business.'

'Roger.'

A moment later another airline official appeared and gestured for Owen to follow him. The two men said cursory farewells and Damon's steward led him to a private luxury lounge. 'We should have you in Byron Bay by four o'clock, Mr Macy.'

Damon glanced at his watch. That was nearly four hours away.

'Joshua at the bar will organise any refreshments that you need. Let him know what you want and if you require use of the business centre. In the meantime, can I get you a drink?'

'Coffee—hot, black and strong.' He hit speed dial for his PA's number. 'I'd appreciate it if Joshua could keep it coming.' He needed his wits sharp and honed. He pressed his phone to his ear. 'Philip, I need you to find out everything you can about the new Greamsman development that's about to start in Mirror Glass Bay. And I need it yesterday.'

'Onto it,' Philip said without hesitation.

'You want to what?'

Kevin Greamsman leaned across the table in the boardroom of one of Byron Bay's most exclusive hotels to stare at Damon with an exaggerated lift of his eyebrows.

Damon shifted his gaze from his competitor's face to the view out of the window. The boardroom boasted a comprehensive view of the coastline. Numerous travel magazines and tourist boards had voted Byron Bay one of the most beautiful beaches in the world. Damon stared out at it with impassive eyes. They were right—it was magnificent.

But he didn't care about the view. He cared about the deal.

He shifted back to Greamsman. 'I want to buy you out,' he repeated. Mirror Glass Bay was a thirty-minute drive from Byron Bay and, from all accounts, sleepy. Where Byron Bay thrived on tourism, Mirror Glass Bay was doing its best to preserve its 'off the beaten track' tranquillity. While apparently beautiful, Mirror Glass Bay lacked Byron's colour, sophistication and the ultra-hippy surf vibe that brought tourists flocking from all corners of the globe.

The older man's eyes narrowed. 'I don't like you, Demon, and I don't like your tactics. What do you know that I don't?'

He used the nickname many in the industry called Damon behind his back, but few had the courage to use it to his face. 'You don't have to like me, Greamsman. I keep telling you—this is business, not personal.'

Though he knew Greamsman wouldn't believe him. He was convinced Damon had used underhand tactics to win two recent government tenders. He no doubt now thought Damon had an inside track on some piece of news that would change the complexion of a development in Mirror Glass Bay in a more favourable way.

Rather than playing games or trying to field questions, he chose to be honest with the other man. 'I find myself becoming sentimental in my old age.' Old? He was only thirty-two, though most days he felt closer to sixty. 'I want to preserve Mirror Glass Bay's natural beauty, its sleepy nature. There's enough development and progress happening here in Byron and further north on the Gold Coast. It's not unreasonable for developers to be asked to leave some places unspoiled.'

'I don't believe you.'

But Greamsman's posture told Damon the opposite. It told him he did believe him and was trying to work out how to take advantage of it.

'I know how much you paid for the site. A little preliminary research shows me there are another two sites in the area that would meet the requirements of the luxury development you're planning. I'm prepared to offer you a fair price for the land.' He wrote a number down and pushed it across the table.

For a gut-wrenching moment he thought Kevin might push it back without even looking at it, shoot to his feet and tell him to go to the blazes just because he could. Damon had risen to the top for his ability to read people, and he could read that impulse clearly in the face of the man opposite. Kevin wanted to tell him that karma was a bitch; he wanted to march out of this boardroom feeling that he'd got the better of Damon.

But that warred with a second impulse—curiosity. When Kevin reached over to turn the slip of paper towards him, Damon knew curiosity had won out. The older man's eyebrows rose. 'This is actually a fair price.'

'I've already told you I'm not playing games.'

'And yet I find myself recalling the sting of having lost out on the container ship contract and find myself unmoved by this particular offer. Though, perhaps another two hundred thousand dollars might help.'

Damon had already factored that in—knowing Kevin would up the price—but he didn't betray that by so much as a flickering eyelash. 'I'm sure that could be arranged.'

'And I'm not signing that site over to you unless you sign a non-compete clause. I'm not handing over a piece of prime real estate just begging for development for you to then go and build your own luxury resort. I don't trust you, Demon.'

'You have yourself a deal, but only on the proviso you can have your man draw up the papers and send them to me for review before the close of business today,' he said, refusing to betray how much he hated that nickname.

Greamsman glanced to the man on his left, who nodded, before rising and sticking out his hand. 'Done. I'll meet you back here in the morning—nine on the dot—to sign the papers.'

Damon refused to let his satisfaction show. 'Till then.'

* * *

The papers were signed and the deal was done by nine-fifteen the next morning.

Kevin eased back, lacing his fingers over his stomach. 'You want to tell me what you're really up to now?'

Damon sipped the coffee Kevin had been good enough to provide, relishing the rich heat and full flavour. For the first time in two days he could finally taste something. Nerves had kept him screwed up too tight. He hadn't wanted to fail Eve. Not again.

Not that she'd ever know about this, of course.

He glanced out of the window at the beach and the sun, at the golden sand and an emerald sea. Would there be time to take a walk on the beach before he left, to dig his toes into the sand?

He shook off the thought. What was he thinking? He needed to get to Frankfurt without delay—had to try and salvage the situation with Herr Mueller who was, from all accounts, far from impressed.

'I had no hidden agenda. I told you the truth.'

'In that case, you should've waited another couple of days, Demon.'

The nickname made his back molars clench.

'Your haste surprised me. It was out of character. And you usually do far more due diligence before embarking on a deal of this magnitude.'

This deal had been far from usual, though, and the other man's words made his gut clench. What had he overlooked? Where had he gone wrong?

'I confess, I enjoyed taking advantage of your…reck-lessness.'

Kevin rubbed his hands together as if enjoying a great joke at Damon's expense. Ice tripped down Damon's back. What the hell had he missed?

'I can't say I'm sorry for it, though.' Kevin chortled

some more. 'Nothing personal, Demon, you understand? It's just business, right?'

Damon calmly sipped his coffee, though his stomach had started to rebel. 'Want to let me in on the joke?'

'That piece of prime real estate you just bought is about to be slapped with an environmental injunction. It appears that it's a breeding ground for some rare seabird. I was walking away from the project—was chalking it up to experience. Instead, I made a killing. At Demon Macy's expense, no less.' He slapped the table and let loose a belly laugh that had his second chin wobbling. 'You win some and you lose some—I believe that's what you said to me last time we did business. I have to say, it's a joy to see you on the losing side for once.'

The hard knot in Damon's stomach eased. 'I got what I came for, Kevin.' Mirror Glass Bay and Eve's business were safe, and he had every intention of keeping them that way. 'Now, if you'll excuse me, I have a plane to catch.'

He turned away to stash the papers he'd just signed into his briefcase when the door to the boardroom crashed open.

'Mr Greamsman,' a female voice said, cutting through the air. 'Is it true you've just pulled out of your resort development?'

A *familiar* female voice. Damon closed his eyes and bit back an oath. *Eve!* He hadn't meant for her to see him, or even to know he'd been here. He'd resisted every bitter impulse yesterday to turn his hire car in the direction of Mirror Glass Bay just to see the place she called home. It took all his strength now not to swing around and feast his eyes on her.

'You're well informed, Ms Clark. Let me introduce you to Damon Macy, who has just bought the development site. I'm afraid I'll be moving my operations elsewhere.'

Two beats passed. 'Damon… *Macy*?'

He counted to five to give her a chance to gather herself—*five, four, three, two...* He turned, met her gaze and froze.

She wasn't wearing make-up. It seemed the most inane of things to notice, but when she'd worked for Spellman and Spelman she'd never walked through the office doors, let alone attended a business meeting, without her armour, a full face of make-up. He didn't know what it meant.

He opened his mouth but snapped it shut again. What was he going to say—*you're not wearing make-up? Looking good, Evie? Can I kiss you?* All of them were totally inappropriate.

And her white-faced shock tore him to the centre of his being. He'd known she never wanted to see him again, but to be presented with such stark evidence made him feel physically sick.

Her familiarity, though, punched through him in a way he hadn't expected, rocking him to his foundations. He hadn't known he had anything left inside him that could still *want*. And he wanted her with a ferocity that had only increased in the four years since he'd last seen her.

He wanted to throw his head back and roar against the unfairness of it.

Only it wasn't unfair, was it? This woman had every reason to loathe him. And she did—he could see that in the endless depths of her green eyes—eyes the colour of sea glass. Some would call it poetic justice.

He'd call it hell. But it was a hell he deserved.

He swallowed and nodded. 'Hello, Eve.'

Greamsman glanced from one to the other, speculation rife in his eyes. 'You know each other?'

Her eyes turned hard and cold, her lips refusing to lift into anything even approximating a smile. '"Know" would be an exaggeration, Mr Greamsman.'

I thought I knew you, but I was wrong.

Her words from four years ago circled through his mind now. His temples started to throb.

'I once had the pleasure…' the word dripped with sarcasm '…of working with Mr Macy.'

'Ah, so you'll be aware of his business practices, then.'

That made his back stiffen. 'My business practices are completely above board. If they weren't, you'd have found a way to have my company brought before an industrial tribunal by now, Greamsman.'

'Perhaps, perhaps not,' the other man said. 'But your tactics…'

'Can leave a lot to be desired,' Eve finished, folding her arms.

'Well, my dear—'

'Don't call me your dear.' Cold eyes turned to his rival and Damon's spine unhitched a fraction with the relief of being released from their cold, penetrating knowingness and the accusation that flared in their depths.

'Yes, well,' Kevin blustered. 'If you'll excuse me, I have a plane to catch.' He gathered up his things before shooting Damon a malicious smile. 'Nothing personal, remember, Demon. Just business.'

Damon wanted to slam a fist into the other man's face— not for the smugness or his ridiculous game of one-upmanship but for continuing to call him that hideous nickname. The impulse made him suck in a breath. For the last four years he'd been incarcerated in some icy, contained world of his own. But one look at Eve had brought all those walls crashing down. Really?

He rolled his shoulders. It felt good, invigorating. Disturbing, too, but…he felt alive again. He straightened. When had he started to feel so dead inside?

He glanced at Eve as Greamsman and the lawyer left the room. She hated him, and he deserved her resentment, her censure, her mistrust—it was an undeniable truth. But he wanted to live again, to feel alive again. He was through with punishing himself. He'd done her the good turn she deserved. Now he was free to go to Frankfurt, do all he could to close the Mueller deal and then...

He lifted his chin. And then he'd take a holiday, walk on a beach somewhere and rethink his life...make some changes.

Her arms were still folded and the fingers of her right hand drummed against her left upper arm. She stuck out a hip and raised an eyebrow. He nodded. Before he could do any of that, he needed to deal with the here and now. 'I know you must hate me, Eve.'

She waved that away. 'Ancient history.'

He tried to gauge what was happening behind her eyes, but he couldn't. Had she really moved on so easily? A dark heaviness settled over him that he tried to shake off. He hoped she had.

'Is it true that you've bought the site from Greamsman?'

She didn't want to talk about the past. Her gaze was firmly fixed on the future—on her livelihood—as it should be. He pulled himself into straight lines and nodded. 'Yes.'

Her eyes didn't waver from his. That was one of the things he'd always loved about her—her unflinching strength.

'And what do you mean to do with it?'

The tightness in his chest started to drain away. Finally, he could give her something of worth. 'Absolutely nothing.'

She blinked as if his words made no sense.

'Mirror Glass Bay will retain its unspoilt character, preserved for generations to come as it should be. I know how special—'

'You're *not* going to build a big, shiny new resort on that spot?' she interrupted him.

'No, I'm not.' He waited for her shock to dissolve into relief...to dissolve into happiness. He didn't expect her to thank him, but one small smile didn't seem too much to ask for.

Her hands clenched and her face twisted. A breath shot out of her lungs and it seemed to leave her diminished, lesser…broken. 'What the hell did I ever do to you to deserve this? From you of all people!'

His mouth went dry. 'What are you talking about?'

She slammed a hand down to the table between them and eyed the pens, the bowls of mints and the coffee mugs as if she was trying to decide which of them to hurl at him first. 'Damn you, *Demon*.'

His jaw clenched so hard pain shot down his neck.

'Mirror Glass Bay *needed* that development.'

What the hell…?

'You *wanted* that development?'

'Yes!'

He took a step back, his veins freezing to ice. Damn it all to hell, how had he got this so wrong?

Eve fell into a seat at the board table and dropped her head to her hands. She'd promised everyone to do her best. *Think!* She had to find a way to fix this. She was an intelligent woman. Her hands clenched into fists at her temples. She should be able to fix this. If she could only get her mind to work.

Except her mind had downed tools at the first sight of Damon.

'Eve?'

Damon's hand came into view and she jerked away. 'Don't touch me!'

He pulled his hand back, his face going white and the lines about his mouth pinching as if he were fighting a spasm of pain. Maybe he had a bad back, or a raging migraine. She really hoped so.

Her reaction to him had never been measured, but the ferocity of her animosity now took her off guard. It was just…

She'd never expected to see him again.

She'd never *wanted* to see him again.

'You *wanted* the development to go through?' he repeated.

'Yes!' The word snapped out of her, full of fire and brimstone, but she couldn't seem to moderate her tone.

'But there was a newspaper article that said local residents were against it.'

She stood, her entire body starting to shake. 'Are you telling me your research of what the residents of Mirror Glass Bay wanted was based on one newspaper article?'

His Adam's apple bobbed as he swallowed. 'I researched the development.' His Adam's apple bobbed again. 'Thoroughly.'

'*One* newspaper article?' she repeated, refusing to let the strong column of his throat distract her.

'The development was slotted for a resort. For holidaymakers. It would've been in direct competition to your motel.'

But his voice wavered as he uttered the words, and she couldn't believe what she was hearing. Had he done no research on Mirror Glass Bay—on her gorgeous, quirky and utterly frustrating community—at all? 'Not in competition,' she managed through gritted teeth. 'We'd have attracted completely different clienteles. The people who come to stay in my motel would no sooner think of staying in a luxury resort than they would take annual trips to Europe.'

He dragged a hand down his face and swore.

'Why?' She tried not to shout the word. 'Why did you get involved at all? Why did you have to meddle?'

'I wanted to make amends.' His lips pressed into a straight, uncompromising line, but he'd lost his colour and it hadn't come back yet. He looked as if he might throw up.

She ignored the stupid skip of her heart, its stupid weakening. 'To you,' he croaked. 'I wanted to make amends to you. I wanted to help.'

She folded her arms across her chest so tightly they started to ache. She would *not* let his words warm her. She wouldn't even let herself believe them. 'If you wanted to help, why didn't you ask me first instead of going off half-cocked and ruining everything?'

He opened his mouth as if to protest but shut it again with a snap and a nod.

'Why couldn't you have left me alone? What the hell did I ever do to you to deserve…?'

She broke off, appalled at how heavily she breathed. It was as if she'd been running a race as hard and as fast as she could but still couldn't win…couldn't even seem to make it to the finish line. She hitched up her chin, desperately wanting to channel ice-cold composure. 'This has nothing to do with me, has it? It's about you wanting to allay a guilty conscience.'

'Maybe they're different sides of the same coin.'

'And maybe they're not. One is selfish and self-interested and the other isn't. We both know unselfishness isn't a trait you're known for.' She wanted to call him Demon again, but she didn't have the heart for it. 'Either way, looks like I'm the one having to pay the price. *Again.*'

'I can fix this, Eve.'

She didn't want him to. She wanted him out of her life for good. She never wanted to see him again.

Except…

She swallowed. It left her throat feeling bruised and sore. Except she'd promised her community, her friends, to do everything she could to make sure this resort went through. And she'd keep that promise, regardless of her animosity… regardless of the pain crushing her chest, as if seeing him now was breaking her heart all over again.

'I swear to you that I can fix this.' He sat at the table and pulled a pad and pen towards him. She remembered then how he'd always liked to brainstorm with pen and paper rather than being chained to his computer and a Word document.

She wrestled with her desire to walk out the door and not turn back. But in the end Mirror Glass Bay and her promise won out. She sat too.

He glanced across at her. He didn't smile, but she had to remind herself that the warmth in his eyes was not reflected in his heart. He'd given her no apology—not for then and not for now. Damon Macy took what he wanted, when he wanted, without apology. And without thought for how it might affect anyone else. She'd be a fool to forget it.

She sat, folded her arms and forced her spine to make contact with the back of the chair. She loathed Damon Macy and all he stood for, but she couldn't let her antipathy harm Mirror Glass Bay. If he really wanted to make amends, she intended to take full advantage of that. 'How will you fix it? Do you now plan to build that luxury resort?'

'I—' He broke off with a curse. 'I signed a non-compete clause. It was the only way I could get Greamsman to agree to the deal.'

Wow. His conscience must be making him feel really guilty. But then the meaning of his words hit her, and it was all she could do not to drop her head to her arms and cry. A non-compete clause meant Mirror Glass Bay could kiss goodbye to a luxury resort for good. The town needed an injection of capital. It needed development, jobs and infrastructure. Local government grants and initiatives were all given to Byron Bay, where the tourist dollar repaid it ten-fold. Mirror Glass Bay didn't aspire to those same standards. It just wanted a little piece of the pie—just enough to support a medical centre and to keep the tiny primary school open. It didn't seem too much to ask.

'Right.'

Damon straightened and the broad expanse of his shoulders squared, as if he were a superhero in a big-budget film getting ready for the fight of his life. It should've made her want to laugh in scorn and derision and call him unflattering names, such as *egotist* and *poseur*. No scorn or derision rose through her, though—at least, not any directed at him.

'I can build several state-of-the-art high-rises on that site—luxury apartments.' He tapped the pen against his mouth. 'As long as I can get the necessary planning permissions.'

She dismissed that with a single wave of her hand. 'And who will live in them? Sure, their construction and outfitting will bring jobs to the area, but it's a short-term solution. Once they're done...'

'I could make them short-term holiday lets.'

'Besides the fact that brings you dangerously close to contravening your non-compete clause...'

'I'd make them family friendly, not luxury, and—'

'In which case you'd be stealing from my client base.'

He cursed again and went back to jotting notes on his pad. 'What about a theme park?'

'What about you do some proper research into the area first and find out the kinds of tourists Mirror Glass Bay—and Byron Bay, for that matter—attract? That is, if you're serious about helping.'

His gaze lifted, his eyes dark and intense. 'I'm serious.'

He'd always been too serious. Though she'd been able to make him laugh, had managed to get him to loosen up—back in the old days. Her hands clenched. Until he'd thrown her over for two million dollars to advance his goddamned career. He'd thrown away everything they'd had for...

She folded her arms. It didn't look as though it had brought him any joy.

Which served him right.

But it didn't seem fair that his hair should be as dark and glossy as it had always been, his jaw just as square and strong or his shoulders as broad and appealing. It wasn't fair that his outside should be so compelling, could make a woman's stomach soften with longing, when inside his heart was black.

He leaned back in his seat, his chin lifting. 'What's wrong with my theme park idea?'

'What am I now—your research assistant?'

Mirror Glass Bay needs help! If this man...

She dragged in a breath, moderated her tone. 'How far are we from the Gold Coast?'

'No idea. Three or four hours?'

'An hour and fifteen minutes.'

If he really wanted to make amends—if he was sincere—then his heart couldn't be that black, could it?

Her lips twisted. Maybe it was just a really dirty charcoal-grey.

'What?' he said, his hand lifting, as if to check his hair.

She snapped back to their conversation. 'How many theme parks are there on the Gold Coast?'

She watched him count them off on his fingers. He held up three and raised an eyebrow.

'Five,' she told him. 'So, if families or singles wanted a theme-park holiday, why would they come to Mirror Glass Bay when they could go to the Gold Coast?'

'Because my theme park would be the best.'

He still had that same old arrogance, the same belief he could make things happen, and it tugged at some secret, hidden place inside her. And for the first time since she'd clapped eyes on him again she was scared rather than shocked and angry. Scared that he still had the power to hurt her.

She set her shoulders and did what she could to get her thumping heart back under control. That'd only happen if she let it. And there was no way on God's green she was going to let it happen. *Ever.* She gripped her hands in her lap to counter their trembling. 'What is Byron Bay known for?'

'An amazing beach. An amazing *surfing* beach,' he clarified. 'The town has always attracted surfers and backpackers.' His lips pursed. 'It's also considered a hub of new age and hippy culture. From what I saw yesterday, very briefly, there are a lot of yoga retreats and holistic wellness centres in the area.'

'And do you think the kind of people who are attracted to those things—who come to this part of the world to experience those things—are the kind of people interested in rollercoasters and water slides?'

His pen started up a quick and annoying *tap-tap-tap* against his pad. She wanted to reach across and halt it, only that'd betray the calm composure she was trying to maintain.

'You're right,' he said slowly.

Hallelujah.

Except...

She frowned. 'About what?'

'I *do* need to research the area. Properly.' His eyes narrowed at whatever he saw in her face. 'I *am* going to fix this, Eve. You'll see.'

She hoped to God he did. Her community needed it. And as for herself... 'As long as you don't expect me to pin a medal on your chest at the end of all this, clap you on the shoulder and tell you what a great guy you are.'

Because he wasn't a great guy. And she had no intention of forgetting it.

'Don't worry, Evie,' he drawled. 'I'm keeping my fantasies firmly grounded in reality.'

She had to glance away at the word 'fantasies'. It conjured up too much, and she'd lost too much to him last time. 'Eve,' she corrected. 'Only my friends are allowed to call me Evie.' It'd taken her too long to pick herself up and find some joy in life again after the last time. That peace had become precious to her, and she wasn't letting him disturb it again.

'There's just one thing I want from you, *Eve*.'

To stay out of his hair?

She turned back and raised an eyebrow, crossing her fingers in her lap.

'I need a place to stay. I need you to find me a room in that motel of yours.'

No!

She didn't want this man anywhere near her beloved town. Mirror Glass Bay had become her haven and refuge. It'd saved her. It'd given her a new direction. It'd given her *hope*. If Damon Macy came crashing into her life now…

She halted that thought dead in its tracks. Mirror Glass Bay needed Damon to undo the damage he'd just done. And if she could hold him the least bit accountable then she owed it to her community.

She forced her lips upwards. 'You're in luck. It's off-season so you can have the Kingfisher Suite. It's our best.' Though he'd be used to much finer these days. 'And I'll charge you through the nose for it.'

His low laugh vibrated in all her hidden secret places. 'I wouldn't expect anything less.'

CHAPTER TWO

EVE DID HER best to assume nonchalance as she led Damon into her pride and joy—the Mirror Glass Bay Beachside Motel—and tried to see it objectively, as if through his eyes.

Tried and failed. The task was impossible. She'd thrown herself into this project four years ago after the scales had been lifted from her eyes—revealing the reality about both Damon and the corporate world upon which she'd pinned all her youthful dreams. The ruthlessness of the former and the savagery of the latter had shattered every ideal she'd ever had about becoming a self-made woman. To her so far never-ending relief, she'd discovered she wanted no part of either. She had no regrets about walking away.

She and her grandmother had jumped into Eve's snazzy little hatchback and had headed north before her parents could shove Gran into a retirement home and forget all about her. The two of them had washed up here in Mirror Glass Bay, eight-and-a-half hours north of Sydney. They'd taken one look at the rundown motel and had glimpsed the future they'd wanted to create.

From the corner of her eye she watched Damon take in every detail. She and Gran had pooled their resources, bought the motel and spent the last four years bringing it back to its former glory. That didn't change the fact that

The Beachside, as it was affectionately known by the locals and its regulars, was nothing more than a three-star family motel.

A spick and span one.

A comfortable one.

A home-away-from-home one.

And a haven for Gran and her.

But a man like Damon wouldn't see any of that. Or, if he did, he wouldn't recognise its value. He'd simply see the lack of ostentation, the lack of five-star luxury, and that was his loss. She loved what she and Gran had achieved, and she refused to let the opinion of a man like Damon Macy belittle that achievement.

She nodded at her reception desk attendant. 'Bettina, this is Mr Damon Macy. He's going to be staying for...?' She turned to Damon and raised an eyebrow. 'For how long would you like to book the suite?'

One powerful shoulder lifted. 'What would you suggest?'

She'd like to suggest he take a hike so she never had to see his handsome face again, but there was too much at stake. And she could be big enough to put Mirror Glass Bay's needs above her own pettiness. *Right?*

She comforted herself with the notion of unearthing whatever better nature he had and taking advantage of it—for the greater good of her community, of course—before his ruthless business sense kicked in and he walked away, dusting off his hands and the challenge Mirror Glass Bay presented.

She kept her expectations within the realms of the possible, though. 'Shall we start with a three-night stay, then?' That would give the town committee the shadow of a chance to showcase the area to its best advantage. He'd at least get a taste for what the place had to offer.

'Do you really think three nights is long enough for me

to get a proper grasp of the unique issues Mirror Glass Bay faces?' he drawled, one eyebrow raised sardonically in enquiry, as if he could see through her mask of calm business composure and was mocking her for her lack of ambition—for not demanding more of him.

But she'd demanded more from him once before and he'd failed her. She had no faith left now.

'Absolutely not. A fortnight might do it justice. But I was keeping my expectations...*realistic*.' She smiled—oh, she made sure she smiled—but her words were laced with a poison that had Bettina's eyes widening.

She doubted Damon noticed, or cared about, Bettina's reaction. He angled his chin towards Eve and placed those long-fingered hands on his hips. 'Let your fantasies go wild, Eve. Ask for what you want. Who knows? You might even get it.'

She recalled a time when she'd have slipped her arms about his waist, tucked her head against his shoulder and relished all of that warm male strength. Her mouth dried and it took all her strength not to take a step away from him. His gaze lowered and she knew he could see the pulse in her throat hammering.

She hated that. Hated that she couldn't control her reaction. Hated that her body betrayed her. Hated that he knew it—*that* was what she hated most of all. She refused to let her chin drop. So what if he knew she wasn't as calm as she pretended to be? The one thing he couldn't be certain of was why.

And she had no intention of admitting that she found him every bit as thrilling and potently attractive as ever.

She swung back to Bettina. 'Book Mr Macy into the Kingfisher Suite for two weeks.'

He wouldn't stay for two weeks.

He handed his credit card over without a murmur.

She sent him a big, fake smile. 'You'll be pleased to

know that we're currently running a deal—stay five nights and get the sixth night free.'

'Absolutely delighted,' he returned, slotting his credit card back into its folder and slipping it into the inside pocket of his suit jacket. 'How…'

If he said *quaint* she might just have to hit him.

'Fortuitous. Some might even say auspicious.'

Smart man.

'Our usual clientele appreciates the chance to stay with us for as long as possible. We like to facilitate that whenever we can.'

'Very generous of you.'

She ignored his sarcasm and took the key from Bettina. 'We're a modest establishment but pride ourselves on our hospitality.' Another big, fake smile. 'We don't have any porters here, Damon, but I'm more than happy to carry your bag for you if you require it.'

He snapped back from his comprehensive perusal of the small motel reception to seize his bag. 'I'm happy to carry my own bag, thank you.' He gestured to the doors—one led left, one led right and there was the one behind them that led back to the street where they'd parked their cars. 'Lead the way.'

She took him through the left door and back outside, where she promptly ascended a set of stairs. 'This is the oldest part of the complex. It used to be a seaman's mission but was decommissioned fifty years ago and turned into a motel.'

When they reached the first floor, with its deep veranda that ran the length of the building, she gestured at the beach spread out before them. 'This is why people pay a few extra dollars a night for the rooms in this part of the motel.'

Because the beach was beautiful.

To their left a residential road perpendicular to the one they'd parked on ran parallel to the beach. To their right was nothing but sand dunes, beach and the headland. 'We parked our cars on Beach Road, and that one—' she gestured to the road that ran beside the beach '—is called Marine Drive. Both roads will bring you back to the motel.'

He didn't answer and she turned to find he'd stopped dead, his mouth agape. 'This is…'

'Rather pretty,' she agreed, deliberately minimising the impact of the view and setting a brisk pace along the wooden floorboards to the door at its very end.

'*Rather* pretty?' he spluttered as she unlocked his door.

She turned to survey the view again, moving to stand by the veranda railing, because it was easier than looking at him. How she loved this place. It fed her soul in ways she needed. She didn't want to imagine life away from here.

And she didn't have to, she told herself.

'You can see why our guests will snap up that extra night for free if they can.'

He'd dropped his bag and joined her at the railing. 'I—'

'But it lacks the grandeur of the main beach at Byron Bay. Or the views of Sydney Harbour from the Toaster,' she added, referring to an iconic luxury apartment complex on Circular Quay—which was probably where he lived these days.

'It has its own charm.'

He smelled of boardrooms—of printer ink, mints and air conditioning—but beneath it was a hint of spice that had her nose wrinkling in appreciation. 'On a good day the surf here can't be beaten, but it can also be uneven and… pernickety. Dedicated surfers prefer Byron. The headland, though, means it's a safe swimming beach. Young families love it.'

She couldn't have said why but the arrested expression on his face satisfied her.

She pointed away from the nearby headland and down

Marine Drive. 'Can you see the scrub at the far end of the road?'

'Yes.'

'That's what you just bought from Mr Greamsman. Beachfront land that abuts national park, which means the site is loaded with both charm…and potential.'

She didn't glance up into his face. She didn't want to see his expression. She had little belief, despite his protestations otherwise, that he would see any project there through. She'd do her best to convince him otherwise— she had to do at least that much. What was it Gran always said? *Where there's life, there's hope.* But she didn't believe Damon would deliver on his promise.

'And this is your room.' She swung away from the glorious view to open his door and motioned for him to precede her. For a moment she thought he might refuse, but then he seemed to recall his status as guest and hers as motel manager, and he strode through the doorway, lips pressed together in a thin line. She meant to make sure he didn't forget that distinction. She meant to preserve the boundary—all the boundaries: guest and worker, small businesswoman and wealthy developer, concerned citizen and potential saviour. Because that was all that mattered here. The fact that they had once been lovers was of no consequence.

Yeah, right. Tell yourself that enough, sunshine, and you might just start to believe it.

Not wanting to look into his face again—not wanting to see the dismissiveness she fully expected to see in his eyes as he inspected his accommodation—she motioned towards the coffee table with its small array of brochures. 'We do what it says in the fine print—provide comfortable accommodation. This is the bedroom.' She opened a door to the left and moved in to open the French doors leading back out to the veranda and those beach views.

When she turned, he was there, staring at her. She knew

he wasn't thinking of her as motel worker or small business-woman, but she refused to let her gaze, her attention or her fantasies dwell on the enormous king-sized bed. Instead she sailed back past him into the main living area where she swept the curtains aside to reveal a glass sliding door at the rear of the room that led out to a balcony. Opening the door, she let in a fresh breeze that swept through from the front doorway—a breeze scented with salt and sun. She closed her eyes and drew it into her lungs.

She felt him move towards her and she opened her eyes and lifted her chin. 'You'll get a better idea of the layout of the complex from out here.'

'The motel is more than the converted seaman's mission?'

She moved outside before he could reach her, letting the warm autumn air move across her skin. She gave what she really, *really* hoped was an expansive gesture. 'As you can now see for yourself.'

There was room for a small café-style table and chairs out here on the balcony, but he ignored them to rest his fore-arms against the wrought-iron railing and gaze out across at her complex.

'We parked on the road, but feel free to drive your hire car in and park it beneath one of the carports.' She gestured to where there was parking for a dozen cars. 'There's over-flow parking on the next block, but as it's not high season it's not in use at the moment.'

The driveway was located on the other side of Reception. She pointed. 'There's a one-bedroom flat above Reception, which is where I live.' On the other side of the driveway a white stucco building stretched away from them, facing the road, and she gestured to that next. 'That's the family accommodation over there.'

'So this is…?' He tapped the railing to indicate the build-ing they were in.

'More for couples and singles. The family accommodation is more budget-friendly, and has easy access to the pool and lawn area where children can play.' She gestured to the large green quadrangle in front of them with an in-ground pool at its centre. 'There are picnic tables down there, showers and a barbecue station.'

Palm trees dotted the area along with an enormous jacaranda, the fronds and branches waving happily in the breeze. Hibiscus bushes in flower added splashes of colour. Damon shook his head. 'This is…'

She told herself she didn't care what he thought, but rather than interrupt him she found herself holding her breath.

'Really nice,' he finished.

She might've taken offence at such an insipid word if he hadn't loaded it with so much wonder.

She shrugged. 'It's home.'

He straightened, rising to his full height, but she kept her gaze trained on the grounds below. 'The bottom floor of the north wing—' she gestured to the white building '—houses the restaurant-cum-breakfast room, cum-café and bar.' It was one of the few meeting places Mirror Glass Bay could boast, and the local residents took full advantage of it.

He gestured to the building directly opposite. 'Is that part of the complex too?'

She didn't blame him for asking. It was in another style entirely—three storeys of plain blond brick. 'Those are the longer-let apartments.' Her grandmother lived in one of the ground-floor ones and she made a mental note to keep her away from Damon.

'So…you cater to different styles of clientele?'

'Within reason. And there is some overlap.'

'How many rooms all up?'

'Sixteen here in The Mission. These are our premier rooms—large, generous, olde worlde.'

'And all boasting that amazing view.'

The view was key.

'We have thirty-two rooms of various sizes and configurations in the north wing. And there are a dozen apartments in that west wing. Some of those, though, are let to permanent residents.'

'Why did you choose this room for me?'

'Because it's the best.' She shrugged. 'And because of the view.' If she'd thought for a moment he'd stay for a fortnight, she'd have considered an apartment for him.

But she hadn't. And he wouldn't. So it was a moot point.

'So you have a beachside wing, a north wing and a west wing.'

'Which are, of course, terribly unimaginative names. This—' she tapped the balcony railing '—is affectionately referred to as The Mission. That—' she pointed to the white stucco building '—is the Shangri La. While the apartment block is called The Nest.'

He gestured to the south. 'And that?'

'Is a nature reserve and can't be built on.'

This odd jumble of buildings shouldn't work but it did. It held all the charm of a bygone era and he found himself responding to its warmth and promise.

She'd called it home. It felt like how home should feel.

He had an apartment on Sydney Harbour—not in the Toaster, but down on the waterfront. He had his own private jetty, but he didn't have a boat. The views were incredible, but he couldn't remember the last time he'd stepped out onto his jetty. It was considered one of the most enviable locations in the country, yet he had a growing suspicion that he didn't love it the way Eve loved her little one-bedroom flat above Reception.

He had everything a man could want—wealth, power, position—yet…

Yet none of it could plug the hole inside him.

The only time he'd ever felt whole was when he'd been with Eve. And he'd sacrificed that.

He glanced at her now. She'd grown her hair and it'd lightened almost to blonde in places. The colour could've come from a bottle…or from how much time she spent in the sun. He suspected the latter, considering the way she wore barely any make-up.

He remembered watching her in the mornings as she'd applied a full face of make-up. He'd always told her she didn't need any of it, that she was beautiful without it. She'd told him it was her uniform. At the time, the thought that he was the only one to see her as she truly was—her unmade self—had dazzled him.

Now it appeared she let everyone see her as she was, and he sensed she was the happier for it; happier in her own skin.

He let no one see him as he really was. The thought had him dragging a hand down his face.

'You look tired. I'll leave you to rest.'

'No!' The word fired out of him too fast and with too much force, taking him as much off-guard as it did her. She raised an eyebrow and his collar tightened about his throat. 'Have dinner with me tonight?'

The request slipped from him—soft and almost begging—and he held his breath.

Surprise flickered across her face, and what looked suspiciously like confusion, before she abruptly turned away to stride back into the living room with its big comfy-looking sofas at right angles to each other, its table for two and large antique desk. She'd made the room feel more welcoming than an entire team of designers had his Sydney apartment.

'I'm sorry, Damon, I have plans tonight.'

Though her tone told him that her answer would've been a blunt no even if she hadn't had plans.

Two things struck him at the same time then. She might've changed her hair, and she mightn't bother with make-up and business suits any more, but her shoulders still went tight when she was angry. And her eyes still held that same remote expression they always had whenever she held her anger in check. She wanted to tell him to go to hell, but something held her back. This development must mean a lot to her.

He swallowed. He'd promised to fix things. That didn't come with conditions. He'd fix this, somehow, whether she was pleasant to him or not. And that was what he should be turning his mind to—making amends, not having dinner with a woman who had no desire to dine with him or to revisit the past.

The second thing that hit him was, was she seeing someone? It was none of his business. *None.* Once in his head, though, the thought refused to let him go. His hands clenched. It was likely, though, wasn't it? At thirty-two, she was still young. And more beautiful than she'd ever been. Somewhere at the centre of his being a howl started up.

What the hell…?

'That wasn't meant to sound like a romantic overture.'
Liar.

'I just want to know more about Mirror Glass Bay, and you're in a position to tell me everything I need to know.'

'The answer is still *I'm busy.*'

Her shoulders remained tight and her eyes remote.

'We don't do room service at The Beachside, but you have tea- and coffee-making facilities in your room. And, as I mentioned before, there's a café-cum-restaurant and bar on the ground floor of the Shangri La. Breakfast, lunch and dinner are all served there. In addition to that, there's a block of shops on Marine Drive including a tiny supermarket, a takeaway, and a café. Remember—Marine Drive runs parallel to the beach, Beach Road runs perpendicular.'

She repeated her earlier directions as if unaware she'd had his full attention from the moment she'd stepped into that boardroom in Byron several hours ago.

She glanced at his business suit and shoes, and he could almost read the 'not suitable beachside attire' in her eyes, but she said nothing.

'I suggest you take your time to familiarise yourself with the town and what it has to offer the potential developer. Most afternoons, I can be found in Reception or the bar.'

It wasn't exactly an invitation, but he clutched the scrap like a lifeline.

'I hope your stay will be very pleasant.'

Then she was gone, and he found himself blinking in the sudden silence. He throbbed all over, as if he'd been hit by a bus, but that made no sense whatsoever.

He shook himself. What the hell was he doing? He needed to ring Owen…and the office. He needed to find out all he could about the environmental injunction on Greamsman's proposed development, pore over the development-control plan and find out all he could about Mirror Glass Bay pronto.

He was a man who made things happen. He had to find a solution and get the hell out of town ASAP because it was clear Eve didn't want to revisit their shared past. He had no right raking it all up and disturbing her peace.

He knew how much he'd hurt her.

Because he'd hurt himself too—just as much.

You didn't get over that kind of hurt overnight. But Eve had rebuilt her life. She'd moved on. He had no right dragging her back and causing her further havoc. He'd come here to help, not hurt her again.

He'd do everything he could to make sure that didn't

happen. Even if everything inside him hungered for a second chance with the only woman he'd ever loved.

Not going to happen.

And the sooner he got over it the better. For everyone.

Pulling out his phone, he started to punch in Owen's number, but caught a glimpse of ocean from his open door and paused mid-dial. That doorway full of sea and sun, the way the light danced and dazzled, had him pulling in a lungful of clean air.

It'd be the middle of the night in Europe. Not that consideration for time zones had stopped him in the past, but… The sun danced on the sea, glinting gold on the sand, and the breeze had everything pulsing with life and play. He pushed his phone back into his pocket and instead strode into his bedroom to retrieve his laptop.

The view from his bedroom's French doors was even better, and he kicked off his shoes, settled on the bed with four big pillows propped at his back and started to compose an email to his VP. *My plans have changed. Not coming to Frankfurt. Apologise to Herr Mueller and return to Australia on the next available flight.*

He went to hit Send but froze. He was being watched. Very slowly he raised his eyes to find a tabby cat standing in a patch of sun just outside the French doors, staring at him with tawny eyes.

Where on earth had it come from?

He blinked. It blinked.

He pulled in a breath and straightened.

It sat, its tail curling around itself in a neat circle.

Should he shoo it away? Ignore it? Was it Eve's cat? The thought made his heart beat harder. Maybe she had a boyfriend *and* a cat.

He rubbed the spot above his left eyebrow. 'Well, puss, while you're not wearing a collar, you look too well-fed to be a stray.'

As if his words were the encouragement it had been looking for, the cat bounded into his room like a dog and jumped up onto his bed with a meow.

What the...?

Before he thought better of it, he reached out and stroked a finger beneath the cat's jaw. A loud rumble of approval greeted him. 'I thought you cats were supposed to be aloof and grumpy.'

The tabby curled against Damon's thigh, its head bumping his hand for more attention. He chuckled. 'I've met your kind before—a con artist, a confidence trickster.'

He stroked the purring cat for several moments and then glanced back at his laptop. 'What am I going to do about Owen, puss? He's put an awful lot of work into the Mueller project.' He bit back a sigh. 'The thing is, though, Mueller isn't the kind of man who agrees to work with an underling.' Still, few people would consider the VP of Macy Holdings an underling.

He stared out at all that dancing blue sea. 'I could give him the go-ahead—tell him to give it his best shot if he wants to, I guess. If he thinks it's a lost cause, he can come home. But if he wants to try...?'

The cat's purr sounded throughout the room as Damon's fingers threaded through the soft fur. It wouldn't hurt to let Owen at least try. With a nod, he sent an email telling Owen to follow his instincts.

Next he rang his PA and told him to reschedule his meetings for the next three weeks, to pass them off to some of the senior executives.

His fingers hovered over the keyboard. He should get a comprehensive report on Mirror Glass Bay, but he couldn't stop his gaze from drifting back to the view of the beach. He closed his laptop with a decisive click. He could research that kind of stuff online tonight when he had nothing better to do except wonder what Eve's *plans* were.

He glanced at his suitcase. He'd packed suits and work-out clothes. That was it. With a sigh he changed into track-suit bottoms, a long-sleeved T-shirt and his trainers.

He paused at the sight of the cat curled up in the middle of the bed. 'I'm going out now, puss.'

It didn't move and he didn't have the heart to disturb it. This was probably the kind of place where people didn't need to lock their doors. He could probably leave one of the French doors open… He glanced at his laptop and shook his head. He couldn't risk it. Instead he left a saucer of water for the cat in case it got thirsty and let himself out of the door, locking it behind him.

A breeze ruffled his hair, its warmth taking him off-guard and reminding him he was eight hours north of Sydney—close to the border of tropical Queensland. In Sydney, people would be wrapping up as autumn took hold. But here he could wear short sleeves—if he had them. Maybe he'd get lucky and discover that Mirror Glass Bay boasted a clothing shop. Regardless, it was time to go and explore.

It took him four and a half minutes to reach the shops. The supermarket was also a post office and boasted a huge range of ice-creams. There were caps and a couple of sou-venir T-shirts, but that was it as far as clothing went. There was also a surf shop that looked like it sold swimwear—including designer board shorts and T-shirts. Except it was only open at the weekend. Ditto with the takeaway. And as it was only Tuesday…

A café sprawled on the corner of the next block. The concertina windows, all pushed wide open, flooded the place with light. He took a seat at the counter that ran the window's length and stared out at the beach.

Mirror Glass Bay was amazing…beautiful. He stared and stared. It was every boyhood dream he'd ever had about the beach and what he'd do with his life if he could ever get away from the dingy inner-city slum where he'd grown up. But, while the town might be a boyhood dream, there was nothing here other than the beach.

Were there any schools? What about doctors or a clinic? Did the town boast a sporting team of any kind? Who lived here—retirees? Singles and young couples? Families?

He pulled out his phone…no service. He shook it, but that didn't make a scrap of difference.

'We're in a black spot here, love,' a waitress said, bustling up. 'A block in either direction, and you can pick up service again, but here…' She trailed off, her shrug eloquent. 'What can I get for you?'

He glanced at the specials board. 'What would you recommend?'

'The fish tacos are particularly good,' she said without hesitation.

He ordered the fish tacos, and was about to add a long black coffee to his order, but glanced out at the beach, changed his mind and requested a glass of iced tea instead.

To his surprise, the place filled up around him. Where had all these people come from?

'Have you heard? Word's out that the resort has fallen through.'

His ears pricked up.

'Nah, mate, it'll be those darn environmentalists up to their old tricks again. What's the bet?'

'What—like them stupid sods who tried to stop that development on the other side of Byron for some rare orchid that had supposedly been found?' a third voice asked.

'Yeah, but turns out they'd planted it themselves to try and scare the developer off.'

'Fingers crossed our guy has more gumption than that.'

'So far all you've got is an unconfirmed rumour, Ron Seymour,' the waitress said, cutting through their chatter. 'I'll thank you not to go starting a panic just yet.'

'Evie Clark'll know,' someone said.

'We can ask her at the meeting tonight.'

A meeting?

Damon swung round on his stool to face the table behind. 'Excuse me, I couldn't help but overhear your conversation. Please allow me to introduce myself...'

CHAPTER THREE

EVE GLANCED UP from her phone and Beck's text message to watch yet another noisy group of Mirror Glass Bay residents stride into the school hall—the school they all desperately wanted to keep. She'd known there'd be more people than usual here tonight, but they'd exceeded her expectations. They'd had to set out more chairs. Twice. At this rate it would be standing room only soon.

Which suited her just fine, as koala conservation was a topic close to her heart. And that was what tonight's meeting was *officially* about. The town might be hopping with rumours, but she was going to make sure they stuck to the order of business first. General town gossip could take place afterwards over a cup of tea and a biscuit.

She glanced at the urn. They didn't have enough biscuits.

Huffing out a laugh, she shook her head. Biscuits didn't matter.

Her phone vibrated. She read the text and then stood and clapped her hands. 'Okay, everyone, Beck is running a bit late, so she's ordered me to start the meeting without her.' Beck Daniels was president of the Mirror Glass Bay Koala Conservation Group and also Parks and Wildlife's resident scientist. Eve was the group's treasurer.

'I'll leave it to her to update us on all of the most recent sightings, findings and numbers. The big thing on the agenda this month is the working bee we need to organise.

The southern and western boundaries of the koala sanctuary are being encroached upon by a variety of non-native plants. If they go unchecked, they'll run rampant through the reserve and overtake...'

She stopped dead when Damon sauntered into the hall with Ron Seymour and his team of carpenters.

What on earth...?

Damon had ditched the suit for a pair of cotton twill work shorts, a high-vis shirt and work boots. She swallowed and glanced away. She preferred a man in a suit.

She glanced back. *Liar.*

Thankfully the entire room had turned to stare or she might've become an object of rumour herself. She wiped damp palms down the front of her jeans.

Damon and his new friends took seats at the back of the hall and all heads swung back to her. What the heck? She might as well use the town's curiosity to her advantage.

Pulling in a breath, she pasted on a smile. 'I suspect most of you will have heard that we have a new developer in town. I will introduce Mr Macy just as soon as we've got through tonight's order of business. So...' she picked up her clipboard '...we need volunteers for the working bee this Saturday.'

So far they only had half a dozen names on the list. A few additional people raised their hands. She jotted the names down, biting back a sigh. 'A good turnout means we'll be done by lunch time. To sweeten the deal, The Beachside will be holding a sausage sizzle afterwards for all of the helpers.'

Damon immediately raised his hand. She tried to stop her eyebrows from shooting up. Did he know what he was volunteering for? Weeding a marshy scrub was mucky work. A murmur went around the room and slowly more hands were raised.

Beck, who'd been standing at the side door, came striding in now. She pointed a finger at the collective crowd. 'I know each and every one of you. If you don't show on Saturday, I'll be demanding an explanation.'

But she said it with a smile and a ripple of laughter went around the hall.

Eve sat as Beck gave her regular report on the small koala population. Thirty koalas currently resided in the Mirror Glass Bay sanctuary. She detailed reported sightings and warned motorists to drive slowly on the strip of road between Cockatoo Avenue and Dolphin Street, as it was the corridor some koalas were taking between pockets of swamp eucalyptus that was their only food source.

'And finally,' she said, 'our treasurer warns me that funds are running low. Our local veterinarians go above and beyond in providing their time and services free of charge, but the conservation group has to cover the costs of all medicines and equipment used. I'd appreciate it if everyone could start thinking about ways we could raise funds. We'll continue applying for whatever grants we can, but every dollar counts, and it'd be an enormous ecological loss if this koala population was to dwindle further. We'll discuss that at our next meeting.'

While Eve heard Beck's words, and agreed with them wholeheartedly, all her attention was focused on the back of the room. Her eyes resolutely looked forward, but she could feel Damon's physical presence in the room. Which was crazy. She told herself it was just her mind playing tricks. But the image of him in that work gear... Her mouth dried. He looked so capable, so competent, so...*hot*.

Stop it.

This had nothing to do with what he looked like. What he looked like should have no bearing on *anything*. Prince or troll, all that mattered was that he held the fate of the town in his hands.

'Thank you, everyone, for your interest. It's heartening to see so many people here.'

Beck's wryness had a smile tugging at Eve's lips. A glance at her watch confirmed it was the quickest meeting ever.

'Does that mean the meeting is officially over?' Ron called from the back.

'It does,' Beck confirmed with a nod.

Ron shot to his feet. 'Then I'd like to introduce Damon Macy to everyone who managed to get here tonight. Come on, mate.'

Eve, who'd started to rise to make the promised introduction, subsided back into her seat as Ron and Damon made their way to the front of the hall.

'Damon here has taken over the development site from that other guy, who for reasons of his own has done a bunk and hightailed it out of here. For legal reasons, Damon can't build a resort on that land, so what he wants from the folks here tonight are some ideas for what we'd like to see developed on that site.'

'A hospital…a modern medical centre…a retirement village!' someone shouted out.

'Shops,' a group of teenagers chimed in. 'Dress shops! Shoe shops! Jewellery shops!

'A business centre.'

'A function centre.'

The suggestions came thick and fast and Damon raised his hands for quiet as everyone started to speak at once. He looked totally at ease in his work gear, which shouldn't have surprised her. He'd never had any trouble commanding the attention of a boardroom. But he must have lackeys to do this kind of on-the-ground reconnaissance for him these days.

Still, it couldn't be denied that when he raised his hands everyone quietened down and waited. Unexpectedly he grinned, and as his gaze roved about the room she was sure that more than one female heart fluttered.

Not hers, though. Oh, no, not hers. She folded her arms and willed steel to her spine.

'First of all, I want to say how pleased I am to meet you all.'

He sounded as if he meant every word.

He's a liar. Don't forget he's a liar.

'I'm impressed already at the number of ideas that have been thrown into the ring. I wish my PR people could be as quick on the uptake with ideas as you have all been.'

Yeah, well, evidently his PR people weren't as motivated as the people in this room. Their town was in danger of becoming a ghost town—a place without amenities. Her stomach screwed up tight.

'But I'm feeling a tad guilty about hijacking the Koala Conservation Group's meeting. So how about we brainstorm a few fundraising ideas for them first?'

She blinked. She couldn't think of a single darn thing to say. Which was fine, as nothing was expected of her, but...

He smiled down at her, his mouth lifting into an amused curve, as if he was fully aware of her confusion. 'So here's an idea I've had off the top of my head—how about an auction? This town has a lot to offer, right?'

Of course, it did. Suggesting otherwise would get him lynched.

A variety of yeses sounded around the room.

'How about auctioning off a variety of services and goods that the people of Mirror Glass Bay can provide to showcase the town's talent and—?'

'Who to?' someone shouted out. 'Who would come other than other Mirror Glass Bay folk? We already know what's on offer in town, so what's the point?'

'Pull your head in, Jeff,' Ron said.

'No, it's a fair criticism.' Damon tapped a finger against

his lips as he strode up and down the front of the room. Everyone held their breath as they watched. Even Eve.

We're all fools, she told herself.

'I can get my PR people to spread the word, but we need something to tempt those from further afield.' He straightened. 'We could make a night of it. We could have a dance. I'll organise a headline band to draw the crowd in if Eve Clark will agree to donate the bar and restaurant at The Beachside as the venue.'

'Absolutely,' she agreed without hesitation.

People started shouting out things they'd donate for the auction—handmade candles and soaps, a pest inspection from the pest controllers. The freelance bookkeeper offered a free tax return…the local seamstress offered garment-mending and alterations.

'We might need your clipboard,' Damon said with a smile to Eve and Beck.

Beck handed the clipboard to Eve. 'You better take the lead on this.'

'Why?' The other woman rarely took a back seat. Beck was a doer. She loved being in the thick of things.

'I'll explain later.'

There was no time to probe her further. Eve joined Damon and Ron on the floor, jotting down the services and products offered. The variety was wonderful—from babysitting to professional photographs, house cleaning to barbecue cleaning, and from free computer training to free websites. Eve offered up a two-night stay at The Beachside.

She read the list out loud, shaking her head when she reached the end. 'This is amazing.' She glanced at Damon. 'It was a nice idea.'

A nice idea? It was a *great* idea.

He shrugged. 'Only because the entire town has got behind it.'

She glanced around the room, because it was far less

confronting and much less confusing than looking at Damon. Why was he doing this? Why was he taking such an interest in Mirror Glass Bay and its doings?

The answer came swiftly. Money, of course. He'd want his investment here to make him money. The far from romantic reality of financial returns had her straightening and the fog in her mind lifting. For as long as he was here, they could take advantage of it. The Koala Conservation Group needed every penny it could get.

As if he sensed her scepticism, he turned to her and one side of his mouth hooked up. 'Do we want to set a date for our auction?'

Beck nodded and mouthed an exaggeratedly urgent, *'Yes.'*

Eve had to fight the sudden urge to hit Damon over the head with her clipboard. Her frustration made no sense—he was doing good, albeit for reasons of his own.

She swallowed. The frustration came from the past she'd thought she'd left behind four long years ago.

He can't hurt you any more.

That was true. But his lack of interest could hurt Mirror Glass Bay.

She moistened her lips, her senses sharpening. The Damon she'd once known had never been able to resist a challenge. She lifted her chin and stuck out a hip. 'How long do you need to find a suitable band and book them in?'

A spark fired to life in the back of his eyes at her thinly veiled challenge. 'I can move fast. I'm a man who makes things happen.'

'Oh, really?' She folded her arms, pressing the clipboard to her chest. 'Then how does six weeks this Saturday sound?'

It sounded impossible to her. He'd be gone before this current week was out. And there was no way he'd still be here in six weeks.

We don't need him. We just need his band.

'Done.'

He had to be joking! She lifted her chin even higher. 'If you can get a quality band in that time, then that sounds perfect to me. What does everybody else think?'

Shouts of assent sounded all around them and the date was locked in.

Damon's smile encompassed the entire room. 'I see this is a town that makes things happen. I'm proud I get to work with people who are so committed. Right.' He clapped his hands. 'Now that I've allayed my guilt about hijacking the meeting, we can return to some development ideas. I like what you've come up with so far, and I'll definitely be looking into several of those ideas, but I'd like to hear more.'

More ideas were touted—from manufacturing and boat-building to a yoga retreat and day spa.

'What about a research facility?' Beck finally said. 'One that could run educational programmes on the local wildlife, review dune rehabilitation…consider ways to protect and enhance the koala population?'

'Nice try, Beck.' Eve shook her head. 'Damon's an investor, not a philanthropist.'

Beck stood, her eyes turning serious and her mouth growing grim. 'I'm sorry, folks, but I need to throw a proverbial spanner in the works. Before I say anything more, just remember I'm the messenger here, not the decision maker.'

She looked as if she were facing a firing squad. Eve touched her friend's elbow. 'Beck?'

'I'm speaking now as employee of National Parks and Wildlife. An environmental protection order has been placed on Damon's development site. Evidence has emerged that it could be the nesting ground of the white-bellied storm petrel—a vulnerable species. I'm sorry, everyone, but until further investigation takes place all development will be stalled.'

Eve swung to Damon and the expression on his face had her sucking in a breath. He'd known!

But…it made no sense. 'That's the reason Greamsman walked away?' The question burst from her, but she didn't care.

He nodded.

But then that meant… 'Why didn't you mention it earlier?' He'd inherited *a mess*.

'Because I didn't have all the facts. I still don't.' He squared his shoulders and met her gaze. 'I promised I'd make this right, Eve. And I'm going to keep that promise.'

She knew then that the money meant nothing to him.

That was the precise moment Eve finally believed him. It was also the first time she looked at him properly, as if she really saw him. She looked him full in the face with those clear green eyes, her gaze not veering from his, and his world tilted.

It didn't just tilt but went whirling off its axis.

He wanted to swear, and swear some more, as the meeting finished up and dissolved around him. People carried the chairs to the back of the room and stacked them in neat rows. He helped and said goodbye to people as they called goodbye to him. But all the while his mind raced.

When he'd betrayed Eve four years ago, he'd broken his own heart. He'd known that was what he was doing at the time, but it hadn't stopped him from choosing his career over her.

If he stayed here, he'd be in danger of breaking his heart again.

His mouth dried and his heart pumped so hard he could barely draw breath. His immediate instinct was to flee. To get the hell out of Dodge before he managed to annihilate all of his hard-won peace of mind.

Peace of mind?

Ha! He didn't have any of that. He didn't deserve any of that. But he'd learned to live with what he'd done. To open that wound again...

His hands clenched. If he could make things right now, though...? Maybe then he'd earn a measure of peace. He craved that—a sense of redemption—it was an ache in his soul.

Eve and Beck continued to talk, their heads close together. He put Beck at around fifty, but she'd seemed to age twenty years when she'd told the assembled meeting about the environmental protection order. The fate of the town mattered to her as much as it did to everyone else who'd attended tonight. Eve said something that made Beck laugh and lifted some of the weight from the older woman's shoulders.

He swore again—softly, under his breath. Eve had always done that. She'd always been focused on her work. She'd always been fiercely clever, ridiculously quick, and yet she'd been shockingly kind. She'd always taken the time to make her colleagues feel good about themselves, had done what she could to help reduce everyone's stress levels. At Spellman and Spelman's her team had been the happiest.

He couldn't get the hell out of Dodge—and it had nothing to do with earning some peace. He'd promised to help fix this problem—he'd promised to help her town. She hadn't asked him to—hadn't demanded it of him. But he'd made that promise just the same. And he wasn't breaking another promise to Eve. He wasn't breaking a promise to a woman who had never broken hers.

Eve and Beck hugged, and then Eve strode towards him. He wasn't a hundred per cent sure why, but he found himself straightening.

'Are you heading back to The Beachside?' she asked.

He nodded.

'Then we might as well keep each other company.'

He fell into step beside her as they walked the two blocks back to the motel. She didn't speak, so he remained silent too.

'Did you want a drink?' she asked abruptly, just as he thought she'd head inside to the bright lights of the bar and bid him goodnight.

'Sure.'

'Scotch?'

She remembered? 'Please.'

She led him up to the bar. 'Hey, Cass, this is Damon Macy. Damon, this is Cassidy Evans, my bar and restaurant manager, right-hand woman and best friend.'

'Pleased to meet you,' he said.

Cassidy was a tall, bronzed brunette—utterly gorgeous—and his stomach clenched at the look she sent him. She didn't return his greeting, just gave a curt nod in his general direction.

She knew.

She knew about his and Eve's history. Acid coated his tongue.

'Two Scotches, please, Cassidy. The good stuff.'

'I'll make them doubles, shall I?' She nodded down the other end of the bar where a group sat nursing beers. 'I heard about the meeting.'

'Good news travels fast,' he said.

The brunette shot him a glare that should've shrivelled him. 'As does the bad.'

He didn't need to be a rocket scientist to know which category she filed him under.

Eve took their tumblers and led the way to a small table at the far end of the room that had a view of the street outside. He couldn't see the beach from here, but he could hear it and smell it from the open windows.

'Cold?' Eve asked.

He shook his head. 'It's mild here compared to Sydney.' He sipped his Scotch. 'Your friend Cassidy knows about our past.' He didn't mean the words to sound accusatory, and they weren't. At least, he didn't think they were, but they held an edge he wished he could temper.

'There are two people here who know our history. Cassidy is one and my grandmother is the other. Neither are going to be big fans of yours.' She sent him one of those piercing glances that had always cut through the nonsense and got to the heart of a matter. 'And if that bugs you then you should take more care not to do things that make you ashamed of yourself.'

He didn't answer that. What was there to say? She had no idea how much he regretted—*hated*—what he'd done. But, even if she did, it wasn't her job to ease his guilt and make him feel better.

'Sorry.' She glanced away. 'That was uncalled for.'

Hell, now she was feeling guilty!

He opened his mouth to tell her to forget it, but a couple of late diners left, shouting out a farewell to Eve before they exited into the night. Eve smiled and waved, and the moment was lost.

He watched them go and then turned back to her, a frown growing. 'Everyone knows you. In four years, you've become part of the fabric of this town—necessary, vital...' *Loved.* 'How'd you do that? I thought it took something like twenty years before you started being considered a local in a small town like this.'

Her lips pulled up into a genuine grin, rather than one of the practised smiles she'd so far reserved for him. It made his heart quicken. 'My grandmother grew up here. She moved when she married, but she brought me here for summer holidays when I was little. So I was practically a local before I bought The Beachside.'

She sipped her drink and then gestured at him. 'Where'd you get the gear?'

It was his turn to smile. He'd become so accustomed to suits, he'd forgotten how good it felt to get around in casual clothes. He told her about meeting Ron and his crew at the café, and how they'd taken him to the industrial site on the outskirts of town, from where he'd been able to buy work clothes from the factory outlet. In return for their time, he'd helped out with their current kitchen renovation job.

She stared at him. 'You spent the afternoon helping fit out Elsie Hitchcock's kitchen?'

The afternoon had been surprisingly enjoyable. 'I need to learn what issues are affecting the town. And Ron and his crew seemed as good a place to start as any. They certainly didn't pull their punches.'

Just for a moment, her eyes danced. 'Ron also wouldn't have minded showcasing his team's carpentry skills to the guy who's just bought the Greamsman site.'

'I told him off the bat what the deal was.' He hadn't wanted to take advantage of the other men.

'He'd have appreciated that. Which is why he dragged you to the meeting tonight.'

'And got word out to all and sundry to turn up if they could.'

She pursed her lips, her brow furrowing. 'I didn't know you had building skills.'

He stared into his Scotch, swirling the liquid around. 'I worked on building sites to help fund my university studies.'

He'd once thought it'd be kind of cool to renovate some old, run-down house and make it his home. But he hadn't bought that kind of house. Instead he'd bought an apartment in mint condition. He shoved the thought away. He didn't have time to play around with hammers, saws and power tools.

He crashed back to find Eve staring at him. He wasn't sure what she'd seen in his face, but he thrust out his jaw, rebelling against the sense of vulnerability that threatened to swamp him. 'I didn't know you had a grandmother who used to take you to the beach in summer.'

'I guess we didn't really know each other very well at all, did we?' she shot back.

Her mouth had never been particularly wide, and her lips weren't particularly full and generous. She didn't have a perfectly formed Cupid's bow. But he'd once told her that her mouth was the prettiest thing he'd ever seen. He still thought so. And, as he stared at it now, an ache stretched through him. She was wrong. They'd known each other in all the ways that had counted. But he didn't say that out loud. He had a feeling it would hurt her. And he had no intention of doing or saying anything that would cause her pain.

'So...' She straightened and sipped more Scotch, moderating her tone. 'What did you learn from your foray into local affairs?'

He eased back. She wasn't quizzing him for the fun of it, or to mock him. She was starting to believe he was serious in his intentions, and he wasn't screwing this up. 'Ron and his wife have two kids and one car, which is Ron's dual cab utility.'

'Yep.'

'If the primary school closes, the kids will have to catch a school bus into Byron Bay.'

'Thousands of kids catch school buses every day.'

'But if one of the kids gets sick, or has an accident at school, Ron is going to have to down tools to go and collect them.'

'Or his wife will have to take his work vehicle for the hour-long round trip. Or she finds someone in Mirror Glass

Bay who can drive her there, or from whom she can borrow a car.'

'You think that's reasonable?' he demanded.

'Or they buy a second car.'

'They want neither the expense nor the environmental impact of a second car. At the moment she can race down the end of the road and walk her kid home.'

Eve didn't say a word.

'One of the other guys and his wife have his father living with them. Her parents live in Mirror Glass Bay too. The two of them are constantly juggling their timetables around taking them to an endless round of doctor appointments. But if the local clinic was to close they'd have to add an hour to their schedules to take them into Byron Bay for their appointments instead.' He shook his head. It'd make things that much more difficult for them. And those two men weren't the exception.

'They also mentioned that there's not much for local teenagers to do—there aren't many casual or part-time jobs for high-school-age kids, and even fewer full-time jobs for those who've finished school. Most are leaving town when they finish school and aren't coming back. And those who do stay are developing drug and alcohol issues.'

She nodded and he bit back a sigh. He'd hoped the men had been exaggerating but evidently they hadn't been. 'All of them were concerned about what the future held for their children.'

'Mirror Glass Bay is in danger of spiralling into obscurity and losing its amenities, and the whole town is desperate to stop it. If the primary school and clinic close, despite making it harder for those who live here it'll also discourage young families from settling here. That in turn will have a knock-on effect. Tradesmen like Ron will need to go further and further afield for work. It means businesses like mine will hire fewer and fewer people in the off season. It might only be viable to keep the bar and restaurant open in the summer.'

He glanced around. If the Mirror Glass Bay community lost this… He stiffened. 'All of those things combined would make the town too hard for people to live in. In some cases, people would have to sell up and move elsewhere.'

'Exactly.'

'And yet this place is their home.' He'd never really had a place like that. 'They love it.' *She* loved it.

'Which makes it all the more difficult to bear.'

He recalled her tone when she'd described the motel earlier. 'It's home,' she'd said. Would she have to leave if that downward spiral she'd described continued?

His hands clenched and unclenched. He'd bet she'd valiantly struggle on until her grandmother passed—and by then The Beachside would be worth next to nothing. She'd have lost her grandmother and her business. Resolution solidified in his gut. He wasn't letting that happen.

'We'll find a way to stop the decline. We'll find a way to reinvigorate your town, Eve, I promise.'

'Which brings me to the reason I asked you to join me for a drink.'

She had a plan?

He leaned towards her, all ears. 'Yes?'

'I believe I owe you an apology.'

CHAPTER FOUR

EVE COULD SCARCELY believe she'd said the words, could scarcely believe she meant them.

His brow furrowed. 'I find that highly unlikely.'

Yeah, she did too. She forced herself to look him full in the face, because she refused to be a coward about this. 'I didn't think you meant what you said.'

'That I'd help fix my mistake?'

She nodded. She'd be in danger of falling for the warmth in those clear brown eyes if she didn't know better.

But she did know better.

She pulled herself back into line. 'But it wasn't your mistake, was it? You had no control over that environmental protection order. You could've told me about it this morning and moved on...like Greamsman did.'

His head rocked back. 'You think I'm like Greamsman?'

That bugged him?

'I'm not talking on a personal level. I've no idea if Greamsman is a barrel of laughs in his personal life or a sourpuss—whether he's faithful to his wife or if he yells at his kids. I don't even know if he is married and has kids. But in terms of what you do in your work lives you're two peas in a pod. It's the bottom line that matters, it's making money that matters.'

She had no idea why her words should make him pale.

In the world he came from, it wasn't just a truth but a compliment.

'I mean, you're both very good at it,' she offered belatedly, realising she'd left that key point out, but she'd have thought it was self-evident.

He didn't say anything so she soldiered on.

'But you've made an exception here…because of me.'

He sipped his Scotch but maintained eye contact with her the entire time.

'Because you feel bad about what happened four years ago.'

'You think I shouldn't feel bad?'

He should be burning in hell for what he'd done, but she didn't say that out loud. Mirror Glass Bay needed this man. And she needed Mirror Glass Bay. If he hadn't stepped in when he had, this town would be back to square one… without resources.

Instead they now had the renowned Damon Macy on their side. *That* was the pertinent fact and the one she needed to focus on.

Four years ago, Damon had taken his two million dollars and in a bold move had invested it in a little-known start-up that had taken the world by storm. He'd sold that stock for ten times the price he'd paid for it. His two million had become a cool twenty million, allowing him to strike out on his own and form Macy Holdings. *That* was the kind of business brain Mirror Glass Bay now had access to.

It meant maybe—just maybe—they could salvage something from this mess. She wasn't asking for miracles. She just wanted to stop her town from sliding into an irrevocable decline.

'Every day for the last four years I've regretted what I did to you, Eve.'

She eased back and did what she could to stop her eyebrows from shooting up towards her hairline. 'What? You'd change what you did—undo it?'

He hesitated, and she counted three beats of her pulse before he nodded. 'Yes.'

She believed he felt bad for what he'd done. But she didn't believe he'd undo the past. She didn't believe he was sorry, regardless of what he told himself.

But, when a girl got down to brass tacks, what did it matter? She rested her elbows on the table. 'I'm going to tell you something shocking.'

His lips twisted. 'That you'd rather see Mirror Glass Bay slide into the sea than ever accept my help or have anything to do with me again, right?'

'Wow. *No!' What on earth...?* 'You want me to ask Cassidy to bring the whole bottle over—' she gestured to his glass '—so you can carry on sliding into some black hole of misery?'

He straightened. 'That wasn't what you were going to say?'

Nope. No siree. 'Let's be clear. I have every intention of taking advantage of your sense of guilt. I'm going to pressure you every way I know how to help my town. I've no intention of letting hurt pride, indignation or moral outrage stand in the way of what you can do here to help.'

She was pleased to see some of the darkness recede from his eyes.

No, not pleased. She rolled her shoulders. Relieved. That was all. She wasn't getting dragged back into this man's orbit—not on a personal level, where she would start to care if he was happy or not. *That* was none of her business. And she wanted to keep it that way.'

'So the shocking thing you wanted to tell me...?'

She set her shoulders. They'd deal with this and then move on. 'You did me a favour, Damon—four years ago. I'm happier now with this life—' she gestured around the restaurant and her motel '—than I'd have ever been as a high flyer in the corporate world. I love Mirror Glass Bay more than I ever loved Sydney. So you need to think again if you imagine I've spent the last four years believing my life is over, that I lost the Holy Grail and that I've settled for some lesser, second-best life. That's simply not true.'

Not that she ever expected him to understand that or appreciate the life she had now.

One long finger circled the rim of his Scotch glass. There was something magnetic, almost hypnotic, about it, reminding her of the way those fingers—and hands—had made her body come alive. Making love with him had been a transformative experience for her. And one that had never been repeated.

For him their love-making had just been a means to an end. And that still hurt four years later. But that wasn't what they were talking about. And she couldn't let her mind go there.

'You're saying I did you a favour?'

He didn't believe her. She could see it in his eyes. 'I'm saying you taught me a hard lesson.' She'd realised that she was nowhere near ruthless enough to survive in the world of finance. More to the point, she hadn't been the slightest bit interested in training herself to become that ruthless. 'The things I learnt from that lesson, the changes I decided to make to my life, have greatly increased my happiness.'

He leaned towards her. 'You're saying we're square?'

Nope, not at all. 'You did a reprehensible thing, and in doing it you deliberately broke my heart. Where do you draw the moral line on that? It's not a course of action I could condone then, and it's not one I could condone now. I'm glad you feel bad about it because it means, somewhere inside, you still have a conscience and a heart.'

Her words made him pale, but she refused to feel bad about that. 'In doing what you did, though, it forced me to look at my own choices. I realised that being some prominent and sought-after financial adviser—a high flyer with the world at my feet—wasn't what I wanted.'

He frowned and opened his mouth to speak, but she cut him off. 'I haven't regretted that decision for a single moment. *That's* what I want you to realise. *That's* what I want you to understand. So, whatever else you feel guilty about, whatever else you're beating yourself up for, you can strike that off your list.'

He stared at her from beneath hooded eyes. 'You really mean that?'

He didn't understand, but he believed her, and that was enough. He opened his mouth and again she cut him off. 'I don't want to talk about the past any more, Damon. I don't want or need to revisit it.' She didn't want to hear about how bad he felt about it. It wasn't her job to make him feel better. 'I only want to focus on the here and now and the problem at hand—how to stop Mirror Glass Bay from figuratively sliding into the sea.'

He dragged a hand down his face. 'Right.'

'Deal?' she persisted. She wanted him clear on that fact. No more discussion about their past.

Eventually he nodded. 'Do you want to shake on it?'

No. And yes. She hadn't touched him yet and she had to know. She held out her hand and he enclosed it briefly in his. The touch was short, perfunctory.

But, damn it all to hell!

She reclaimed her hand—unhurried, careful not to betray herself. She'd always had a good poker face, but she had to draw on all her vast reserves to keep it in place now. She wrapped her hand around her glass, praying it would help to cool the rush of heat that had sparked through her veins at his touch. So…that same old pull still existed, then. *Brilliant. Just brilliant.*

She tossed her head. Well, fine. She simply needed to

make sure they didn't touch again. *Ever*. End of story. His touch had always tempted her to wildness, had broken down her everyday guard. She couldn't let that happen if she was to survive working with him now.

She glanced at him, recognised the tightening of his jaw and her pulse went erratic. He felt it too, then—that old pull—and that didn't help. Neither one of them wanted this thing between them.

She pulled in a shaky breath. They were adults. They could ignore it.

And as an adult she could still apologise—which was what she'd been trying to do before this trip down memory lane had hijacked them. She refused to focus on the fact that he still hadn't apologised for what he'd done four years ago, even though he'd said he felt bad about it. Not once had he ever said, *I'm really sorry for what I did to you, Eve.*

Well—she squared her shoulders—she could do better than that. 'I'm sorry I didn't believe you when you said you wanted to help. It's clear that you're sincere.'

He waved her apology away. 'If you'd been forewarned that I was getting involved... And if I hadn't stumbled in, in all my glorious arrogance, thinking I had all the answers... But I did, and you rightly called me on it. I don't blame you for your scepticism, Eve. But...'

The expression in his eyes stopped her heart. 'But?'

'But you're prepared to work with me now?'

'To save Mirror Glass Bay? You bet.'

'Then I suppose the first thing we need to do is find out what kind of environmental evaluation is being done on the site, and for how long it's likely to halt work. And then discover what kind of development is more likely to be looked upon with a favourable eye. Ron and his team were telling me about some "mad hippies"—their term— who've been causing trouble, planting fake evidence and the like. If that's what has happened here, then it'll delay the development but it won't railroad it.'

True, but…

'Beck looked worried, which makes me think there's more to this.' The older woman wanted to reinvigorate the town as much as Eve did. But she wouldn't do it at the expense of the local habitat. 'But even if it is true, and that's a storm petrel breeding ground out there, it's possible that the protection order could be downgraded to a conservation order instead.'

Which would allow development at a prescribed distance from the breeding ground.

'In which case we could build…'

'A conference centre?' she suggested.

He pursed his lips and nodded. 'Weddings are a big business in Byron.'

She glanced up, surprised. He'd familiarised himself with the views of individual locals in an attempt to understand their needs and concerns. He'd attended a town meeting and, it must be said, had come up with an excellent fundraising idea; and he'd also found the time to do some research. She'd forgotten his energy. Not his drive and ambition—she remembered those vividly—but she'd forgotten exactly how much he could cram into an eight- or ten-hour day.

He tapped his fingers against his glass. 'A convention centre has definite potential. I'm looking for a place to run staff retreats. Mirror Glass Bay would be perfect.'

'Really?'

'Yep.'

Once word got out, especially given his connections, then a convention centre's success would be assured. She sucked in a breath. A convention centre would be…*perfect*.

'It won't bring in as much money or as much work as a fancy resort.'

'But it'll help. Like I said, we don't need anything crazy or over the top. We just need...*something*.' She gestured to his now empty glass. 'Would you like another?' When he shook his head, she tried to force her heart from beating so hard. 'What do you have planned for the morning?'

'Nothing yet.'

'Then I propose we go and take a good look at that parcel of land you just bought.' She forced the suggestion out before she could change her mind.

'Excellent plan.'

She gathered up the glasses and stood. 'It's time for me to grab some shut-eye. I'll see you tomorrow...around nine?'

He rose and pointed. 'Here?'

'Or Reception.'

He bade her goodnight and she took their glasses to the bar and waved goodnight to Cassidy, before letting herself out of the same doors as Damon had. They led out into the internal quadrangle with its gardens and she ambled for several yards, relishing the stillness of a quiet night.

'Dolores?' she called out softly. 'Come on, Dolly, where are you?'

'Who's Dolores?'

She whipped round to find Damon sitting at one of the picnic tables.

'Sorry, I didn't mean to startle you. I stopped to admire the sky.'

She glanced upward automatically. The night sky was amazing here. It had mesmerised her when she'd first arrived too.

A loud meow carried on the still night air. Eve lifted a finger. 'That's Dolores—my cat.' She peered into the darkness, which admittedly wasn't all that dark, given the safety lights in the garden and the light from the moon and the stars. 'Where are you, Dolly?'

Another two meows and she finally located her. She was on the balcony of Damon's room. Eve planted her hands on her hips. 'What are you doing up there, miss?' Had she snuck into Damon's room and inadvertently been locked in? She'd be starving!

'I...uh...'

Damon came to stand beside her. The smell of the boardroom had started to dissolve, replaced instead with the scent of cotton and soap, the leather of his steel-capped work boots and salt-scented breezes. A definite improvement.

He gestured to his balcony. 'That's my fault. She came to visit earlier and curled up on my bed for a nap. I didn't have the heart to wake her. I left a dish of water for her. When I got home again in the afternoon she didn't seem inclined to leave. I left all the doors open, but...'

'You didn't think to pick her up and put her out?'

One shoulder lifted. 'It seemed a bit mean.'

She blinked.

'I went to that little supermarket and bought her a tin of tuna.'

He'd fed her cat? This man, who was considered a corporate shark in boardroom negotiations, hadn't had the heart to put her cat outside? And had then gone out of his way to buy a can of tuna to feed said cat?

'The company's been nice,' he muttered.

She tried to hold back a smile. 'Well, I'm afraid whether you enjoy her company or not you're now stuck with her for the duration of your stay. She will refuse to budge—especially if you keep feeding her tuna.'

'You won't mind?'

'Absolutely not.' She turned to face him fully. 'But we have one golden rule where Dolores is concerned. She's fifteen, which is old in cat years. She spends most of her time sleeping in the sun. But she's still a cat with a cat's instincts. We keep her indoors at night—there's too much nocturnal wildlife she can hunt and harm.'

'Okay.'

'She'll test your limits—meow and make a fuss.'

'I promise to keep her in. I won't let her out till the morning.'

'And if she isn't in your room one night you need to let someone know—me or Cassidy—so we can hunt for her. We inherited Dolores with the motel and she divides her time between my grandmother's unit, Cassidy's place and my place.' She pointed to her unit above Reception.

Just for a moment, their gazes caught and clung. His gaze lowered to her lips and a low thrum started up inside her. Temptation swelled. It'd be so easy...

No!

She reefed her gaze away but forced her legs to hold firm. With a deep breath she met his gaze again—forced her eyes to narrow and pulled her lips into unsmiling lines.

'I want to make this clear, Damon. We're not revisiting the past in any way, shape or form. It's probably not something that needs stating—' like hell it wasn't '—but I want us crystal-clear on that point.'

He took a step back. 'Absolutely! I would never...'

He shook his head, his nostrils flaring, and then he smiled, but she sensed the effort it cost him.

'Eve, I appreciate your frankness. It's always wise for a woman to set boundaries she's comfortable with. I promise not to overstep them.'

Good, she told herself. That was...*good*.

She edged away from him, feeling the magnetic pull of the man but determined to ignore it—determined he shouldn't become aware of her weakness. She had no idea if he'd exploit it, and she had no intention of finding out. But as she walked away she found a smile touching her lips.

Hot damn!

The man had fed the cat. He evidently had a weakness or two of his own.

Damon was ready and waiting on the dot of nine outside Reception the next morning.

Inside Eve exchanged a couple of words with her receptionist and then joined him. She wore jeans, hiking boots and a long-sleeved shirt. Everything was covered, as if she were trying to hide her body from view. His gut clenched. She'd made it clear last night that she wasn't interested in him. Was she worried he wouldn't keep his word?

With one comprehensive sweep of her eyes, she raked him up and down, and his gut clenched in an entirely different way. 'Are you wearing sunscreen?' she demanded without preamble.

It took a moment for her words to penetrate the fog surrounding his brain, but when they did he wanted to laugh. Not a mirthful belly laugh, but a scornful laugh, directed solely at his own over-inflated sense of self. Her covering up had nothing to do with him. If yesterday hadn't proved beyond all doubt that she'd moved on from the events of four years ago, then this moment now hammered another nail in the coffin of his vanity.

'Slathered in the stuff,' he assured her. He'd spent the last four years in a hell of his own making, while she...

She'd chalked it up to experience and moved on.

'Bug spray?' she asked.

He shook his head. Insect repellent hadn't occurred to him. In Sydney the mosquitoes and flies were only a problem in summer.

She disappeared back into Reception, emerging a moment later to toss him a small tube of cream. 'We have wetland areas around here, and when you combine that with the warm autumn weather...'

She didn't want him getting eaten alive by bugs. It was only a little thing, but he'd take whatever crumbs she offered. And, if that made him pathetic, he didn't care.

'Thanks.' He applied the stuff and then put the tube in the pocket of his cargo shorts in case they should need more later.

Surveyors had pegged out the perimeter of the site with wooden stakes and plastic tape, while an access road ran through the middle of the fourteen-hectare site. The southern boundary shared a border with residential homes. To the west and north it bordered National Park, and to the east it had direct access to the beach.

Eve planted her hands on her hips and turned a slow circle. 'This is such a great location.'

Her jeans fitted her like a glove and it made this mouth go dry. He forced his gaze away, chiding himself for noticing. 'It's a *pretty* location,' he corrected. 'It's only going to be great if we can develop it.' He kept his gaze trained on the land. 'If you were a white-bellied storm petrel, where would you make a nest?'

'They're seabirds so…near the water, but protected from the strong winds we can get here, I guess. What do you think?'

He nodded. It sounded like she'd read the same research articles he had.

They started in the north-eastern corner and worked their way westwards. Nothing. They swept back again. They kept that up for an hour. Eventually he pulled to a halt. 'Look, Greamsman was about to start clearing the lot, right? That means he'd have already been granted DA approval, which means someone from the local council had to have come out here to assess the site.'

'Unless he bent the rules…paid someone off.'

It happened, but it was risky. Greamsman had a ruthless streak a mile wide, but he wasn't an idiot. 'Let's say it was assessed and that nothing was found. If the nesting ground is just outside my boundaries, that would still impact on what I can do with the site, right? I could still be slapped with a stop-work notice while further investigations were carried out.'

They started scouting through the National Park to the north. And found Beck. 'I had a feeling I might see you two out here today,' she said by way of greeting.

'Have you found anything?' Eve asked. She wore a cap that shaded her face, but he saw the way her gaze sharpened beneath its brim.

'Come with me.'

He fell into step behind both women when Beck gestured for them to follow her.

'Here,' she said, gesturing around. 'I've found a dozen nests in total so far, but I think there'll be more. From what I can tell, though, these are the ones closest to your boundary.'

He glanced back the way they'd come. 'So…in all likelihood this'll mean a conservation order rather than a protection order.' That would mean, within certain parameters, he could still develop the site.

'As long as you can guarantee a generous green corridor on your northern boundary.'

He pulled the site plans from his pocket. He and Eve consulted them, pointing out likely new perimeters for any building work.

'That's not all I found.' Beck heaved out a sigh. 'There's also evidence of a small squirrel-glider colony here.' She pointed to a spot on his western boundary.

'Which is great news for the squirrel glider,' Eve said glumly.

'Because we love our native fauna and want to protect it where we can,' Beck said just as glumly.

'But our convention centre is becoming smaller and smaller,' he finished for them.

'But not impossible, right?'

Eve bit her lip, worry darkening her eyes. In that moment Damon swore again to make this right somehow. He injected confidence into his voice. 'Not impossible at all.'

The thing was, if he really wanted to shore up this town's viability he was going to need more than a single-pronged approach.

'What? You're looking worried. What's wrong?'

Eve's questions hurtled him back with a thump. He shook his head. 'Nothing. Just thinking.' He turned to Beck. 'You'll get your report in ASAP?'

She nodded.

'In the meantime, I'm going to contact an architect I know. He's making a name for himself with his environmentally sympathetic designs. By the time he gets back to me with some ideas, the relevant authorities should have rubber-stamped the necessary covenants and lifted the temporary embargo.' Especially if he lit a fire under the necessary authorities. 'Once that happens, building can start.'

'My vote is still for the research centre,' Beck grumbled.

Eve patted her on the shoulder. 'Keep trying, Beck. Keep lobbying for all the government grants you can, and petitioning universities. You'll get your research centre one day.'

They left Beck to her inspection and started back towards the motel. 'What did you mean by that?'

She pulled her cap off and ran a hand through her hair, the blonde highlights glinting in the autumn sunshine. Everything about her breathed warmth and vigour. Just walking beside her made him feel happier, more content, more relaxed than he'd felt in...

Not just four years but *forever*.

'Beck has been petitioning Parks and Wildlife, local

council and state government for years to set up a research centre here, and it sounds as if her case is starting to grow. Not only do we have an isolated koala population, but now a squirrel-glider colony and a white-bellied storm petrel breeding ground.'

A research centre made sense.

He glanced at his watch. 'Are you busy for the next hour or so? I have a guy coming from Byron Bay to show me around some of the warehouses in the industrial estate.'

She glanced up so quickly, her gaze so intent, he nearly stumbled. 'Why?'

They halted beside his car and he widened his stance, trying to regain his balance, forcing himself to focus on what mattered to her—and that *wasn't* his physical reaction.

'Okay, full disclosure here.' He pulled in a breath. 'I think it's wise to have a back-up plan. Mirror Glass Bay should *not* be relying on your motel and my hypothetical conference centre for its continuing financial viability.'

He punctuated each point with a stabbing finger, then realised he might be coming across as too intense and pulled his hand back to his side. 'What if your motel burns down? What if an even better conference centre gets built nearby, or people decide beach weddings are passé, or—'

'Or there's another down-turn in the market.' She sighed. 'I have no idea what potential these warehouses hold, but I figure it can't hurt to look. And two heads are better than one.'

'Especially when they're our heads.' Her lips twisted, almost in self-mockery. 'You have an inside track into the corporate world while I've got the skinny on the local community.'

Her eyes suddenly gleamed and he sensed her mind racing the way it used to in the old days, whenever she'd discovered an exciting new investment opportunity. Was she really no longer interested in the financial markets or following stock and futures prices? She'd said that she was happy with her life now and he had no reason to disbelieve her. But it didn't stop him from wondering.

The tour of the five empty premises that were located between the small work-gear clothing factory, with its tiny outlet, a panel beaters and the rural fire brigade quarters ranged in size from a huge site, that could be turned to any number of uses, to a small office block and everything in between. After their inspection, he and Eve hunkered down at a picnic table in the gardens of The Beachside with their laptops, the local newspapers and some sandwiches. Best office ever.

'Right,' he said after forty solid minutes of research. 'I'm dreaming big. I want this guy to build his boats here.'

He swung his laptop round, and her mouth fell open, not in surprise but in chagrin. 'Hot damn. Really? It'd be a hell of a coup.'

She then turned her laptop towards him. 'This is what I was thinking. Craft beer is huge at the moment—and cider.'

She had a list of equipment needed and the specifications required for such an operation, as well as the names of all the local brewers.

He tapped a finger against the table top. 'How are we going to do this?' They could cold call these guys or...

'Your ship-building guy is having a huge party at his house in Byron Bay a week Saturday.' She flipped over the pages of the local paper and pointed to an article in the social pages.

Perfect.

'I'll find a way to get us in.'

CHAPTER FIVE

EVE FASTENED THE leg rope of her board around her ankle and headed straight into the surf. At 7:00 a.m., the beach was utter perfection. The sun had slipped above the horizon, painting the sea gold and orange, and, untouched by even a breath of breeze, the water looked like satin. Out the back a perfect swell built to curling sets of breakers that would allow her to practise her rail-to-rail surfing and bottom turns to her heart's content.

She waved to another couple of riders—evenly spaced and too far away to drop in on each other. They waved back, no one shouting out a greeting, no one wanting to break the spell of the morning quiet.

It was nearly June—nearly winter in the southern hemisphere—but the water temperature was twenty-four degrees Celsius. Some mornings she wanted to weep with gratitude and happiness.

She caught waves and tried to lose herself to the magical sensation of being buoyed by a force so much greater than herself, one that could never wholly be predicted.

But the same concerns, and the same face, that had kept her tossing and turning for the last three nights kept intruding into her thoughts. She'd manage to push those thoughts from her mind and catch a wave, only to have them reappear a moment later when paddling back out to catch the next wave.

Exhausting.

She was tempted to head back in, but sheer bloody-mindedness had her determined to stay at her usual morning post for her traditional forty minutes.

She sat on her board and glanced around, and something inside her settled. *This* was the life she loved. She didn't want to be anywhere else. She loved Mirror Glass Bay. She loved her motel. She loved her community.

And yet none of that changed the fact that when she'd been scouring the paper and Internet for local investment opportunities two days ago something had come alive inside her. She'd loved rising to that challenge. She scrubbed both hands back over her hair. It didn't mean she wanted to return to the corporate world, though. She couldn't think of anything worse. And that was the truth.

She caught a wave to shore and, with her board tucked under her arm, walked up the beach to where she'd left her towel. Young Pru—a local youngster Eve had befriended and taken under her wing...or had *tried* to take under her wing—was sitting on it, but she leapt up to hand it over as Eve approached.

Eve's heart started to pound when she saw who sat beside Pru.

Damon.

He stared at her and his jaw dropped. 'That was *you* out there?'

Pru grinned, taking a seat on the sand. 'I knew he thought you were a guy, so I just let him keep thinking it.'

She forced herself to laugh. Damon had been watching her surf? She was glad she hadn't known that when she'd been out there.

'You...you rat!' Damon feigned outrage. But then he grinned and shook his head, glancing back at Eve. 'You're really good.'

A man's praise shouldn't warm her. It shouldn't matter.

It *didn't* matter.

'I didn't know you surfed.'

'Eve learned when she was a kid—my age—but she was pretty crap when she first came here.'

That made her laugh for real. 'Thank you, Pru.'

'Yeah, but you know you're really, *really* good now.'

The wistfulness that crossed the young girl's face made Eve's heart burn. So much about Pru made her heart burn. 'Hot chocs up at The Beachside?'

Damon blinked but followed them into the café section of the motel. A waitress came bustling up with three steaming mugs of hot chocolate. Eve watched Damon wrestle with his curiosity—he wanted to ask questions, lots of questions—and she was almost proud of him when he bit them back and just watched, submitting to taking events as they came. It'd be an alien concept for him.

'You should auction surfing lessons at the fundraiser,' Pru said. 'I'd bid on them. I have thirty-eight dollars and fifty cents. Do you think that'd be enough?'

'As I expect you'd be the only bidder, it should be more than enough.'

The smile dropped from Pru's face. 'Except I don't have a board, so it wouldn't matter even if I was the highest bidder.'

'We'd find a way around that—we could borrow one.' Pru's face lit up again. Eve nearly offered to give her lessons for free but managed to stop herself at the last minute. 'You really think I should auction off lessons?'

Pru nodded vehemently. Damon watched them both with a still intensity she found impossible to ignore and that sent her pulse fluttering in the strangest way.

'All right, then. I'll do it.'

Pru gave a cheer.

'You know,' Damon said, 'it occurs to me that we should

run a raffle in conjunction with the auction. And Pru has hit on the perfect prize—a surfboard. What do you think?'

Pru's eyes went wide. 'I'd buy a ticket. And Mum would too.'

He grimaced. 'I'd need some help choosing the right surfboard, though. I know nothing about surfing. While you...' he addressed Pru '...know everything.'

'You want *me* to help you choose the surfboard?'

'You and Eve.'

'We'd be delighted to, wouldn't we, Pru?' Eve said promptly, even though not twenty minutes ago she'd been reminding herself to spend less time with Damon, not more.

Pru nodded, her eyes shining as she finished her hot chocolate. She glanced at the clock on the wall and wrinkled her nose. 'I've gotta go to school now. Bye.'

They waved the young girl off.

'What's the deal with her?' Damon asked once she was out of earshot. 'She seems lonely. Reminded me of myself as a kid.'

Had Damon had a lonely childhood? He hadn't talked much about it four years ago—had always deflected her questions. She'd always thought he'd tell her more once they'd been together a bit longer—that she'd earn his trust. She'd been prepared to wait. But things hadn't turned out the way she'd thought they would.

She pushed the thought away.

'Pru is what my gran's generation called a latchkey kid. Her mum is a single mother and is working three part-time jobs just to make ends meet. She's a nice woman but she's doing it tough. She doesn't spend anywhere near enough time with her daughter as either one of them would like.'

'And she can't afford to buy her daughter a surfboard.'

'Nope.' She glanced at him and then swiped her finger through what remained of her hot-chocolate foam and stuck it in her mouth. 'You know you can't rig that raffle, Damon. You can't make sure that she wins the surfboard.'

'But if she buys a ticket she's in with a chance, right?'

A slim one. She was swiping her finger through more foam when he suddenly leaned across the table, pinning her with merciless eyes.

'Why didn't you offer to give her surf lessons for free? That seems like the kind of thing that should happen in a place like this.'

Was he disappointed in her? The thought bemused her.

'It took me weeks to talk her into having a hot chocolate with me, and she only does it because I told her there's no one else to talk to about surfing—or that everyone here is too busy to have a drink with me in the mornings. I once asked her if she'd like to have some breakfast. I didn't see her for a week after that.'

He sat back and she popped her finger in her mouth. His gaze immediately darted away and her stomach started to churn. She pushed her mug aside.

'Pru is insanely sensitive when it comes to anything she thinks might be charity. Which is why you can't buy her a surfboard.'

His lips thinned into a grim line and he gave a hard nod. 'It's not uncommon among poor kids. They don't have anything except their pride.'

'Were you and your family poor when you were growing up?' She couldn't believe the question had slipped out, but there was something in his face. And it might help to explain why he'd sold her down the river. It might explain why success was so important to him.

Her spine suddenly stiffened. What was she doing? His answer didn't matter. It changed nothing.

'Sorry, don't answer that. It's none of my business.'

'We were dirt poor,' he said. 'My mum was a single

mother too until she married my stepfather when I was fourteen. Things got easier after that.'

She stared at him. It was more than he'd ever told her in those few months when they'd been seeing each other. She wanted to get up and walk away—she didn't want to hear his story—but she didn't have it in her to be that rude, that heartless. And it would be heartless. He had shadows in his eyes—she had no intention of asking about them, but she couldn't leave him alone with them.

'Considering your humble beginnings, you certainly reached exalted heights. You must be pleased with all you've achieved.'

She didn't ask him if his parents were proud of him because she knew how complicated family could be. She didn't ask him if he was proud of himself because he'd stomped on her on his way up that ladder of success—and she didn't want to hear him admit that he thought it had been a worthwhile thing to do.

'My success makes me feel safe in a way I never felt as a kid.'

Her chest burned. Her temples started to throb.

'Your family were very different.'

She nodded. 'I was lucky. My parents were both professionals—very successful. I'm not talking Vaucluse area of Sydney kind of money, here, but I grew up in a beachside suburb in Sydney. I could walk to the beach.'

'"Successful"?' His lips twisted. 'Isn't that code for never being at home because they were always at work?'

The latent sympathy beneath his words had her gripping her empty mug too tight. She loosened her grasp and eased back in her chair. 'Don't go putting me in the same category as you and Pru. My parents might not have spent much time with me.' It was hard to understand why they'd ever had a child. 'But there was plenty of money for surf lessons, surfboards, dance classes and the best university money could buy. Money does make a difference—a big difference. I entered the workforce debt free and with all of my ideals intact.' Back then she been completely unaware of her own privilege.

'With the weight of your parents' expectations on your shoulders, no doubt. It was why you were so determined to prove yourself at Spellman and Spelman wasn't it?'

'What does any of that matter now?'

He searched her face. She concentrated on keeping her expression smooth and unruffled. 'It doesn't,' he finally said.

'Whichever way you look at it, my route to Spellman and Spelman was easier than yours. And my childhood was easier than Pru's as well. I had my grandma and my school friends. I wasn't lonely as a kid.'

He leaned forward, intense again. 'Pru doesn't have school friends?'

Her heart chugged, burned and did things she had a feeling it'd be better to not understand. 'It's a small school. The kids are generally pretty good to each other. But Pru's two best friends left last year—their parents had to move for work.'

His fingers drummed against the table. 'It all comes back to revitalising the town.' His gaze sharpened. 'These are reasons it matters so much to you.'

She fought the automatic roll of her eyes and a sarcastic, *Duh!* 'Yes.'

His lips twitched, as if he'd read that struggle. 'Then you'll be pleased to know that I've managed to get us on the guest list to the Sorensen party.'

She straightened. Simon Sorensen was a yacht-building tycoon. 'How did you manage that?'

'Saturday, seven p.m., black tie. You in?'

'Yes!' She wouldn't get such access to so many local business people and wheeler-dealers again. She didn't know how Damon had managed it, what strings he'd pulled, but she'd be an idiot to knock back an opportunity like this. 'I better dust off one of my old frocks.' She stretched her neck first one way and then the other. 'You wouldn't happen to know who else is on the guest list?'

'Of course I do. I'll email the list to you.' He stood. 'I'll talk to you later, Eve.'

Cassidy came up the moment he left and took his vacated seat. 'Are you really going to a party with him?'

Cassidy had been eavesdropping! Eve shook herself upright. 'Of course I am. It's too good an opportunity to miss. If I can make just a few local connections…' She rolled her eyes at Cassidy's expression. 'Cass, this isn't a date. It's business.'

'I know that's what you're telling yourself, but you need to be careful, Evie. I have a feeling that man is your kryptonite. None of us should be playing with kryptonite.'

'Kryptonite doesn't hurt mortals.'

'We're not mortals, Eve. We're super women.'

That made her laugh. 'Sorry, my mistake.'

Cassidy leaned forward, serious again. 'Be careful.'

She sobered too. 'I will be. I promise. I know spending time with him is dangerous. But he'll be gone again before we know it.'

Worry flooded Cassidy's eyes. 'You still find him attractive.'

'C'mon, Cass, the guy's hot. And I'm not dead.'

'Kryptonite,' her friend intoned darkly.

'But all I have to do to counter the danger is remember what he did. And any tiny hint of temptation that raises its head will be shot down in flames. Don't worry, Cass, I'm not getting involved with that man ever again. I promise.' She clasped her friend's hand briefly. 'Now, I better go have a shower and get down here to help with the morning rush.'

* * *

That Saturday night, Damon could barely breathe when Eve removed her wrap to reveal the stunning dress she wore. Not that he noticed the dress so much as *her*.

Colour mounted high on her cheekbones when she glanced at him. He kicked himself mentally and smoothed out his face, hoping like hell it hid the heat in his eyes. She'd made it clear that she wasn't interested in pursuing any kind of physical thing with him.

He respected that, and only a jerk would mount any kind of protest and make her feel uncomfortable.

And he wasn't a masochist. He wanted her—everything inside him clamoured to be near her. But he wanted all of her, not just a scrap or crumb. And he would never have all of her—she'd never allow it. She'd never trust him with her heart again. And he didn't blame her.

So he smoothed out his frown and forced a smile. 'You look stunning.'

Did he imagine the relief in her eyes? 'You already said that, Damon.'

He tucked her hand into the crook of his elbow.

'That was merely customary politeness, what a man is supposed to say when he arrives to collect a woman—any woman,' he hastened to add. 'This is proper appreciation.' She wore a calf-length dress of extraordinarily fine silk in a warm buttery yellow that clung to her every curve. It's low cowl neck made his mouth water.

'This was the last dress I bought when I was still living in Sydney.' She named a well-known Australian designer. 'Terribly extravagant, but I couldn't resist. It's the first time I've worn it.'

'Whatever you paid, it was worth it.'

She laughed and some of the tension drained out of him. His earlier ogling hadn't left her feeling indelibly uncomfortable. He'd make sure to stay on his guard against such slips for the rest of the evening.

She glanced at him. 'You're not looking too bad yourself. You always did a tux proud.'

Her words made his heart hammer, ache and burn all at the same time. 'I'd want to do this one proud.' He made his voice wry and self-deprecating. 'It's tailor made.' He'd had it couriered up from Sydney. 'Whatever your dress cost, I bet this cost twice as much.'

She laughed again and this time he found he could manage a grin. 'Ready to work the room?'

'Absolutely.'

The Sorensen mansion—probably more of a complex— was strategically perched on the Byron Bay headland. Below were spectacular ocean views that were incredible at night and would therefore be ten times more impressive during the day.

The open-plan living area was filled with people. French doors opened out to a terrace and the most spectacular pool and gardens. He let out a breath. The Sorensens' neighbours were movie stars and celebrities, and more than a few of them had chosen to grace the party with their presence.

'Nice,' Eve murmured at his elbow, though he noted she was staring at the pool rather than the apparently swoonworthy film star who'd just strode across their line of vision.

He took two glasses of champagne from a proffered tray and handed her one. She touched her glass to his and just for a moment their gazes clung.

She blinked and broke the moment. 'See the man over there?' He glanced to where she indicated. 'That's Mr Dalton…a local brewer.' Damon filed the information away.

'And that man over there is our host.' He nodded in the direction of the luxury-yacht builder.

She stared. 'I think you should take Dalton while I take Mr Sorensen.'

'Divide and conquer?'

'You bet.'

He feigned outrage. 'You just want the kudos of closing the bigger deal and leaving me with the small fry.'

'Mr Dalton is not small fry! He's also a fan of Australian soccer—he's thinking of buying a club in the national league. From memory, that was your thing too, right?'

He feigned further outrage. 'It's called *football*, not soccer.'

It was an old argument that had her grinning. 'Whatever. But I have a point of contact with Mr Sorensen—I once had a cruise around Sydney harbour in the *Joyful Jade*.'

He eased back in genuine admiration. 'That was his first big yacht.' That was when the Sorensen brand had become synonymous with luxury and quality.

'I know. And it's an in.'

She'd done her homework but so had he. 'You have an in with the Daltons too. His goddaughter is one of your housekeeping staff.'

It was her jaw that dropped this time.

'And he's a big reader of mystery novels—his favourite author is Agatha Christie. You once told me that you spent your summers re-reading your favourite Agatha Christie books.'

She blinked. 'You remember that?'

In the same way she'd remembered that he was a football fanatic. 'Sure I do.' He spoke the words lightly enough, but the atmosphere between them threatened to turn tense. He made himself gaze back out at the crowd.

Keep it light. Don't make her feel uncomfortable.

'While I'm considering buying a luxury yacht.'

'Ah, so you want me to take Mr Dalton while you have a shot with Mr Sorensen.'

He shook his head. 'I don't think divide and conquer is our best strategy. I'm thinking that together we make a crack team. Why halve our power and impact if we don't have to? There's time for us to chat with both the Sorensens and the Daltons.'

'A joint charm offensive?'

He grinned down at her. 'Precisely.'

She grinned back. 'Game on.'

The fire in her eyes did something to him. She couldn't hide how much she enjoyed the thrill of the chase, even if she wasn't aware of it herself.

They greeted their host and hostess first. Mr Sorensen's eyes narrowed when they rested on Damon. 'I'm intrigued to know what you're doing in town, Mr Macy. Kevin Greamsman has been saying some…interesting things about you.'

'The name's Damon. And you shouldn't believe every-thing you hear. Come and find me when your host duties are less urgent and you can have the story straight from the horse's mouth.'

'I'm going to do that,' the other man promised.

Damon and Eve slowly worked their way around the room until they'd reached the Daltons' circle. Introductions were made. 'I'm feeling a little envious,' Damon said to the other man, who was probably twenty years his senior. 'I hear you're thinking of buying one of the football teams.'

'Not exactly. I'm trying to get a syndicate of business-men together—a joint-ownership scheme. And I'm actu-ally pushing the national soccer federation to expand the league to include a team from the Gold Coast. Things are looking promising.' He sent Damon a cheeky grin. 'I don't suppose you'd be interested in coming on board?'

A little over a week ago, he'd have said no. But that was before he'd promised to get himself a life.

'ROI is going to be…well…probably non-existent,' the older man confessed.

'But what price do you put on the enjoyment of owning

a team in the national league and sitting in a corporate box to enjoy the games?'

'That's what I keep telling Barbara here. What do you think, Eve?'

She rolled her eyes at Barbara Dalton. 'It sounds like every boyhood dream come true.'

Everyone laughed. 'Keep me in the loop, Garry,' Damon told the other man.

Talk turned to recent movie releases. Garry Dalton turned to them. 'Have you seen the latest Agatha Christie adaptation?'

Eve wrinkled her nose. 'I don't know if I dare risk it. The movies are never as good as the books.'

Damon smiled as the two started discussing the ins and outs of the book and film, and he contented himself making small talk with Barbara. Usually he found such events oner-ous but that wasn't the case tonight. Barbara had a passion for animal welfare and was heavily involved in the local dog shelter. 'I had a rescue dog as a kid,' he said. Which strictly speaking wasn't true. The dog had been a stray that he'd taken home with him and had somehow managed to feed. Most of the time. 'He was the best friend I ever had.' That much was true.

'Pets are great for children,' she agreed. Her eyes sud-denly gleamed. 'You wouldn't be interested in owning an-other dog, would you, Damon?'

'Not for myself. At least, not at the moment. But…' Pru's face popped into his mind. 'I might know someone.' He grimaced. 'Dogs can be expensive, though, right? Vet bills and vaccinations.'

Her gaze sharpened. 'We're also looking for foster car-ers for our dogs. When someone fosters a dog, all of the dog's expenses continue to be covered by the organisation.'

Would Pru be interested in that? 'Do you have a card?'

She handed it to him. 'Ring me if you have any questions.' At the same time Garry Dalton swung back to them.

'Eve here owns the motel that our Danielle works at, Barb. And between us we've come up with a grand idea—murder mystery weekends at the motel! Isn't that the most splendid idea you've ever heard?'

The older man's enthusiasm was infectious and Damon found himself grinning. *Well played, Eve!* He had to resist the impulse to reach across and high-five her.

They discussed the idea for a while, Eve moving to the side when some of the women asked about the stunning necklet that she wore. He caught snatches of the conversation.

'Mirror Glass Bay resident...'

'Self-taught...'

'Freelance...'

'I'll send you her details...'

And then, as if the thought had only just occurred to her, she said, 'Hey, we're having a fundraising auction for koala conservation in four weeks' time. And this particular jeweller is donating a really lovely piece for the cause. You should all come. There's going to be a fabulous band—Damon is pulling some strings, but their name will make your mouths drop when we finally get to announce it. It should be a lot of fun.'

The woman was a one-man band. She was amazing. She hadn't hit up a single one of them, the cream of Byron Bay society, to donate anything. These men and women were used to petitions on their pockets and resources, but she hadn't attempted to appeal to their better natures or their consciences. Instead she'd promised them a great night out and the opportunity to score a unique piece of jewellery.

'So spill, Damon,' Simon Sorensen said, sauntering across to him. 'What are you really doing in town?' All the other men in the circle immediately honed in on the conversation. Damon didn't kid himself. How he handled the next five to ten minutes was going to be crucial to Operation Mirror Glass Bay.

'Besides catching up with old friends?' He indicated Eve, who he knew was listening but was pretending not to be. 'I'm finding Mirror Glass Bay a bit of an…under-used resource. There's potential there that I wouldn't mind harnessing. I've been after a place to run team-building retreats for a while now. Somewhere quiet and out of the way in an inspirational location.'

'Ah, the Greamsman site.'

'My site now—an ideal beach-front parcel of land surrounded on two sides by national park that can't be built on. And the price…' He shook his head. 'It's impossible to get beachside land further south at those kinds of prices. Greamsman was crazy to sell to me. The environmental embargo scared the silly goose off.'

'That's not the story he tells.'

Damon grinned. 'Of course it's not.' Sorensen wasn't a man who could be easily influenced, and Damon had no intention of lying to him. 'Greamsman only had one vision for that site. If he'd expanded his thinking outside the square… But he didn't.'

Sorensen still didn't look convinced, but Damon needed to convince this man that he would be a safe bet to work with—for Eve's sake. 'Compare Greamsman's staff retention rates to mine. That reveals the differences in our business cultures and approaches. Carrots work better than sticks, gentlemen. It's the perks and conditions that Macy Holdings offers its employees that attracts and keeps the best staff.'

'And being offered a week or two each year to enjoy the sun and sand when you're working on so-called team building is a nice perk.'

'And in a place like Mirror Glass Bay, where there's no real nightlife to distract the staff,' Dalton added.

Damon didn't answer immediately, just let the beginnings of a smile tickle the corners of his mouth.

'Studies show that relaxation and the positive ions from moving water are conducive to creativity and problem-solving.' He sipped his champagne, still the same glass he'd taken when he and Eve had first walked in. 'It's been working for me...so let's hope it works for my team.'

'Working for you?' Sorensen pressed.

'There's an old industrial area on the way into town— a bit run-down now, with over half the warehouses either sitting vacant or under-utilised. There's potential there for the right investor.'

The women joined the group. They were as curious as the men—and, as several of them had business degrees and were active business partners with their spouses, he was only surprised they'd not joined the conversation sooner. He suspected the local rumour mill had been working over-time this last week.

'It has occurred to me recently that all work and no play makes for a dull life.'

Eve's eyes felt like a physical presence on his skin, but he didn't turn to meet them.

'It's why I might be persuaded to buy into your football team, Garry. Eve called it a boyhood dream come true, but I don't see that there's anything wrong with that. Owning a brewery comes under that same umbrella.'

'The market is already flooded here,' Dalton said promptly.

He laughed. 'Which is exactly what you would say to deter new competition.'

Dalton rubbed a hand across his chin. 'However, I am looking to expand my operations. I'm not looking to move my entire operations to brand-new premises, mind—it currently makes no sense to do that—but if there's something suitable on this industrial estate of yours…?'

Damon nodded slowly. 'We should talk.'

'Darling.' Valerie Sorensen slipped a hand through her husband's arm. 'This sounds like an interesting opportunity.'

Eve turned to him. 'Valerie was just telling us that Simon is diversifying into smaller craft—jet skis and skiffs.'

'I was hoping to buy a site not too far from my shipyard, but the price isn't right yet.'

'And the owner is an odious man,' his wife said. 'Look, Damon, why don't you and Eve, and Barbara and Garry, all come to dinner on Wednesday night? We can have a good old natter about it all over steak and salad.'

They all agreed and settled on a time. Eve sent him a grin that made him feel as if he could fly.

'I can't believe how much we accomplished,' Eve said on the way home in the car later that night.

Even in the darkness he could see the way her eyes danced. Excitement shimmered off her in waves; she could barely keep still in her seat.

'You won Dalton over with your murder-mystery weekend idea.'

'It was his idea.'

'Correction—you let him think it was his idea. I was there, remember? I heard what was said.'

She waved that away. 'You won both Barbara and Valerie over with your interest in the dog shelter.'

'How'd you know about that?'

'Barbara told us about it when you were talking about team-building retreats with the men.' She turned in her seat to face him. 'Who were you thinking of getting a dog for? I can't have a dog at the motel, it'd—'

'Pru.' He told her about the foster care option and how that might suit Pru's mother's tight budget.

She nodded slowly. 'That's a really nice idea.' She sent him a sharp glance. 'You better be careful, Damon. You're in danger of losing your reputation as a shark.'

He didn't care. Not when it put such a spark in her eyes.

He drove down Beach Street towards her motel and blinked at all the lights that blazed from the restaurant and bar. 'I didn't know you had a function on tonight.'

'We don't. This is called small town nosiness. Word will have circulated about where we were headed tonight and what we were up to.'

Really? He wasn't sure what to say. His stomach started to clench. 'Well, at least it's good for business, I suppose.'

CHAPTER SIX

EVE STARED AT the light spilling from The Beachside, at the smiling faces and general laughter inside, and something hitched in her chest.

These were her people.

This was her home.

What she and Damon had done tonight…

You haven't closed any deals yet.

But they *had* set wheels in motion. Not just one but several. Damon was right. They shouldn't be relying on only one or two sources of local industry to provide revenue and employment opportunities in the area. Not if they wanted to maintain and eventually enhance Mirror Glass Bay's infrastructure.

She turned back to Damon. 'Thank you for everything you're doing and have already done.' She was reaping untold rewards from the bad turn he'd done her four years ago. It'd be churlish not to acknowledge that.

And tonight she wasn't feeling churlish. Tonight, she felt euphoric. 'I want you to know I really appreciate it. The whole town appreciates it.'

He shook his head, not smiling. 'It's the least that I could do.'

'No.' She wondered how his eyes could look so vibrant in the darkness of the car. 'You're doing far more than Greamsman would've done. And you're doing far more than you ever had to. I wouldn't have blamed you for walking away.'

The light in his eyes darkened, became more subdued. 'Are you so sure about that?'

She thought about it and then grimaced. 'I'd have blamed you for getting involved. *Until* I'd found out about the stop-work notice.' But he hadn't walked away. He was doing what he promised—he was fixing things.

Neither of them made reference to the past. But the past suddenly didn't seem to matter so much. 'Come on.' She hitched her head in the direction of the bar. 'Let's go join in the fun.' She didn't want the night to end.

'You're saying the whole town knows we went to that party?'

'Looks like it.' She leaned back in her seat and folded her arms when he didn't move. He really didn't get it, did he? 'Who did you mention the party to?'

'Ron—but only in passing. I didn't make a big thing about it, just said I hoped it'd give us a couple of leads and maybe some contacts. I didn't want to get anyone's hopes up. Nothing has come yet from tonight's foray and there's no guarantee that there will.'

But he was going to do his best to make sure something did come from it, and so was she. They'd been an unstoppable team. Tonight, it had felt as if they couldn't fail.

'Cassidy knew about it, and I told my grandmother. So, if Ron knew, between the three of them that means the whole town will have known what we were up to.'

The furrows in his brow deepened. 'Right.'

Her stomach started to churn. 'You're not okay with this?'

'We haven't achieved anything yet!'

'But we *are* a step closer to making something happen.' His frown didn't abate.

She turned more fully in her seat. 'What do you care

about, Damon?' He blinked. 'Well, come on,' she badgered. 'Even if your list is short, there must be one or two things on it.'

'My mother. My friends.' His gaze shifted from hers to the view outside—the brightly lit bar and all the people. She didn't need to turn to know what he saw. 'I don't have a large circle of friends like you do—you can count them on one hand—but I care about them.'

It hit her then how closed off this man was. Had he always been like that? He'd never been closed off with her. She grimaced. At least, she'd never felt closed off. But she'd never known about his background, his parents. She'd never realised all he'd sacrificed in the pursuit of success.

His gaze swooped back to hers. 'I care about making *this* right.'

She didn't doubt that for a moment… '*This*, Damon—' she gestured towards the bar '—is a community. They don't just want a *fait accompli*. They want to feel a part of the journey. They want to feel they have a say in what happens.'

'But what if we disappoint them?'

What on earth…?

'And what if we don't? Look, nobody is counting chickens—everyone knows what we're trying to achieve here is a gamble—but that doesn't mean we can't celebrate small successes along the way, or the potential for big successes. It doesn't mean we can't hope. This—' she gestured to the bar pulsing with life, vitality and friendship '—builds community spirit. If things don't work out, then we'll find solace in each other. And we'll come back together with renewed vigour to find a new solution, a new way forward. So for heaven's sake, dude, lighten up.'

Her words made him blink. His frown cleared and then reappeared, but humour lit his eyes. 'So you're saying that tonight I'm…part of the community?'

She didn't hesitate. 'Yes.'

And then it hit her what his problem was, and her stomach started to churn. 'Nobody has any expectations that you're going to become a permanent fixture here, Damon, so relax. We all know that when you're done you'll be off back to Sydney and your jet-setting life.'

She pushed open her car door. He'd been here for nearly a fortnight. It would be ludicrous to think he'd be here in another fortnight. 'Look, you don't have to come in if you don't want to, but—'

He reached out and grabbed her hand. 'I'm sorry. I've tempered your enjoyment of the evening and I didn't mean to. I…it's just…it matters to me that I pull this off. I feel like I'm losing control because I care—because I've become invested.'

And he found that a challenge—that much was obvious. Her heart gave a funny thud. 'I'm not going to talk you out of feeling invested.'

'And nor should you,' he agreed. He smiled and she didn't know if he meant it or if it was just for her benefit. 'So I'm going to take your advice and go in there and enjoy it.'

He squeezed her hand. She'd forgotten he'd been holding it. She rubbed at it absently when he let it go. 'Right, well…' She pushed out of the car, feeling suddenly lightheaded. 'Let's go.'

The moment they entered the bar, they were pulled into the crowd, which demanded to know what had happened at the party, if any potential developments had occurred and who'd been there. Eve didn't hold back anything. She wanted her town on board. People knew people; they could keep their ears to the ground; unforeseen serendipitous encounters and chance meetings could occur. She worked on the principle that knowledge was power. And the more people working towards the common goal of shoring up Mirror Glass Bay's future the better.

Damon followed her lead. In fact, he was so good at bringing the evening's earlier party to life that he held people spellbound as he painted a glamorous and fascinating picture.

It made her euphoric all over again.

It made everyone euphoric. Cassidy brought out the karaoke machine and demanded that Eve sing.

Eve allowed herself to be hustled onto the small platform at the end of the room to lead the town in a stirring rendition of Queen's *We are the Champions*, aware the entire time of Damon's open-mouthed shock. And the fact that his cheer was the loudest of all when the song came to an end.

'You can sing,' he said when she jumped down.

'I know!' But she said it with a laugh. 'What about you?'

He shook his head. 'I'm terrible, truly terrible.'

'What you've got to remember, Damon, is that the trick to karaoke is that it's one's enthusiasm that counts—not whether you can hit the high notes, or any notes for that matter.'

His eyes narrowed. 'Why are you telling me this?'

'Because you're next, mate,' Ron said, clapping him on the back.

She handed him the microphone, her grin full of challenge, and he visibly swallowed. 'You want me to sing?'

'More than anything. Now, what song would you like?' She flicked through the selections. 'Madonna, Jimmy Barnes, The Rolling Stones...?'

He pointed a finger at her. 'You were warned.'

'Noted.'

'The Beatles.'

He sang *With a Little Help From My Friends* very badly but with such gusto. It had everyone clapping and joining in.

Eventually Cassidy called for last orders, and Eve took the microphone and reminded the crowd that it was the koala sanctuary working bee the following day and threatened everyone with a painful death if they didn't show up for it.

With groans, the bar cleared.

'That was fun,' Damon said, following her outside in the direction of their separate sleeping quarters. 'A lot of fun.'

He could barely get the grin off his face and she couldn't help but grin back. 'I hate to say "I told you so".'

'I'd believe you if you didn't sound so smug.'

She just grinned.

'You have a great voice, Eve. You could've been a professional singer.'

'It wasn't a path I was ever encouraged to follow.' She shrugged. 'Besides, you need more than just a good voice. I wouldn't have made it in the profession. I never had the passion for it.'

He mulled that over for a moment. 'But you do have a passion for saving this town.'

She halted at the door that led up to her flat, 'I do.'

'Why?' he asked. 'Why does it matter so much to you?'

She pulled her wrap more tightly about her. She wasn't going to invite him in, but... 'Are you up for a walk?'

He nodded.

They strolled in the direction of the beach, not speaking, but the silence was companionable and easy and she found herself relaxing into it as she slipped her sandals off at the top of the path and dug her toes into the sand. A million stars dotted a night sky that was so clear and crisp that each of them sparkled with the clarity of a diamond. A new moon formed a perfect crescent high above them.

'Dear God,' Damon breathed, staring up at it all. 'This has been here all this time? And I'm only just discovering it?'

'I thought you discovered it your first night here.'

'Yeah, but all this—' he gestured skyward '—here on the beach is utterly amazing.'

'I know what you mean.' She kept her gaze trained on the crescent moon. 'It's how I felt when I came back here. I'd forgotten.' She glanced at him then, saw how it all held him spellbound, and something in her stomach twisted. She had an awful feeling that he'd never known that this existed. At least, not like this.

She swallowed and forced her gaze back to the sky. 'This is why people come back year after year. Being close to this, just for a week or two, renews people's spirits. It tops them up, reminds them of what's important. It just gives them a chance to…breathe.'

She felt him turn towards her.

'And it's important to you to facilitate that?'

'It's why I've resisted turning The Beachside into some mega resort. I don't want to price my regulars out of the market. And, before you tell me what a noble sentiment that is, following that route would mean Gran and I would no longer own the motel outright—we'd need investors, would have to go into debt.' And neither one of them wanted to do that.

'I see.'

Did he? She treasured the simplicity of her life now. 'Four years ago, I found out that my parents were planning to put my grandmother into a home. They were badgering her to assign them power of attorney and enduring guardianship.'

'Could she no longer live on her own?'

'Of course she could. She still can. I mean, she needs some help every now and again, but she doesn't need to go into a home. It's just that my parents felt like she was one thing too many on their to-do list and putting her into a home was the expedient solution.'

'That's…' He looked appalled.

'Heartless,' she agreed. 'I suspect they wanted to get their hands on her house too. Gran owned a rather sweet little cottage in Balmain. It sold for a ton of money.'

'I bet. So…you and your gran did a Thelma and Louise to here?'

'We did. And we've not looked back since. This place suits her so much better than Sydney ever did. She doesn't have to catch a bus to do her groceries or to go to the doctors for her monthly vitamin B shot—it's all just a short walk away. The restaurant's kitchen delivers her a hot meal every evening. And she goes to the raffles and the bingo three to five times a week at the bowling club. Again, she can walk there. If she has a funny turn, someone will drop her home. Or they'll ring me at The Beachside and I can nip down the road to collect her. Or if I'm not here Cassidy or one of the other staff will do it.'

He was silent for a moment. 'Everyone here really does look after each other.'

'Uh huh.'

'Does she have many funny turns?'

'No, but she's nearly eighty and none of us lives forever.'

'Your grandmother!' He spun to her so suddenly it made her feel dizzy. *He* made her feel dizzy. He pointed at her. 'She's the reason this town means so much to you.'

Was she really so transparent? The thought made her swallow. 'That's part of it,' she hedged. 'She's my family. I love her, want to see her happy. But I've made good friends here and I make a contribution—I feel like I belong. I don't want to give that up.'

She hesitated. She wasn't sure if he'd understand…

'Four years ago, I realised I was in danger of becoming exactly like my parents. When I finally recognised their priorities, I was horrified. Money and success should never matter more than people…and doing the right thing. They were so selfishly concerned with protecting and maintaining their lives that they were going to just throw my grandmother away as if she didn't matter.' Her stomach churned in outrage at the memory. 'I didn't want to be like that. So when I look up at that night sky I'm grateful I realised that before it was too late. I'm grateful for that every single day.'

'People should always matter more than money or success.'

She knew he thought he meant those words. But she didn't think he felt them in his soul the way she did.

But he didn't have to and it was none of her business. What mattered was that he was searching for some kind of absolution and Mirror Glass Bay was reaping the benefits.

'I can be my best self here,' she said softly. 'I don't want to ever lose that again.'

'Eve, you were never in danger of becoming like your parents. *Never*. You were always a beacon…a bright light.'

He smelled of a heady mix of amber, spice and the sea. It could tangle a woman's senses if she let it. Eve reminded herself that she was her best self these days and no longer a weakling who succumbed to temptation. She was a woman who had left her old life behind, and she had no intention of ever going back.

She dismissed his words with an airy wave of her hand. 'Oh, I was clever, I'll give you that. And I knew how to make a good impression. I could make people laugh and be oh-so-charming.' She'd been charming tonight and it'd been fun. But it didn't mean she hungered for her old life.

'You were kind, Eve. You were always kind. That's what made the difference.'

Eve turned to him as he spoke and he had to suck air into his lungs at the vulnerability reflected in her eyes.

But stars were reflected there too.

She'd been kind tonight. And she wanted to write that off as a character flaw? Not on his watch! 'You were charming tonight but, Eve, your charm is kindness—it's genuine. And it brings out the best in people, lets them shine.'

'I was charming because I wanted something in return.'

He shook his head. 'You had an agenda tonight, sure, but you weren't prepared to walk over anyone to achieve it. People instinctively sense that. Anyway, parties like the one we went to tonight are deliberately tailored to bring together people whose agendas might align. There's nothing wrong with that.'

He watched her mull his words over. Her eyes were almost silver in this light, making them appear otherworldly and fey. It pushed him off-balance, and something inside his chest started to ache.

'You're a giver, Eve, not a taker like your parents.'

Her gaze lifted for a moment and it felt as if the two of them hung suspended between breaths. 'And what are you, Damon?'

She shivered in the cool night air and he immediately slipped his jacket off and laid it across her shoulders. 'I'm trying to become a giver, like you. That's what I want to be.'

She'd stilled, frozen, when he'd moved in closer with his jacket. He eased away immediately, not wanting her to feel uncomfortable with his proximity. And not wanting her to see how being this close to her affected him—had desire and need slugging through his veins with the force of a steam engine.

'Feel free to laugh at that if you want,' he added in as wry a tone as he could manage. But his voice didn't sound wry or flippant. The words emerged gruff and vulnerable, and they made him grimace.

'I don't want to laugh at it.'

He glanced back at her in time to see a flash of heat in her gaze that had his world tilting.

'Why should I laugh at your desire to be a better person?'

'I...'

A luscious, tempting smile curved her lips, though he doubted she meant it to be either luscious or tempting. And then she moved in closer to place her hand over his heart and his pulse went wild. 'That wouldn't be very kind, would it?'

He couldn't help himself. He had to touch her. Reaching up, he brushed the backs of his fingers across her cheek, her quick intake of breath finding an unequivocal answer in the tightening of his groin.

This was madness. He should step away. Kissing her would not make her happy, and he'd sworn to do only what would make her happy. But he couldn't move, couldn't stop his fingers from brushing across her cheek in a slow caress that made every atom come alive.

Under her palm, his heart pounded.

'I had a lot of fun tonight,' she whispered.

Something in her words made him frown. 'You don't often have a lot of fun?' It wasn't the picture of her life he'd drawn in his mind.

'I've found peace and satisfaction.' She leaned into his caress almost absent-mindedly. 'I have a lot of contentment, but not a lot of fun.' She moistened her lips. 'I didn't realise that until tonight. I thought what I had was enough, but...'

His mouth went dry.

Her eyes had gone dark and slumberous. She tilted her chin...almost in invitation. He swallowed and tried to cling to his sanity, his reason...

'But I'm starting to wonder if that's enough.'

'Eve, I—'

'I know you're wondering what it'd be like to kiss me now.'

His chest rose and fell. 'I don't have to wonder. I *know* it'd be sensational.'

She blinked, as if his candour surprised her. He'd sworn to himself not to lie to her again. He'd be as honest and vulnerable as she needed him to be. Even if it meant she'd stomp all over his heart.

She moved in a fraction closer. 'Well, I've been wondering all night. I can't seem to help it. Maybe it's the stars, maybe it's the tide, maybe it's the champagne.'

She'd hardly drunk any champagne.

'Maybe it's because you haven't taken advantage of the situation when I can see how much you want me.'

And, no matter how much he wanted to, he wouldn't.

She laughed—a low sound that feathered over him. 'Or maybe it's because I've held myself on too tight a leash for too long.'

She stepped in even closer until her breasts touched his chest. She was going to kiss him! Everything inside him roared to urgent, eager life. It was all he could do to stop from seizing her and devouring her like some starving beast.

Lifting up on tiptoes, she let her breath mingle with his. 'Do you have a girlfriend, Damon?'

'I haven't been with a woman since you.'

The words were wrenched from him. He hadn't meant to admit it, but in this moment he could hold nothing back.

Somehow his hands had gone to her waist and he steadied her as shock rippled through her, his fingers tightening against the softness of silk and the firmness of her flesh beneath it. Something flashed through her eyes. Passion? Definitely. And maybe possessiveness? But then she touched her lips to his and Damon lost the ability to think.

He lost the ability to hold himself back. And yet in losing himself he gained so much back in return. Eve's warmth, her ardour and her very essence surrounded him and he pulled her close to savour every delectable taste of her, grateful beyond measure for this moment, for this chance to have her in his arms again.

She'd been wondering what it would be like to kiss him

so he set himself to making this a kiss that would rock her world. He concentrated his every effort on a long, slow awakening of their old desire, which it appeared hadn't diminished in the intervening years. He refused to rush—he wanted her to feel cherished. He wanted her to know how much this moment meant to him.

Her arms slid about his neck and she kissed him back with a passion that stole his breath, moved against him restlessly. With one hand he cupped her face to hold her still, wrapped his other around her waist and kissed her with all of himself—with everything he had. He kissed her thoroughly—gently, firmly, nibbling, drawing her lower lip into his mouth and lathing it with his tongue.

He loved this woman—heart and soul. His heart was hers. It was pointless denying it. For the last four years he'd been living a half-life. But he'd come alive again and he'd do anything to win Eve back—give up anything, be whatever it was that would make her happy. He poured all of that into his kiss. All of that and more.

She gasped, she moaned. A tremor shook her entire frame. Catching his face in her hands with a half-sob, she did what she always did—she gave. She kissed him with a slow intensity that had the pulse pounding in his ears and his groin straining in his pants.

The last of his restraint snapped. He slid his hands down the side of her breasts. He made lazy circles around the tight buds of her nipples with his thumbs until she cried out his name, desperation and need lacing her voice.

He loved her with his hands and his mouth, dropping to his knees at her feet, pushing up her dress and sliding aside the barrier of her panties to his questing fingers and tongue. He worshipped the texture of her skin, her scent and her very essence, savouring her unalloyed pleasure at all he was doing, taking delight in her abandon and wonder, wanting to make her feel as good as he could, give her as much delight and pleasure it was in his power to give. Her gasps and moans urged him on.

And when she came apart in his arms he gave thanks to whatever force that had brought her back into his life, because he wanted to show her that he could cherish her like this forever.

He held her close as she drifted back to reality. He felt her still as she registered what just happened. In a moment he'd tell her what a monumental impact it'd had on him. In a moment he would tell her he loved her—that he'd never stopped loving her. In a moment he would beg her to give him a second chance. Tell her he wanted to build a life with her here in Mirror Glass Bay because it was the home of her heart. And that he wanted her to have everything that would make her happy.

When she shivered, he reached down to pick up his jacket, which had fallen to the sand, and wrapped it back around her.

'Kryptonite.'

Her whispered word made no sense to him.

She pulled away, clasping the lapels of his coat tightly to her chest. 'I can't believe I just let you do that to me.'

The expression in her eyes shattered every dream he'd just dared to let himself dream.

'I can't believe...' A sob left her throat. 'I didn't even put up a fight.'

Her face had gone pinched and pale, and it wrung his heart inside out. Bile burned the back of his throat. 'Eve, I'm sorry.' He reached out a hand to her and then swallowed when she batted it away. 'I thought it was what you wanted.'

'While you,' she continued as if he hadn't spoken, 'played the perfect gentleman and didn't take advantage of my weakness. And now you no doubt think that gives you some moral high ground.'

'I don't have any moral high ground. None,' he assured

her, searching for a way to make things better, to make them right.

Her eyes flashed. 'You're darn right you don't!' And then those eyes filled with tears.

His throat thickened. 'Please, Eve. Don't cry.' How had he misread things so badly? How could he have made such a mess of things?

Darkness, betrayal, pain—they all swirled in her eyes. 'You never said sorry—not once—for what you did four years ago.'

His head snapped back. And then his stomach dropped... and his heart dropped with it, and kept right on falling.

'And you needn't think that what just happened makes a jot of difference. You're...you're just trying to make yourself feel better at my expense.'

No, he wasn't!

'You stay away from me, Damon Macy.' She reefed his jacket off and slapped it to his chest.

And with that she turned and stormed off.

You never said sorry. Not once.

He braced his hands on his knees and tried to find his centre of balance, tried to make his brain work. Tried to think of a way he could make all this up to her.

CHAPTER SEVEN

EVE SPENT THE next three days avoiding Damon. He'd walk into the bar of The Beachside and she'd walk out of it. He'd walk through the gardens and she'd walk out of them. Catching the slightest glimpse of him made her pulse pound and her body ache. It didn't matter how much she tried telling herself that what had happened on the beach was an aberration. It hadn't felt like an aberration—not then and not now. It had felt right. And that was a lie. She knew it was a lie.

Four years ago, he'd betrayed her. *For two million dollars*. How had she let herself forget that? How could she *ever* forget it?

She believed he felt bad for what he'd done, but it didn't change the fact that he was the kind of man who put a price on love. She was *never* getting involved with a man like that again.

So why on earth had she let him touch her and kiss her so intimately?

Heat flamed in her face and she seized a cloth and wiped down the bar vigorously. What had happened on the beach on Saturday night had reminded her how good things had once been between them. But it had also brought back the devastation of his betrayal, her sense of loss—the sense that she'd never really known him when she'd thought that together they'd made more sense than anything she'd ever known.

She'd pinned all of her dreams and happiness on him—on them. Saturday night had brought back the unravelling of her sense of self in the days following his betrayal, the realisation that he'd played her for a fool and she'd been totally blind to it.

She closed her eyes, her hands clenching about the cloth. Yet on Saturday night she'd given herself to him wholeheartedly…recklessly…without a second thought. How could she have been so stupid, unguarded, forgetful?

Had she no pride?

Apparently not because when he'd stared at her as if she were the whole world a lump had lodged in her throat. It'd been so long. So long since she'd felt beautiful, desirable…like a woman. He'd kissed her as if she were his every dream come true.

And she'd been lost and so greedy for him, so hungry. That hunger still coursed through her now—and only increased whenever she saw him. Perhaps that was what frightened her most of all. Because she wasn't dancing that particular dance with him ever again. She had to find the strength to resist him.

Dragging in a breath, she scowled as she watched his car drive away from The Beachside. She *would* find that strength.

Cassidy moved to stand beside her. 'Evie, I know I probably shouldn't say anything, should keep my mouth shut, but—'

'Don't say a word, Cassidy. Just…don't.' She didn't even look at her friend as she said it, but from the corner of her eye she saw Cass raise her hands in a gesture of appeasement.

'You're the boss.'

Her chest clenched and she swung to her friend. 'I didn't mean it like that.'

'I know, hon.' Cassidy's blue eyes were filled with concern. 'But you've gone so quiet…and everyone is starting to get worried.'

And Cassidy was bearing the brunt of everyone's concern and curiosity—no doubt fielding questions and doing what she could to deflect attention from Eve's sudden withdrawal.

Damn.

She had to get over herself and move on. It was selfish to wallow in all…this. But she had no idea how she was going to face Damon, let alone look him in the eye. The very thought made her want to die a thousand deaths.

Tonight, they were going to dinner at the Sorensons. She had to pull herself together before then.

'You know I'm here, Evie. If you need to talk or…for anything.'

'I do and it means a lot.' She loved these people and they loved her. Four years ago, they had helped her find her centre again. That centre was still there, even if the events of Saturday night had left her feeling flung off-course. That thought helped to steady her. She forced her spine to straighten. She even found a sort of smile. 'Hey, have you seen Dolly in the last few days?'

Cassidy rolled her eyes. 'Looks like she's still as besotted with Damon as ever.' She leaned in closer. 'But I just saw him go out. I also happen to know for a fact that housekeeping will be doing the rooms in that part of the motel right about now. Perhaps you need to go and supervise?'

She stretched her neck to the right and to the left. She hadn't clapped eyes on Dolly in days.

Cassidy bumped shoulders with her. 'Go and cuddle your cat, Eve.'

Eve didn't need any further encouragement.

Damon's room had already been cleaned and the house-keeping staff had moved to the one other room currently occupied on this floor, but the doors to all of the rooms stood wide open to embrace the fresh air and sunshine.

Dolores lay curled up in the middle of Damon's bed. Eve moved to lie beside her. 'You old reprobate.' She stroked her fingers through soft fur. 'You've changed allegiances, huh?'

Dolly immediately stood and smothered Eve with affection. She batted her head against Eve's chin and hand, purring and giving funny little half-meows, rolling against Eve's chest and tummy, falling onto her back to bat Eve's hand with her paws. It made Eve smile. It made the sun shine a little brighter.

'You're a disgrace to the cat world, Dolores, you know that? You have the soul of puppy.'

'I tell her that too.'

Eve froze. *Dear God.* She was utterly incapable of moving a muscle, except her eyes. And they confirmed what her senses already knew—Damon stood in the doorway.

'I… I just wanted to cuddle my cat,' she whispered.

'Totally understandable.'

She was lying on his bed like some kind of invitation, having deliberately snuck in here when he was out. She should be mortified. And yet the warmth in his eyes told her he understood, that he didn't mind, saving her from the worst of her embarrassment. And it nearly undid her.

'I didn't mean to disturb you. I forgot my phone and wallet. Mirror Glass Bay is obviously making me too relaxed.'

And now he was apologising to her!

He hadn't moved from the doorway and she forced unco-operative limbs to shuffle her to the side of the bed where she stood on legs that felt like jelly. 'I'm sorry. I shouldn't have disturbed your room.'

'Except I seem to have commandeered your cat. And

it's your motel, Eve. You have the right to disturb this room any time you like.'

She focused on his first sentence rather than the latter with all its accompanying disturbing images. 'I suspect it's more accurate to say Dolores has commandeered you.'

His mouth twitched. 'She's still enough of a cat to believe she deserves accommodation in the best room in the house.'

That almost made her smile. 'Right. Well…sorry again. And now I really should get back to work.'

'Can I have a word before you go? If you have the time.'

If she made some excuse he wouldn't try to stop her—he wouldn't argue. She could see that in his face. He was also doing his best not to look physically intimidating—slouching rather than looming, ducking his head, keeping a pleasant smile on his face.

She almost made that excuse anyway. But then she remembered Cassidy, her grandmother and the rest of the town—knew how closely everyone was watching her. So, instead of fleeing, she made herself shrug. 'Sure, but can we move the conversation into the living area?'

She was too aware of the king-sized bed. Too aware of everything she shouldn't be.

Without a word he turned and she followed, but the sight of a bright-pink litter tray in his bathroom pulled her up short. 'You bought a litter tray?'

'I… It seemed like a good idea.'

She stared at him, mouth agape. She stared at the tray. He'd bought her cat *a litter tray*? That it had even occurred to him…

Close your mouth, Eve.

'Um…thank you. That was very kind of you.'

He waved that away. 'It's my own fault. If I don't have the heart to put her out then I have to make sure accidents aren't going to happen in the room.'

'For which I'm grateful.' She dusted off her hands and hoped she looked businesslike 'Now, you wanted a word?'

'About what happened on the beach—'

'*No!*' Her vehemence startled them both. She dragged both hands down her face and pulled in a breath. 'Look, Damon, I *really* don't want to talk about it. What happened was a mistake. I was stupid and reckless, and I can promise it won't happen again.'

He'd gone still, his eyes throbbing, and she had to look away.

'Can we pretend it never happened? Please?'

She closed her eyes, mortified at how pleading her *'Please,'* sounded.

'If that's what you want,' he finally said.

'Oh, it is. It really is.' But when she turned back to face him she could tell that somehow she'd hurt him, and she had to roll her shoulders against a growing sense of guilt.

'Okay...' He pulled in a breath then and let it out, as if he were trying to release something. 'Right, it's clear you've been avoiding me for the last three days.'

She didn't bother denying it. She'd look like an idiot if she did.

'But I want to assure you that you've nothing to fear from me. I'm not going to push my attentions on you—I won't try to kiss you again. I don't expect anything from you. I swear I'll abide by the boundaries you're setting. You won't have to tell me again. I don't force myself on unwilling women.'

It wasn't him she was worried about, but her own deplorable lack of unwillingness. Saturday night had shown her precisely how willing she was where this man was concerned. Not that she had any intention of confiding as much. She couldn't give Damon any kind of power over her again.

'I just wanted you to know that.'

She eyed him uncertainly. He didn't look as if he'd slept

in the last three days. She did what she could to harden her heart. 'Thank you.' Was that it? She edged towards the door, before she weakened and asked if he was all right.

'There's one more thing.'

He widened his stance and her pulse went berserk. *Kryptonite.* She held herself tight. 'Yes?'

'You said that four years ago I didn't apologise, Eve. I—'

'No.' She cut him off, waving both hands in front of her face, wanting desperately to dismiss all mention of their past and the memory of how much he'd hurt her—how much he might still be able to hurt her if she let him. 'I don't want to talk about our past. I don't want to talk about what happened four years ago. Bringing it up now will only make working with you more difficult.'

He paled. And for some reason his words on the beach came back to her now. *'I haven't been with a woman since you.'* She didn't know if that was true or not, but she couldn't let herself care.

She drew in a breath and let it out, trying to tame the way her heart raced. 'Damon, all I want is to focus on the here and now and do what I can to ensure Mirror Glass Bay's future. That's all.'

He pinched the bridge of his nose as if he had a raging headache and she had to stop herself, again, from asking if he was all right.

'You and I are only going to focus on the practical. Not the emotional—that's too fraught. I know you started this whole crusade to make amends—to make yourself feel better—but it's not fair to ask me to provide you with absolution or—'

'You're right.'

He sounded sick and for a moment she hated herself. But…he was her kryptonite—Cassidy was right—and she couldn't reveal any weakness around him. It'd taken her too long to get over him. It wasn't that she didn't want him to find the peace he was searching for or that she didn't applaud his desire to become a better person.

It was just…she wasn't going to help him gain his peace at the expense of losing her own. Kissing him, letting him touch her so intimately, had been a crazy mistake, but at least it had brought home to her, with a clarity that still shocked her, her weakness for this man.

She'd work with him because she wanted her town to benefit from his contacts, his money and his know-how. But she couldn't get close to him emotionally. Not again. They didn't have a future together. They had…nothing.

She glanced at him again. 'If that's all…?'

Before her eyes, he transformed. He shook himself and became businesslike and efficient. 'Three practical things.'

She couldn't explain why but she didn't feel relieved or comforted.

'The first—are we still on for the Sorensen dinner tonight?'

'Absolutely. I'll drive this time.' She wanted no hint of this being a date. She wanted an excuse to stay away from the champagne too. Not that she blamed champagne for what had happened Saturday night, but she wasn't giving her defences any opportunity to weaken. 'Shall we leave at six-thirty?'

He nodded his agreement. 'The second—last Sunday Pru helped me choose a surfboard for the raffle fundraiser.'

He'd got the younger girl's input. That was nice of him.

'And I have raffle books.'

'Oh!' Of course, he did. 'Right, I'll take at least ten books, and we'll keep one on the bar and another in Reception. Actually, give a stack to Cassidy. She'll distribute them to any townsfolk who pop in for a coffee or a beer. Excellent, that's great, Damon. Thank you.

'And the third thing?' she prompted when he remained silent.

'Barbara Dalton contacted me about the dog shelter, so I spoke to Pru's mum, floated the idea of Pru becoming a foster carer, and she thought it was a good idea.'

'I'm so glad.'

He stared at her carefully. 'But Pru needs to attend a training session a week Saturday.'

'But her mum works Saturdays.'

'I offered to take her, of course, but she doesn't know me well enough to entrust her twelve-year-old daughter to my care.'

Her stomach clenched at the question she could see coming.

'But she said it'd be okay if you made up one of the party.'

How could she refuse? She'd been searching for months to find a way to help the younger girl. And, seriously, where was the harm? It wasn't as if she'd be spending the time with Damon on her own—Pru would be with them the entire time. Nothing could happen... Plus, dogs. She'd get to spend a few hours playing with dogs.

She nodded. 'Okay, count me in.'

The Beachside's café-bar-restaurant was roughly divided into two sections. The three-sided bar was located in the middle of a long rectangle of a room. To the left was the café and informal eating area, to the right was the restaurant, though Damon had noticed a lot of overlap on Friday and Saturday nights. The Beachside didn't stick to rigid and clear rules about who could sit where, and he could see the clientele loved the establishment all the more for its democratic attitude.

He didn't sit in cafés in Sydney, idly read the paper and sip a leisurely coffee, certainly not at ten-thirty on a Thursday morning, but here in Mirror Glass Bay it seemed the natural thing to do. Not to take the time to appreciate the coffee Cassidy served him would feel wrong—rude somehow.

And sitting here like this felt…freeing.

Which was making him realise how rigid his own life had become.

He glanced up from the paper when the other chair at his table was pulled out and an older woman seated herself there. 'Damon Macy, I believe?'

'That's right.'

Behind her he saw Cassidy halt in her clearing of a nearby table and bite her lip. But when she noticed him watching her gaze turned mocking and she turned away again with a shrug.

'And you are…?' he asked. By now he was used to the residents of Mirror Glass Bay introducing themselves and telling him how great their town was, making suggestions in relation to his building site.

'*You're* the man they're calling the town saviour.'

He shifted, fighting back a frown. 'That's not how I'd put it.'

'No, nor would I.'

She didn't smile. No humour lit her eyes or face. She stared at him as if he were a bug that she'd like to squash beneath her shoe. He stiffened. Who on earth was she? Was she an environmentalist who thought all he was interested in was raping and pillaging the land? Was she…?

And then he realised *exactly* who she was. She might not look like her granddaughter, but she was one of only two people in Mirror Glass Bay, besides Eve, who had any reason to loathe him. 'You're Eve's grandmother. She told me how the two of you came here and made Mirror Glass Bay your home. I'm pleased to meet you.' He held out his hand, but she ignored it.

'Bethany Ford,' she clipped out. 'So *you're* the two-million-dollar gigolo.'

He choked. *What* had she just called him?

'Ah, I can see you don't like that, but what else would you call yourself, Mr Macy? My granddaughter slept with you and it cost her two million dollars.' She shook her head. 'You're a good-looking man, but you're not worth two million dollars.'

She rose. 'Can I make a suggestion?'

He couldn't make his voice work. He couldn't even nod or shake his head.

'It'd be greatly appreciated if you didn't stay in Mirror Glass Bay longer than necessary. You might have the rest of the town fooled, but you and I both know the truth—you don't belong in a place like this. We both know you're not good enough for a woman like Eve.'

She left and everything inside him ached. He couldn't recall a lower point in his life—and he'd had a few. An elderly woman had just called him a gigolo…and she had every reason to do so.

Bitterness filled his mouth. She was wrong, though. He hadn't sold his body. He'd sold his soul. If he'd only sold his body, he might still be able to find redemption.

Cassidy's face broke into his field of vision, consternation in her eyes and something that might've been sympathy. 'Eve has been trying to keep Granny Beth away from you.'

He stared at the piece of carrot cake she set in front of him and shook his head. 'I—'

'Eat it. It'll make you feel better.'

And then she was gone, so he did. And at least, after he'd finished it, he didn't feel any worse.

While the Sorensen dinner on Wednesday night had gone exceptionally well, and he had business meetings set up with both Simon Sorensen and Garry Dalton, Eve still continued to avoid him over the following week. Damon did what he could to keep busy. He sent instructions to his office to send him a lawyer and an administrative assistant. He hired temporary office space and living quarters for them in Byron Bay. He spoke to Owen who, amazingly enough, was still in Frankfurt and slowly making inroads on the deal with Herr Mueller. But none of that could stop his mind from returning to Eve.

She didn't avoid him with the same assiduity as she had the previous week—whenever she did see him, she sent him a cheery wave, and might exchange a few words, but she was always on her way somewhere to do something…

His hands clenched. Why on earth would she want to spend any time with a two-million-dollar gigolo?

You never said sorry.

He flinched. As he did every single time Eve's words replayed themselves through his mind—which they did with startling frequency. At least that was something he could rectify.

At seven o'clock on Friday morning he took a brand-new surfboard he'd bought the previous day and paddled out into the surf—not directly towards Eve, but nearby—and tried to catch a wave. Pru had given him some preliminary instructions and he'd watched a couple of 'how to' videos on the Internet.

It was a whole lot harder than anyone had made it look. He gritted his teeth as he fell off the board for the umpteenth time, all but face planting into salt water and sand. He was starting to hurt. He suspected that tomorrow he'd discover muscles he'd never known he had.

'What are you doing?'

He glanced up to find Eve sitting on her board nearby, perfectly at ease on the treacherous, shifting water. He scowled. 'I thought I'd give surfing a go. I watched some videos—surfing basics.'

She folded her arms but still stayed on her surfboard

without falling off. 'And those videos told you to leap straight to trying to stand on your board in chest-high water, did they?'

He grabbed the surfboard as a wave tried to tug it free. 'Well, no. They said to catch small waves on your knees in the shallows first, but…'

Her eyebrows rose. 'But you think you're so good you can skip ahead a few steps?'

In a word—yes! He kept himself fit.

But apparently he wasn't fit for surfing.

With a laugh she headed back out again. He watched her catch a perfect wave, switching back and doing some fancy turn that had him shaking his head.

Right. He patted his board. They'd take it back to basics, then.

He didn't know how long he practised but eventually he managed to travel a few metres on his knees before falling off. Then, and only then, did he turn his board in Eve's direction.

'You look like you were making some progress,' she said.

He tried to sit on his board with the same ease and grace that she did. He doubted he managed it, but he did finally find himself sitting on the board. The swell of the sea moving beneath him felt oddly soothing. 'I'm crap.'

'We're all crap in the early days.' She sent him a sidelong glance, her brow furrowing. 'You want to tell me what you're really up to?'

He didn't understand the sudden anger that ballooned in his chest. 'You want to see me hurt and humiliated. And I want to make you happy.' He gestured at his board. 'Two birds, one stone.'

Her lips pursed. 'So…this is about my grandmother and whatever it was she said to you yesterday? Cassidy told me about it.'

He should've known she'd hear about that. 'What did Cassidy say?'

'I think the words she used were "shell-shocked" and "shattered".'

He winced. 'She brought me a slice of carrot cake after your gran left.'

Eve's eyebrows lifted before she smoothed her face out again. 'Granny Beth has a remarkable ability to make one feel the size of a pea when the mood takes her, and—'

'Eve, she didn't say anything to me that I didn't deserve. She held a mirror up and I didn't like what I saw. That's all.'

She gestured to his board. 'So now you want to punish yourself?'

'In part, probably. So far it's not working.' He didn't feel the slightest bit better for the beating he'd so far taken in the surf. 'But I live in hope. The other part...'

Her eyes widened like a startled deer's. 'The other part?'

'Out here I can talk to you alone without anyone overhearing.' She made as if to lie down on her board and paddle back to shore. 'In an environment where you're at home and comfortable and where I'm not.'

She stilled and then sat upright again.

'Out here I'm hoping you don't feel intimidated by me... Out here I'm hoping you feel you have the advantage.'

Her eyes flashed. 'I don't feel intimidated by you at all—out here or on dry land.'

'So you're saying you haven't been avoiding me?'

Her gaze moved from his to scan the shore. 'I run my own business, in case you forgot. There are demands on my time, things I need to do.'

'I understand that, which is why I'm making the effort to meet with you at a time that's convenient to you and on your terms.'

'If you want to discuss any of the local development

opportunities or the fundraiser, you only need to say. I'll make the time.'

'And what if I want to talk to you about something that's not business?'

'Like what?' She stared at him as if they couldn't possibly have anything other than business to discuss. Her face cleared. 'Oh, you mean Pru. Has something happened? Are we no longer going to the dog shelter next Saturday?'

'I could send that kind of information to you in a text, or wait till you'd returned to shore. I didn't need to go to this effort, let the sea use me as its punching bag, to tell you that.'

'Punching bag?' She snorted. 'You big baby—that's nothing. You've been playing in the little pool.'

Would she feel more kindly towards him if a monster wave dumped him? 'Here's the thing, Eve. I made you a promise to not bring up the past, and I'm not going to break any promise I make to you. Not in the here and now. But that doesn't mean you can't raise the past with me. And I mean to be here in case you ever decide to do that.'

'Not going to happen. And here's a tip, Damon. You're fighting the sea's power when you should be harnessing it. I'm harnessing your power for the greater good of Mirror Glass Bay and that's all I need from you. End of story.'

And with that she lay flat on her board, paddled onto a wave and caught it all the way back to shore. She didn't turn and wave to him. She didn't turn and look back once.

He'd known this wasn't going to be easy. But the only way he could think of to tell her how sorry he was for all that had happened between them was to continue to show up. And he planned to keep doing exactly that.

She'd said she didn't need anything from him. But she needed to hear his apology. The expression in her eyes after their encounter on the beach that night… Bile burned his stomach. When he'd broken her heart, he'd broken her belief in herself—her belief in her judgement and in her ability to read people. She needed to know that he hadn't deliberately played her false or for a fool. She needed to know that he hadn't deliberately, coldly and ruthlessly made her fall in love with him just so he could gain an advantage over her.

She needed to hear the truth. It wouldn't change anything between them, but it might bolster her belief in herself again. And he owed her that.

Damon surfed every morning for the following week. Sometimes he was there before Eve, sometimes after. He always waved to her and she always waved back. Most days, once he was worn out from trying to master the skills he needed to, he'd paddle out the back to where she was and just sit there. Not talking. Not asking anything of her. Just being present.

One week to the day that he'd started showing up, she swung on him. 'Fine, Damon, tell me what this is all about. What is it from the past that you want to tell me?'

His every muscle stiffened. He dragged in a breath over the pounding of his heart. 'Sorry.'

'You got water in your ears? I said—'

'I'm not asking you to repeat yourself, Eve. I want to say I'm sorry for what I did four years ago. I wanted to apologise then, but you were so angry and said you never wanted to see me again—and I didn't blame you, not in the slightest. And then you left. Without a word.'

He'd known she'd leave him after he'd destroyed everything. He just hadn't realised she'd leave everything else too—the promising career she'd created for herself, the city he'd thought she loved and her family. He'd understood then exactly how badly he'd hurt her. 'I hated myself so much for what I'd done that afterwards I didn't try to find you, and I never told you how sorry I was. I just slunk away like a coward.'

Two million dollars richer.

She paled at his words, but her chin didn't drop. 'What exactly are you apologising for?'

The breath he pulled in hurt his lungs. 'I'm sorry I betrayed your trust and stole your client. I only won the grant because I managed to score the Otto Farnham account. I deliberately used the insider knowledge I'd gained from you to woo him and steal him out from beneath you.'

Inside information she'd given him when they'd been in bed together—both of them physically replete from their love-making but not yet ready to sleep because they'd wanted to continue revelling in each other for a little longer. It had felt like their own little world, precious and fragile, and he'd treasured it. It was where Eve had shared her hopes and dreams with him, transporting him and giving him a picture of a life he'd never thought possible for himself. It was also where she'd shared her worries and concerns—including work problems and difficulties.

He'd been honoured by her confidences. While their company had positioned the two of them as business rivals, pitting them against each other to win particular accounts, she'd trusted him. They'd both known that the powers that be at Spellman and Spelman were watching them, wondering which of them to fast-track, to whom to offer a junior partnership first...and to which of them to award their prestigious industry grant.

That grant had guaranteed the winner a place within the company's hierarchy—a recognition of excellence. It had guaranteed career success, financial security and a place at the top. They'd both been hungry for that. But she'd trusted him enough to share her difficulties at work and to ask his advice. And he'd done the same, knowing she'd never betray him.

He'd never meant to be anything but supportive. He'd never expected...

He'd loved her! *Her* triumphs and successes had felt like *his* triumphs and successes. And she'd been *so* close to closing that deal with Otto. He'd been holding his breath for her.

And then…behind her back he'd wooed Otto himself—using everything he knew about the man and his insecurities to give himself the edge. He'd betrayed her. All so he could win that damn grant.

'I knew how many months and how many hours you'd put into winning Otto's trust. I knew you were battling old-fashioned sexism and prejudice.' Otto was old-school, believing men were better at finance than women. The inroads Eve had made and the fact she'd nearly won him over did her credit. 'So I used that to my advantage.' And he'd thrown everything he'd had into winning the other man's trust, playing on his belief that only a man could do such a job properly.

'Wow.' She paled. 'So…no pussyfooting around about what you did, then.' Cupping her hands, she scooped up seawater and splashed it over her face.

'I can't pretty any of it up. I was completely ruthless.' He forced himself to continue. 'Did you know that Otto thought you and Clay were still engaged?'

Clay Spelman was the son of one of Spellman and Spelman's senior partners, and Eve had been engaged to him for six months before Damon had met her. And for two months after. They'd all become friends—these days Clay was Damon's best friend.

It was only after Eve and Damon had become lovers that she'd told him she and Clay had basically fallen into their engagement—a path of least resistance, a mutually easy arrangement encouraged by their families. On paper, they'd seemed perfect.

She'd said she'd broken off the engagement because of her attraction to Damon—the strength of her desire for him had made her realise what was missing from Clay's and her relationship. It'd made her realise that she wanted more—that both she and Clay deserved more.

'I did wonder,' she finally said now. 'I didn't deliberately keep the truth from him, but I also knew if he thought I was that closely allied to the Spelmans it'd be a tick in my favour.' She glanced at him. 'I take it you disabused him of the notion.'

He nodded.

Her nostrils flared, and she shook her head, as if she still couldn't believe what he'd done.

Damon swallowed the hardness that did its best to lodge in his throat. It settled in his chest like a stone. 'I knew the board's decision about whom to award the grant to was drawing closer. When Mr Spelman asked me if there was any reason why he should award me the grant over you, I knew they'd chosen you as the grant's recipient.'

Her eyes throbbed. But she didn't utter a word.

'So I asked him…' It was hard to push the words out. 'I asked him what would happen If I handed him the Otto Farnham account by the end of the day—all signed, sealed and delivered.'

She flinched.

'He said if I did that then the grant was all mine.'

She refused to look at him and he wanted to throw his head back and howl. 'I'm sorry I did that to you, Eve. I've regretted it every single day since.'

She tossed her head and swung back to glare at him. 'Really? So if you could turn the clock back you'd do things differently?

Would he? He dragged a hand down his face. She laughed—a harsh, ragged sound—and made to paddle away.

'Wait!' Panic rose through him at the remote expression on her face. 'I want you to know that I didn't plan it. I didn't set out to make you fall in love with me to take advantage of you or the situation.'

Eyes the colour of sodden seaweed met his and his mouth went dry. 'I loved you, Eve. I broke my own heart that day too.'

But he could see she didn't believe him. 'You chose the two million dollars, though, Damon. You didn't choose me. You'll have to excuse me if I don't have any faith in your version of love.'

'If I tell you why I did it, though, you might—'

'Nope. Not interested.'

And then she was on a wave, moving away from him, looking free, lovely and utterly beyond his reach.

CHAPTER EIGHT

PRU CHATTED ALL the way from Mirror Glass Bay to the Byron Bay Dog Rescue Centre, for which Eve gave thanks, because it took her the full thirty-minute drive to force every cell from focussing wholly on Damon. His apology the previous day had messed with her head—blown all her concentration—and she'd barely been able to think of anything else since.

She'd checked in customers, spoken to her bookkeeper, had lunched with her grandmother and had pulled beers in the bar—but it had all been by rote. Her mind had been elsewhere.

Ever since that apology she'd been in turmoil. It made no sense—his apology shouldn't change anything. But his stark recitation of what he'd done four years ago hadn't soothed her at all—it'd brought all the pain, confusion and disbelief rushing back.

And then he'd told her how sorry he was and there'd been no mistaking the sincerity in his eyes. But it hadn't drawn a line beneath those long-ago events, as it should've done. Instead of easing the burning in her chest it had increased it tenfold, and she wanted to throw her head back and scream.

And then he'd had the affront to show up on his surfboard again this morning—getting knocked off wave after wave, time and time again, but gritting his teeth and getting back on that damn board.

It was enough to make anyone scream.

Even more infuriatingly, he hadn't come near her. He hadn't tried to pick up the thread of yesterday's conversation, hadn't tried to force his point of view or interpretation onto her—as he'd promised he wouldn't. He was letting her set the pace. He was letting her choose what she wanted to know and what she didn't want to know.

She folded her arms and glared doggedly out of the window, sticking out her chin. It wasn't going to happen. There was no pace to set because *they* weren't going anywhere. She felt him glance briefly at her, but she didn't return it. The *why* of what he'd done four years ago didn't matter. All that mattered was that he'd chosen that two-million-dollar grant over her, and he'd done it in the most brutal fashion possible. That was all she needed to know.

'And there's even a mother dog with five puppies,' Pru was saying from the back seat. 'That'd be like fostering six dogs for the price of one—how cool would that be?'

She forced her mind from thoughts of the man sitting beside her and to the twelve-year-old in the back seat. 'Five puppies could be fun, but that's an awful lot of toilet training.'

Pru giggled. 'Yeah, it could get messy.'

'Six dogs would need a lot of exercise too, don't you think? And a big yard.'

Pru's yard was large, but only a tiny portion of it had a dog-proof fence.

'Uncle Ron and his team are putting a brand-new fence up—for free. Well,' she countered a moment later, 'for ANZAC biscuits. I have to bake them ANZAC biscuits every week for the next month. They wanted to do something good for the dog shelter. Ron wants to check out the dogs I foster and have first dibs on one for his family.'

Ron was...? She glanced at Damon. She'd bet he'd set that up. His answering glance gave nothing away but it had her pulse chugging all the same. She turned in her seat more fully to look at Pru. 'Won't you find it hard to give them up to their forever homes when someone adopts them?'

'Mrs Dalton talked to me about that. She said that finding foster carers for the dogs was really important—it means the pound doesn't have to put them down. That's a really big thing, don't you think?'

'Huge.'

'So, I'll miss the dogs when they get a home for real, but there's always going to be more dogs who need fostering. This way I'll get to know lots and lots of dogs, and that'll feel like I have lots and lots of friends in the world.'

'Oh, Pru, what a gorgeous thought. And it's true. What you're doing is such a good thing.'

Pru's chin lifted and she beamed back. 'I'm doing something for the greater good.'

The younger girl's words made Eve's chest burn. She turned back to the front and swallowed down the lump that lodged in her throat. It settled in her chest, a hard and heavy weight. Pru was doing something for the greater good. So was Damon. While she...

While she was holding on to a four-year-old grudge. Tightly. With both hands. As if it were a life buoy. Wasn't it time to let it go?

She had no idea. And then they were at the dog shelter and she looked forward to putting it all out of her mind for a couple of hours while she played with the shelter dogs. A yard full of fun, playful, rowdy dogs—it was exactly what she needed.

When they entered the office, not only did they find Barbara Dalton, waiting to take Pru through for the foster-care training, but Valerie Sorensen too. 'Simon and I planned to surprise you,' she said. 'We wanted to treat you to a couple of hours on the boat.'

'Boat?' Barbara snorted. 'This thing is like a palace with a hull and sails.'

'Simon is rather proud of it.' Valerie rolled her eyes. 'I suspect he thinks you're in the market for one, Damon.'

'He could be right.'

No, no. Eve glanced from one to the other. She wanted dogs and noise…time *away* from Damon.

'But Simon has been called away on business.'

She let out a relieved breath. Very quietly. She wouldn't offend the Sorensens for the world—and not just because of the business negotiations currently underway, but because she genuinely liked them. They were nice people. So were the Daltons. That said, negotiations were still at a delicate stage. Offending them could prove fatal to Mirror Glass Bay's hopes.

'Never mind,' she said brightly. 'Maybe some other time. We understand he's a busy man. But it was really lovely of you both to think of such a thing.'

'Oh, no,' Valerie said. 'We haven't cancelled the treat. Everything has been arranged. We've organised a jaunt just for the two of you. Just for a few hours—but I made sure to order you lunch and champagne.'

She beamed at the two of them. Somehow—just—Eve managed to beam back. 'Wow! It sounds amazing.'

'And Barbara has spoken to Pru's mother, and she's fine with the two of you leaving Pru to her care for a couple of hours.'

Eve's mind whirled, trying to find a way out. 'Honestly, though, Valerie, that's much too generous. We couldn't possibly trespass on your goodwill like that.'

Shadows chased themselves through Damon's eyes when she met them, but he took his lead from her. 'And I'm sure Simon would much rather be there to point out all the yacht's features and answer all of my questions.'

'We'll organise another jaunt for the four—or the six of us,' she added, swinging back to Barbara.

Damon glanced at her and Eve gave a tiny shake of her

head. They'd have to submit or risk alienating the Sorensens…and that was something they couldn't afford to do. 'It sounds wonderful.' She pasted on her brightest smile. 'But…you are going to join us, aren't you?'

'No, no! The two of you go and have a lovely time.'

'We're going to be busy anyway,' Barbara said.

Eve couldn't help herself. 'You do know that Damon and I are just friends—there'd be no third-wheel thing happening if you did join us.'

The other woman leaned across and patted her hand. 'Of course—whatever you say, dear.'

She didn't believe her! Which left Eve with nothing to say.

Half an hour later, she and Damon were sailing the placid waters off the Byron Bay main beach in the kind of luxury she'd had only ever dreamed about.

And she couldn't enjoy any of it because she was supposedly enjoying 'couple time' with Damon—the last man on earth with whom she wanted to spend couple time.

'I'm sorry,' he murmured as he came to stand beside her at the yacht's railing. 'I know you'd rather be anywhere but here. If I'd realised what they had planned, I'd have found a way to get out of it.'

'It doesn't matter. It wasn't worth making a fuss over. Look.' She gestured. 'Isn't the view spectacular?'

He frowned. 'It really is.'

Since he'd been grounded in Mirror Glass Bay, he'd been forced to stop and smell the roses. The combination of bewilderment, awe and pleasure that flitted across his face did things to her insides. It reminded her of their shocking intimacy on the beach that night—how his kisses and caresses had set her free. It reminded her of what it had been like to spend long afternoons making love with him. She missed it so much it hurt.

'Oh, and look!' She pointed. 'They've organised some dolphins as well.'

His surprise, and then his delight, tugged at her, daring her to throw away both her resentment and her caution. He moved to the bow to watch them frolic in the waves caused by the yacht as it ploughed through the water. 'That almost makes it worth it.'

She blinked. Didn't he want to be here with her either? She had to fight the sudden urge to jump overboard and swim for land.

He turned back to her with a self-conscious grin. 'I was really looking forward to playing with puppies.'

Something in her chest eased. 'Me too.'

His eyes narrowed as he studied her face and he straightened. She sensed he was about to say something awkward and hard, and panic gathered beneath her breastbone.

As if sensing her resistance and trepidation, he eased back, but she'd have had to be blind to miss the hurt that flashed through those warm brown eyes.

That wasn't her fault.

But it felt like her fault.

'Did you know that this yacht is forty-five metres of un-rivalled luxury?' He started talking dimensions and engine sizes and she could've hugged him.

They talked about the yacht, the scenery and the view until they'd exhausted all those topics and had nothing left to say. So they settled to touring the yacht's layout below deck. The luxury took her breath away but couldn't divert her attention from Damon and his broad shoulders and lean length—the same clean, broad lines she did her best not to notice every morning while he tried to teach himself how to surf. The master bedroom—apparently called a stateroom—had her tongue cleaving to the roof of her mouth and temptation coiling through her.

Damon didn't look at her.

And she knew. She knew he was remembering what it had once been like between them. He was remembering what they'd once have done with a couple of hours like this. He was wondering what it would be like if they closed that door and tossed all caution to the wind.

And so was she.

She stared at the enormous bed and swallowed, every cell on the surface of her skin becoming more and more sensitised until her mouth dried with need and temptation.

When she glanced across she found Damon's gaze on her—hot, heavy and filled with the same passion she remembered from four years ago. Before Damon, love-making had been pleasant. But making love *with* him had been a revelation. She hadn't known that such pleasure existed—pleasure that could make her pant and beg and lose herself. She'd not understood the irresistible urge to make someone lose control, or the freedom in losing control herself. Until Damon.

She couldn't look away.

She didn't want to look away.

She wasn't sure who moved towards the other first. She was only aware of the elation that filled her soul when Damon closed the gap between them and lifted his hand to her cheek. She nuzzled it, closing her eyes as she dragged in a breath of his skin.

'Eve.'

Her name was a breath, a whisper...a question. And, when his lips descended to hers, her parted lips answered it with a hunger and need she could no longer deny.

His greed matched hers. He slammed the door shut and then hauled her so close she could feel his every muscle moving beneath the softness of her curves. He kissed her with a wild abandon, as if he'd been holding himself on too tight a leash and could no longer contain himself.

And something inside her sang at his wildness, sang at the knowledge she could still drive him insane with need.

'I need to taste you.' She didn't recognise the growl that emerged from her throat and she didn't stop to care. She hauled his shirt over his head, pressed her lips to the spot where his neck met his shoulder and licked him, wanting to weep at the familiar scents and tastes that assailed her. How had she lived without this?

She raked her fingers down his chest, her lips following to find one hard, flat male nipple. She circled it with her tongue, groaning in approval when it hardened as she drew it into her mouth and scraped it gently with her teeth.

Damon swore, and she suddenly found herself upright again and with her shirt pulled over her head, her arms bound and tangled in the cotton. His grin grew wolfish as he stared down at her, making her heart beat like a tattoo in her throat. Swiping the lace of her bra aside, he drew one nipple into his mouth and suckled hard. Her cry sounded about the cabin as she arched into him, and she'd have fallen if he hadn't swept an arm about her waist. She trembled from the soles of her feet to her fingernails as he lathed and pleasured her breasts with a thoroughness that had need roaring in her ears.

With another growl she wrestled her T-shirt over her head, her hands going straight to the belt buckle at Damon's waist. She needed this man inside her now! And she wasn't going to be denied…

A knock on the door had Damon stiffening. Eve ignored it.

'Ms Clark and Mr Macy,' a steward called out from the other side. 'When you're ready, your lunch has been served on the main deck.'

'We'll be right there,' Damon called back,

Not if she had any say in it. She pressed kisses to his jaw, letting her mouth rove down his throat, her fingers busy at his belt, while he sucked in great breaths of air. She wanted to drive him wild again, to the edge of all reason.

She scrabbled for purchase as he put her away from him. Very gently he eased her bra back into place, and she blinked. He picked up her T-shirt from the floor and handed it to her, not meeting her eyes. 'I'm sorry, Eve, I lost control.'

She swallowed. 'I…um…you weren't the only one.' She frowned. They were adults. They could…

Her heart sank at the expression in his eyes. Apparently, they couldn't. She did what she could to hide the disappointment that stretched through her.

His lips pressed into a grim line. 'I promised not to kiss you again.' He hauled his shirt on over his head and covered up that glorious naked chest.

Her heart thumped in protest.

'I am truly sorry.'

He was sorry? He was apologising? Did he wish he hadn't kissed her?

Swallowing, she tried to slam herself back into her shirt, her arm getting caught in the process, and she had to tolerate the supreme indignity of Damon coming to her aid before she strangled herself.

'You hated me for what I did that night on the beach. And I can't repeat that. I…'

She closed her eyes.

Dear God, what had she been thinking?

She hadn't been thinking.

'And I made you a promise.' He swore. 'I lost my head and—'

'Let's forget it, Damon,' she cut in, everything inside her hurting, though she couldn't explain why. Other than the fact that she ached for him, for the release she knew he could bring her.

Oh, but it'd be too foolhardy, because making love with

Damon had never just been about pleasure and finding release. For her it'd been about connection.

Being with Damon had made her feel…not whole, because she'd always felt whole, but somehow more than whole, better than whole. She'd never known that such a feeling could exist. It'd taken her a long time to realise that feeling hadn't been mutual.

She glanced up. The darkness in his eyes, the guilt that swirled there, made her stomach clench. Pulling in a breath, she slowly let it out again. She had to get things back on track. She had to get things back to normal again. 'Okay, now we're even.'

'Even?'

'I lost control that night on the beach.' Her skin continued to fizz and spark. 'And now you've lost control here.' She managed to roll her eyes. 'But at least you found your control again.'

'Only because we were interrupted.'

'Then…then we'll be thankful for small mercies, right?'

But as they made their way back up to the main deck she didn't feel thankful. Not in the slightest.

They seated themselves at the ridiculously romantic table that had been set for them—all white linen and crystal—and stared at the amazing meal spread before them. 'Crab salad, lobster, artisan rolls and steamed vegetables,' she said, pointing to each dish. 'This looks amazing.'

'And vintage champagne.' He hefted the bottle in his hand.

'Mr Sorensen must really want you to buy one of his yachts.'

'I guess he must.'

She did what she could to get her raging hormones under control—a feat Damon seemed to have accomplished with barely any effort at all. Her back molars clenched. She could do this. She would make polite chit-chat if it killed her. 'Are you really in the market for one of these beauties?'

He shrugged. 'It could be fun, don't you think?'

'How much would one of these cost?'

'I'd put this one at twenty-five million, but I wouldn't want one this big.'

Her jaw dropped. He'd grown up poor, and she wondered what it must feel like to be so rich now, but she refused to ask a question so personal. She cleared her throat instead. 'I wonder who Mr Sorensen sells these too.'

As they ate, he regaled her with the names of the celebrities and princesses who made up Sorensen's clientele. He told her a funny story about a bidding war between two business rivals for one of these yachts. She understood exactly what he was trying to do. He was trying to dispel her tension. He was trying to make lunch as painless for her as possible. He was trying to distract her and take her mind off her worries and concerns.

The care he took with her now was the same care he showed her every day when he turned up on the beach with his surfboard—only speaking to her when she spoke to him; letting her set the pace and course of their conversations... Her mouth went dry.

It all spoke of... It all pointed to the fact that...

Did Damon still care about her? Or was she being fanciful?

In her chest, her heart turned a slow somersault. She did her best to ignore it. 'What does this all feel like? You had next to nothing growing up. You could buy one of these now if you wanted. Doesn't that feel amazing to you?'

So much for not asking personal questions.

He touched a white linen napkin to his lips. 'It should.'

'But?'

'But I don't give myself the time to enjoy it.'

Was it because of her? Because of how he'd earned his first big break?

He was showing her every kindness and consideration, and had done so ever since he'd arrived back in her life a month ago. He...cared for her. She couldn't deny that knowledge any longer.

It didn't mean he loved her. It didn't mean anything beyond the fact that he wanted her forgiveness. And even if it did mean more... She moistened her lips. She'd never give him a second chance and risk her heart to him again. *Right?*

But she recalled the way she'd flashed to life when he'd kissed her just then. Even now she could taste the euphoria, the delight... And the temptation kept circling through her.

Her heart started to pound. He'd told her he'd not been with a woman since her. That had to mean something. It had to mean something big.

Was she going to ask him why he'd betrayed her four years ago?

Or was she going to leave it all firmly in the past?

She glanced at him. While he had a lot of money, she had everything that mattered—a home, a community to belong to, a business she loved...and a grudge it suddenly seemed petty to keep.

She sat back and pulled in a breath. 'Fine, Damon, you win.'

He lowered his cutlery back to his plate. 'What do you mean?'

She gave up all pretence of eating. 'Why did you really betray me four years ago? Why was that grant so important to you? If you loved me—really loved me as you say you did—then the money shouldn't have mattered at all.'

Damon's heart pounded so hard that for a moment he couldn't catch his breath.

Was she prepared to listen to him?

What he was about to tell her wouldn't change a damn thing—it wouldn't change what he'd done—but it might give her a different perspective on the events of four years ago.

He'd always known, deep down inside where he knew the truth, that she deserved that from him.

'I mean, if you've changed your mind...'

Her shrug was nonchalant, but it didn't fool him. He knew the courage it'd taken her to ask the question. 'I haven't changed my mind. I'm just gathering my thoughts. You took me by surprise, that's all.'

He poured sparkling water into a crystal glass and drank deeply. Sunlight glinted on the bay and waves splashed against the side of yacht. The beach glowed golden and mansions graced the headland in magnificence and splendour. But in his mind's eye he saw none of it. What he saw was the knocked-over garbage cans and trash that littered a dark alley and a doorway that led upstairs to the one-bedroom apartment he'd shared with his mother.

'I told you that I grew up in... Well, we weren't financially well off.'

'You said you were poor.'

'The truth is I grew up in inner-city squalor. My mother was a drug addict. There were times she turned tricks to get the money for her next hit.' His lips twisted. 'There were times I stole food because I was hungry.'

Her hand flew to her mouth and her eyes went wide.

'We lived above a Vietnamese bread shop owned by the Nguyens. They'd sometimes give me the leftovers at the end of the day. That kindness probably kept me out of juvenile detention.'

Eve pulled her hand away from her mouth. The pulse in her throat fluttered. It was all he could do not to lean across and touch his lips to it. 'I'm so sorry, Damon. I had no idea.'

Because he'd made sure nobody had any inkling about his background.

'That's an awful way to grow up.' With a visible effort, she swallowed. 'Two million dollars must've felt…it must've felt like a dream.'

His lips twisted. That kind of money had always seemed like an inconceivable sum. 'You want to know what I was really afraid of when I was a kid, Eve? Going into foster care. I know now I'd have been better off, but back then…'

He remembered the fear with a clarity he could almost taste—it'd been a dark, constant presence. It was why he'd done his best not to draw the attention of anyone in authority. His attendance record at school had been impeccable; he'd kept himself and his clothes clean; he hadn't got into fights or disrupted class. But it'd meant he had kept to himself. He'd never made the kind of friends he could invite home.

'My mother didn't really start going off the rails until I was seven. Seven through to eleven were the tough years.'

She blinked hard, but her gaze didn't waver from his. 'What happened when you were eleven? What changed?'

'Scott came into our lives. He was an old school-friend of my mother's and had been trying to track her down for an upcoming reunion. He told me later he'd always had a bit of a thing for her.'

'He became your stepfather?'

He nodded. 'He got my mother off the drugs, found us a place in the suburbs and got her a job—working in a clothing factory that made leisure wear. A factory full of women, so suddenly she had friends, and…' He was toying with a piece of lettuce, pushing it about his plate with his fork, and he lifted his head to meet her gaze. 'Hell, Eve, I can't tell you how good life was. I felt like we'd won the lottery. And then when I was fourteen Scott asked Mum to marry him and she said yes—and I felt like we'd won the lottery twice over.'

'He sounds like a wonderful man.'

'I hero-worshiped him.'

'Of course you did. He…he saved you. And he definitely saved your mother.' Her gaze turned uncertain. 'Is he still alive?'

A shaft of pain splintered his chest. 'He died a year ago. Cancer.'

She reached out and covered his hand. 'I'm so sorry.'

'Thank you.'

He stared at her hand, everything inside him throbbing. Almost without volition, he turned his hand over and laced his fingers through hers. And then held his breath. He had no right to touch her, to hold her to him—even just her hand. Especially after what had just nearly happened—and would've happened if they hadn't been interrupted. He'd nearly broken his word to her. *Again.*

Her grandmother was right—she was too good for him. But she didn't pull away. A fine tremor ran though her—transmitted from her hand to his—but, with a tiny sigh she probably thought he couldn't hear, she left it there.

Gratitude rolled through him, fierce and fervid, and he had to fight the overwhelming and intense urge to tell her he loved her.

She didn't want to hear that. She'd moved on. He was here to do what he could to make things better for her, not worse. If he was lucky, at the end of this he might get the chance to call her a friend.

'Damon.' Her fingers tightened fractionally. 'Why didn't you ever tell me about your mother and Scott when we were together?'

He rubbed his free hand across his brow. 'When I was at university there was a girl I thought I was in love with. I took her home to meet the family…told her about my background.' He gave a low laugh. He'd been such an idiot. 'She came from a very nice upper-middle-class suburb and couldn't handle the grittiness of my childhood.'

'The insensitive…' She called her a name that made him laugh. 'You're better off without her.'

'I know that now, but at the time I was gutted. Scott and I talked about it and agreed it might be best if I didn't share details about my background with a lot of people.'

'Oh, Damon.' Her eyes went soft with sympathy and it made things inside him ache. 'Anyone with half a brain would've admired you all the more for what you'd over-come and what you'd made of your life.'

'We thought it might jeopardise my career chances.'

'So you got used to not talking about your childhood and family?'

He gave a heavy nod.

She was quiet for a moment. 'You thought I would treat you like your university girlfriend?'

It was hard to hold her gaze. 'I didn't know.'

Pain flashed in her eyes and he tightened his fingers about hers. 'Eve, when I first met you, you were engaged to Clay. Clay came from such a privileged background, and so did you.'

'But it wasn't on the same scale as Clay's,' she protested.

'No, but both your parents were professionals, and I knew how much pressure they were putting on you. And you have to remember how insecure I was. I hid it well, but when I compared myself to Clay…' He shook his head 'I couldn't work out what you saw in me.'

Her eyes widened, filling with tears, but then she swallowed and nodded. 'Okay, I can see that. You were wrong to short-change yourself, but given your background I can understand your insecurity.'

'I was scared too.' He wasn't ashamed to admit it. Not now. 'I'd never loved anyone with the intensity I did you, and it scared the hell out of me. It made me sensitive—ridiculously so. And it made me a bit paranoid...suspicious.'

She leaned towards him. 'What do you mean?'

His heart beat hard. 'You and Clay broke off your engagement, but I sometimes wondered if the only person who knew about it was me. It wasn't shouted from the roof tops. It was kept pretty hushed up.'

'But you knew the reasons behind that. We didn't want to embarrass the company. Plus, our families were hoping we'd change our minds, so...' She shook her head. 'Clay and I knew it was over, though, and so did you. I figured that's all that mattered.'

'I knew what you and Clay had told me. But all the time a part of me couldn't help wondering if you were just having a bit of fun with me on the side and that you saw Clay as your future.'

'How could you think that?' She pulled her hand from his. 'I told you how much I loved you. *All the time.* I told you how much I wanted to build a life with you.'

He saw in that moment how much he'd hurt her, and he'd never loathed himself more.

'Why didn't you share any of this with me back then? Why didn't you talk to me? Damn it, Damon, all that time I thought I was building a future with you while you were waiting for it to break apart.'

'Not talking to you was the biggest mistake of my life.'

She pulled her arms in close to her body as if closing herself up...or preparing herself for a blow. 'That's why you threw me over for the grant.'

'No!' He dragged a hand down his face. 'Behind the scenes other things had started to snowball. And, yes, I should've told you about them—I see that now.'

Her shoulders unhitched a fraction. 'What things?'

'My mother...' Even now it was hard to push the words out.

Eve turned grey. 'She went back to drugs?'

He forced himself to laugh. 'Not quite, but it's evident she has an addictive personality. She took to gambling. Unbeknownst to Scott, she gambled all their money away. Now, that's an attractive family to marry into.'

'That's not what I'd have thought.'

'I know that now.' She'd never know how bitterly he regretted not confiding in her. 'Scott got her help—counselling. But he's proud, just like our Pru. He wouldn't let me help. I could've taken a mortgage out on a house for them, but he wouldn't let me.'

A breath left her. 'Until you were awarded that grant money.'

'No, not even then. Besides, this was all in the year prior to the grant.' He scratched both hands through his hair. 'Given some time and space, Eve, I'd have got over my inferiority complex and my insecurity—would have allowed myself to believe in your love.'

She glanced at him uncertainly. 'Okay.'

She didn't fully believe him, he could see that, but she was still willing to listen.

'But then Scott was diagnosed with cancer.'

For a brief moment she covered her face with her hands. 'I can't believe you tried to deal with this all on your own.'

'I was an idiot.' *Such an idiot.* 'Scott fixated on the grant. He told me he could die happy if I won it because he knew it'd mean I'd never face financial insecurity again…that I'd have the means to look after my mother.'

And *that* was why he'd betrayed her. Though, neither one of them said it out loud.

'If you'd told me all this at the time, I'd have taken my name out of the running.'

'I know that now too.' He swallowed back the bile that burned his throat. 'I returned to work one afternoon after having taken Scott to an oncology appointment earlier in the day. Mr Spelman called me into his office and asked me if I knew of any reason why he should award me the grant instead of you. I figured then that you'd won.'

'Idiot. He'd called me into his office earlier that same day and asked me the same question. If you'd swung by my office first, I'd have warned you.'

He stared at her. 'You're joking!' He'd always thought... 'What did you say?'

'I told him to toss a coin, because we were both as good as each other and that he couldn't go wrong either way.' She wrinkled her nose. 'It wasn't an answer that pleased him. It wasn't cut-throat enough.'

Neither of them spoke. He pulled in a breath. 'In the interests of full disclosure, Eve... I'm ashamed to say this... part of the reason I never confided my fears to you at the time is I'd have given anything I had to keep you in my life. And there was a part of me that was afraid you'd ask me to take myself out of the running for that grant so you could win it. I knew how much pressure your parents were placing on you. And if you'd asked it of me—even after Scott's diagnosis—I was afraid I'd do what you wanted.'

She stared straight back at him. 'I'd have never asked you to do that.'

'No, you wouldn't. But all I could see back then was how much I owed Scott. He'd been the one person in my life I could rely on.'

'You gave up what you most wanted to give him what he most wanted.' Her shoulders sagged. 'So that's why you hesitated the day I asked you if you regretted doing what you'd done. You couldn't actually say you regretted making Scott's final wish come true.'

'I hate what I did. But I can never regret giving Scott the sense of peace he needed. What is unforgivable is that I hurt you in the process.'

CHAPTER NINE

EVE STARED AT Damon and for a moment everything hurt. 'Why didn't you try and tell me all this at the time…or at least afterwards?'

He had to know it would've made a difference.

'Not only was I your social inferior, but I also saw myself as morally reprehensible. I'd never felt I deserved you. And, doing what I did, it was like I proved that to myself. When you said you never wanted to see me again, I figured getting out of your life was the best thing I could do for you.' His lips tightened. 'I became the morally bankrupt businessman I considered myself after that—cold, ruthless, unfeeling. I walked away from you and lost a part of myself.'

He'd hurt himself even more than he'd hurt her. 'If you'd told me all this four years ago, I'd have forgiven you.' For the first time she wondered if leaving Sydney had been a mistake. She'd handed in her notice and fled—she'd needed the space to lick her wounds and get over her hurt and humiliation in private. Walking away from the world of finance hadn't been a mistake. But maybe she should've given Damon a chance to try and explain.

'I didn't deserve forgiveness.'

She wanted to slam a hand down on the table and shout at him. 'What about what I deserved?'

He leaned towards her and everything inside her yearned for him. 'You deserved better than me.'

'And what gave you the right to decide that on my behalf?' Her insides screwed up tight. 'What is it with men? They think the little woman needs protecting and—'

'I never thought of you as the little woman, Eve.'

A seagull landed on the deck, squawking at them for leftovers. They both ignored it.

'I was screwed up, confused, not thinking straight.'

And he'd been grieving for the man he loved—she could see that. Her heart ached. But she also saw what he couldn't—he hadn't loved her enough to fight for her. She'd never been enough for her parents, and she hadn't been enough for Damon.

Her eyes burned and her throat ached. Ancient history. None of it mattered any more.

'But, when I saw you in that boardroom a month ago, I didn't want to be that morally bankrupt businessman any more. I wanted to be the man you once thought me.'

Things leapt inside her. She did what she could to pull them back into line, reminded herself that what he was telling her didn't mean anything in the here and now. They didn't have a future together. They hadn't had a future four years ago, and perhaps they had even less of a chance now. Their lives were so far apart. Damon would return to his corporate life and the bright lights of the city with his conscience eased, and she'd stay here in her gloriously low-key life where she belonged without the burden of an ugly grudge.

Win-win.

Only it didn't feel like a win. She felt like the biggest loser on the planet.

'Besides…' His smile didn't reach his eyes. 'If I'd done that, you wouldn't have all this.' He gestured at the bay—the sparkling water and golden sands, the sun shining down on it all. 'You said your life now is so much better than if you'd stayed in the city and the corporate world.'

It was.

And it wasn't.

'And this life suits you, Eve.'

She moistened her lips. She had nearly everything she wanted. Forcing her lips into a smile, she met his wary gaze. 'While you got on with things and made a success of your career, when all the odds were stacked against that.' He should be proud of himself.

Her words dragged a harsh laugh from him. 'I made a lot of money. But I stopped living. I stopped being who I wanted to be.'

He eyed her for a moment and then thumped his elbows on the table, a fist running back and forth over his mouth. It took a super-human effort not to let her gaze linger on that mouth and those lips.

'It's time for me to stop punishing myself and to start living again.' The knuckles on his fist whitened. 'What I need to know, Eve, is if you'll be okay with that.'

She jerked back, the spell broken. 'Of course I am!' What kind of person did he think her? 'I'd have forgiven you four years ago if I'd known the whole truth. And I forgive you now.'

He closed his eyes, his shoulders sagging as if released from a weight they'd been carrying for far too long. 'Thank you.'

He smiled then—really smiled—and she couldn't help smiling back, even though she wanted to cry. He looked so happy, and she'd helped him to find that happiness. She couldn't regret it. 'So…' She placed a dessert in front of him. 'Honey and chai *panna cotta*. Sounds delicious, doesn't it?' She had no appetite whatsoever.

'Eve, I'm not really hungry.'

She fixed him with her best boss glare. 'The Sorensens have gone to all this trouble.'

He eyed the dessert dubiously. 'So I'm going to eat the *panna cotta*?'

'*And* you're going to enjoy it.'

He laughed. She lifted a spoonful of dessert to her lips. Oh, the stuff was delicious! 'So,' she started, needing conversation, not wanting to let dark thoughts overtake her. 'What does this new life of yours look like? What's going to change?'

One gorgeously broad shoulder lifted and it was all she could do not to whimper. 'I've barely had a chance to think about it. I'm going to work less—much less—and delegate more. I know that much. My VP is currently in Frankfurt doing an incredible job closing a deal.'

He frowned, but he didn't look unhappy, just perplexed.

He gestured with his spoon. 'I'm surrounded by great people. I should be giving them more responsibility and a chance to shine without me constantly looking over their shoulders.'

Warm brown eyes speared hers. 'It seems to work for you at The Beachside.'

'I might be the overall manager, but I defer to Cassidy on anything related to the bar and restaurant because she knows her stuff. Same goes for my housekeeping manager.'

'It appears to work seamlessly.'

She shrugged. 'There's the occasional hitch, but we pull together when that happens and can usually fix it or come up with a temporary solution. So, yeah, it works most of the time.'

'And it frees you up to do the things that give your life extra meaning—like surf, and get involved in koala conservation, and…'

His face suddenly went so wistful, her heart started to throb. 'And?'

'Take the time to have a coffee and chat with people. You've made the time for friends.'

Oh, Damon.

'And you can now too,' she told him, refusing to let her sadness for him show. What a difficult life this man had led. 'You obviously have a knack for it.'

He blinked.

'Oh, for heaven's sake. For someone so smart you can be really dumb sometimes. Look how easily you made friends with Ron and his carpentry team on your first day here. And now both the Sorensens and the Daltons.'

'But...that's just business.'

'Only if you want it to be.'

His mouth opened, and then he closed it, as if turning her words over in his mind. As he did his eyes became brighter and his shoulders lost more of their hard cast.

'Believe me, you're not going to have trouble making friends.' She ate more *panna cotta*, suddenly hungry again. 'So, I surf and get involved in koala conservation. What are you going to do that you're passionate about?'

His gaze dropped. He stared out at the water and she didn't understand his sudden remoteness. 'Maybe I'll get a boat like this one. I have an apartment on the harbour with its own jetty.'

Wow. That sounded fancy.

She squinted out at the water too. What on earth was she thinking? He didn't need her help. He'd find his own way.

'I'm going to take a holiday.' He swung back, his eyes sparkling. 'Maybe I'll buy a holiday house in Mirror Glass Bay.'

She froze. *What?* That'd mean she'd be forced to see him...what...two weeks a year, maybe more? And every year she'd be forced to face the fact that he hadn't loved her enough. And never would.

'Scrap that.' The words ground from him as if he'd just taken a punch to the gut. His eyes lost their brightness. 'That's a daft idea.'

She shook herself. Where were her manners? Where was her *kindness*?

'Nonsense! It's a great idea. You'll always be welcome in Mirror Glass Bay. You've done so much for the town, Damon. You're one of us now.' How could she be so damn selfish? 'Everyone is very grateful for all you've done. You have friends here, and we'll always be happy to see you.'

'Everyone except you,' he said with a straightforward candour that made her blink.

'Not true, I—'

'I just saw the look of absolute horror that passed across your face, Eve. You couldn't hide it.'

Her mind raced. She couldn't tell him the truth—that she still loved him...that she'd never stopped loving him.

How pathetic!

The only thing worse than his pity would be if he told her he loved her too in an attempt to continue making amends. She'd rather die!

'And you can't deny it now.'

'Fine.' She glared right back at him. 'It felt like a weird collision of my present and my past, and it felt confronting. I mean,,, God!' She threw up her hands. 'What if my parents show up next? But it was just a momentary thing and that weird moment has passed. My logical brain has kicked in again.' She forced her chin up. 'It'd be lovely to see you come back to Mirror Glass Bay year after year.'

'Liar.'

He said the word softly, but she sensed the anger that had built behind it. Anger she probably deserved. 'You've earned a place in the Mirror Glass Bay community, Damon—if you're not too afraid to seize it.'

'I'm not the one who's afraid.'

Maybe he was right, but she wasn't admitting as much. 'Besides, the deals you and everyone are counting on aren't sealed. Not yet.'

She gestured at the yacht and the luxury that surrounded them. 'My instincts tell me they are, and my instincts are still good.' She tried to pull the threads of her scattered mind together. 'I know you've bought those warehouses.'

'How the hell...?'

'And I know you're promising to fit them out to Sorensen's and Dalton's specifications. You're saving them time and trouble, which equates to money.'

He eyed her, looking as if he was doing his best to channel righteous outrage. 'Those were private deals!'

She waved that away. This was Mirror Glass Bay they were talking about. 'Don't worry, the details are private. What I'm saying is that you've paid whatever debt you imagined you owed me ten times over. You can live your life in whatever way you see fit without any thought to what I want or don't want.' She leaned across to drive her point home. 'I shouldn't be figuring in your considerations at all.'

He thrust out his jaw. 'Then you'd be wrong.'

She couldn't help it. Her heart leapt.

'I came here with one goal, Eve.'

Her mouth went dry. Hope wrung her from the inside out. Was he going to tell her he stilled loved her? Was he going to say he'd come to Mirror Glass Bay to win her back? If he did...

Her heart thundered in her ears. If he did, she had a feeling she might just launch herself across the table at him. She couldn't hide what she felt any longer. Her heart pounded. For better or for worse, she loved Damon Macy.

'Do you want to know what that one goal was, Eve?'

She nodded. She couldn't speak. She couldn't take her eyes from his. After all this time, did they finally have another chance at love? What they'd had together had always been too big, too strong...too much to throw away.

It was why he hadn't been with another woman since her. It was why she hadn't been with another man.

'For four years I've been waiting for an opportunity to make it all up to you, Eve. I betrayed you, hurt you, and threw away the best part of my life. But helping you to shore up Mirror Glass Bay's future has meant I can finally pay my debt and give you something of real worth. I only wish I could've done it sooner.'

She stared at him, and slowly everything inside her collapsed and she laughed—watching herself as if from a long way away. Damon didn't love her. Maybe he had once, but now.

Kryptonite.

She was *such* an idiot. He saw her as an obligation, nothing more—a problem he'd needed to fix. While she was as big a fool as ever where he was concerned. He hadn't shunned other women because nobody else could live up to her memory. He'd been punishing himself.

While she'd been living some stupid half-life because she'd never been able to exorcise him from her mind.

Well, no more!

'I wanted to do something to make your life better, not worse.'

An obligation. A god damned obligation. Was there an uglier word in the English language? It was right up there with guilt and self-flagellation.

The hope that had gathered beneath her breastbone became a cold, hard lump that pressed on her heart until she could barely breathe. The kiss they'd just shared, that crazily intimate episode on the beach, hadn't meant anything. She'd been stupid to think otherwise. She'd been stupid to think that him showing up on his surfboard at the crack of dawn day after day meant anything either.

'You can tick that off your list, Damon. You've saved my community—you're providing it with at least two sources of industry that will translate to ongoing employment, all of which will lead to better infrastructure for the town.

So, if you want to turn the Greamsman site into your ideal holiday house, feel free—you've earned it. Just don't forget to invite me to your house warming.' She didn't want to go to his god damned house warming!

She stabbed a finger at him. 'What I want you to do is to stop using me as an excuse from leading the life you want to lead.' While she was going to work on wrenching this wretched man out of her heart for good! 'You're welcome in Mirror Glass Bay—part-time, half-time, full-time, whatever you damn well please. Just as long as you realise that you and I are never going to be anything to each other ever again. We don't have any kind of future together. We're...*nothing*!'

His eyes widened at her anger. And then his mouth twisted and his face became dark, fire flashing from his eyes. 'Oh, don't worry, Eve. You've been crystal clear on that particular point.'

Good!

'That's one message I couldn't possibly mistake!'

'Good, because I wouldn't want to have to repeat myself.' She'd turned into a shrew, but she couldn't stop herself. 'I like my life exactly the way it is.'

'Oh, keep lying to yourself, Eve. Who knows, one day you might even believe it.'

What the hell...? He *couldn't* know.

'Four years ago, you ran away. And you're still running away now.'

'Not running away,' she managed through gritted teeth. 'Running to. Running to a better life, filled with people worth spending my time with.'

His eyes narrowed and the lines about his mouth deepened. 'And in the process you sacrificed your ambitions— because they scared the hell out of you. You can deny it all you want, but you came alive when we were working on ways to woo potential developers. You shone at that party—charming everyone and working towards several deals all at once. It filled your belly with a fire I bet you haven't felt in four years.'

She stared at him. He was wrong. Her mouth dried. 'You never needed me to save your town. You could've dusted off the skills you'd spent years at university learning and then perfecting at Spellman and Spelman, and you could've saved the town on your own.'

She shot to her feet. 'Oh, but why do that when it would've robbed you of the opportunity to come in and save the day? You swooped in too quick for anybody else to have the chance to make their mark.'

His head rocked back at her words and he shot to his feet. 'You've been wrapping up your reasons for being here in a nice, big, bright-red bow—*I want to make up for my shabby behaviour, Eve.* But, really, it's the thrill of the deal that matters to you. It's what's always mattered, what you've always loved.' More than he'd ever loved her. 'Regardless of the personal cost to yourself!'

His entire frame shook, and she watched it with a sick kind of fascination. 'You know what, Eve? It's finally occurred to me that you're right—we never really did know each other.'

She couldn't answer him, couldn't speak for the lump that had lodged in her throat.

His nostrils flared as he drew himself up to his full height. 'I vote we end this discussion right now.'

'Best idea I've heard all day,' she shot back.

Without another word, he spun on his heel and strode towards the back of the yacht. She blindly made her way to the front, only stopping when the railing halted her progress. She gripped the metal tightly until her hands ached with the same ferocity that made her eyes burn. Hauling in breath after breath, she told herself she wouldn't cry. She wasn't crying over Damon Macy ever again.

CHAPTER TEN

THREE NIGHTS LATER Damon found himself alone in The Beachside bar. He sat on a high stool at the bench that ran the length of the window at the far end of the room and stared outside at the darkness. A wind had whipped up and all the windows were closed to protect those inside. Low clouds scudded across the sky, hiding the glory of the stars he now knew sparkled behind them.

He scowled at the darkness and wondered if Cassidy would have a fit if he opened one of the windows just a crack to let the wind lash his face. He lifted his second glass of beer to his lips. Maybe it'd help him feel alive again.

Because, ever since that look of horror had passed across Eve's face when he'd tentatively proposed buying a holiday house here, something inside him had died.

He didn't deserve anything more, he reminded himself. She'd said she'd forgiven him—and the sympathy in her eyes when he'd told her his ugly story had been sincere— but it didn't mean she wanted him as a permanent or even semi-permanent fixture in her life.

The fight they'd had afterwards only reinforced that fact.

He'd still betrayed her. His actions four years ago, while mitigated by other circumstances, were barely excusable.

The Demon was reaping what he had sown.

With a bitter laugh he drained his beer in one long swallow. He should head back to his room and do some work—

see how Owen was getting on. Except he didn't feel like doing any work.

And he didn't feel like going back to an empty motel room. For the last three mornings he hadn't gone surfing. He'd given Eve her space. They'd exchanged stilted but oh-so-polite apologies about losing their tempers and Eve had been assiduously pleasant to him ever since. He had a feeling he preferred it when she yelled at him. At least that had felt real. Even Dolores had abandoned him, as if she'd sensed the darkness of his mood and wanted to be away from it.

Still, he should never have kissed Eve. It'd made things too hot and heavy, frustrating and fraught. All of that tension had sparked their tempers.

He glanced up to his right. The flat above Reception was in darkness, which meant Eve was out somewhere, enjoying herself…living her life.

He glanced around. There were a couple of other tables still occupied. He wasn't keeping Cassidy from closing. Striding up to the bar, he signalled for another beer.

Cassidy took his empty glass and slotted it into a rack beneath the bar. She pulled him another beer, not saying a word, but she raised a single eyebrow. She was a woman who could say a lot with just one eyebrow. Setting the beer in front of him, she leaned on her forearms. 'You look like crap, Damon. You coming down with something?'

The beer halted halfway to his mouth. Cassidy's solicitousness, brusque as it was, took him off-guard. 'I'm fighting fit.'

She snorted.

It took all his willpower not to fidget beneath her stare. 'Why'd you snort? What's so funny?'

'You said you were *fighting* fit. Doesn't look like you're fighting at all. Looks to me like you're surrendering—waving a big white hanky in the air and crying uncle.'

What the hell…?

He nodded at the bottles of liquor lined up on the wall behind her. 'You been sampling the goods?'

'Have you told her you love her?'

He froze.

Another speaking eyebrow made him swallow. 'So… not going to deny it, then?'

Denying it seemed wrong—like another Judas kiss—and he had no intention of wronging Eve ever again, whether she knew about it or not. But it didn't mean he was going to talk about it. 'None of your damn business, Cass.'

She straightened from her slouch. 'So you're in love with Eve, but you're not prepared to fight for her?'

'She hates me.' A strategic retreat seemed the best course of action.

'God, don't be so pathetic. Eve doesn't hate anyone.'

He dragged a hand down his face. 'You're right. But it doesn't mean she wants me in her life. And even if she did—' his hands fisted '—I don't deserve her.'

Cassidy stuck out a hip and folded her arms. 'So, for all your hero status in town, you're nothing but a faint heart.'

Her scorn stiffened his spine.

'She appears to have forgiven you, but you're too much of a mouse to win her back.'

'You're not hearing what I'm saying, Cassidy.' He ground the words out. 'She doesn't want me.'

'You know that for sure?'

He recalled the horror in Eve's face and it was all he could do not to flinch. 'Yes.' She didn't want him anywhere near Mirror Glass Bay, not even for a couple of weeks a year.

'A hundred per cent sure?' Cassidy persisted.

He went to say yes, and then out of nowhere he recalled Eve's earnestness when she'd told him he'd earned a place in Mirror Glass Bay. He scowled. 'Well?' Cassidy demanded.

'Ninety-five per cent certain,' he growled.

'So there's a five per cent chance you're wrong.'

He took a drink, pointing a finger at her when he lowered his glass again. 'Those are seriously bad odds.'

Her eyes narrowed. He had a feeling he preferred it when she raised an eyebrow. 'You're prepared to risk your money on a long shot, but not your heart...or your dignity?'

'This has nothing to do with my dignity!' He didn't give two hoots about his dignity.

His voice had risen and several people turned in their direction. He lowered it again. 'When I came to Mirror Glass Bay, I swore to only do things that would increase her happiness, not lessen it.'

'And you think pursuing her will make her unhappy?'

'Unwanted attentions,' he muttered.

'You let Eve decide if they're unwanted or not. You've no right to make that decision for her.'

Eve had said something similar to him on Sorensen's yacht.

'Anyway, that just sounds like one of those crap excuses men make when they're afraid of feeling vulnerable. If you're not prepared to put everything on the line for Eve, then it's better she forget about you.'

Did Cassidy think he had a chance?

Though, knowing Cassidy, she'd simply take great pleasure in watching Eve wipe the floor with him. Except they both knew Eve wouldn't take any pleasure in that. Cassidy was Eve's best friend. She wouldn't tell him to pursue Eve, declare himself, if she thought it would bring Eve pain or disturb her peace of mind.

He recalled that night on the beach when he'd worshipped Eve's body. There'd been magic in their kisses, in the heat of his caresses, and in her temporary surrender to the pleasure he could give her. So much magic, it'd left him reeling and had sent Eve into a spin—and she'd retreated, fled.

That kiss on the Sorensen yacht had been magic too. But…was he the one fleeing this time?

He recalled the mornings on the beach when he'd been struggling with his surfboard, when Eve—as if she couldn't help herself—would tell him to try moving higher up his board, or to speed up his paddling to get onto a wave properly. They'd only been tiny scraps of advice, but she'd still taken the time to give them to him when she hadn't had to.

Five per cent?

'Five per cent is crap odds.'

'Then I'd make my gesture a big one, if I were you.'

The next morning Damon tucked his surfboard under his arm and made for the beach. The wind was still up, and high, grey cloud masked the sun, but it hadn't rained. And he figured it wouldn't much matter if it did. He was going to get wet either way, right?

Eve, wearing a pair of black trousers and a long cardigan, intercepted him in the park before he reached the path down to the beach. 'What are you doing?' she demanded.

He stared at her. 'Why aren't you in a wetsuit?'

She looked great in a wetsuit—sleek, lean and strong.

She looked great out of a wetsuit too. She looked great in anything.

'You're not surfing?' He couldn't keep the disappointment from his voice.

'Have you actually looked at the surf this morning? Spared it a passing glance from your balcony on your way down?'

Um… He'd been in too much of a rush to get down to the beach—to see her. He'd hoped bobbing in the sea for a bit, and admiring her skill on a board, would help him come up with a plan, provide him with inspiration for a big gesture.

Eve gestured seaward. 'Oh, Grasshopper, you have much to learn.'

He followed the direction of her hand and swallowed at the churning mass of ocean that greeted him. That wasn't the kind of sea one bobbed around in.

'That, my friend, is a dangerous surf, and not for the likes of beginners.' She followed his gaze and added, 'The guy on the yellow board is currently ranked three on the Australian circuit, while the guy on the white board is a former Argentinian champion. They have the experience to deal with these kinds of conditions.' She glanced at him again. 'You really want to go out in that?'

He shook his head and turned back towards the motel. 'You ever surfed seas like that?'

'A couple of times, but I didn't enjoy it.' She glanced back behind them. 'I only risk swimming in seas like that when there are a lot more people around.' She stopped then and stared right into his face, her eyes serious. 'You can't ever take the ocean for granted, Damon. Always check the conditions before you go in. And, if in doubt, don't.'

Wise advice for surfing. It was often wise in business too. But Cassidy was right—it was the wrong approach to love. He loved Eve—with everything he was—and he'd find a way to show her and convince her of his love. And maybe, just maybe, if he were lucky, she'd take a chance on trusting him again.

'Go put your board away and come have some breakfast. There's something I'd like to run by you.'

And then she was gone, and he was racing upstairs to his room to get changed like an eager fourteen-year-old getting ready for his first date.

'I ordered us both a full English breakfast,' Eve said when he slipped into the seat opposite. 'I hope that's okay.'

'Sounds perfect.' He studied her face. 'What's on your mind?'

She blew out a breath, her gaze sliding away for a fraction of a moment before returning. Worry spiked through him. 'Has something gone wrong with the Sorensen or Dalton deal?' If it had, then he should be the first one to know. But Eve had access to some kind of bush telegraph that gave her an inside scoop well before everyone else. 'Or have you heard back from the Environmental Protection Agency?'

'How would I know? I thought you were handling all of that.'

'Yeah, but you seem to hear things a good eight hours before I do.'

That made her laugh, lightening her eyes and easing the weight in his chest. 'Rest easy, Damon. I haven't heard anything to the contrary.'

Good.

'What I want to talk to you about is—' her gaze slid away again '—me.'

His absolutely favourite topic of conversation. He sat a little higher in his chair. 'Okay.'

'But first... Damon, that fight we had—'

'You don't have to say anything.'

'I want to.'

He stilled and then nodded.

She kept her gaze trained on his. 'I want you to know I didn't mean the things I said. I'm honestly grateful for everything you've done. I was angry because...' Her gaze dropped and she shrugged. 'Because four years ago you didn't confide in me, and it seemed that we lost so much when we didn't have to. But it was childish of me to lash out like I did, and I'm sorry.'

'While I lashed out at you because I was angry at myself.' He grimaced. 'The height of maturity, I think we'll both agree.' She huffed out a laugh and he found his lips lifting. 'I'll accept your apology if you'll accept mine.'

'Done.' She bit her lip and held out her hand, looking adorably uncertain. 'Friends?'

He shook her hand, things inside him clenching. 'Friends.' He eased back and tried to still the hammering of his heart. 'Now, what did you want to talk about?'

She moistened her lips. 'I've been thinking about what you said to me on the Sorensens' yacht. About it maybe, possibly, being a mistake to have turned my back so completely on…on my training.'

He studied her carefully. She looked neither peeved nor resentful and he let out a slow breath.

Cassidy chose that moment to set two plates piled high with food in front of them. 'Enjoy, folks.'

They thanked her, and Damon lifted a piece of toasted sourdough to his mouth. Before he bit into it, he said, 'We were both a bit het up—emotions were running high. I'm sorry if I overstepped the mark.'

'I don't know about overstepping the mark. What I do know is that you hit it dead centre—you hit a big, fat bullseye.'

The toast dropped back to his plate.

'You were right—I have missed it. And I didn't even realise it until you pointed it out.' She shook her head, as if appalled at her own cluelessness.

'Understandable. You've had a lot on your plate.' It was all he could do not to reach across and clasp her hand.

'I suppose.'

'And I think you equated the ruthlessness and ugly cut-and-thrust of a few people within the corporate world with the entire industry.'

'I don't want to go back to that world full-time.' She gestured around. 'This is my life and my home.'

'But?'

She suddenly leaned towards him. She hadn't touched her breakfast yet. 'Do you think I could make a tiny little investment firm here in Mirror Glass Bay work? I'm thinking of only one or two days' worth of work a week. I don't think there'd be the demand for anything more than that, but…what do you think?'

'You're asking my advice?'

She picked up her fork and speared a mushroom, before setting the fork back on her plate, mushroom untouched. 'It's just, I've been out of the game for four years.'

'Garbage.' He tried to hold back a grin. 'I've seen you reading the financial pages while you sip your coffee. I've seen people in here ask you what you thought about certain stocks and shares.'

'That's just small stuff. Nobody's paying me—it's just an opinion.'

'An opinion backed by experience and a savvy business sense, Eve.'

She met his gaze. 'I trust your advice on this, Damon. You have one of the shrewdest heads in the business.' And then she outlined her plans for a small investment firm, just servicing the local community, and explained how she thought it might work. He sat there and listened, his heart starting to sing. 'Well?' she finally demanded.

He wanted to lean across and kiss her. Well, okay, he always wanted to kiss her. But he specifically wanted to kiss her in this particular moment because she'd come alive.

Her courage made his heart leap. She was facing her fears and was pushing through them to create a solution and find a way forward. She was amazing. He wanted to tell her she was amazing, but it would come out too intense—too much too soon. So instead he grinned, and she blinked, as if dazed. 'You already know it's a brilliant plan.'

She pondered his pronouncement and then shook her

head. 'No. I thought it was an okay plan, but not brilliant. It's why I wanted to run it by you.'

'It's better than okay—it's a great plan. But there's one thing you haven't considered.'

She leaned towards him, so close he could count the spattering of freckles across her nose. 'What?'

'Expansion.'

'Oh, I don't think—'

'In time it *will* become a full-time gig.' Clients would flock to her. 'If you don't want to do it full-time, you need to think about attracting good staff.' She'd be crazy to think otherwise.

Without letting her gaze drop from his, she called Cassidy over. 'Hey, Cass, would you be interested in becoming a partner in The Beachside?'

'In a heartbeat.'

'Want to discuss it over pizza tonight?'

'Can't. Remember?'

Eve slapped a hand to her forehead. 'That's right! Well, what are you doing in a couple of hours, around ten?'

'I'm pencilling in a meeting with you,' Cassidy said, before heading back to the counter to take an order.

'What are you doing tonight?' He hadn't meant to ask, but the question slipped out.

She sent him a smile that made his heart beat faster. 'Big plans. I hope you're free.'

'I am.' He'd be whatever she wanted him to be. If he'd had plans, he'd have cancelled them.

'I seem to recall that you used to like poker.'

'I still do.'

'Well, I've organised a poker night. Here. Tonight.'

He glanced around in search of a flyer.

'It's invitation only.'

Something in her tone had him swinging back to face her.

'I wanted to apologise for making you feel so bad the

other day on the yacht, Damon. For making you feel you weren't welcome here. You'd be a great asset to Mirror Glass Bay. And tonight, at the poker game, you're going to see exactly how well you fit in.'

She grinned at him and determination solidified in his gut. His five per cent suddenly felt like seven, or maybe even ten, per cent. 'I can't wait,' he said, finally starting to attack his breakfast—now cold—with gusto. It was the best damned breakfast he'd ever eaten.

CHAPTER ELEVEN

EVE FINISHED THE last of her breakfast and set her knife and fork into a neat line on the plate before blotting her mouth with a paper napkin and glancing at the man opposite, so acutely aware of him it almost hurt. Damon only had a few more days in Mirror Glass Bay—the auction was this coming Saturday night—and after that he'd return to Sydney with its bright lights, his apartment on the harbour, his business...and with the past firmly behind him.

She told herself she was glad for him. He'd carried a burden of guilt these past four years that was entirely out of proportion to his crime.

She cringed again at the memory of the way she'd flown off the handle at him. Her hurt had got the better of her, and it made her want to die a thousand deaths. All he'd been doing was trying to put things right. After the childhood he'd had, and all the difficulties he'd had to battle, the one thing he hadn't deserved was her anger and resentment.

She was only grateful he hadn't realised the true reason behind that hurt and anger.

She had an urge to order another entire full English breakfast, but she suspected it had nothing to do with hunger and everything to do with comfort—an attempt to plug the aching gap that yawned through her.

Get over yourself.

They were saving her town; she was going to embark on

an exciting new business venture; she'd learned the truth about the past and it helped to know she hadn't been some sucker Damon had manipulated for his own ends. She was surrounded by friends. It was time to draw a line under the past and move on.

She pulled in a breath and sent Damon a smile. 'Thank you for listening to my plans—for letting me pick your brain—and for being so encouraging. I just took unashamed advantage of you and...' She trailed off with a shrug, not sure what she was trying to say.

One corner of his mouth hooked up in a wicked smile that tilted her world to one side. 'You can take advantage of me any time you want, Eve.'

She swallowed. He almost sounded as if...he was flirting with her!

Oh, don't be absurd. That was just wishful thinking.

Outside the wind had died down but it had started to rain—a gentle, nourishing patter that the local farmers would welcome, not to mention The Beachside's gardens.

'I appreciate that more than I can say.' She smiled to hide the sadness circling in her chest. 'I was really awful to you when I first saw you again in Byron Bay.'

'It was a shock. You hadn't been forewarned. And you had every reason to loathe me. It was understandable.'

He'd tensed, but someone who didn't know him as well as she did wouldn't have noticed. His eyes didn't leave her face and it made her mouth dry. 'I was wrong, Damon, and I'm sorry I made you feel so bad.'

'Eve, I—'

'You're the best thing that could've happened to Mirror Glass Bay—a thousand times better than Greamsman and his resort. You've poured money into this place that you didn't have to. And you're not going to get a high return on your investment.'

Those whisky-brown eyes suddenly gleamed. 'You never know. Maybe I will.'

She went to clasp his hand, but at the last moment pulled back. If she touched him, he'd know—he'd sense how she felt about him—and she wasn't putting that kind of pressure on him. She wasn't taking advantage of any lingering guilt or sense of obligation he might still harbour. She moistened her lips. He followed the action and everything inside her clenched tight. 'Thank you, Damon. Truly—thank you for everything you've done.'

Things throbbed behind his eyes that she couldn't identify and didn't understand. 'What would make Mirror Glass Bay perfect?' he finally asked.

Him. He would make Mirror Glass Bay perfect. Not that she could say as much.

'Sealing the Sorensen and Dalton deals, which you tell me are nearly in the bag. I don't need anything more than that.' *Liar.* 'Mirror Glass Bay doesn't need anything more than that.'

He nodded, but not in agreement. More as if he were pondering something imponderable.

'That kind of local industry will keep our primary school and medical centre open.' And that was all she'd wanted to achieve. 'Your conference centre will be a boon for The Beachside and local eateries if you decide to go ahead with it.'

His lips curved upwards. 'Not to mention a boon for my staff.'

And maybe it'd mean she'd get to see him once in a while. 'And the boss, if he decides to take some time out of his busy schedule,' she said, desperately hoping she didn't sound as if she was fishing.

He nodded, but didn't commit himself. 'What else would make Mirror Glass Bay ideal?'

She pushed on to hide her disappointment. 'Oh, I don't

know. Maybe a research centre for Beck. She could do good things here. We need to conserve and preserve what we can where we can, and she's on top of all the latest research, so…' God help her, but she'd still rather he built a holiday house in Mirror Glass Bay than for Beck to get her research centre or for his employees to get their corporate beachside retreat.

'And?'

She stared at his raised eyebrow. 'And nothing. This place is perfect the way it is.' But he raised his eyebrow even higher. She didn't want to dwell on the intriguing planes of his face or the faint shadow accenting his jawline, so she searched her mind for things to add…*anything*! 'Okay, then, to get my little investment company off the ground without a single hitch.' There'd be hitches, of course, there always were… 'I'm excited by that.' She loved running The Beachside, but it didn't have to be either-or. She could do both. And somehow that seemed the perfect solution.

'Eve, Eve, Eve.' He shook his head in mock disappointment. 'All of those things are so predictable. Go wild, let your imagination soar.'

Oh, right. They were playing *that* game—if she found a genie in a magic lamp…if money and resources were no object.

She leaned back and let her creativity take flight. 'Okay, it'd be beyond fun to hold an annual surf competition here.'

'Hell, yeah. I'd come to see that.'

Excellent. What else would he come for? Maybe an annual poker competition. *Don't be an idiot*. That'd be laying it on too thick.

'What else?' he urged.

'Anything I want?'

He nodded.

'This is utterly indulgent, but I'd love it if there was a little boutique in town that sold cute dresses and shoes, funky jewellery...'

'Handbags,' Cassidy said, coming up to clear away their plates and obviously catching enough of the conversation to want to play along. 'And a hairdresser,' she added. 'They wouldn't need to be open every day of the week, just one or two.'

'Ooh, and a spa—facials and massages.' Eve sighed.

A dreamy expression crossed Cassidy's face. 'A bit of waxing, tinting and fake tanning.'

They both raised their hands at the same time and wiggled their fingers. 'Manicures.'

Damon leaned back and stared at them. His grin hooked up the right corner of his mouth, making her want to swoon. She shrugged, suddenly self-conscious. 'You told me to dream big.'

'In that case,' Cassidy said, balancing plates, 'add a bus-load of hot, eligible men to that list.'

Eve and Damon laughed at the staged look of longing that crossed Cassidy's face as she walked away. Eve shook her head. 'But we can live without those things...or make a trip into Byron Bay for them.'

His expression sobered and his eyes searched her face. 'Isn't there something you want—something just for you?'

Him. But she couldn't say that out loud.

'What do you want for yourself in the long term?'

She'd barely let herself think about it. 'I...'

When she hesitated, he shifted a fraction on his seat. 'Do you want to keep living in your tiny flat above Reception?'

She gripped her hands together beneath the table. 'We're dreaming big, right?'

'Absolutely.'

'Then one day I'd like to buy a house somewhere along

Marine Drive with a beach view and a good back yard for a dog. I'd like to have a dog.'

She'd like to have a family too—a husband and kids—but she couldn't think about that. Not while she was looking at Damon. She'd never be able to think about that until she met a man who touched her the way he did, and she didn't even know if that was possible.

'That sounds…nice.'

Had she imagined that wistful note in his voice?

He suddenly stood and clapped his hands together. 'I better get a kick on—there are some things I need to do.'

She swallowed as he walked away. His old life was pulling him back already. She hoped he meant what he'd said to her that day on the yacht—that he'd make time to have a life outside of the office. He deserved one. He deserved to be happy.

'You look stunning!'

Cassidy's wide-eyed approval helped to bolster Eve's nerves as she strode into the restaurant wearing a satin cocktail dress in fire-engine red. Maybe it was perverse, but she wanted Damon to see her, to notice her, wherever she might be in the room tonight.

She smoothed a hand down the chiffon overlay, fingering the satin band that tied into a square bow beneath her breasts. 'Not too much?'

Cassidy shook her head. 'It's perfect.'

'You're not looking too shabby yourself.' Her friend was poured into a midnight-blue number that was fitted from collarbone to mid-thigh and then flared out around her knees and calves. 'Can you breathe in that?'

'Just about,' she said with a wink.

Eve had a feeling that quite a few men this evening would have trouble catching their breath when they caught sight of her.

'The band are setting up,' Cassidy said. 'I still don't know how Damon managed to get them—the man's a magician—but they're such a draw-card. We're going to have a heck of a crowd tonight.'

Both women took deep breaths and Cassidy said, 'Looks like our first guests have just arrived. Ready?'

Eve went to nod, but Damon chose that moment to walk in wearing a dinner jacket and white tie and her tongue stuck to the roof of her mouth.

Beside her, Cassidy let out a long, low sigh. 'Your Gran called him a two-million-dollar gigolo…said he wasn't worth that kind of money.'

She'd what?

'But, looking at him now, I'm not so sure.' Her friend winked at her. 'I'm thinking you'd pay that price twice over.'

Eve snapped upright. Was she that obvious? Cassidy sauntered off towards the waiting staff lined up behind the bar before Eve could make any reply. And then Damon stood there, lifting her hand to his lips, his eyes warm with masculine appreciation. Her heart crested a wave and then hurtled down it with dizzying speed.

'You look beautiful.'

'So do you.' He didn't let go of her hand, and warmth radiated from where his lips had touched her bare skin. He moved in closer, bending down as if to whisper something in her ear, but a burst of laughter from the doorway as the guests started to arrive had him easing back. She reclaimed her hand and sent him a tight smile. 'Let the fun begin.'

When she'd found out the band Damon had organised, she'd known they'd draw a crowd, but it exceeded even her grandest expectations. The bar and restaurant became so crowded people spilled into the gardens and onto the footpath outside the motel. Eve was grateful she'd had the foresight to hire big outdoor heaters. Winter was balmy here, but the nights could still be cold and crisp—especially in a cocktail dress.

She glanced around and shook her head. Mirror Glass Bay had just put koala conservation on the map. *Go, Mirror Glass Bay! And thank you, Damon Macy.*

When the band finished playing their opening set, Damon chose that moment to move to the makeshift stage. 'We have a few minors here tonight who all have to leave by nine o'clock and I promised them we'd announce the winner of the raffle before they left. Eve, do you want to come on up here and draw the name of the winner for this top-of-the-line surf board from Joey's Surfhouse? The one-stop shop for all your surfing needs.'

She hadn't known he was going to ask her to draw it. He should've asked one of the Sorensens or the Daltons. She so wanted Pru to win! She wouldn't be able to hide her disappointment if it went to someone else. Pulling in a breath, she made her way to the platform. 'Good luck, everyone,' she said, but she stared straight at Pru as she said it. The hope in the young girl's face tugged at her.

Crossing the fingers of her left hand behind her back, she reached inside the tombola barrel and pulled out a ticket. She handed it to Damon, but he gestured for her to read it. She unfolded it, stared at the name and her jaw dropped. A big lump lodged right in her throat. She held the ticket out towards him, wanting proof that she wasn't dreaming.

He read the name, grinned and then spoke into the microphone. 'And we're delighted to announce that the winner is… Pru Atkinson!'

A big cheer went up. Pru stared up at them in open-mouthed shock before giving a huge squeal of delight and hurtling up on stage to hug both of them and collect her prize.

'Please tell me you didn't rig that,' Eve murmured to

Damon later. 'We sold something ridiculous like seventy books' worth of tickets.' He wouldn't have…

Would he?

His eyes danced. 'How many books did you buy?'

'Ten.'

'And who's name did you write on each of the tickets?'

'Pru's, of course.'

'Cassidy bought a book and did the same. Ditto for your gran. And so did Pru's mum.'

'But that still only accounts for thirteen books. I mean, I know it helps to increase the odds, but only slightly, and—'

'I bought fifty books.'

She did a double take. 'You did what?'

'So that's sixty-three books all in Pru's name.'

She wanted to hug him.

'That *really* helps the odds.'

She wanted to hug him and never let go.

'Look, the auction is about to start.'

They turned, but before they could move closer Granny Beth blocked the way. Dear God, had she really called Damon a two-million-dollar gigolo?

Before Eve could usher her away, Gran fixed Damon with an unblinking eye. 'Mr Macy, my granddaughter has fully explained to me the circumstances surrounding the events four years ago. Now, Eve has a big heart—bigger than mine, it must be said—but I wanted to acknowledge that I might've been a little harsh in my words to you the other day. I'm prepared to reserve judgement for the time being and give you a chance to prove me wrong.'

His jaw dropped. 'I…um…appreciate that.'

'I like what you've done for the town.'

'Thank you.'

With a nod, she held out her hand. He shook it, and then without further ado she turned imperiously on one heel and marched away.

He picked up his jaw to stare at Eve. 'Did you put her up to that?'

She shook her head. *But...wow.* 'I think you can take that as an official seal of approval.'

Damon ushered Eve—the most stunningly beautiful woman there tonight—to the side of the room where they could watch the auction unhindered.

While the band was an undeniable hit, the auction also exceeded expectations. He glanced around at the excited faces of the Mirror Glass Bay residents that he'd come to know and care about...people like Ron and his team of carpenters, Beck and Cassidy...but his gaze kept returning to the flushed face of the woman he loved. Eve.

All evening, unbeknownst to her, she'd captured his entire attention, had held him in thrall. Oh, he'd chatted and laughed with other people, had even danced with Cassidy and a couple of other women, but the entire time he'd ached to be with Eve.

Except...every time she glanced at him her smile faded.

He did that to her—he dimmed her light. Somehow, and without meaning to, he sucked the joy from her life. And every single time her smile faded it was like a knife sliding in between his ribs.

The ten per cent chance he'd given himself to win her heart dwindled to one thousandth of a per cent.

But he was still going to prostrate himself at her feet. It didn't matter how slim his chances. He wasn't leaving Mirror Glass Bay without knowing for sure, without knowing he'd given it his all.

Both Eve and Cassidy had chided him for making assumptions. He had no hope—couldn't help assuming Eve would be glad to see the back of him—but he wasn't acting on that assumption. She would get the choice. He'd leave his fate in her hands. The risk of humiliation didn't matter in the face of such a prize—a lifetime with the woman he loved.

When the band stopped for their penultimate break, he strode up to the microphone. Amid cheers, he thanked everyone for supporting the koala conservation project. He announced the official sum raised. And then he paused. The room hushed, as if it could tell from the expression on his face that something of great moment was about to take place. He waited until Eve stilled and glanced up, meeting his eyes across the crowded room.

He would not be a faint heart. Not this time.

'A lot of people made tonight happen, and I want to thank each and every one of you. I started on a journey here to help improve Mirror Glass Bay's local economy because of Eve. It's her love and passion for this town that has made things happen. And I want to make a couple of official announcements in relation to Operation Mirror Glass Bay. First, two very respected local businessman—Garry Sorensen and Simon Dalton—will be moving branches of their existing businesses to the industrial site on the edge of town. The final contracts were signed yesterday.'

A big cheer went up.

'In addition to that, on the old Greamsman site two new initiatives are underway. The first of these is Beck Daniels' much-yearned-for research centre. It'll be small to begin with, but there'll be the potential for expansion, which we're hoping will attract government grants. The research centre will be located on the north-western side of the site. On the rest of the site, I'll be building a small boutique conference centre.'

An excited murmur went about the room, but he was barely aware of it. He couldn't drag his gaze from Eve's face, her eyes wide and vulnerable as she stared at him.

He knew she was grateful for all he'd done and was doing. And in all likelihood she'd be appalled when she found out why he'd done it—because he still loved her. He had a speech prepared for that eventuality too, so she wouldn't blame herself and feel bad for hurting him. Something along the lines of the fact that he couldn't think of a more worthy way to spend his money than safeguarding Mirror Glass Bay's financial future.

He hoped to God he wouldn't have to use it.

His hand clenched about the microphone. He probably would. And he *would* find the strength for it.

'With this influx of new industry, the local infrastructure such as schools and medical centres should actually improve rather than decline. The likelihood of Mirror Glass Bay now becoming a ghost town is almost zilch.'

Another big cheer went up, even from those people in the room who weren't local residents. 'And I wanted to celebrate that in a special and memorable way. Eve once joked to me how much fun it'd be if the town could host a surfing competition. Through the week, I spoke to the National Surfing Board, and we've agreed to a five-year sponsorship deal. In September next year, the very first Mirror Glass Bay Surf Festival will take place.'

Eve's hands flew to her mouth—in shock, he suspected—but they couldn't hide the way her lips widened into a huge smile or the way her eyes started to dance.

He spared Cassidy a glance. 'Cass, I think that will also answer your special request.' A town full of hot, eligible men!

She grinned and sent him a thumbs-up.

'I've also been in negotiations with a hairdresser-cum-beautician who's interested in a sea change. Yesterday I took her through several houses that are for sale in town and she's settled on a place on Beach Road that she thinks will make the perfect home business.'

Eve's hands dropped back to her sides and she shook her head, wonderment shining from her eyes. A smile rose through him. Regardless of whether she loved him or not, he had this moment and the knowledge that, in the end, he had helped to improve her life rather than ruin it. In this moment he'd made her happy.

'I was reliably informed that a hairdresser, beautician and manicurist would make many of the women in Mirror Glass Bay very happy, and I'm a guy who likes to deliver.'

Laughter rippled around the room. Someone called out, 'Three cheers for Damon,' and the cheers that followed nearly lifted the roof.

Damon gestured for quiet. 'It's not me you need to thank—it's Eve. She's been the driving force behind all of this.'

And then Eve was moving towards him, and his throat closed over, and he could barely draw breath. She nudged him out of the way so she could speak into the microphone. 'Damon, as usual, is being ridiculously humble. None of this could've been possible without his perspicacity, his determination and—'

She broke off to meet his gaze and the sincerity in her eyes threatened to unbuckle his knees at the same time as it fired his blood.

'And his kindness,' she finished.

It didn't mean she loved him, but... 'Eve's wrong.' He spoke into the microphone again but his eyes never left hers. 'I'm just the man who's determined to do whatever will make her happy—who's one goal in life is to do exactly that.' His mouth went dry. 'The man who wants that job for the rest of his life.'

Her mouth opened and closed, and then she leaned towards the microphone again. 'And now you're all going to have to excuse us. The band are back for their next set so...um...enjoy.'

And then she seized Damon's hand and led him out the nearest door into the gardens, which were littered with people cooling off, taking a little couple time or simply enjoying the fresh air. Eve shivered and he immediately shrugged out of his jacket and slipped it about her shoulders.

'Your role is to give me whatever I want?' she whispered, her eyes huge in her face.

He nodded.

A thread of humour briefly lit her eyes. 'Do you think you could find us some privacy?'

He knew the perfect place. Taking her hand, he led her along Marine Drive with its glorious beach views. Partway along, he veered them down a path and onto the beach. She let go of his hand, kicked off her sandals and sank her toes into the sand. Only then did she meet his gaze again. 'What you said back there, Damon.'

'I meant every word.'

She moistened her lips. 'It sounded a lot like you were saying that you…'

'That's exactly what I was saying.' He reached out and touched her face, just the backs of his fingers to her cheek. 'I love you, Eve. I've always loved you. I never stopped loving you.'

Uncertainty raced across her face. And vulnerability. His heart started to race. Did he see hope there too? He leaned towards her. 'You don't believe me?'

'I don't *not* believe you. I just…' She hesitated, her hands clenching and unclenching. 'What I'm wondering is, if you've sensed how I feel about you, and in your misplaced guilt are trying to give me what I want…'

She wanted…*him*?

'But, Damon, you have to understand that you don't owe me anything. And certainly not a sacrifice like that. Just because I love you doesn't mean—'

He didn't wait to hear any more. He swept her up into his arms and claimed her lips with his, kissing her with all the hunger in his starved soul. She seemed to bow under the onslaught, but flung her arms around his neck, held tight and kissed him back with a matching hunger.

They eased apart several long moments later to gulp oxygen into starved lungs, holding onto each other to keep their balance, to keep from falling.

'That,' Eve gasped, 'wasn't a pity kiss.'

His heart thundered in his ears. 'I feel a lot of things for you, Eve, but pity isn't one of them.' He cupped her face. 'Please say it again.' He was begging, gut-wrenchingly needy, but he couldn't help it.

She didn't laugh at him. She didn't tease him. She didn't even smile. She stared deep into his eyes and he recognised the tenderness reflected there. 'I love you, Damon. I love you so much it frightens me.'

'You don't need to be frightened. I'm never going to hurt you again. I promised.'

She nodded.

'I nearly made the same mistake now that I did four years ago. I nearly left without telling you how I feel—because I don't deserve you. I know that, but...'

'But you gave me a say in the matter.'

He wanted her to know that he'd listened, had taken her words on board when she'd told him how she felt and how his actions had made her feel. 'It only seemed fair to give you the chance to reject me.'

She reached up on tiptoe to press a swift kiss to his lips, and it sent fire licking along his veins. 'That was never going to happen. Also, just for the record, you do deserve me—every bit as much as I deserve you.' She suddenly frowned. 'What on earth made you think I would reject you anyway?' She shook her head, as if she couldn't fathom how he'd ever come to that conclusion.

'Every time you looked at me tonight the smile disappeared from your face and your eyes went dark, almost haunted. I know you said you'd forgiven me, but I figured no matter what you said you couldn't forget what I'd done.'

She smoothed her hands across his chest. 'No, Damon, it was because I was in a hundred different kinds of agony tonight knowing that tomorrow you'd be out of my life for good. I didn't know how to bear up under that knowledge and keep my happy face on. And you'd been beating yourself up so badly for what happened four years ago, and were so determined to made amends, I didn't feel I had the right to tell you I still loved you. I thought you'd stay because it's what I wanted, not because it's what you wanted.'

He'd read the situation so appallingly inaccurately that he made a silent resolution then and there never to keep anything from her again.

A smile, tremulous and beautiful, trembled on her lips. 'But you are staying, aren't you, Damon?'

A sunburst of something pure and joyful shot through him. He turned her to face the road. 'See that house there? I bought it this week.'

She clutched his arm. 'That house has the best beach view in the entire street. How did you convince Molly Collins to sell?'

'I made her an offer she couldn't refuse.' He glanced down at the woman by his side, something inside him taking flight at the expression on her face.

She grinned up at him. 'You really are staying.'

It hit him then—she didn't care about that house or the view. She cared about *him*.

His throat thickened. He swallowed. 'I'm staying.' He was going to turn that house into Eve's dream home. He didn't tell her that, though. There would be time for that later.

'What about your work?'

'I plan to become a master delegator. I want to work remotely. I'll probably need to fly down to Sydney for a day or two here and there.'

'I... I could come with you.' She laughed at whatever she saw reflected in his face. 'Only if I won't be in the way, of course.'

'You'll never be in the way.'

'I just want to be where you are.' She slid one warm hand across his cheek. 'Where *you* are is my home. If you need or want to live in Sydney, then—' she shrugged '—I can do that.'

Would she relocate for him? The realisation stunned him. He knew how much she loved this place. He'd started to love it too. He'd never ask her to leave. Her generosity, her kindness, the size of her heart cast him adrift and reeled him in both at the same time.

Concern shone from her eyes. 'What is it? What's wrong?'

'Nothing! I just... I don't deserve to be this happy.'

Her face gentled. 'Yes, you do. You really do.' She lifted her chin. 'You said your role in life was to make me happy, right?'

'And I stand by that.'

'Then I want the first item on that "making Eve happy" agenda of yours to be for you to understand that you deserve to be this happy. And to cherish being this happy. You work hard, Damon, and you're good to people. And I love you. I have good sense and good taste—I'm not a stupid woman.'

'Of course, you're not!' Pity help anyone who suggested otherwise!

'Then trust my judgement.'

He stilled.

'Please?'

Slowly he nodded. 'I'll try.' Because he did trust her but, more than that, he wanted nothing to mar her happiness, and that included his own insecurities.

Solemnly he put her away from him and went down on one knee, pulling out the velvet box that had been burning a hole in his pocket all evening. 'Eve, I love you. I want to spend the rest of my life with you. Will you please marry me and make me the happiest man on the planet?'

He opened the box to display the champagne diamond nestled inside.

She glanced with trembling wonder from him to the ring. Her bottom lip trembled, she clasped her hands to her chest and his heart swelled, because he could see her answer plainly in her face.

And then she did a double take. 'Damon!' She stared at him, scandalised. 'What did you do? Walk into the jewellery store and buy the biggest diamond you could?'

He grinned. *She was going to say yes!* Maybe not right now…she might insist on a long engagement. And he didn't mind. She could have whatever she wanted. But she'd told him she loved him. She wanted to be with him as much as he wanted to be with her.

'Not the biggest—the prettiest,' he corrected. 'The colour and brilliance of this stone reminded me of you. Eve, your soul shines as brightly as this diamond. We can change it if you don't like it.'

If possible, her expression became even more scandalised. 'We'll do no such thing!'

If possible, his grin widened. 'Is that a yes?'

She pulled him to his feet. 'Of course that's a yes. I love you, Damon.'

He kissed her then, and it was a long time before either one of them spoke again.

* * * * *

THEIR SECRET
SUMMER FAMILY

CHRISTINE RIMMER

For Gaye McGill, in honour of her golden retriever–German shepherd mix, Flip, who was the inspiration for the hero's dog, Owen, in this story. Gaye would like readers to know that Flip was the best of the best and Gaye misses her greatly.

Chapter One

Grace Bravo was going too fast and she knew it.

But she really needed to cheer herself up. And it was a beautiful, sunny first day of June on the Oregon coast, the perfect kind of day to drive with the windows down, playing "Shut Up and Drive" really loud. The fir-scented air blew in and swirled around her, stirring her hair as she bopped right along with Rihanna. She was beating out rhythm on the steering wheel and swinging around curves with abandon.

Too bad she wasn't really feeling it—not the beauty of her home state, not the sunshiny day, not the warm summer air whipping her hair around her face, not even the hard-driving beat of the music turned all the way up.

And then the light bar started flashing behind her. A siren blared.

"No!" she cried. "This cannot be happening..."

But it was. Grace turned off the radio and took her foot off the gas. Easing her eight-year-old RAV4 to the side of the road, she put it in Park and switched off the engine. The white Valentine Bay police cruiser, lights still flashing, pulled in behind her, the nerve-shredding siren cutting off in midshriek.

A ticket was definitely in her future.

She shouldn't be the least surprised. It was all just more crap piled on top of an already crap-tastic day.

Thinking dark thoughts, she raked her wind-tangled hair back off her forehead and watched in her side mirror as the officer—tall, dark haired, broad shouldered, tanned and very fit, in Valentine Bay PD blues and black wrapback sunglasses—emerged from the cruiser.

It took her a second or two to realize who he was.

Dante Santangelo?

No way.

Grace had known Dante forever. His only sister

was married to one of her brothers. Once or twice a week, he dropped by the Sea Breeze where she worked. They got along great, Grace and Dante. She'd always considered him a friend.

Until now, anyway.

"Are you kidding me?" she muttered sourly when he leaned in her window.

"Gracie, you were speeding," he chided—like he was really sorry, but being sorry wouldn't stop him from doing his job. He took off those black sunglasses and gave her a melty look as his plush mouth curved in a warm smile. "License and registration?"

"This is so wrong," she grumbled.

He just kept on leaning in the window, those velvety, coffee-brown eyes patient, like he could wait forever for her to stop being grumpy and pass him her papers.

"Fine." She leaned across the console, popped open the glove box, got out her registration, handed it over, then fished her wallet from her bag and gave him her license, too.

"Thanks," he said. "I'll be right back…"

"I was afraid you'd say that."

He turned for his cruiser. With a groan of frustration, she flopped her head against the seat and closed her eyes.

He was back in no time with a clipboard. "Here you go." He handed her documents through the window.

She took them. "Thanks," she sneered, and couldn't resist reminding him, "I give you the good beer. I don't even let you tip me." Actually, he always tipped her, anyway. But she always meant it when she told him not to.

Did he chuckle as he wrote on his clipboard? Sure sounded like it to her. One big shoulder lifted in an easy shrug. "And I'm giving you the good ticket."

"That makes no sense. There is no good ticket." And yeah, it was a stretch, but she might as well try her feminine wiles on him. Tossing her messy hair a little, gazing up at him with sad, wide eyes, she pleaded pitifully, "Do you *have* to?" He just kept writing out the ticket. "It's been a bad day," she whined. With feeling. "And now *this*."

He passed the clipboard in the window and handed her his pen. "Initial here and here. And then sign here."

"A hundred and sixty bucks? You can't be serious."

He said nothing, just continued to look at her with that thoroughly annoying expression of gentle patience on his handsome face.

She huffed out an exasperated sigh, took her sweet time reading the whole damn thing and did what he told her to do, giving back the clipboard and pen when she was done.

He passed her the ticket and launched into a little spiel about the deadline to respond and how to contest the citation. When he finally shut up about it, he leaned in the window again. "Okay, that's out of the way. Now. Are you all right?" His expression had morphed from patience to real concern.

She glared at him, just to drill it home that she would be a lot better if he hadn't pulled her over. "Not really."

"You need someone to talk to?"

Share her problems with Dante? The idea never would have occurred to her. Yeah, she considered him a friend. But not a cry-on-your-shoulder sort of friend. She'd known him her whole life, practically. And she'd always considered him hot and all, with those smoldery good looks and that broad, hard body.

But he was nine years older, thirty-two to her twenty-three. He'd been married and divorced and he had twin daughters. The guy was a settled, responsible sort of man who would no doubt consider her flaky and immature if she griped about her fight with her bossy eldest brother and whined over her paltry bank balance, which was keeping her from getting her own place.

And about her miniscule bank balance? That was all on her. She'd inherited a little money back when she turned eighteen. If she hadn't enjoyed spending it so much, she would have plenty of money to move.

She should thank Dante for offering to listen to her problems, insist that she was fine, say she would see him the next time he stopped by the bar—and then wave goodbye.

But the thing was, his offer kind of gave her the warm fuzzies. Dante was a tough guy. He didn't let many people close. That he seemed to really want to be there for her made her feel better about herself, somehow.

"You'll be sorry," she warned and waited for him to back out.

But he didn't back out. "I get off at five. I'll see you at the Sea Breeze."

"No, you won't."

"Why not?"

"I can't cry on your shoulder at my place of work. That would be totally unprofessional—and besides, I'm off tonight." She was pretty sure that would do it. He would tell her to drive carefully and turn for the cruiser.

Didn't happen. "How about my place, then?"

Dante's house. She hadn't been there in years—not since she was sixteen and babysat his twins that one time when his then-wife, Marjorie, couldn't get her regular sitter. "You don't have to do this, you know?"

"Hey, come on. What's a friend for?" He upped his offer. "I'll open a bottle of wine."

She waved the ticket at him. "After this, you owe me a nice bottle of tequila. I'll bring the tacos."

He didn't even blink. "Six o'clock?"

For the first time since he'd pulled her over, she gave him a smile. "I'll be there."

Dante had a really nice house—a shingled, rambling, ranch-style place on an acre of wooded land overlooking the ocean. He'd bought it about a decade ago, in the midst of the last housing crisis, when a house like Dante's went for half what it was worth now.

Grace admired the pretty setting as she carried bags of take-out tacos up to his front door. On three sides, the house was surrounded by trees. In back, it overlooked the ocean.

Dante, in worn jeans and a gray crewneck T-shirt that showcased his muscular arms, pulled the door open before she rang the bell. "Right on time. And you brought the tacos, too—here." He took the bags from her. A friendly-looking dog bumped around him, tail wagging. Dante gently warned, "Owen, play nice." The dog had short floppy ears, a sweet face and a red-brown coat with a blaze of white at the throat. His paws were white, too.

She greeted him. "Hello, Owen." With an eager whine, the dog sat and gazed up at her hopefully. "Part golden retriever, right?" she asked Dante.

He nodded. "Golden and German shepherd."

"He's very handsome." She knelt to scratch his thick ruff, glancing up as she let Owen lick her face. "You get the good tequila?"

"Come on inside." He stepped back and ushered her in. "You can see for yourself." He led her to the kitchen area, which was open to the living space, with concrete tile counters and glass backsplashes.

"The counters are beautiful," she said.

"Thanks. I like to change stuff up now and then."

Back when she was sixteen and the pinch-hit babysitter, the counters were white tile—and right now, the bottle of tequila was waiting on the island. She picked it up. "Anejo." The word meant "smooth" or "restful." Tequila Anejo had to be aged in oak barrels that did not exceed six hundred liters for at least a year. "Thank you."

He gave her a nod and gestured at the limes in the wire basket nearby. "You want to shoot it?"

"Have you met me? I'm a purist."

"Perils of being a bartender, huh?"

"That's right. You develop definite opinions when it comes to enjoying good liquor." Actually, bartending was an interim job for her while she'd waited for a teaching job to open up locally.

She had a degree in history with a minor in education from Reed College and she'd recently snagged her dream job. This fall, she would be teaching history at Valentine Bay High. In the meantime, she was still working at the bar, sometimes days and sometimes nights. She liked the flexible schedule.

Dante took a couple of stemless wineglasses from a cupboard. "Will these do?"

"Perfect."

They decided to sit out on the deck and enjoy the view. She helped him carry everything outside, including a pitcher of ice water, which made her laugh. It was so Dante, to make sure they stayed hydrated while they were getting blasted.

It was gorgeous outside and wouldn't be dark for hours. The deck faced a stretch of wooded yard. Farther out, twisted, windblown evergreens framed the edge of the cliff and the top of a narrow trail leading down to a nice stretch of beach below. Off in the distance, the ocean gleamed, pearly blue to the horizon.

Grace sat in a cushioned deck chair at a cast iron table beneath the shade of a big white umbrella. At Dante's insistence, she drank a tall glass of water and ate two tacos before settling back to sip tequila. Owen had stretched out at her feet.

"Okay, I gotta admit." She tapped Dante's glass with hers. "*This* is the life—how are the girls?"

Dante took a slow sip. It went down smooth and hot.

It was nice, really, sitting out here with Gracie. He'd always liked her. She was fun and easy to be with.

And she'd grown up to be gorgeous, with all that silvery blond hair, those soft lips the rich pink color of the inside of a conch shell and those sapphire-blue eyes. Her skin was so pale. She looked like she might bruise from a touch—not that he'd ever make a move on her or anything. They had a way-too-complex history.

Her third-born brother, Connor, had been Dante's best friend all their growing-up years.

But then Connor had broken the bro code. He'd fallen in love with Dante's sister, Aly, and married her. Dante had barely forgiven Connor for that, when Connor divorced Aly for reasons that really weren't reasons at all. Dante had sworn never to speak to the jackass again.

Then last year, Aly and Connor had gotten back together. They'd married each other for the second time last October and Aly had given birth to their daughter, Emelia, just last month. Dante and Connor were friends again now.

And really, Dante had always thought of Gracie Bravo as a kid.

Well, until lately, anyway. Today, she wore faded denim shorts and a cropped top. Following her out here from the kitchen, he couldn't help staring at her ass and her strong, pretty legs, at all that gorgeous, delicate skin...

"Dante. Helloooo." Laughing, she reached across the table and lightly batted his arm. "Nicole and Natalie? How are they doing?"

"Good. Real good." He ordered his dirty mind off Gracie's ass and back to the much safer subject of his twin daughters. They were eight now. They mostly lived with his ex-wife, Marjorie, in Portland, where they went to school. He had them every other weekend and for seven weeks in the summer.

Gracie asked, "When do they come for vacation?"

"A week from this coming Saturday."

"You're counting the days."

He tipped his glass at her. "I always do." He was a family man, through and through. His ex-wife was a good mother. Still, he just felt better when his girls were with him.

Gracie asked, "So how's it going with the new stepdad?"

At Easter, Marjorie had married Dr. Roger Hoffenhower. Roger was a family psychologist and a really nice guy with a big heart. "Terrific." He drank more tequila.

Gracie scoffed. "Smile when you say that."

"I like Roger." He set his glass on the table and turned it slowly. It was almost empty. Against his own better judgment, he added, "I also kind of hate Roger."

"Why?"

He put the glass to his lips again, sipped the last of the golden liquid inside and then slowly swallowed. "Roger is an open wound of feelings and sensitivity." In other words, pretty much everything Dante wasn't. "Plus, Nic and Nat like Roger. A lot. Can you blame me for hating the poor guy?"

She gave a husky little laugh that he found way too attractive. "I think anything I say right now will probably be wrong."

"Smart girl—and why are we talking about Roger, anyway?"

"Er, because you like him—but you hate him, which means you're conflicted about Roger and that's not only interesting, it's the kind of thing you need to talk about with a friend."

He stared at her, unblinking. "But we're not here to talk about Roger."

"You started it. Officer." Those sapphire eyes twinkled at him.

"You're the one who asked about Roger."

"But then you told me how you really feel about the guy. That's my cue to encourage you to tell me more."

"Wrong." He raised his glass to her. "We're risking liver damage for your sake, remember? You need to tell me all about what's bothering you so I can take a crack at saying all the helpful stuff that will make you feel better."

"Clearly, you are at least as sensitive as Roger."

He grunted. "Don't bet on it. But I'm here and willing to listen."

She picked up the bottle and poured them both more tequila. They sat back, just sipping, for a few peaceful minutes. It was nice, he thought. Companionable.

She was staring off toward the ocean when she said, "I had a fight with Daniel this morning." Daniel Bravo was the eldest of the Bravo siblings and something of a father figure to all of them. When their parents died years ago on a trip overseas, Daniel had gotten custody of them and raised them to adulthood in the house where they grew up. "It was a stupid fight and we both apologized after. Daniel and I used to get into it all the time, but it's been better lately. Truly. We get along really well now, as a rule. But I'm sick of living in the house I grew up in and frankly, my big brother is sick of having me there, though he would never admit it…"

They both continued sipping the excellent tequila as Gracie rambled on, looking way too cute and kind of sad, too, explaining about the small trust fund she and her siblings had each inherited from their lost parents. She went on to explain about her trips to Europe in the summers while she was in college, about the writer she lived with one summer. And the sculptor the next and the inventor the year after that.

"That was in Italy, the inventor," she said. "His name was Paolo and he invented things that had a tendency to explode."

Mostly, she explained, she supported these guys with her inheritance while she was with them. "You have to understand, Dante. They were brilliant and interesting. It was England and Ireland and Italy. Best of all, Daniel wasn't there to call me foolish and wasteful and taken advantage of by irresponsible guys. I had the time of my life."

"But…?"

She rolled those big blue eyes. "But Niall and Keegan and Paolo were expensive. And that means that by the end of that third summer, I was kinda, sorta broke."

"How broke?"

She plunked her glass down and poured herself another. He probably should have suggested they put the brakes on the drinking. But he was enjoying himself. That was the thing about Gracie. He'd discovered in the nights he'd hung out at the Sea Breeze with her that she was not only easy on the eyes, she was funny and smart—with a lot of heart.

Gracie Bravo was the whole package, really. He felt better about life in general somehow, when he was hanging around her. He held out his glass and she gave him more, too.

"There's good news, though," she said, after she'd put the bottle down and sipped again from her glass.

"Tell me."

She raised her glass high, as though saluting the trees and the cliff and the whole damn Pacific Ocean. "My perfect job has finally opened up at Valentine Bay High. I'll be teaching world history in the fall."

"Congratulations. That's terrific." He tapped her glass with his.

"Thank you. Also, I've been budgeting responsibly for the last two years, saving what money I can. By Christmas, I'll have enough to get my own place."

So what was the problem? "Okay, then. You had a fight with Daniel, but you already patched that up."

"Yeah."

"And you've got your money situation under control."

"I do. It's true."

"That doesn't sound so bad."

Her forehead got scrunchy as she considered what he'd said. "You don't get it. Dante, I need my own space *now*, I really do. Daniel and Keely are good to me." Keely was Daniel's second wife.

His first wife had died shortly after giving birth to twins—a boy and a girl— almost four years ago. "And the house is really big, I know. But still, they've got the twins and now Marie." Marie was Daniel and Keely's daughter—and about a year and a half old now, if Dante remembered right.

Gracie drank more tequila. Dante did, too.

"Keely and Daniel have a right to their own house," Gracie said. "And I want a life without my big brother breathing down my neck. I want that life now. My BFFs Carrie and Erin are already roomies—with no room for me. I could move in with Harper and Hailey." They were two of her sisters. "They've got that rambling old cottage Aislinn owns." Her sister Aislinn had married recently and moved to a ranch owned by her new husband. "But Harper and Hailey are like a team, you know? I always feel like a fifth wheel around them. So anyway, I thought I had an interim solution to the problem, a room in the house of a nice older woman named Sonja Kozlov down on Cherry Street. But then, early this afternoon, Sonja gives me a call. Her son has moved home unexpectedly and my interim space is no longer available. She gave me back my first, last and deposit and that's that. I'm still living in my brother's house. Probably till Christmas."

The good news was, he actually had a solution to her problem. "You want the cabin? It's yours."

"What cabin?" Squinting, she craned across the table toward him. "Are you drunk?"

He gestured toward the thick copse of trees behind her, on the south end of his property. "I have a guest cabin, I guess you could call it. Over there. See the trail going into the trees?"

She turned and stared where he pointed. "Wait. I see it. A log cabin, green tin roof?"

"That's it. It's one room—and a bathroom. Nothing fancy, but it has everything you need. Power, basic appliances. Running hot and cold water. A woodstove for heat if you need it. I even had Wi-Fi hooked up in there last year when one of the station house dispatchers needed a place to stay for a few months."

"How come you don't just rent it out on a regular basis?"

He shook his head. "I don't want some stranger living a hundred feet from my back deck. Luckily, you're no stranger. You can have it for as long as you want it, free of charge."

She sat back in her chair. "That's not right."

"Sure, it is."

"I can pay you what I would've paid Sonja, at least."

He put up a hand. "Stop. Let me do this for you. Like you said, you need a place of your own and the cabin is just sitting there empty."

She slapped the tabletop. "Wait."

"What?"

"We should discuss this tomorrow when we're both sober."

"Oh, come on, Gracie. I solve your problem for you and you can't just say thanks, I would love to stay in your log cabin for free?"

"Nope. Not tonight. Tonight is for tequila and commiseration." She let out a heavy sigh. "Right now, we need to get on to a more interesting topic. Let's commiserate about love."

"That does it."

"Huh?"

He grabbed the bottle and moved it to his side of the table. "No more tequila for you."

"You're such a hard-ass, Dante—but I still intend to talk about love."

He helped himself to another glass. After all, the bottle was in his control now. Might as well take full advantage. "Go right ahead."

She'd slipped off her pink sneakers and was giving a very happy Owen a tummy massage with her toes. "I love your dog."

Owen knew she was talking about him. With a gleeful little whine, he rolled over and got up.

"Come on, sweetheart," she coaxed.

With a sigh of pure contentment, Owen put his head across those amazing white thighs of hers. She petted him, stroking down his back, scratching him behind the ears. Owen shut his eyes and basked in the attention.

She asked, "Does he just stay home alone when you're working?"

He explained about the nice lady named Adele who lived on the next property over. "Adele runs a sort of doggy daycare, but it's casual. She's there all the time. I can drop Owen off and pick him up pretty much anytime that suits me. When I work nights, he stays here, but I can always manage to get home sometime midshift to check on him, give him a little attention and a short walk outside."

She made a humming sound low in her throat and petted the dog some more. Dante began to hope that maybe they'd left the subject of love behind.

But then she sat back in the chair and stared up at the sky. "Where were we? Right. Love. I can't say for sure that I've ever really been in love." A long sigh escaped her. "But I have been infatuated, like head over heels, you know? Sadly, I always

go for the brilliant ones, the ones nobody understands, the emotional fixer-uppers, I suppose you
could say." She slanted him a quick glance. "You
know about fixer-uppers, don't you?"

He did like watching those pink lips move. "Explain it to me."

"Fixer-uppers are expensive. I've blown my wad
on fixer-uppers." She let out a giggle, and then got
serious again. "So right now, I can't afford another
relationship—and could you maybe not look so
completely disapproving?"

He blinked. "I'm not." Was he?

"Yeah, you are. You're reminding me a little
of Daniel. Talk about a buzzkill." She pushed her
glass across the table and gave him the evil eye
until he poured her some more.

He set the bottle down again and decided that
he might as well be honest with her. "Okay, the
way I see it, Gracie, romantic love? It's a crock."

She whipped out a hand and slapped him lightly
on the arm for the second time that evening. "Take
that back."

"Can't. Sorry. What you call love is just an excuse to misbehave."

"Not true. So wrong."

"Take my parents."

"Dante. Slow down. You're telling me that romantic love's a crock and your parents are your example of why that's so?"

"Exactly."

"But your parents have been married forever and they're *happy*. Aren't they?"

"Blissfully so," he replied in disgust.

"Dante. You're making no sense. I mean, if they're happy, well, isn't that the point?"

"The point is, my mom was seventeen and pregnant with me when she married dad."

"So what? They're happy. They've been married for more than thirty years. Give it a rest."

"They're crazy."

"No."

"Yeah. Crazy in love after all these years. And they always have been. Do you know how many times I walked in on my folks having sex when I was a kid? It was traumatic. No surface was sacred. Apparently, it's still that way." Which was proven out by the fact that a year ago, at the age of forty-eight, his mom had given birth to his littlest brother, Mac. "And look at my sister. Loved your brother since she was barely in her teens. Chased him shamelessly until she finally caught him. Married him. Got wrongly divorced by him. Seven years later, she gets hit in the head and comes running back for more."

Gracie put both her hands out to the side, palms up. "And they're making it work now. They're very happy together, Connor and Aly."

"Romantic love is just another name for insanity." Dante finished off what was left in his glass. "I love my girls. That's a love that matters, a love with dignity and purpose."

She bent down and kissed the top of Owen's hairy head, which was still in her lap. The dog had his eyes closed and a blissed-out expression on his face. "You just haven't met the right woman yet. It will happen."

"No, it won't. The truth is, I'm bad at relationships and I'm just fine with that."

She stuck out that plump lower lip of hers. "That is too sad."

"No, it's not."

"Yes, it is. And I'm sorry it didn't work out with Marjorie. Don't feel bad, Dante."

"Did I say I *feel* bad? I didn't say that. I said I *am* bad at relationships."

"Everyone fails at love."

"Not my parents."

"Okay, *except* for your parents—and my parents, now that I think about it. They were totally in love till the end. And Daniel and Keely. And your brothers, Pascal and Tony, they're happily married, too, right? And let's not forget my sister Aislinn and—"

"Stop." He set his empty glass down harder than necessary. "All these happy couples. I can't take it anymore."

"My point is, you just have to be patient. It will happen. I've been in five failed relationships—if you count Joseph and Randy in high school. And after Paolo, well, I've been going through a bit of a dry spell if you know what I mean, avoiding sex and relationships and all that—but that doesn't mean I'm giving up, you know? I'm just having a break, that's all. I could have a wild fling any day now. And one of these days, I'll find the kind of love your mom and dad have. *I'm* not discouraged."

"Meaning *I* am? I've already said twice that I'm not."

"But you are." She gave Owen another scratch behind the ear. The dog nuzzled her hand and then flopped back down at her feet, rolling to his back in a shameless invitation to another toe massage. Gracie obliged.

Dante watched her pretty, turquoise-painted toes rubbing Owen's belly and laid it out for her *again*. "You're not getting it, Gracie. I'm fine with things just as they are. More than fine."

"But…you never have sex with other people anymore?"

"I didn't say that."

"Ohhh," she said slowly, eyes going wide. "Just flings and hookups, then, is what you're saying?"

"What I'm saying is I like my life. I've got a job that matters, one that interests me, with good potential for advancement." He gestured widely at the trees, the deck, the cliff and the ocean below. "I've got a great house in a beautiful spot, a good dog and most important, two smart, beautiful daughters."

The sun had sunk below the water. It was almost dark. The light by the slider, set on a timer, came on.

Gracie put her hands to her throat and made choking noises.

"Whatever that's supposed to mean," he said flatly, "I don't get it. You need to use words."

"Fine. A life without the prospect of someone special to love just makes me want to strangle myself."

"How many different ways can I say that I'm perfectly happy with how things are?"

"No. Uh-uh. I refuse to believe that you have no interest in finding love again. Dante, you're a great guy. And hot." She peered at him more closely, that pillowy, pink mouth softly parted. "Seriously. You're really hot…" She stood.

Before he could figure out what she was up to, she'd stepped over Owen and plopped down in his lap. With a happy giggle, she wrapped her arms around his neck and stuck her tongue in his ear.

He knew what to do—take her gently but firmly by the arms and hold her away enough that he could look in those big blue eyes and say in a soothing tone, *Gracie. No. Bad idea.*

But there was a problem.

Her tongue in his ear? It felt really good. Almost as good as her pretty, curvy body pressing against him. She smelled fresh and clean and sweet, too. And he liked the way she felt. He liked it a lot. The evidence of how much he liked it was growing beneath his fly. She knew it, too. He could tell by the way she gasped and whispered his name.

Tell her this can't happen, he said to himself.

And he opened his mouth to do that.

But then, her tongue left his ear and her soft lips were right there, meeting his. He sank into that kiss like a drowning man, going down and down, looking up at the sky through the water, realizing that drowning was a good thing—as long as it was Gracie he was drowning in.

Because Gracie, well, she tasted of tequila and

summer and the promise of something so perfect and right.

Of course, it didn't exist, that promise.

He knew that—or rather, the fulfilment of that promise, *that* didn't exist. The promise itself? That was the problem. The promise was so tempting. The promise made the world seem like a much more beautiful place.

And right now, on his back deck, as night came on, just the taste of her mouth and the soft weight of her pretty body and the scent of her skin, it was all magic to him. She practiced the best kind of sorcery, equal parts innocence and heat.

She pulled back a little, but only to slide that mouth of hers along the ridge of his jaw. She gave his chin a little bite.

And then her lips met his again. He went down a second time, plunging below the surface of all his own objections.

Dragging her tightly to him, he speared his tongue into her beautiful mouth. He was drunk, but not *that* drunk. He knew that he shouldn't, that they were friends and this was how friendships ended, that he was violating the very rule he'd once beaten the crap out of Connor for breaking. Because Gracie was Connor's little sister and a guy didn't make moves on his best friend's little sister.

No. Uh-uh. He shouldn't, couldn't, wouldn't…

But she tasted so good, like excellent tequila and the best bad decisions. All the shouldn'ts in the world could not hold out against the flavor of her, the feel of her, so soft and wild, in his arms.

She pulled back violently and blinked at him. "We're both kind of drunk. Maybe this shouldn't be happening. I'm kind of taking advantage of you in a weakened state, aren't I?"

"What the…? Of course not."

"I'm not?"

Wait. He should probably just agree with her, shouldn't he? Put an end to this incredible craziness.

She kissed him again. His brain got all scrambled in the best possible way.

This time, when she put her hands on his shoulders and pulled her mouth from his, she said, "Then again, since we're both hosed, nobody's taking advantage of anybody. It's mutually consensual. Wouldn't you say?" His head started nodding of its own volition. And she gave him her beautiful, glowing smile. "That settles it. We should go inside where the condoms are. You do have condoms, right?"

It was yet another opportunity to tell her they weren't doing this—or even to lie and say he had no condoms. Whatever it took to discourage this completely unacceptable behavior.

This was so wrong. He couldn't have sex with Gracie for any number of reasons, none of which were all that clear to him right at this moment.

And her mouth...

Her mouth was so tempting, all swollen from kissing him. Her skin was flushed a hot, dewy pink and her eyes were the deepest, purest blue.

He scooped her hard against his chest and got up.

"Whoa!" she cried happily, tightening her arms around his neck, kicking her feet a little like she just couldn't contain her glee.

He carried her to the slider. She reached out an arm and pushed it open. Owen went through ahead of them.

Inside, the lights were still on from earlier. Dante turned toward the door again to shut it. Gracie did it for him. Without a word, she pushed it shut and latched it.

His better judgment tried to surface, to put a stop to this insanity. He opened his mouth to gently put the brakes on.

And she kissed him. Her scent was all around him and her skin was so soft, her naughty little tongue all wet and delicious.

His objections flew away. There was nothing in his head now but lust and longing. She felt too perfect in his arms and she tasted like heaven and the scent of her was driving him out of his mind.

Hoisting her higher, he made for the hallway that led to the bedrooms.

Chapter Two

Grace woke to morning light.

She opened her eyes and saw Dante, sound asleep on the other pillow, his eyelashes so thick and black against his tanned cheeks. He looked really peaceful.

And that made her smile.

How much tequila had they drunk? A lot. She deserved to have a hangover—a headache, at least.

But she didn't.

Gently, so as not to wake him, she rolled to her back and shut her eyes. Her smile got wider.

Seriously, what a night.

And with Dante. Who knew? Yeah, she'd always considered him hot. But way too controlled. He wasn't a happy man, really—a good man, but not happy. She'd always assumed he was the kind of guy who would have trouble getting loose in bed.

Wrong.

She sighed in pure bliss as X-rated scenes from the night before played out on the dark screen of her eyelids.

After the first go-round, which had been nothing short of spectacular, they'd raided his freezer and gobbled Tillamook Mudslide straight from the carton, each with a spoon, passing the chunky chocolate deliciousness back and forth. He'd then ordered her to drink more water to prevent a hangover later. She'd laughed and called him a control freak, but she did drink the water.

Gracie frowned. About then, he'd started acting kind of distant, hadn't he? She'd had a really bad feeling he was going to start backing off, start saying that maybe it hadn't been such a smart idea for them to fall into bed together.

But she'd known how to shut him up about that.

She'd kissed him. Worked like a charm. He scooped her right up and carried her back down the hall to his bed, where the good times rolled some more.

Sometime after midnight, they'd fallen asleep. She'd closed her eyes for a minute—and slept straight through until morning.

What a night.

She could not wait to do it all again.

Carefully, so as not to wake him, she eased her legs over the side of the bed and slid out from under the covers. Her clothes were right there on the bedside chair. She put them on swiftly and tiptoed to the door.

Sweet Owen was waiting on the other side. Pulling the bedroom door silently shut behind her, she asked in a whisper, "Need to go out, boy?"

He let out a low whine and turned to lead the way.

Outside, she found her pink Chuck Taylors right there on the deck by her chair, where she'd left them. Her purse was there, too, still hanging on the back of her chair. She put on the Chucks, hooked the purse over her shoulder and walked Owen into the trees to do his business. As she trailed along behind him, she got out her phone to check messages.

There were two texts from Daniel asking if she was all right.

Oops. They had an agreement that if she wasn't coming home, she would let him know she was okay—and he would refrain from asking questions about what she'd been doing and with whom.

She answered, Sorry. A little too much tequila at Dante Santangelo's place. Stayed here to be safe. (And to have the best sex ever in the history of sex. But her big brother didn't need that kind of TMI.) I'm fine. Home in a while.

He responded right away. Okay, then. Thanks for letting me know.

Was he pissed at her? Probably. Daniel hated it when she didn't keep her agreements. But she was going to call this a win. She'd messed up and he'd been civil about it when she apologized.

It could've been so much worse.

On the way back inside, she grabbed the remains of their dinner, the glasses and the nearly empty bottle from last night.

In the kitchen, Owen went straight to his food bowl. He sniffed at it and then looked up at her with those sad doggy eyes. She took the hint and found him a can of dog stew in the pantry closet. After dishing the food into his bowl, she freshened up his water.

"Good, huh?" She stood over him as he wolfed down his meal. "And now I need coffee."

Dante had one of those pod machines. She loaded up some Peet's French Roast.

Five minutes later, she was standing at the counter savoring that first cup when Dante, in jeans and a fresh T-shirt, emerged from the back of the house.

She watched him come toward her, her heart lifting just at the sight of him.

God, he was gorgeous. All that thick, wavy almost-black hair, those smoldering eyes. The eight-pack, the V-lines, the ebony treasure trail leading to fun and fulfilment—and no, she couldn't see all that amazingness right now. But she *had* seen it and thoroughly enjoyed it last night. It was all burned into her brain in the best sort of way.

And then she met his dark eyes. Instantly, she *knew*. It was so painfully clear to her before he even opened his mouth.

Mr. Control was back with a vengeance.

"Hey," he said.

"Hey."

He knelt to give his dog a good-morning scratch down his back and a pat on the head. "You found the coffee all right?"

As if that even required an answer. She raised her mug to him as he rose. Sliding to the side a little, she made room for him at the coffee maker.

The silence had weight as he loaded the machine and put his cup under the spout. He pushed the button and turned around to lean against the counter as it brewed.

For a good thirty seconds, they stood there, side by side, the coffee maker gurgling and hissing behind him. She drank her coffee and waited. It seemed only fair to give him a chance to *not* disappoint her.

"Gracie, I…" The sentence wandered off unfinished.

Okay, yeah. Message received. He regretted last night and was about to tell her all about how it could never happen again.

Well, okay then. He would say what he had to say. As for Gracie, she refused to help him in any way, shape or form. She enjoyed her coffee and waited for the rest.

"Gracie, will you look at me?"

Stifling a sigh, she turned her head to face him. Those melty brown eyes were full of self-recrimination and regret.

"I'm sorry," he said. "I never should have touched you. I'm too old for you and I'm not any kind of relationship material, anyway. I don't know what got into me, but I swear to you it's never going to happen again."

Hmm. How to respond?

Too bad there wasn't a large blunt object nearby. The guy deserved a hard bop on head. What was *wrong* with him? No wonder it hadn't worked out with Marjorie. The man didn't have a clue.

But never mind. Gracie held it together as he apologized some more. She watched that beautiful mouth move and pondered the mystery of how such a great guy could have his head so far up his own ass.

Maybe if she yanked him close and kissed him, he'd get over himself and admit that last night had been amazing, the two of them had off-the-charts chemistry and he didn't want to walk away from all that goodness, after all.

Yeah, kissing him might shut him up and get him back on track for more hot, sexy times. It had worked more than once already.

But come on. She couldn't go jumping on him and smashing her mouth on his every time he started beating himself up for having a good time with her.

No. A girl had to have a little pride.

He thought last night was a mistake?

Fair enough. She'd actually let herself believe for a minute or two there that they had something good going on, that her long dry spell man-wise might be over.

But never mind about that. Let him have it his way. She would agree with him.

And then she would show him exactly what he was missing. And *then*, when he couldn't take it anymore and begged her for another chance, she would say that they *couldn't*, that he was too *old* for her and it wouldn't be *right*.

Not that she was vindictive or anything...

"You're right, Dante," she said with exaggerated sincerity. "It was a big mistake. One that can never happen again—and about the cabin? I'll take it. You are a lifesaver. Thank you so much."

For a fraction of a second, he looked kind of stunned. But then he gave a solemn nod. "Well, all right then."

"Is there furniture out there already or will I need to bring my own?" She could use her bedroom suite from Daniel's. Plus, Daniel and Keely had a lot of random pieces stored in the attic and basement of the Bravo house. Getting the cabin furnished wouldn't be a problem.

"There's a bed, a table, a chest of drawers, some chairs and some kitchen stuff." He moved down the counter, took something from a drawer and came back to her. "Here you go." He handed her a key, which she stuck in a pockct of her cutoffs. "Anything that's in there you don't need, no problem. I've got space to store it."

"That'll work. I'm off from the Sea Breeze again today, so I was thinking I would just go ahead and move in."

He frowned. She was sure he would start back-pedaling, saying maybe they ought to rethink this, that now they'd shared a night of fabulous sex, it wasn't such a good idea for her to live on his property.

But in the end, he said only, "All right. I've got today and tomorrow off. I'll help."

"Thanks, but I can handle it." She would need to scare up a truck and get one of her brothers to take on the heavy lifting. If none of them were available, she had friends. Someone would come to her rescue.

Dante scowled. "I said I would help. We can use my pickup."

She gave a him big smile. Really, he was a terrific man—well, aside from that stick up his butt. "I hate to keep taking *advantage* of you."

"You're not. Come on, let me help."

"Then thank you. Again."

He still looked way too serious. "Gracie, is this going to wreck our friendship?"

She had such a deep longing to make him squirm. It took serious effort to not put on an innocent voice and probe a little, ask him what, exactly, he meant by *this*?

But no. If she did that, he might just tell her. "No, it's not going to wreck anything. Not for me, anyway." She met his eyes straight on. Was he going to insist they talk about it? Really, the last thing she needed right now was Dante getting down in the weeds with all the reasons last night couldn't, shouldn't, wouldn't be happening again. "Your coffee's ready."

"Right." He gave a slow nod and took his full mug from under the spout. For a moment, they just stood there, sipping and staring at anything but each other.

Finally, he offered, "How 'bout some breakfast?"

"I would love some."

After they ate, Dante showed Gracie the cabin.

She walked in the door, took a slow look around and said, "I love it," which made him feel pretty damn terrific in spite of his doubts about having her living so close after last night. "There's room for a sitting area *and* my bed, not to mention it has an actual kitchen."

The kitchen consisted of a small range and a compact fridge with a counter and cabinets between them, a sink in the middle. "It's pretty basic," he said.

"Don't you disrespect my new kitchen," she commanded, looking way too adorable in those damn sexy Daisy Dukes and that T-shirt that exposed her flat stomach and clung to those fine breasts he wouldn't be fondling again. "Everything's so clean, too."

"I got a Groupon for cleaning services a couple of weeks ago. I had them go through the house and then went ahead and paid extra for them to clean this place, too—never hurts to get rid of the cobwebs now and then."

"There's even a window above the sink." She leaned over the sink to peer outside, causing her right butt cheek to peek out from under the tattered hem of those cutoffs that really ought to be illegal. He gritted his teeth and ordered himself to forget about last night and simply appreciate the spectacular view of her shapely behind. "Perfect," she said with a happy little sigh.

Next, she went through the cabinets and got all enthusiastic about pots and pans, dishes, mismatched glassware and the drawer of utensils and flatware. He watched her bending to look in the lower cupboards and stretching to peer in the high ones. Her butt cheek reappeared more than once and that damn T-shirt kept drawing tight across those breasts he needed to stop staring at.

"I'll keep the sofa," she said, "and the drop-leaf kitchen table and chairs." She wanted to bring her own bedroom furniture. "You said you have somewhere you can put this bed and bureau?"

"No problem. There's a shed behind the garage. Plenty of room in there."

She babbled on, all sunny enthusiasm, about planting rhododendrons by the front door and a rag rug she thought might be stored in the attic at the Bravo house. "That rug would so tie the room together."

He agreed to all of it. Whatever she wanted. Because she was a friend and a guy helped his friends. Even if, after last night, he was never going to be able to look at her and not see her naked inside his head.

She looked incredible without any clothes on, all that pale, firm skin. Her whole body flushed the prettiest shade of pink when she was turned on.

But he wasn't going to think of that. From this moment on, he was wiping thoughts of Gracie Bravo naked right out of his brain.

He plugged in the fridge. Together, they moved

the chest of drawers and the bed to the shed. Then he followed her in his pickup to the Bravo house up on Rhinehart Hill. Daniel wasn't there. Keely was, though, along with the kids and Ingrid Ostergard, who was Keely's mother and also the owner of the Sea Breeze bar where Gracie worked.

Keely took Gracie's arm. "We need to talk."

"You're right," Gracie agreed.

The two women vanished into Gracie's room off the kitchen, leaving Dante with Ingrid, the twins, Frannie and Jake, and the toddler, Marie. The twins were busy making what looked like a village of Duplo blocks over by the breakfast nook, the family basset hound stretched out nearby. Marie toddled Dante's way and kind of landed against his leg. She was a cute little thing, with wispy strawberry curls.

She beamed up at him, causing a tightness in his chest as he thought of his daughters. It seemed just yesterday they'd been Marie's age. "Up." So he swung her up in his arms and she patted his face and babbled out nonsense syllables. "You don't say?" he asked. She babbled some more and he nodded. "No kidding…"

Ingrid, who had green hair this week and wore a purple tank top, sat over at the breakfast nook table. She'd been the lead singer and guitarist for a one-hit wonder rock band back in the eighties. Now she lived with her widowed sister, Gretchen Snow. "Gracie tell you I'm losing her come September?"

"She did. She seems excited to start teaching." He caught Marie's fat little hand before she could poke him in the eye.

"I hate to see her go. But you can't keep the good ones forever, you know?"

Unfortunately, he'd had Gracie for only one night—way short of forever. And maybe "had" was the wrong word. Too objectifying. Or something.

"Dante?" Ingrid seemed to be hiding a grin. "You with me?"

"Uh. Yeah—and you're right. Good things never last forever." *Some of them last only one damn night.*

"Gwamma Ingwid," said Frannie, with a Duplo in each hand. "Come help."

Ingrid, who was slim and fit and maybe in her fifties, got up and joined the twins on the floor.

Gracie emerged from the short hall next to the pantry, Keely right behind her. "I'll head up to Warrenton, tell him in person," Gracie said. Dante knew she meant Daniel. Her eldest brother ran Valentine Logging. The family company had its offices on the Columbia at the Warrenton docks. "Just as soon as we get all my things into the cabin at Dante's."

"That'll work," agreed Keely.

Gracie shifted her glance to Dante. He felt the force of her gaze all through him. Did he have it bad for her? He decided it was better not to think about that.

She asked, "Ready to haul some heavy furniture out to your truck?"

"I'm ready." He put Marie down and she toddled over to join the Duplo builders on the floor. "Let's get after it."

She led him back to her room and they got to work taking the bed apart.

A few hours later, they had her bedroom furniture and all of Gracie's clothes and random other stuff loaded into the two vehicles. They caravanned back to his place and transferred everything into the cabin. Dante had had a graveled side driveway added a few years ago. It branched off to the cabin from the main driveway, so they were able to drive right up to the cabin door.

By a little after three, they had everything out of the vehicles and stacked up in the cabin, ready to be put away. He helped her reassemble the bed.

Once that was done, she fell back across the mattress with a groan that made him start thinking about last night again—not that he'd ever really stopped. "Thank you so much, Dante. You're a lifesaver on so many levels. Now, I'm going to see if I can find a towel and a bar of soap in one of those boxes somewhere. I'll take a quick shower and then go tell my big brother that a miracle has happened and I've found somewhere other than the room off his kitchen to live."

He realized he was starving. They hadn't eaten since the eggs and sausage they'd had at breakfast. "Come on over to the house first. I've got plenty of stuff for sandwiches. You should eat."

She remained sprawled across the bed, looking way too inviting, with her arms thrown out wide, her pink Chucks dangling an inch from the floor. "Can't."

Owen, who had followed them around as they brought in her things, trotted over to her, dropped to his haunches and whined at her hopefully.

She sat up and gave him a pat on the head. With her free hand, she pulled the elastic free of her high ponytail. The silvery mass spilled over shoulders and down her back. He wanted to grab her arm, yank her up off the bed, wrap her hair around his fist and pull her head back so he could bite her smooth, pale neck.

"I need to get going," she said. "I want to catch Daniel before he heads for home."

"It's been hours since breakfast." He should shut up. He sounded like some fussy old mother hen. But then he just kept on talking. "You've got to be hungry and you really should eat."

She laughed. The happy sound kind of reached down inside him, making him yearn for something he was never going to have. Between completely unacceptable bouts of pure lust for her, he kept thinking that maybe they should talk about what had happened last night, kind of clear the air a little, get their friendship back on track. But then, what were they going to say?

No. It was probably better to just leave it alone.

"I'll grab a burger on the way," she said. "Promise. Don't worry about me. I'm fine."

If she wanted to starve herself, how was he going to stop her? He let it go.

She thanked him again. He clicked his tongue at Owen and the dog followed him back to the main house.

At the Warrenton docks, Gracie went straight to the barnlike building where Valentine Logging had its offices. Daniel was still there. The office manager told her to go on in.

A big man, broad shouldered and square jawed, with hair a little darker than her own, Daniel sat at his desk punching keys on his laptop. He glanced up at her when she entered. "Scotch?"

"No, thanks." Daniel always brought out the good Scotch during important discussions, to mark life transitions and for big occasions. Apparently, he already knew why she was here. "Keely told you, huh?"

He rose, went to the liquor cart in the corner and poured himself a small one. "She said you'd be dropping by. I asked what was going on. She said you would explain everything."

"You don't know what I'm here for and you offered the good Scotch anyway?"

He saluted her with his glass. "Just in case I'm going to need it."

She laughed. "Yeah. I get that. You never know what kind of crap I might pull next."

He had on his wary face. "I didn't say that."

"But maybe you thought it?" She held up her thumb and forefinger with a sliver of space between them. "Just a little…"

He went to the sofa and chairs across from his desk and gestured for her to join him as he sat. She took one of the chairs and Daniel said, "So what's going on?"

"Dante Santangelo offered me this little cabin he has on his property. I took it. Moved all my stuff in there today."

He asked, very carefully, "So, you and Dante…?"

She almost gave him a dirty look, but somehow managed to stop herself in time. "We're friends." *Yeah, okay. With benefits—for last night only and never again.* But all that was TMI as far as her big brother was concerned. "We got to know each other at the bar. He likes to stop in there for a beer a couple of times a week."

Daniel now looked thoughtful, like maybe he was pondering the mysteries of the universe. "Dante's a good man."

She realized then that this conversation was actually going well. Her overbearing eldest brother was treating her like an adult. And that was the second time he'd seemed to imply that maybe she and Dante had a thing. And they kind of did. A very short thing that Daniel never needed to know about. "Like I said, Dante's a friend."

Daniel studied her for several seconds, long enough that she almost started to worry about what he might say next. But then he only reminded her gently, "Your room is there for you. Come home to stay anytime you need to."

Her throat clutched. Just a little. "I'm going to

try really hard not to. You should use my room for a guest room. It's downstairs, private, with its own bath. I already took all my furniture and stuff, so you don't even need to clear it out."

"It's not going to be the same without you there." His voice was kind of gruff. Like he might be just a little choked up, too.

Strange. It seemed like she and Daniel had been at odds since she turned ten or so. But right now, all she felt was affection for him—and gratitude that he'd kept them all together, kept them a family, when their parents died.

"I'm sorry that we haven't always gotten along. I think my moving out on my own will be good, you know?"

"Yeah."

It was the right time, she realized, to tell him what she really thought of him. "You are amazing and strong and we all count on you far too much. I love you a lot, Daniel."

He gave her a slow nod. "And I love you. I'm proud of you, too, Gracie. You do things your own way and I'm slowly learning to accept that you're all grown up, not my little baby sister anymore."

When she got up to leave, he held out his arms. She stepped into them and they shared a hug.

"You need help with the move?" he asked.

"Thanks, but no. It's handled."

"Whatever I can do, you just let me know."

"That works both ways." She smiled up at him, feeling really good about everything right at that moment.

Grace stopped for a burger and then to get groceries before heading back to the cabin. It was a little after seven and she'd almost finished putting the food away when someone tapped on the door.

She figured it would be Dante.

And it was.

Sweet Lord, he looked good. All dark and broody. He must have showered. His tanned cheeks were clean-shaven, he smelled of some yummy aftershave and he'd changed to black jeans and a faded plaid shirt with the sleeves rolled up to reveal those sculpted forearms of his.

"Just the man I wanted to see," she said. "I have something for you."

His dark eyebrows drew together in a worried frown. "What?"

"So suspicious," she chided, and ushered him in. Owen was right behind him. "Here you go." She had a check already made out to him, but when she took it from her pocket, he put up both hands like she'd pulled a gun on him.

"Gracie. Come on. I said that's not necessary."

"It's the five hundred I was going to pay Sonja."

"Keep it."

"No."

"Gracie…"

"Listen. I know it's hardly what a homey little cabin in the woods with a nearby trail leading down to a gorgeous stretch of beach would bring you if you actually rented it out, but at least it'll cover utilities."

"I said no. Forget it."

"Five hundred a month," she repeated, her chin high. "If you don't take it, that's a deal breaker. You'll be forcing me to load all this stuff into my Toyota and move back to Daniel's. And you know that will be bad for the Bravo family dynamic. I love my big brother and he loves me, but it's definitely time for me *not* to be living in his house." Dante had lowered his hands by then. She grabbed one and slapped the check in it.

He looked down at the scrap of paper and then back up at her. Owen, who'd dropped to his haunches at their feet, whined up at them.

"It's okay, boy," she said to the dog. "Your human is stubborn, but we're working it out."

Annoyance flashed in Dante's eyes and his gorgeous high cheekbones suddenly looked like they might poke right through his skin. "You're not going to give the hell up on this are you?"

"Nope. And you need to cash that in the next few days. Unless you'd really rather I didn't stay here. If you don't cash it, I'll know you want me gone and I'll make that happen."

"See how you did that? You turned it all around on me. If I don't take your money, I want you gone?"

"So, then. You *don't* want me gone?"

"Of course not." He really seemed to mean it.

And she felt considerable relief. She had kind of worried that after last night, he would prefer that she lived elsewhere. "Good, then," she answered softly. "Five hundred a month."

He threw up both hands again. "Have it your way."

"Thank you. It's a steal and we both know it. So much better than a room in someone's house." She went back to the kitchen counter to finish empty-ing the last grocery bag.

He was silent. A quick glance over her shoulder confirmed that he was just standing there in the middle of the room, surrounded by plastic bags and a few boxes and more than one suitcase full of her stuff.

"What can I do to help?" he asked.

She stuck a giant box of Cinnamon Toast Crunch in the cupboard and turned to him. "You helped me all day. Go home. Take a break. Head on over to the Sea Breeze for a beer."

He didn't budge, just stood there frowning at the piles of stuff she'd yet to put away. "You eat something?"

"Yes, *Mother*, I did."

"You must be exhausted."

She wasn't, not really. She'd always had a lot of energy. And she was excited to have her own space at last. It was beautiful here. Maybe, before bed, she would take the trail down to the beach, enjoy a stroll along the shore. "I think I'm getting my second wind. And hey, the bed's made." It had stacks of towels and two suitcases on it, though. "When I get tired, I can just shove everything off it and climb in."

Now he was staring down at the rag rug, which they'd left rolled up near the sofa when they brought it in from his truck. "Let's roll the rug out, why don't we?"

She braced her hands on her hips. "You just can't stop helping, can you?"

He flashed her a mouthful of straight white teeth and she swooned a little inside. "Please. You know you need a hand moving the furniture out of the way."

She really could use some help with the rug. "Well, since you asked so nicely..."

They set to work, shoving the bed, the night-stand, the coffee table and all her stuff against the walls, rolling the rug out, positioning it just so, and then putting the furniture in place on top of it.

"It looks so good," she said, standing back by the window to admire the effect. "My great-great-grandmother Cora Valentine made this rug as part of her trousseau." The braided rug was a treasure, with a rainbow of colors woven into it. "So cozy and homey."

Dante had already moved on to the next job. The two suitcases were still on the bed. He grabbed one and pulled it to the edge of the mattress. "We should clear off the bed, figure out where you want all this stuff to go."

She knew what was in that suitcase and almost stopped him. But then she remembered the little promise she'd made to herself.

Really, she shouldn't.

He'd gone way above and beyond to help her out when she needed a hand, not only providing a place for her, but pitching right in to help her make it habitable. The guy was a true friend.

Even if he had given her a speeding ticket.

It wasn't right for her to hold a grudge just because he said he wouldn't have sex with her again.

But, well, some grudges were too much fun to give up.

And besides, Dante Santangelo was wound way too tight. He needed to loosen the heck up.

Grace was only too happy to help him with that. She crossed the space between them and stood at his side.

He unzipped the suitcase and tossed the lid back, revealing stacks of pretty bras, sexy panties and a froth of different nighties she hardly ever wore. For a moment, he stared down at all those goodies—not embarrassed, exactly.

More like not sure where to take it from there.

"I confess," she said wryly. "I've got this thing for lingerie. I've controlled my fancy-panty addiction the past year or so in my ongoing effort to get the budget under control, but I still have more undies than will fit in my drawers—if you know what I mean." She snatched up a fuchsia-pink satin thong and another pair of panties that was mostly lace. "What do you think—a thong?" She dangled the bit of satin by her index finger. "Or cheekies?" She waved the black lace.

He gave her a look of great patience, with just

maybe a touch of sexy smolder there in his eyes. "All your drawers are full, you said?"

"Yup." She popped the *p* and pressed both pairs of panties to her breasts. "What shall I *do*?"

Dante was all business. "I say we bring back that bureau from the shed." He pointed to a bare corner next to the window on the other side of the bed. "It should fit there."

She gave him a blinding smile. "Brilliant."

And really now, exactly how far should she take this? He didn't seem to have noticed yet, but tucked in with all that lace and silk and satin was a personal pleasure toy—or five. Because a girl who's steering clear of romantic complications for a while definitely needs a little stimulation now and then.

She was just about to grab her favorite magic wand and wave it at him with gleeful enthusiasm when he said, "Let's go get it, then." And turned for the door.

They brought the bureau back.

Again, she tried to tell him he'd done enough.

But he refused to stop there. He helped her empty the big black plastic bags, the other suitcase and the boxes. Somehow, they found a place for everything. As for her lingerie and personal pleasure devices, he steered clear of them, so she put them away herself without brandishing a single one.

He didn't go back to the main house until after nine.

She stood at the door as he left. "I can't believe I'm pretty much moved in already. Thank you. Again."

"Anytime. Come on, Owen." His dog at his heels, Dante headed off through the trees.

She watched him stride along the footpath until he reached the cleared area that surrounded his house. No, she hadn't given up on her plan to drive him mad with unsatisfied lust.

But that was going to take time. He was a tough nut to crack. Luckily, she lived here now and would have all sorts of opportunities to work on bringing him to his knees, sexually speaking.

Operation Make Dante Beg for It was going to be a whole lot of fun.

Chapter Three

Dante stood at the slider that led out to the deck. Staring out past the twisted trees that framed the path down to the beach, he watched the last orange fingers of sunset fade into the growing dark.

He'd seen those sex toys of hers.

How could he miss them? One was two-pronged and purple and one was as aggressively pink as that thong she'd dangled at him from her finger. One even looked like a microphone.

At least she'd put them away in the bureau without making a show of them. Her sudden attack of discretion had surprised him. After all, she'd asked him about his preference in panties, hadn't she?

He'd figured she wouldn't pass up the chance to taunt him with her, er, sensual devices.

But even without all the sexy underthings and the battery-powered pleasure enhancers, the woman would still be driving him insane. He wanted to touch her, pull her close, kiss those beautiful, bubblegum-pink lips of hers. He wanted to spend a couple of hours sitting out on the deck in the light of the moon with her. He wanted to whisper with her about nothing in particular, to listen to her laugh and bask in her bright, gorgeous smiles.

It all sounded so damn romantic.

And it wasn't going to happen.

He'd really messed up. He'd had too much tequila and then given in to the urge to have sex with someone he considered a friend, someone he cared about who he didn't want to lose. Now he wanted his friend back, at the same time as he was never going to forget the way she looked naked.

And that moment with the panties? She *had* been tormenting him on purpose. He knew that she had.

She was young and free-spirited. So different from him on so many levels. That she had no shame about provoking him with her sexy underwear was just more proof of all the ways the two of them were not any kind of a match—not that he was even looking for a match in the first place.

He'd meant what he told her last night. His life worked just fine as it was and trying for something meaningful with a woman was more likely to screw everything up than to make things better.

They were friends, damn it. He shouldn't have slept with her, though he couldn't quite bring himself to regret that he had. It had been nothing short of perfect, spending the night with Gracie. The sex was mind-blowing and yet, she was still Gracie, with her smart mouth and her bubbly laugh. Gracie, who, as it turned out, felt just right in his arms.

But that was last night and last night was over.

All he wanted now was to still be her friend and put last night behind them.

And he would. Over time.

Because, come on. It had been less than twenty-four hours since he'd had her in his bed. The powerful desire to do it again was bound to fade as the days went by. He'd gotten her settled in at the cabin. Now all he had to do was steer clear of her for a while, give his mind and his body some distance. Let that distance solve the problem for him.

It was all going to work out just fine.

Since he'd made detective, Dante mostly worked day shifts, and then was on call at night for major crimes, of which there were few in Valentine Bay.

However, when he didn't have his daughters with him, he tried to be flexible, help the other guys out so they would have his back scheduling-wise when Nat and Nic were home.

As a result, he'd taken C Watch for the next five days, 10:00 p.m. to 6:30 in the morning. In Valentine Bay, night watch was about fighting boredom more than anything else. Now and then you got a rough domestic to sort out or a burglary to solve or drunks acting up, but it was hardly like some big-city departments where you took your life in your hands every night on the street.

Working all night had a side benefit this time around. For five days straight, he got home at 9:00 a.m., after an hour at the gym and then breakfast. He would sleep until late afternoon. That meant he'd have little opportunity to see Gracie. She worked either early afternoon to ten at night, or six to closing. They were on completely different schedules. All he had to do was *not* stop in at the Sea Breeze and he would never see her.

Out of sight, out of mind. Right?

Except he couldn't stop thinking about her.

Plus, well, she was right there in front of him most afternoons, planting rhododendrons outside the cabin in a tiny little top that showed off her flat stomach and those battered jean shorts that ought to be illegal. Or heading down to the beach in a swimsuit made of what looked like three tiny handkerchiefs and a few pieces of string.

Apparently, she had the closing shift at the bar that week, leaving all afternoon and most of the evening for him to spot her outside. And really, he knew way more than he should about her schedule, didn't he? Plus, he found himself looking out the damn windows constantly now. Never in his life had he felt like a creeper.

Until now.

Also, there was Owen. The damn dog was in love with her and had grown nothing short of crafty about slipping out any door Dante opened and heading for the cabin. If she was home, Gracie would bring him back, which was nice of her. He would order the dog inside, thank her and shut the door on her, knowing that he was being borderline rude to her.

But it was hard enough on his equilibrium staring at her out a window when he shouldn't be, trying not to think of what she looked like naked. Up close, it was even harder—*hard* being the operative word.

Saturday afternoon, she called him to tell him she had a leaky pipe under the bathroom sink. "I stuck a pot under it, but it's not looking good. I need either a bigger pot, to stop using the sink or to hire a plumber," she said. "I'm happy to handle it. Word on the street is that Santangelo Plumbing is the best around. I'll just call them if that's okay?"

"Word on the street is right for once." His dad had inherited the plumbing business from his father before him. "But I'll take care of it." He'd worked alongside his father in the summers back in high school and to bring in extra cash when he and Marjorie first got married.

"How 'bout soon?" she asked hopefully.

"How 'bout now?"

"Works for me."

When he got there, she was wearing a short kimono-type robe and just possibly nothing under it. She knelt to pet Owen, and Dante tried not to look down at her sleek bare legs and the way the top of the robe kind of gaped where it wrapped between her breasts.

"I was about to take a shower when I saw the water on the floor." And that had him picturing her naked in the shower—really, there were so many ways he could picture her naked. The possibilities were endless. And he needed to cease and desist on that front.

She rose. "Come on. I'll show you." He tried really hard not to stare at the rounded perfection of her ass beneath the revealing silk of her robe as he followed her into the bathroom, where the door to the small cabinet under the sink was wide open.

He flipped on the water and then knelt to watch the water drip into the pot. The seals had failed in at least two places. Reaching in there, he turned the valves at the back wall that shut off the water to the faucet.

"If I patch the joints, it will probably just start leaking again, so I'm going to replace the whole assembly," he said as he stood. "I'll need to run to the hardware store to get parts."

She stood by the door, barefooted in her short kimono, her arms wrapped around her middle. "Can I go ahead and shower while you're gone? I'll make it quick." Owen, seated at her side, his floppy tongue hanging out, panted and gazed up at her adoringly. Really, how could Dante blame the damn dog for panting over her. She was too tempting by half.

"Dante?" She asked again. "Is it okay if I have a shower?"

He gave himself a mental shake. "Uh, sure. I've turned the water off under the sink, so you can't use that faucet, but the shower's a go."

"You have to work tonight?"

"Ten to six thirty."

She chewed on the corner of her full lower lip. "And there goes the rest of your afternoon and evening. Sorry."

As though he had anything all that important to do. He didn't—and that was another thing having her around made him all too acutely aware of: life was short and he was spending way too much of it just kind of going through the motions.

Okay, yeah. He was set in his ways and not likely to change. But having Gracie around sure made life a lot more interesting.

Was she trying to drive him a little bit crazy with her Daisy Dukes and that short kimono that gaped in the front when she bent down and showed off her spectacular behind every time she turned around? With her teasing smiles and come-and-get-it glances—not to mention her sexy underwear and personal pleasure devices?

Probably.

Right at the moment, though, he kind of hoped she never stopped.

Which made him only too happy to spend his afternoon fixing the drainpipe under the sink for her. He liked doing things for her. On top of the whole burning-lust thing he had going on for her, he also wanted to take her in his arms and reassure her—of what, exactly, he had no idea. Whatever she needed, he wanted to make sure she got it.

At the same time, he'd made it his mission *not* to give in to his consuming need to grab her close and peel off whatever skimpy piece of nothing she happened to be wearing at any given moment.

"Not your fault," he said. "Pipes leak now and then. It's a fact of life."

The trip to the hardware store took almost an hour. When he got back, the cabin smelled like tropical flowers, probably from her shower gel. She was dressed in dark-wash jeans and a Sea Breeze T-shirt, all ready for work.

"I need to get going," she said. "It's summer and it's Saturday. We're packed from four or so straight through till closing. Ingrid needs all hands on deck."

And he felt let down, though he'd been avoiding her all week. "No problem. I'll lock up when I'm done."

"Thanks—oh, and one other thing." She grabbed an envelope off the counter. It was addressed and had a stamp on it. "My check for that ticket you gave me. Can I just drop it in the slot of that group mailbox near the end of your driveway?"

"That'll work."

"Great." She knelt to give Owen a quick cuddle.

A moment later, she was at the door. Turning back to him, she asked, "You doing all right, Dante?"

"Of course," he said too quickly and then made it worse by adding, "Fine. Why?"

She gave him this sweet little smile, kind of tender and knowing. "When's your next night off?"

"Tuesday."

"Perfect. I'm off Tuesday, too. Let me cook you dinner. Show my appreciation. For the cabin and the, er…"

"Do not make a dirty joke about your plumbing," he warned.

She stifled a giggle and then tried to look innocent. "Never, ever would I do such a thing. So, Tuesday? Dinner?"

He shouldn't encourage her—except there was nothing in the world he would rather do than spend his night off with her. "I would like that."

"Terrific. You're on."

Sunday, Grace went to dinner with the family at the Bravo house. Her brother Connor and his wife, Aly, Dante's only sister, came, too. They brought their month-old daughter, Emelia.

The baby was the center of attention. Everyone wanted to hold her, including Grace. After dinner, she finally got a chance to have that baby in her arms.

"She is gorgeous." Grace held Emelia's tiny hand and kissed her perfect miniature nose.

Aly said, "She's a handful, but in the best way possible—I heard you moved into that little cabin at my brother's place."

"Yeah. I love it. It's gorgeous there and the cabin is nice. I feel right at home."

"He treating you right?"

What, exactly, did Aly mean by that? Grace answered cautiously. "He's a good friend—and he would have let me have the cabin for free. I had to twist his arm to get him to take what I would've paid for a room in someone's house."

"A good friend, huh?"

Grace smoothed the blanket around the baby's adorable, squinty little face and looked up to meet Aly's eyes directly. "Okay, whatever you're getting at, just go ahead and say it."

It was only the three of them—the baby, Grace and Aly—on one end of the big sofa in the family room. Everyone else was still hanging out at the table in the dining room or in the backyard or grouped around the island in Keely's big kitchen.

Aly said quietly, "Connor and I saw you together."

"Me and Dante?" Except for a few hours last Tuesday night, they'd never been "together" anywhere that she could remember. At least not "together" the way Aly seemed to imply. "When?"

"Last summer, at the Sea Breeze. You looked—I don't know. It was just a moment. You were behind the bar and he was getting a pitcher or something. You were both laughing. There was this energy, you know, a certain chemistry between you. It was pretty obvious. I thought so and Connor did, too. He was really pissed off."

"Why?"

Aly shrugged. "Can I just say it's a guy thing and leave it at that?"

"Sure. I suppose…"

"You'll be happy to know I got all up in Connor's face about it and he ended up agreeing that it was your business—yours and Dante's—and he would stay out of it." Now Aly grinned. "I don't know what it is with guys sometimes, but I make it my mission to call them on their stupid crap whenever necessary."

"The women of the world are grateful—me included. But you said this happened last summer? Wow." That seemed forever ago. Absolutely nothing romantic had been going on between Grace and Dante back then. And there was nothing going on between them now, either. Because Dante considered himself too old for her, and because he didn't do relationships. Grace slowly shook her head. "We really are just friends."

Aly laughed. She leaned in close and whispered, "I so do not believe that. If Dante hasn't made a move on you, he's a fool."

"You don't think I'm too young for him?"

"No way. You're just what he needs. A little joy and sunshine in his life for a change. And that's nothing against his ex, either. Marjorie's a good person. It was just…not really happening with the two of them, you know? They'd broken up. It was over. She'd moved back to Portland. But then it turned out she was pregnant with the twins, so they got married at the county clerk's office and tried to make it work."

"I didn't know."

Aly forked her hands back through her thick dark hair. "Dante will be giving me hell when he finds out I told you that."

"I won't say anything to him."

"No worries." Aly waved a hand. "Honesty is the way to go, I believe that. Tell him what I said. Dante and me, we're always getting into it. I can handle my brother. He gives me grief, I give it right back to him. He's a good man and he means well.

But he thinks he knows how things should be and at least half the time, he's wrong."

On Tuesday, Dante got up at three in the afternoon. Outside, the sun was shining and he had a really strong sense of…what?

Promise, maybe.

Anticipation.

He reminded himself not to be an idiot. It was just dinner and nothing was going to happen between him and Gracie tonight—or ever again. He wouldn't let it.

But that didn't mean they couldn't enjoy each other's company now and then, did it?

They were friends and friends spent time together.

He made coffee and wandered around the house in old sweats and a Portland State T-shirt, thinking he probably ought to get dressed and drive over to his mom's house for a quick visit, see how she and his eight-and-a-half-month-old brother, Mac, were doing. But the coffee tasted really good and he was enjoying being lazy on his day off.

He ended up standing at the sink, looking out the kitchen window, staring at the trees and the gravel driveway leading to the cabin. As he watched, Gracie emerged. She wore busted-out jeans and one of those silky cami tops. It was printed with big tropical flowers and she had no damn bra under it. All that silver-blond hair was loose on her shoulders.

She looked like a fairy princess in some Disney movie—only better. Hotter, too.

She came straight for him, hips and breasts gently swaying. He clutched his second cup of coffee like a lifeline and told himself to turn away.

Didn't happen. She disappeared from sight as she mounted the short stairs to the deck. Behind him, Owen let out a happy little whine and padded straight for the slider.

Dante followed, reaching the glass door at the same time as Gracie did. For a moment they just stood there, staring at each other through the glass. Owen dropped to his haunches and whined up at Dante to open the door and let in the object of the mutt's complete adoration.

Very slowly, Gracie smiled. She lifted her right hand and pantomimed knocking without actually touching the glass.

"Stay," he commanded the dog.

Owen might be in love with Gracie Bravo, but he was a good dog and always obeyed a direct command. He stayed right where he was when Dante shoved the slider wide.

"Want some coffee?" At his feet, Owen quivered with eagerness, but he kept his butt to the floor.

"No, thanks. I just came to tell you dinner's at seven and you should be over at six—and yeah, I could have texted you. But what fun is that?"

"I'll be there." He stared straight into those fine blue eyes. It was a pleasure to do so and it also kept him from looking at her unconfined breasts.

"I'm roasting a chicken. Nothing fancy."

"Sounds good. I'll bring a bottle of white."

Owen was already over there when Dante arrived at six on the nose. Gracie was still wearing that silky, distracting cami.

But really, since last Tuesday night, everything about her distracted him. She could wear a burka and he would still spend every moment near her obsessing over what was under it.

He handed her the chilled bottle of wine and she carried it to the counter to open it.

"Smells good in here." He knelt to pet the dog, who greeted him by rolling over for a stomach scratch. "You've got bowls for him, too?" They were on the floor at the end of the counter. One was empty, the other had water in it.

"Have a seat at the table," she said as she popped the cork. "I never feed your dog, I promise."

He pulled out a chair and sat. "But I'll bet you have kibble."

"Well, just in case." She got down two wine-glasses and carried them and the opened bottle to the table, where she filled a glass and held it down to him.

He took it. "Thanks."

She claimed the chair opposite him, poured a glass for herself and sipped. "Yummy wine— and you know, I'm more than happy to watch him whenever I'm here."

That made him laugh. "You already watch him all the time."

"If you're here, it's not watching him. He's just coming over to visit, that's all."

He studied her face, wondering how it was that she always seemed to have a certain glow about her. "That's a distinction without a difference."

"Wrong. And the offer stands. Just let me know if you need me to look after him."

He glanced over at the dog, who lay on his back with his tongue hanging out. Dante probably ought to put more effort into keeping him at home. But Owen was happy and Gracie liked having him around, so why mess with what seemed to be working out for everyone? "I think I'll just say I appreciate the offer and we should move on to some other, more interesting topic."

"Works for me."

They stared at each other. He wanted to touch her and knew that he wouldn't at the same time as he regretted saying they ought to talk about something more interesting.

Interesting topics could be dangerous—at that moment, *all* topics seemed off-limits. Anything they said could lead to an honest conversation. He might just blurt out something totally unacceptable, like how he couldn't stop thinking of her and he hadn't changed his sheets since the night she spent in them. They still smelled of her, though only faintly now. Of flowers. And sex.

She set her glass back on the table. "The chicken needs another half hour and then a little time to rest before we carve it. How 'bout a walk down to the beach?"

He set his glass next hers. "Let's go."

Owen led the way along the twisting, narrow path to the sand. This time of day, the beach was deserted. The lowering sun glittered on the water and the waves were slow and lazy, drifting in, sliding out.

They took off their shoes and strolled the shoreline, the dog running ahead and then doubling back to follow for a while, then taking off in front of them again.

It was nice, but too quiet. They were being careful with each other and he hated it. At the same time, he knew that saying anything too meaningful could lead somewhere he wasn't prepared to go.

They went to back to the cabin. She served the dinner. He tried not to stare at her sleek bare shoulders, at her thick, pale hair. At everything he wanted that he really needed *not* to let himself have.

Grace sat across from him at the small gateleg table and didn't really know where to go from here.

Tempting him until he broke didn't seem to be working. Plus, it was kind of childish. She realized that.

But the guy was impossible. They could have a great thing together if he'd only stop behaving like it was his sworn duty *not* to touch her ever again.

For once in her life, she was attracted to someone who didn't want her to fund his art or his writing or his next experiment. All Dante really wanted from her was companionship—and hot, sexy times, even if he refused to admit it.

He was the first traditional male who'd ever interested her in the least. And since the night they'd shared a bottle of great tequila and his bed, he interested her a whole lot. He was protective and considerate and smoking hot—when he wasn't being a damn idiot and turning her down.

After the meal, he helped her clear the table and volunteered to wash the dishes. It didn't take all that long.

He thanked her for the evening and said he had to go. She felt so disheartened, she didn't even try to stop him.

Maybe, really, she needed to simply accept that they'd shared one amazing night and it wasn't happening again.

For the rest of the week, she wore a bra when she hung around the cabin. She gardened in her oldest pair of baggy cargoes and she saw Dante only when she brought Owen back to him or waved at him because they both happened to be outside at the same time.

She figured she'd seriously messed up, lost a really good friend by getting naked with him. It was just another life lesson, she tried to tell herself. Constructive and depressing. Like blowing her inheritance supporting interesting men in Europe.

Some women never really worked it out, manwise. That didn't mean they couldn't have a rich and meaningful life. Look at the first Queen Elizabeth. They called her the virgin queen, though most reliable sources claimed the epithet was an exercise in irony. But whether she'd actually died a virgin or not, Elizabeth I never found a life partner. Yet she'd been the greatest ruler England ever had.

Time to face facts, Grace decided. She and Dante were over before they'd even really begun.

Chapter Four

That Saturday morning at ten, Dante arrived at the specified wide space in the road about midway between Valentine Bay and Portland to pick up his girls.

As always, he got there right on time.

And as usual, Marjorie and the girls were late. Dante played Fortnite on his phone and tried not to feel impatient as twenty minutes crawled by.

And then, finally, there they were, with Roger at the wheel of the white Toyota Sienna he'd owned before he and Marjorie got together. Because leave it to Roger Hoffenhower to drive a minivan even before he had a family to ferry around in it.

Roger pulled in behind Dante's Ram crew cab and Dante got out to help the girls move their mountains of belongings from the Toyota to the truck. Nic and Nat jumped out and came running as Marjorie called out the window, "Stay out of the road, you two!" They were on the passenger side of the minivan, nowhere near traffic, but Marjorie was a mother to the core.

His daughters squealed as he held out his arms. They landed against him, one on each side.

"Daddy!" cried Nicole as Natalie shrieked, "We're here!"

Had they grown since their last visit four weeks ago? Kind of seemed like it. They smelled of Sour Patch Kids and that all-natural mango-and-shea-butter shampoo Marj bought for them, and he forgot all about his annoyance at Roger for arriving late. It was everything in the world to him, just to have them in his arms.

For about a half a second.

Immediately, they were dropping to the ground again, whirling around to start grabbing their stuff, babbling on about their cousins and friends in Valentine Bay that they couldn't wait to see. They'd been coming to Dante every summer since they were three. It was pretty much the life they'd always known. They had friends, Marj's family and school in Portland and a whole other set of friends and family in Valentine Bay.

Roger got out and shook Dante's hand and they made friendly noises at each other for a minute or two as Marjorie tried to supervise getting the booster seats out of the minivan.

"We know how to get our seats," insisted Natalie.

"Yeah, Mom," moaned Nic. "We'd rather do it ourselves."

"Well, pardon me." Marj stepped back with both hands up.

The change-off went pretty smoothly, overall. And the girls weren't fighting or crying or complaining, so that was a win. Not ten minutes after Roger pulled in behind Dante, he and Marj were waving goodbye.

The girls buckled up in the back seat and off they went. The drive home took about an hour. Five minutes into the trip, they started working on him to stop at Camp 18 for burgers.

It wasn't even eleven yet. They could have sandwiches at the house.

But he was a single dad and he hadn't seen them for a month. Whatever they wanted, he wanted to give them.

And they knew it, too.

"Daddy, please?"

"Can we?"

"We *never* get to stop at Camp 18…"

They stopped at Camp 18. First came the pictures. He took a bunch of the two of them posing in front of various pieces of logging equipment on view out by the parking area. Then they started in on him about cell phones.

"We need our own phones, Daddy, we really do," insisted Nat as Nic stood beside her, nodding with enthusiasm. "If we had our own phones, we could take our *own* pictures…"

So far, he and Marj had held the line on the phone situation. The plan was to put off going there until the twins reached eighth grade. Yeah, he knew it was a losing battle, but at this point he and his ex were still presenting a united front on the issue. "We've talked about phones. A lot," he said patiently. "I don't think we need to go over all that again right now."

They aimed identical scowls at him.

But then Nic asked so sweetly, "Can we at least use your phone and take some pictures of each other?"

There went another half hour as they giggled and chattered together and took turns posing for each other in front of and on the giant chainsaw sculptures scattered around the series of porches leading into the log cabin–style restaurant and gift shop. Not that he minded them taking their time. They were having a ball and he had the weekend off and the plan was to spend it all with them, anyway.

When he finally herded them inside, they wanted to order everything on the menu. He just kept shaking his head until they narrowed it down to burgers with fries and lemon-lime sodas. The burgers were big, so he really tried to get them to split their order between them. But they looked at him through matching sets of wide brown, hopeful eyes and he was a goner. Food would be wasted.

But as it turned out, they were both hungry and really put it away. He was glad he'd let them have what they wanted. It was all going great—until Nic picked up her full soda just as Nat leaned close to her ear and whispered something.

Nic burst out laughing and stopped paying attention to the drink in her hand. The corner of her big plastic cup caught the edge of the table and sent ice and sticky soda raining into her lap, drenching her turquoise tank on the way, soaking her faded rolled-up jeans and even sliding down her calves to fill her pink-and-white-checked Vans.

She let out an outraged cry of surprise and stared down at the mess with a look of absolute horror.

And then Nat said in a gently chiding tone,

sounding just like their mother, "Nic, you really need to be more careful."

Nicole promptly burst into tears. "Oh, shut up, Nat," she sobbed. "You made me do it."

"Did not."

"Did so…"

The nice waitress came running with clean towels and gentle words. Dante was sent to the truck to get Nic some dry clothes as the waitress and Nat took the sobbing Nic to the restroom.

Of course, he brought back the wrong things.

"I'm not wearing those," Nicole moaned. He could hear every word clearly through the restroom door. "Nat, you have to go with him and show him what I need."

A moment later, Nat emerged carrying the clothes he'd brought from the pickup. "She's soaked all the way through," Nat said sternly. "And she's very upset." He must have looked pretty worried, because then she reassured him. "Come on, Daddy." She patted his arm. "It's going to be fine."

Back out to the truck they went. Nat dug around in one of Nic's suitcases, coming up with a top and some pants that, to him, looked pretty much like the ones he'd chosen in the first place. She also found clean underwear and another pair of canvas shoes.

They headed back to the restaurant and straight

to the restroom. He lurked near the door as his daughters spoke in whispers on the other side.

When they came out, he thought Nic looked pretty composed. She handed him a plastic bag provided by the waitress. "Here's my stuff," she said with distaste. "Everything's sticky."

"We'll dump them in the wash at home and they'll be good as new."

Though her tears had dried, her eyes were red from crying. "I know, Daddy. It's just *embarrassing*, that's all."

"Happens to everyone now and again."

She stuck out her lower lip with a tiny *humph* of sound and then added softly, "I'm sorry, Daddy."

"It was an accident." He dared to offer a hug and she accepted as Nat looked on approvingly.

"Ready to go home?" he asked them both, though as a rule with them he tried not to ask questions he might not like the answer to.

This time, though, he got the answer he was hoping for. Both of them nodded.

By nine that night when the girls went to bed, he was exhausted. He grabbed a quick shower and then checked on them. They were both sound asleep.

Grabbing a beer from the fridge, he went out to

sit on the deck, only realizing that Owen had escaped to Gracie's again when she emerged from the cabin with the dog right behind her. The light by the cabin door made a halo around her bright hair as she paused to pull it closed behind her.

He watched her coming toward him through the twilight, wearing jeans and a white T-shirt—with a bra underneath, he couldn't help but notice with more disappointment than he should have allowed himself to feel.

"Owen." He clicked his tongue and the dog loped up the deck steps and right to him. "Lie down."

Owen dropped to the deck boards and put his head on his paws. With a wave, Gracie started to turn back for the cabin.

He'd spent the whole day with a couple of eight-year-olds and he really couldn't help longing to look at a pretty woman, not to mention, talk to an adult. "Gracie."

She turned back to him again and braced her hands on her hips. "What'd I do now?"

"Want a beer?"

She tipped her head to the side, like she wasn't sure she ought to accept his invitation.

He got that. He'd been avoiding her and, judging by the bra she was now wearing and the disappearance of those revealing Daisy Dukes, she'd taken the hint.

"C'mon," he coaxed. "Just one." With a shrug, she came toward him. "Have a seat."

She dropped into the chair across from him and he got up and went in to get an IPA, handing it to her before he sat down again.

For a couple of minutes, they just sat there, sipping. He thought about how superfine she looked in the light by the slider behind him and couldn't help missing all that gorgeous skin she had hidden now under faded jeans and a plain shirt.

"Your daughters are adorable," she said.

He frowned at her. "You met them?"

She laughed. The sound tugged on something deep inside him, something that wasn't quite an emotion, something more basic. Something needful and hungry—and lonely, too. "I babysat them once, back when they were toddlers. It was here. At this house."

"I'd forgotten."

"They were a handful back then, but sweet. Kind of like Daniel's twins." She set the bottle down on the table, but didn't let go of it. "This afternoon, they came to the cabin to get Owen."

"Owen." At his feet, the dog lifted his head. Dante gave the dog a pat. "I should have known.

That must have been when I was trying to get their karaoke machine up and running. I had some trouble with the disco lights."

"But you got it working?" At his nod, she went on, "For identicals, I find them pretty easy to tell apart."

"Yeah, Nat's more athletic, more outgoing and opinionated. Nic is more in her own head, I guess you could say. She weighs maybe five pounds more than Nat, but she's pretty sensitive about it."

"They're both gorgeous."

"I couldn't agree more."

"Spoken like a really good dad."

He grinned at her across the table. "Hold that thought."

"Once you got the disco lights working, did they sing for you?"

"Let me put it this way. I don't really ever need to hear 'Let It Go' again."

Gracie ran a hand back through all that beautiful hair. What was it about her? Even in unrevealing clothes, she pretty much sucked the breath clean out of his lungs. She asked, "So they wore you out, huh?"

"They did. And I try to keep in shape, too. Valentine Bay is hardly a hotbed of crime, but I've taken down my share of bad actors and fleeing offenders.

None of them had half the energy of my two girls. Every time they come home, I realize all over again how nonstop they are. Always talking, on the move."

She was watching him. "I meant it when I said that you're a good dad, Dante."

"Thanks." He confessed, "I miss them so much when they're gone." Their eyes met and held. He never wanted to look away.

She was the one who broke the spell, slowly turning to stare off toward the shadows of the twisted trees that framed the path to the beach. "They're excited to be here. They told me they always do the day camp in Valentine City Park and have lots of friends they can't wait to see."

"Yeah. I get banker's hours when they're with me so I can work while they're at camp. Today, they were home for maybe two hours before they started begging to go to Grandma's. They can't wait to have sleepovers with their cousins and friends here in town. And they're already on me about where they can get the right costumes for the Medieval Faire—according to some all-knowing authority they somehow can't quite name, it's no good to just go to a discount store and pick up something simple and easy out of a box. It has to be 'special,' though neither of them seems that sure what 'special' involves."

Gracie turned those shining eyes on him again. "My sisters are running the Medieval Faire."

"Harper and Hailey?"

"Who else? They're the Barnum and Bailey of Valentine Bay, those two. I might be able to hook your girls up with what they need for the Faire. Harper's kind of a genius with costumes. She can take a bunch of random fabric and some rickrack and whip up something any medieval lady would be proud to wear."

He really wanted to kiss her. He wouldn't. Uh-uh. But he wanted to. Bad. It didn't matter in the least that she'd stopped running around braless in short shorts. Whatever she wore, he was interested. He would never forget their one night together and he kind of hated that it wasn't going to happen again.

"Dante?" She leaned toward him across the table. "Where'd you go?"

"I'm right here." It wouldn't take much to get his mouth on hers. He could lean in to meet her.

Not that she was necessarily interested anymore. She sat back and picked up her beer again.

He ordered his brain to stay on task. "Getting two eight-year-olds the 'special' costumes they require is kind of a lot. I don't want to take advantage of you."

She let out a snort. "Oh, please. Look at all

you've done for me. I'm no longer living in my brother's house. Instead, I've got the perfect little cabin in a beautiful setting for five hundred a month, all because of you. Getting Nic and Nat costumes for the Faire is nothing, the least I can do. And it'll be fun, too."

Seeing her naked again, now *that* would be fun…

And what was the matter with him? He needed to get his mind out of the gutter.

He was hopeless when it came to her, no doubt about it.

Twin lines had formed between her smooth brows. "You okay, Dante? You seem kind of… I don't know. Sad, maybe. Or preoccupied."

There was nothing wrong with him that another night with her wouldn't cure—at least temporarily. Until the next night, when he would only be wanting her all over again.

"I'm fine," he lied. "'Nother beer?"

"Thanks, no." She set her empty bottle down and stood. "I need to change and head over to the Sea Breeze. Ingrid's short a bartender. She asked if I could make it in from eleven to closing—listen, tomorrow I'll reach out to my sisters about costumes for the girls."

"'Preciate it."

"I'll let you know."

He gave her a nod and then watched her walk away, feeling low that she was no longer sitting across from him.

Was he ridiculous? Damn straight.

Somehow, he needed to get over himself, either stop yearning for what he was never going to let himself have.

Or reach out and take it.

If she was still willing. If he hadn't already blown any chance he might have had with her.

During the family dinner at Daniel's the next day, Grace talked to Harper. She said she would love to put together costumes for Dante's twins. The Faire opened in two weeks. Harper said that was plenty of time to fix the twins up, as long as they got on it right away.

It wouldn't be right to get the twins' hopes up if Dante had changed his mind about Harper helping the girls out, so Gracie planned to wait until after nine when she knew the kids would be in bed to talk to him about it. She got home from Daniel's at a little past eight. It was weirdly nerve-racking, sitting in the cabin, waiting for the right time to go looking for him.

She'd been missing him. They *were* friends and

she hoped that someday they would get past what had happened on what she'd come to think of as the night of the tequila. She longed for them to be easy with each other again.

And okay, hard truth? Even with the current tension between them, she *liked* being alone with him. The way he looked at her caused small, fluttery creatures to buzz around in her belly in the best kind of way. Sometimes she even dared to imagine the day would come when he would admit that he ached to spend the night with her again.

Would she turn him down flat, as originally planned?

Better not to even think about what would happen if…

Dante was sitting on the deck with Owen when she went over there at ten past nine. With a nod at the chair across from him, he went in to get her a beer.

When he came back out, she explained that Harper would make the girls their costumes. "So we were thinking that on Tuesday, I could pick them up at the park after day camp and drive them over to the cottage where my sisters live. Harper will take measurements and sketch out what the finished dresses will look like. She says she can have them ready in a week or so."

"Sounds great. How much do I owe you and Harper?"

She gave him a serious eye-roll. "I told you last night. Nothing. I'm taking care of it."

"What does that mean?"

"It means my part of this is minimal. I'm taking the girls over there and bringing them home. And I already agreed with Harper on the price of the costumes. I'm paying that."

"No, you're not."

"This is ridiculous. Let it go, Dante."

He had on his bad-cop face, unreadable and harsh. "Okay, I'm willing to take advantage of *you*." She had to press her lips together to keep from making some silly, suggestive comment in response to that one. He went on, "Because you're so damn stubborn and I'm tired of arguing about it."

"Jeesh. Thanks?"

"But if Harper is making my girls their costumes, she's going to get paid for it by me."

They went back and forth a couple of times, Grace maintaining that she had it handled, Dante insisting she take his money, or else. In the end, she gave in and he went inside again, emerging a few minutes later with a check for her to give to Harper.

She reluctantly accepted the money and stood up to go.

"Sit back down," he commanded as he dropped into his chair. "Finish your damn beer."

She made a face at him. "Why? Because you're so much fun to be with?"

He gazed up at her through those fine dark eyes. His eyelashes were so thick and black. She wanted to reach out and touch them, feel them brush against her fingertips. She wanted to bend across the iron table between them and kiss that sexy mouth again, to have those big, muscular arms of his wrapping tight around her, pulling her in good and close to his heat and strength.

"Please." He said the word a little roughly. But kind of earnestly, too. Like he really, truly wanted her to stay.

When, exactly, did she become such a complete pushover for this man? The night of the tequila? Maybe.

More likely, it had started long before that, when he was always coming into the Sea Breeze and sitting at the bar, keeping her company while she worked. He would nurse a beer or two, maybe have sliders or fish tacos and fries. When things weren't too busy, they would talk. He was a good listener. Too serious, maybe. But the thing about

Dante was, he really did *care*—how a friend was doing, if everything was all right.

She sat down and picked up her half-finished beer. "Bad day?"

Dante set his beer down. "Tomorrow, I have to work. The girls will go to day camp."

She gave him a small shrug. "I'm aware of the schedule."

"All I mean is, two days into having them with me and I'm so ready to drop them off at City Park and spend the day reviewing arrest reports and conducting background investigations."

Gracie rested both forearms on the table and plunked her chin down on her folded hands. "You feel guilty, is that what you're saying?" She gave him a tiny smile and a hint of a dimple tucked itself into her left cheek.

He had a raging case of lust for her. And he liked her, too. So much. Too much?

Probably.

"Talk," she said.

"It's partly Roger," he grumbled.

"They use Roger against you?"

"Exactly. It's 'Roger lets us do this.' And 'Roger says we don't have to do *that*.' And 'Roger understands that we're eight and we need to have some independence—and lip gloss. Daddy, we're old enough for lip gloss.'"

Gracie laughed, a quiet little laugh, and sat back in her chair again. "I'm sure it's frustrating. But they really do seem like great kids. And it's natural for them to test boundaries and limits with you. Also, think about it—is there a kid alive who doesn't play one parent off against the other, at least a little?"

He couldn't stop himself from reminding her, "Roger isn't a parent. He's their stepdad."

"Oh, come on." She slanted him a look both ironic and reproachful. "Stepfathers count, too, in a child's life. And even you said he's a great guy. You're just jealous."

"Hey," he grumbled. "Whose friend are you, anyway?"

"Yours." She reached across and clasped his arm. It felt so good. Her palm was cool, her fingers soft. He wanted...

Never mind what you want, fool.

She took her hand away—too quickly, as though she'd caught herself doing something she shouldn't. He wanted to reach out and catch it, to lace his fingers with hers.

How bad did he have it for her, really?

Pretty damn bad. And it wasn't only that gorgeous face and rockin' body. She was good at heart and wise, too. Sometimes, when they talked, he forgot that she was almost a decade younger than him. He liked hearing whatever she had to say on any given subject.

"Be patient with them *and* with yourself," she advised.

"I'm working on it. I try to remember not to *always* draw the line on them, to be more permissive now and then. Being permissive isn't my strong suit, though."

"Really?" She poured on the sarcasm. "I never would have guessed..." But then she softened. "Honestly, though. They do seem happy and it's obvious they adore you."

He scoffed. "They think I'm a dinosaur who doesn't understand them the way Roger does."

She leaned in again. "They love you. You never have to doubt that. Show a little faith that they can love you and love Roger, too."

Tuesday, Gracie picked up Nicole and Natalie at the park after their day camp. They'd kept their booster seats that morning when Dante dropped them off and now, they hooked them up in the back seat of Grace's RAV4 themselves.

The two were bouncy and bright-eyed, going on about their best friends at camp and their first sleepover of the summer at their cousin Heather's house Saturday night.

"Aunt Lisa lets us stay up late," Natalie announced with glee.

"It's so much fun," Nicole chimed in. "They have a fire pit in back and we roast hot dogs and marshmallows for s'mores. Carly, our friend from camp, is coming, too."

A glance in the rearview mirror showed Grace that Natalie was nodding. "We can't hardly wait. We'll bring our sleeping bags and sleep outside and tell scary stories all night long."

At the rambling one-story cottage on a hill above the beach at the north end of town, Hailey whipped up strawberry smoothies. Harper had ten different costume sketches for the twins to choose from, each consisting of two layers. First, a long undertunic in a lightweight fabric. Then another, heavier tunic went on top. The overtunic designs, in damask and velvet, featured deep, strong colors. They were embellished with ornamental bands at the ends of the flowing sleeves, around the hem and dropped waist and at the neckline.

Harper had also provided a selection of wimple sketches so the girls could mix and match their headdresses with the gowns they chose. Grace, who'd studied medieval dress in college, had always considered the wimple to be about the ugliest thing a woman could wear on her head—no offense to all the excellent nuns the world over. However, the wimple was an authentic part of any medieval lady's wardrobe and Harper had done a beautiful job of sketching out various wimple styles. Gracie kept her opinion of that particular article of clothing to herself.

But then it turned out Natalie and Nicole felt the same. The two whispered together and then Natalie spoke up. "Can we skip this bandage thing on our heads?"

Harper had no problem with that. "Absolutely. Who needs a wimple, anyway? You should love what you wear or why bother?"

"I'm glad," declared Nat.

"We really love these dresses," added Nic.

Nat agreed. "It might take us a little while to choose…"

And it did. For more than an hour, they sipped their smoothies and ate apple slices and debated the strong points of this or that gown.

Grace took Harper aside as the girls pored over the different designs. "I planned to treat them to the dresses, but Dante wouldn't let me." She handed over the check.

"Whoa," said her sister. "This is more than I expected. Really, Gracie, I was only going to charge you for the fabric and notions."

"Cheap at the price. The girls are going to love those gowns and Dante was insistent that you should get paid for your work."

"Tell Dante thank-you."

"I will."

"How's it going, with the cabin and all?"

"I love it there."

Harper seemed to be studying her a little too closely. "But?"

"But nothing. It's a really cute place. Like this place, there's a private path down to the beach and the price is ridiculously low. Dante's a good, um, friend."

Harper looked at her sideways. "What's an 'um' friend?"

"That's a long story and I'm not tellin' it."

"Gracie." Harper reached out and stroked a hand down her arm. "I'm here. Hailey's here. For you."

It felt so good, just to hear her sister say that. Maybe she'd misjudged the situation with Hailey and Harper. Maybe feeling like an outsider around the two of them was more on her than on them.

The truth was, Grace had felt somewhat adrift lately, in terms of having other women she trusted to talk to. Her lifetime besties, Carrie and Erin, were still partying hearty all the time, ready for anything, while Grace was starting to be more about making a place for herself in life and succeeding at her chosen career. She'd kind of drifted away from them in the past year.

Now she was the one squeezing Harper's arm. "I appreciate the offer for some girl time. I really do. And I'll probably be taking you up on it one of these days."

"Anytime, the sooner the better. I mean that. We know Daniel used to be too hard on you."

"Well, we're okay now, Daniel and me. We really are."

"Good. He was always kind of grim about having all that responsibility dumped on his shoulders after Mom and Dad died."

"Yes, he was," Grace said with conviction.

"But then I kind of think it was also hard for him to let go of being a second dad to all of us. As the youngest, you had the toughest time getting him to see that you are all grown up."

Grace was kind of blown away at all this insight from her sister. "You are absolutely right."

"Just remember." Harper caught her hand and gave it a quick squeeze. "We've got another bedroom here and the price, for you, is even better than what you're paying Dante—I mean, you just can't beat free."

Somehow, Grace hadn't expected Harper or Hailey to be that thrilled at the idea of her moving in on them. Apparently, she'd been wrong about that, too. Which had her throat going tight and her eyes turning misty. "Thank you."

"Nothing to thank me for. This house is for anyone in the family who needs it. And Hailey and I would love to have you here."

Grace didn't know what to say. She pulled her sister into a quick, tight hug. "It means a lot—you know, to have the option."

"Anytime." Harper whispered, "And I gotta ask. You and Dante? Maybe?"

"Like I said, we're friends." The words tasted sour in her mouth.

Harper was grinning—and still whispering. "No doubt about it now. I'm picking up an undercurrent, hot goings-on with a hot cop. You need to talk about it. With me."

"Uh-uh. Not happening."

"Shake your head all you want," said her sister. "I'm not convinced. You've got to come over some evening, and tell all—or tell nothing if that's how you want it. But come over and spend some time with us, please."

Grace promised that she would.

When Nat and Nic had finally made their choices, Harper took their measurements and said she expected them back for a final fitting a week from today. Then she would make any necessary alterations and the dresses would be ready that following Friday, the day before the Faire opened.

Dante had chicken cooking on the grill when Gracie brought the twins home at a little after seven.

She pulled in at the front gate and the girls got out, unhooked their booster seats and carried them into the garage.

He called to Gracie from the top step, "Barbecued chicken? I've got plenty."

She leaned across the seat and hollered out the open passenger window. "Can't. I'm closing at the Sea Breeze. Gotta be there by eight. Rain check?"

Disappointment he shouldn't be feeling twisted inside him, but he tried not to show it. "You got it."

"Harper says thank-you for the check."

"Worth every penny," he replied with a friendly wave—because that's what they were. Friends.

She waved back and drove off around the house on her way to the cabin. He went inside and on out back to the deck, where he turned the chicken over and then called the girls to set the table.

While they ate, the twins talked nonstop about the costumes Harper Bravo was making for them and the fun they'd had that afternoon with the beautiful, grown-up Bravo sisters.

"Grace is the best," declared Nat. "She's almost like another kid, a really nice kid, and smart. A kid who *knows* stuff, someone you can talk to."

"Talk to about what?" asked Dante.

Both girls frowned at him. Finally, Nat answered, "Everything," and went right on talking before he could try to get some specifics out of her. "Hailey made us smoothies."

"They were *so* good." Nic beamed.

"Strawberry," Nat said. "We had the smoothies while we picked which costumes we wanted. Mine will be gold underneath with red velvet on top and lots of gold trim."

"And mine's green," said Nic, "and kind of silvery underneath, with silver trim. Harper drew these beautiful pictures of the dresses she could make for us. It was really hard to choose which one."

"And it took a long time, too," Nat added, eyes going wide.

"But it was worth it," said Nic.

"*So* worth it," Nat agreed. "We have to go back next Tuesday…" She paused to sip her milk.

"For a final fitting," Nic finished for her as Nat carefully set down her glass.

The girls chattered on. Dante got the memo, loud and clear. In bold, all caps. His kids and his dog couldn't get enough of the gorgeous, generous, big-hearted woman he kept telling himself he couldn't have sex with again. Ever.

Because he was too old for her and he didn't do actual relationships. He was no damn good at them, a complete slacker in the love department. The only one in his family who'd been born without the talent for being in love and staying that way. And let us not forget that Connor would probably knock his teeth down his throat if he ever found out what had happened between Dante and Connor's baby sister.

Dante wished she'd come over for dinner. But it was probably better she hadn't. Keeping his hands off her was an exercise in constant diligence. He could break at any time.

It was getting to the point where he kind of couldn't wait to break.

And that was wrong. So wrong. He should be avoiding her, not trying to lure her to the deck nightly with barbecued chicken and beers. Yet, as each day went by, he grew less certain of all the very good reasons he really needed to keep his greedy hands to himself.

"Daddy," said Nat, clearly perturbed.

"Huh?"

"You aren't listening," Nic chided.

"We're telling you all this important stuff." Nat set down a chicken bone and wiped her hands on her napkin. "And you're just sitting there looking like this." Nat let her mouth drop open and put on a vacant stare.

"Oh, come on. I'm not *that* bad."

Nic reached over and patted his arm with her soft little hand. "You need to pay some contentions, Daddy," she instructed in a gentle tone.

"You mean 'attention,' that I need to pay *attention*." Now and then, the girls still got the bigger words turned around.

Nic looked puzzled—but only for a second or two. "Yeah. That. It's important."

He promised them he would do better. They resumed their endless chatter and he did his best to listen to every word they said and not to let his mind wander to dangerous thoughts of Gracie Bravo.

Chapter Five

Saturday around six, Dante arrived home from dropping the twins off at his brother's for a sleepover. Owen was waiting just inside the front door when he entered the house. The dog looked up at him pleadingly.

"Walk?" he asked. At Owen's eager whine, he grabbed the leash he rarely used and a baggie for cleanup and took the dog out the back slider for a run down on the beach.

Gracie's ancient Toyota was parked in the graveled parking spot on one side of the cabin. Light shone through the windows on either side of the door. He could see her at the kitchen counter in there.

"Hey!" he called as he went by.

"Hey!" she answered from inside.

A moment later, she opened the door. He drank in the sight of her, in a tank top—with a bra under it, damn it—and shorts that were unfortunately *not* those magical Daisy Dukes he so fervently admired. She had all that silver-blond hair corralled in two pigtails. He tried really hard not to imagine wrapping them around his fist from behind, giving them a good, hard tug so she tipped her head back and gave him her mouth for a deep, wet kiss.

She asked, "What's up?" Owen detoured to the front step and plunked to his butt in front of her. "Hello, handsome." She knelt to properly show her affection and he wished he was Owen, getting a scratch around the neck, being allowed to lick her face.

"Just a walk down to the beach." He shouldn't ask. But then he couldn't stop himself. "You working tonight?"

"I'm off." She rose to her feet again and Owen trotted back to his side. "And on a Saturday, no less. I traded with one of the other bartenders. I had the Fourth off and she really wanted it—family coming into town, she said."

His next question? Yeah, pretty much inevitable. "So what are you up to?"

"Just hanging at home, taking it easy."

"I've got some steaks and baby potatoes. I'll be firing up the grill as soon as Owen and I get in a quick run along the beach. Join me for dinner?"

For a moment, she just looked at him, those jewel-blue eyes unreadable. He braced himself for a no. But then she said, "Nicole and Natalie are at their cousin's tonight, right?"

"That's right. First sleepover of the summer."

"They mentioned it the other day."

"It's a very big deal," he said. "Momentous, even."

"Yeah, I heard rumors of untold delights. Hot dogs. S'mores. Scary stories all night long…"

"Don't tell me the details. I'll only worry they're eating too much junk food and not getting enough sleep."

"They're going to have a wonderful time." She said it kind of tenderly, like he needed reassurance that his girls were all right and sleepovers were an important part of an eight-year-old's social life. At his side, Owen was eager to be moving on. The dog whimpered with impatience as Dante and the gorgeous creature in the cabin doorway stood silently gazing at each other. And then she said, "I'll bring a salad and a bottle of red."

After dinner on the deck, they cleared the table and came back outside to watch the sun sink below the water way out on the ocean. The bottle of wine was still more than half-full. They were both being careful this time not to drink too much.

Something about her made him start blabbing stuff he never told anyone. Like how he and Marjorie were essentially broken up when she found out she was pregnant.

Grace didn't seem the least surprised at the news. "So you decided to try again?"

He studied her face and realized he would never get tired of looking at her. "Somebody already told you that Marjorie was pregnant when we got married, right?"

She gave him the barest hint of a smile. "Women talk. You need to get used to it."

"Must've been my sister. When did you have time to talk to Aly about me?"

She only tipped her head to the side, causing one of those sexy pigtails to swing down along the silky skin of her bare arm. The damn pigtail seemed to be taunting him, tempting him to reach across and give it a tug.

He dragged his gaze back up and focused on meeting her eyes. "You're not going to tell me if it was Aly, are you?"

"Nope."

Did he care that much who'd told her? Not really. He let it go and went back to saying more than he should about what went down with him and his ex-wife. "Marjorie had moved here to be with me after college, but she missed her family and friends in Portland. It wasn't working out for either of us, really. We broke up and she moved home— and then she found out she was pregnant. I asked her to marry me. She came back to Valentine Bay. The girls were born. We lasted as a couple until they were two and then Marjorie said she just couldn't do it anymore. She said that she and I were over and we needed to accept that."

"So…she filed for divorce and returned to Portland?"

"Yeah. The rest is history. At least, it should've been."

"Except…?"

"For the next three years or so after Marj and I called it quits, I remained fake married to her anyway."

"What does 'fake married' mean?"

"It means I couldn't let go. If I had a day off and the girls were with her, I drove to Portland to check on her and see my daughters. While I was there, I would fix stuff around Marj's house, change the oil in her car, whatever she needed."

"You wanted to get back together with her?"

"I wanted to be a family with my girls and their mother."

"You're saying you felt that you and Marjorie *should* get back together?"

"That's it. That's right. Eventually, Marj drew the line on me. She said we weren't married and we would never be married again and I had to stop appearing at her doorstep, coming to her rescue all the time. It wasn't good for either of us, she said—and it wasn't fair to our daughters because it was too confusing for them. She said we had to face reality. It was over and it had been over for a long time."

Gracie smoothed both of her braids forward over her shoulders and held on to the ends of them. She looked so young, tugging on her pigtails, one sleek bare leg crossed over the other one. "Were you still in love with her?" she asked.

"No." Sometimes he doubted that he'd ever been in love with Marjorie. "I just wanted to make it work. I really did. For the girls' sake. And because Marj is a good woman. Because making it work is the right thing to do."

"I have to ask." Gracie wrinkled her nose and stared off into space.

"Go ahead."

She turned those unforgettable eyes on him again. "Are you saying you didn't have sex with anyone for three years, while you were driving back and forth to Portland to fix your ex-wife's... whatever?"

He shouldn't be talking about sex with her. He shouldn't be talking about his failed marriage or the wife he'd never loved the way a man should.

And yet, once again, he laid it right out there. "For about a year after Marjorie moved back to Portland, she and I would hook up occasionally. Then she told me she wouldn't sleep with me again and she was going to see other guys. I was so pissed off about that. There I was, knocking myself out to get us back together and she just announces she wants to go out with other men. I hit the roof, said things I shouldn't have. Marj never raised her voice. She just held firm. She was moving on. So, I started seeing other women. I'm no monk, for God's sake. I've just learned my lesson when it comes to love and marriage and forever after. I'm not cut out for that. I'm not looking for anything serious and I'm not getting married again and I make that very clear to any woman I spend time with."

"I see." She let go of her braids and recrossed those beautiful legs.

His mouth was dry and he ached to kiss her—to do a lot more than kiss her, if he was honest about it. "I'm sorry. You didn't need to hear all that."

"Didn't I?" Those deep blue eyes of hers seemed

to look right inside his head, to know every hot, sexy thought he kept trying really hard not to have about her. Sometimes she made him feel that *he* was too young for *her*. Another of those mysterious smiles curved her plump lips. "I've got a few things to tell *you*, too."

He grabbed his wine and knocked back a big gulp of it. "Why am I nervous, all of a sudden?"

She giggled then, and suddenly she was once more the young, carefree Gracie, ready for fun, up for anything. "The morning after we shared that bottle of tequila and ended up in bed together, when you said we could never do it again...?"

He realized he was holding his breath and let it out carefully. "Yeah?"

"I decided to torment you, to punish the crap out of you. My plan was to drive you insane with desire and then, when you finally begged me for one more night, to turn you down flat."

He liked her so much. Liked everything about her. Liked her enough that it kind of freaked him out. Maybe. A little. "You've been a very bad girl."

She snickered. "Oh, yes, I have." Her expression grew more serious. "Or I was. But then I kind of decided I was being childish. I put the short shorts away and put on a bra."

"Gracie?" He really needed to watch himself or he'd be saying what he shouldn't say.

"Hmm?"

That stuff he shouldn't say? He said it anyway. "Bra or no bra, your plan worked."

She uncrossed those spectacular legs and leaned into him. "Is this it, then?" It came out breathless and her eyes were softer, the pupils dilated. He ached to reach for her. She asked again. "Is this the moment you break?"

It was. Absolutely. "Yeah. You might as well go ahead and tell me right now to forget it."

She looked…stricken suddenly, every last trace of that breezy seductiveness gone.

The wounded look in her eyes kind of freaked him out. "Gracie. What's wrong?"

"Who am I kidding? I won't say no. I want you, too, Dante. Way too much to turn you down."

Chapter Six

Am I a complete fool? Gracie wondered.

Yeah. Probably.

Didn't matter. There might not be a tomorrow for her and Dante. But sometimes right now can be a very fine thing.

She got up and held down her hand to him. He took it without the slightest hesitation. A dark, heated shiver skated up her arm from just the touch of his fingers on her skin.

"Come here." He rose and pulled her around the small table until she stood in front of him. Only then did he release her—to clasp her by the waist.

"You're so beautiful." His mouth swooped down. "God, I missed having my hands on you."

She lifted up.

And finally, after far too many days and nights, they were kissing again. His mouth tasted of wine and the gelato they'd had for dessert. She'd missed him, too. So much.

His big, broad hands skated up her torso and she lifted her arms to wrap them around his neck. He smelled so good, like cedar and cloves and sheer, burning need.

She broke the kiss.

He opened his eyes. She saw such yearning in his face and found herself thinking that he didn't really understand how deeply he cared. He denied the power of his own emotions, seemed to take a dark kind of pride in being tough and calm and always in control of himself.

"Self-denial," she said. "It's kind of a thing with you."

"Not tonight, it isn't." He growled the words— and then he narrowed those midnight-dark eyes at her. His sensual mouth turned down. "Wait. Did you just change your mind?"

She reached up and framed his face with her hands. His cheeks were smooth now, though he'd been sporting some serious five o'clock shadow when he stopped by the cabin earlier to ask her over for dinner. He'd shaved for her. She didn't mind a little beard scruff. But she loved that he must have had some hope they might end up in each other's arms tonight, that he wanted to be smooth shaven for her.

Oh, she couldn't wait to kiss him some more, to touch him all over, to memorize again every muscled ridge, every dip and hollow. His body ran hot. She wanted to press herself tightly against him, to melt into him until there was nothing between them but the hunger and the pleasure they stirred in each other.

Until the only reality was the two of them moving together, naked and shameless, all through the night.

"No," she said, her voice soft, her intention firm. "I haven't changed my mind. No way. I want to be with you tonight." She surged up and took his mouth.

That kiss lasted longer than the first one, until she felt boneless. Liquid. Breathless, too.

"Let's go inside." He caught her earlobe between his teeth and gave it a tug.

She moaned and pushed away enough to see his eyes. They were dark as onyx, heavy lidded with arousal. "The cabin," she said. "*My* place this time." If he got freaked out like before and wanted to escape her in the morning, he could just go. She wouldn't have to suffer through the awfulness of him trying to get rid of her.

"However you want it."

She gave a low laugh then. "Now you're talkin'. Grab my salad bowl, lock up and let's go."

In the cabin, they pulled down the shades.

"Leave the lights on," he commanded.

"Works for me."

He pointed to the dog bed over by the fireplace. She'd bought it last week so Owen would have his own spot in her living space. "Go lie down." The dog trotted right over there and made himself comfortable. Then Dante turned those dark eyes on her. "Come here."

He caught her hand. She stepped out of her flip-flops and into his arms. His mouth came down to claim hers in a scorching kiss.

"Everything off." He breathed the command against her parted lips. But when she tried to un-button her shorts, he made a growling sound and pushed her hands away. "Uh-uh. I'll do it."

"So controlling..."

A low, rough chuckle escaped him. He kissed her slow and deep as he set about undressing her. Tugging the zipper wide on her shorts, he shoved them down, taking her panties right along with them. Those panties were a favorite of hers. Cheekies in cherry-red lace.

They fell unnoticed to the rag rug along with her shorts. And then his big hand was sliding between her legs. An approving growl escaped him as he stroked her wetness.

"Beautiful," he muttered thickly. "Perfect." He grabbed the globes of her bottom and pulled her up to him, hard and tight, so she could feel how much he was enjoying this. His big fingers digging into her backside, he licked and bit his way over her jaw and down the side of her throat. "This, too." He had the hem of her top in his hands and was already pulling it up. "It has to go." His voice rumbled against her collarbone.

She simply lifted her arms and he took it away, leaving her standing in front of him in only her red lace bra and two pink hair elastics, one at the end of each braid. When she reached up to pull off one of the elastics, he caught her hand.

"Leave the braids. I like them." His eyes promised things—lovely, sexy things. She sighed and dropped her hand.

He was gazing at her red bra now. "Pretty." Lifting a finger, he traced the lace of one cup, following it across the top slope of her breast, then moving on to the other one, drawing a sweet cascade of goose bumps along her skin, making her nipples go hard and tight. "Let me see..." He tugged on the lace, pulling it down, using his other hand to lift her breast up and push the lace below it. He did the same with the other cup, creating quite the display.

"You know, I'm all but naked with my boobs sticking out," she remarked, trying her best not to sound as breathless and needy as she felt. "And you're still wearing all your clothes."

"No complaining." He actually had the nerve to shake a finger at her. "I'm busy here." He bent close then and took her nipple in his mouth. She tried not to groan at the stab of sheer pleasure as his teeth closed around the hardened nub and he started to suck.

"You are so bad," she whispered, gathering him even closer, spearing her fingers in his thick, wavy hair, breathing in the heat and the dizzying scent of him. "Just a bad, bad man."

He kissed the tight flesh over her breastbone as he moved on to the other nipple, biting a little as he drew on it. It felt so good, painful in the most delicious way. And his hands weren't idle. They played her below. She could feel his erection, full and hard, against her hip.

When he lifted his head and looked in her eyes again, he said, "Get on the bed."

She might have talked back to him, just to let him know he wasn't the boss of her. But then again, what was there to argue about, really? Getting prone on the bed seemed like an excellent idea to her. She climbed up and stretched out with her head on the pillows. "Now what, oh lord and master?"

He watched her, his eyes dark fire, burning her, searing right down to the core of her, as he emptied his pockets, setting three condoms, his keys and his phone on the nightstand. Then he undressed, turning first to sit on the edge of the mattress and get rid of his boots and socks, then rising to peel everything else away.

She got to watch. It took him only a minute to strip himself bare, but it was a terrific minute. She drank in the sight of his broad, muscled shoulders and big arms, his deep chest and flat belly with its perfect trail of silky black hair leading down to the ready evidence that he really, really liked her. Every bit of him was just right. Just as she remembered from that first night.

Even drunk as she'd been, she did remember. All of it. The sheer glory of it.

And it was even better now, with her senses completely awake and attuned to him. Whatever happened in the morning, she would have tonight.

He came down to her.

And then he kissed her.

Time kind of flew away. There were only his strong arms around her, his mouth claiming hers in a long, thorough kiss before he moved down her body, settled between her thighs and guided her legs up over his shoulders.

"The taste of you..." He spoke the words against her core, rough and low and hungry. "I remember, Gracie. I remember everything. I won't ever, ever forget..."

"Good," she replied. "So, so very good..." And it was. The best. Even better than the time before. "Yes. Oh, absolutely. Beyond the faintest shadow of a doubt... Yes!" She speared her fingers into his hair, braced her heels on his hard shoulders and opened her legs even wider. Lifting her hips eagerly, she pressed her eager body up into his wonderful kiss.

She could lie there forever, moaning and writhing, with his mouth making magic, his fingers driving her crazy, curling inside her, finding that perfect spot that sent her straight to the moon.

How did he do it? How did he know just how to touch her, how to kiss her, how to drive her happily out of her mind? It really was not fair that he was so good at this. Not fair in the least.

And oh, please, if only he might never, ever stop…

Too quickly, she was flying over the moon and straight to the stars. She pulled on his hair and yanked him harder against her as she moaned out her climax and cried his name.

When she finally went lax, he prowled up her body, dropping a chain of kisses along the way, finally taking her mouth, slow and so sweet. She laughed against his lips, pressing her hands to his cheeks to rub her own wetness away.

"You're much too good at that," she scolded.

"I live to serve." He caught her lower lip between his teeth and tugged, stretching it deliciously before letting it pop free.

With a snort of affectionate derision, she shoved at his shoulders. She couldn't wait to give him a big dose of his own medicine.

But he was already reaching toward the nightstand, grabbing a condom.

"Give me that." She snatched it from him.

And for once, he let her have her way. She took it out of the wrapper, pushed him over onto his back and straddled him.

"Who's bossy now?" That sinful mouth of his curved in a lazy smile and his gaze roamed over her, possessive and so hot. He reached up and cupped her breasts, which were still in their cradle of lace. Using his thumbs, he idly flicked at her nipples. "You wreck me, Gracie. You blow me away."

She sighed in sheer pleasure, at the feel of his hands on her flesh and also at the rough, needful sound of his voice. For a moment, she just sat there on top of him, staring into his eyes, wishing...

But no.

There was now, tonight, and it was just beautiful. But he showed zero inclination to get over his conviction that he wasn't cut out for a lasting relationship.

No need to go wanting something she would never have.

Better to fully enjoy what was offered and let the future take care of itself. Really, she'd always been good at both.

Those big hands slid around to her back and he unclasped her bra. One at a time, he guided the straps down her arms. Still holding the unused condom, she stretched out her arms so he could take the bra away. "There," he said, his hands back beneath her breasts again and then trailing down her torso. Gently, he grasped her hips. "Well?"

"I'm on it." She rolled the condom down over his thick, hard length, easing it all the way to the base, taking care not to tear it as she worked. Once she had it in place, she lifted up to her knees and guided him to her. Slowly, she sank down on him, letting her head fall back. A luxurious groan escaped her as he filled her.

He groaned, too.

She looked down into those ebony eyes and they shared a smile. Then he reached up and took hold of both of her braids and slowly pulled her down until her lips met his.

He took her face between his hands. "You are spectacular. I never want to let you go."

Then don't, she thought. But all she said was, "Feels so good..."

She began to move, lifting and lowering, rolling against him, loving the feel of him, so thick and hot, deep and then deeper, so perfect. Just right.

He clasped her hips again, pulling her down tight, then letting her rise—only to drag her close once again.

She moaned in delighted surprise when he flipped her over and took the top position. Kneeling up, his hands still holding her hips, he pulled her lower body with him and guided her legs over his shoulders. By then, she was flying.

"So close," she whispered. "I'm almost…" A soft cry of pleasure escaped her.

"Now," he commanded as he surged deep within her.

And that did it. Her climax opened her up, spilling a shimmer of purest sensation. Starting at the core of her, the pleasure radiated outward in glorious waves. As she reached the peak, she felt him begin to pulse deep within her.

"Going," he groaned at her.

"Gone," she moaned back.

She woke to someone whining.

Carefully opening one eye, she found it was daylight and she was nose to nose with Owen, breathing in his doggy breath. "You need a mint," she grumbled.

A sleepy voice behind her said, "He wants to go out." Dante lifted his arm from its spot in the curve of her waist and tugged on one of her braids. She turned her head back to him and he kissed her, a sweet, chaste brush of his lips across hers.

Then he was rolling away from her, getting out on the other side of the bed. "I'll take him."

She braced up an elbow and watched Dante pull on his jeans. He zipped up and then dropped back to the mattress to put on his socks and lace up his Timberlands. When he stood again, he raked his hands back through his hair to kind of minimize the bedhead. Actually, he looked downright delicious, all rumpled and manly, with those muscles everywhere.

And she had no doubt at all that her braids were a mess, her hair sticking out every which way, with last night's mascara smeared where it shouldn't be.

"Be right back," he promised.

She realized she'd kind of been expecting him to start making excuses, acting all apologetic, saying he had to get going. But no. He was coming back. That pleased her no end. She couldn't stop herself from beaming him a huge, happy smile. "I'll make the coffee."

"Deal." Pulling open the door, he clicked his tongue. "Owen. Come." The dog went out and Dante followed.

As soon as he was gone, she jumped up and ran to the bathroom, where she rinsed away her raccoon eyes, combed her hair and brushed her teeth.

She had her clothes back on and was spooning grounds into the coffee maker when Dante and Owen returned. The dog went to his water bowl.

Dante came up behind her, wrapped his arms around her and kissed her neck. It felt really good. Also, domestic. Like they were a real couple.

Down, girl, she ordered her romantic heart. *It's a kiss on the neck, not a promise of forever.*

Not that she would want forever anyway. She had a lot to do in her life and she didn't need some man to make it all worthwhile.

However, the *right* man would be nice. One of these days. When the stars finally aligned.

Dante bit her earlobe. It felt so good. "You took out the braids. I really liked those braids."

She laughed, pushed the button to start the brew cycle, and slithered around to face him. "You like to pull on them."

He put up both hands. "Shoot me. I like to pull on them a lot."

"Be nice to me. You might see those braids again."

"Whatever it takes." His eyes had that smoldering look she very much enjoyed.

Did that mean last night was more than a one-time thing? She would really like that. Maybe too much. "You want some eggs?"

"I do. Got bacon?" He arched a thick, dark eyebrow at her.

"Yes, I have bacon." Owen sat at their feet staring up at them hopefully. "Kibble's in the bottom right cupboard if you want to pour him some."

Dante waited until after they'd eaten to bring up the elephant in the room. He poured them both more coffee first.

When he sat back down, he took a slow sip and said, "I'm through lying to myself about you and me, Gracie. I want more. Of you. Of this."

She stared across the battered old table at him. *More of Dante.* The prospect excited her. And scared her, too. What if she came to care too much? What if she already did? Cautiously, she asked, "So…what are you thinking?"

He looked down at the table, then dragged his gaze back up to meet hers. "Could it be just between us? Just you and me? I don't want the families to know. We would never hear the end of it. And I have no idea how Connor might react."

"I do not get what Connor has to say about it."

"We have history, me and Connor. You know that."

"Come on, it's none of Connor's business what you and I do in our own private lives."

"Yeah, well. Connor might think otherwise."

She put up both hands. "Fine. Whatever. The families won't know. Can we move on?"

He looked as relieved as she felt. "Absolutely."

"So you're saying a secret fling?" And actually, given that what they had wasn't really going anywhere, keeping it just between the two of them wasn't such a bad idea.

"I really like you, Gracie. And I want you. So damn much. I'm through pretending I can keep my hands off you. I want to be with you, but I'm still the same guy and I'm not going to change."

She dropped her head back and groaned at the ceiling. "Just answer the question."

"Yeah. A secret fling."

"What about seeing other people?"

That had him leaning in again, his face turned hard and dark. "No way. Just you and me. For as long as it lasts. No one else. For either of us."

"Not real big on sharing, huh?"

He looked almost hurt. "You are?"

"No." She gave him a slow grin. "But I sure do like yanking your chain."

He studied her for several endless seconds. "Okay, then. You and me. Nobody else and nobody knows."

"Until one of us calls a halt?"

"Yeah."

She thought of his daughters. "As long as the girls are here, we're not going to have a lot of chances to be together."

He reached across the table, as though to take her hand. But then he pulled back without touching her. He picked up his cup and drank. "Not exactly an irresistible offer, is it? Just tell me to shove it."

She walked her fingers to the middle of the table, turned her hand over and waited, palm up.

It took him a minute, but he put his mug down and covered her hand with his. It felt wonderful. Right. To have his hand wrapped around hers.

She said, "So then, what with keeping it secret and the girls living with you, we won't be spending all that many nights together. It's my considered opinion that we need to make the most of every moment we get."

All of a sudden, his dark eyes seemed to shine with the brightest light. Still holding her hand, he got up. She rose at the same time. It took only a tug on her hand and she was in his arms.

He wrapped her up tight and kissed her slow and deep. When he lifted his head, he asked in a rough whisper, "Did you just say yes?"

"Yes, Dante. Yes."

Chapter Seven

Dante was more than happy to seek out opportunities to be alone with Gracie.

He rarely drove home for lunch. But the next day, Monday, he took a flyer on the off chance that Gracie might be there.

She was. He spotted her little SUV parked beside the cabin and drove the cruiser on back there. Wearing those dinky shorts he so greatly admired and a T-shirt with History Buff printed on it beneath a flexing bodybuilder, she was waiting in the open doorway for him when he sprinted up the pebbled walkway.

She laughed and wrapped her arms around his

neck as he scooped her high against his VBPD blues. "I do believe I'm about to experience my first luncher," she said.

"Nooner," he corrected, nuzzling her neck.

"Oh, Officer." She heaved an over-the-top sigh. "Whatever you call it, I need it. Now..."

And he got to spend forty-five minutes in the cabin with Gracie, naked. Those minutes raced by. He relished every one of them.

Monday night, after the girls were in bed, he texted her and she came over. They had a beer on the deck and compared daytime schedules. Her hours at the bar changed every week and he sometimes got stuck at the station house or out working a case and had to skip lunch. They agreed it would be easier if he just called or texted when he could get away in the daytime. That way he wouldn't waste his time driving home if she couldn't meet him there.

When she got up to go, he grabbed her hand and pulled her down onto his lap. "Don't leave. Not yet." He kissed her.

Eventually, he had to let her mouth go. She said, "I have to be at work at..."

He kissed her again before she could finish. "There isn't enough time for us."

She nipped at his earlobe. "It's a secret fling.

Deal with it." Her voice was light and teasing, while he felt all dark and twisted inside, full of needs he really didn't want to address.

He wanted her. Constantly.

And he was going to have to lighten up and count his damn blessings. At least now, for as long as it lasted, he could have her whenever their schedules lined up.

It just wasn't often enough. Not by a long shot.

"Dante…" She said his name in a sweet little singsong. And then she kissed the side of his throat. "I really do have to go." He stole one more kiss and somehow kept himself from grabbing for her when she rose from his lap, leaving his arms empty and his pants too tight. "Tomorrow," she reminded him. "I'm picking the girls up from day camp."

"Right. The all-important costumes for the Medieval Faire."

"Yep. I'll have them home earlier this time."

"Stay for dinner? I'll have the food ready when you get here."

"Can't. I've got a hot date." She laughed, the sound musical. Teasing. "You should see your face."

"We have rules," he said darkly. "You. Me. No one else."

She bent down to him, nuzzled his cheek and

whispered, "It's so much fun to mess with you." Somehow, he kept from grabbing her and yanking her back down across his knees. She pulled away just enough to capture his gaze. "I'm meeting Erin and Carrie at Beach Street Brews."

Now he just wished he could go, too. Secret flings, he was quickly learning, had a whole raft of drawbacks.

His disappointment must have shown on his face, because she added, "They *are* my best friends. And I hardly see them these days, you know?"

"I get it." He needed to back off and he knew it. "Have a good time."

She put her mouth to his ear a second time. "I would rather be with you," she whispered. And then, with a quick brush of her cool lips to his cheek, she straightened and headed for the steps leading down off the deck. He watched her go until she disappeared into the shadows of the trees.

At a little past ten the next morning, Dante got a text from Connor Bravo—Lunch? Noon. Fisherman's Korner.

Alarm rattled through him. Suddenly he was certain Connor knew about him and Gracie. They would end up beating the crap out of each other the way they had a decade ago when Dante found out about Connor and Aly.

But then he reminded himself to get a damn grip. How would Connor know? Gracie wouldn't have said anything, and no one else knew. And besides, who even knew if it would bother Connor that Dante and Gracie were having a thing? Not all brothers went ballistic over stuff like that.

Still, it would be awkward, eating fish and chips with Connor, knowing that he'd been in Gracie's bed yesterday and couldn't wait to go there again.

Well, too bad, Dante decided. He and Gracie were nobody's business.

And he and Connor *were* friends—a hard-earned, lifelong friendship that had gone off the rails more than once, yet somehow always managed to end up back on track. A man needed to spend a little quality time with his friends.

Dante replied, I'll be there.

And it went pretty well. Connor was all about his baby daughter. They agreed that daughters made a man's life complete.

"Oh, and don't forget," Connor reminded him. "You're coming to the party next month, you and the girls."

On the fourth Saturday in July, at Oceanside Gardens, a fancy wooded estate and event venue

just outside of town, Connor and Aly were celebrating their remarriage to each other. The original
plan had been to have the party in October because they'd been married in October—both times.
But Aly ended up deciding it would be more fun
to have their reunion celebration in the summer.
She wanted a sit-down dinner outside and dancing under the stars.

"We'll be there," promised Dante. Along with a
whole bunch of friends and just about every Bravo
and Santangelo in the USA.

"So how's it working out having Gracie living at the cabin?" Connor asked. Dante must have
blinked or otherwise looked busted, because his
best friend's forehead crinkled in confusion.
"What?"

"Not a thing."

"You're acting weird, man."

Dante played it off with a shrug. "Gracie's great.
My daughters and my dog are crazy about her."
And they are not alone. "Owen spends half the
damn time at the cabin with her. And she's got
Harper fixing the girls up with costumes for the
Medieval Faire. Nat and Nic are thrilled about that."

"I'm glad it's working out. Gracie really needed
her own place."

"I'm glad to have her there." So glad. Connor

had no idea. Dante stared across the table at his friend and brother-in-law. For several years, he'd been certain he would never willingly speak to Connor again. And yet, here they were, sharing a booth at Fisherman's Korner, tight with each other just like it used to be. "Connor, I…" Where was he going? He wasn't quite sure. Somewhere he shouldn't, probably.

Connor ate his last steak fry. "Yeah?"

"I keep thinking about that fight we had."

"Which one?"

"When you and Aly first got together."

Connor arched an eyebrow and shook the ice in his nearly empty cup. "Yeah, that was a messy one."

"I was a complete jerk to have come after you like that. I acted like I owned you *and* my sister, like the two of you had no right to be together."

Connor set down the cup, his blue gaze assessing. "What's going on with you?"

Gracie. For as long as she'll put up with me. "I've been thinking that I never apologized to you for being such an ass."

"And this is it, then? Your apology?"

"Yeah. I'm sorry, Connor. I was wrong. You and Aly are good together. More than good. I think it was always supposed to be you and her. I'm glad that you worked it out and got back together. And I'm pissed at myself that I ever tried to stand in the way of what you guys have."

Connor's expression was completely unreadable—for about ten seconds. But then he nodded. "It's okay," he said gruffly.

"Is it?"

"Hell, yeah. You were out of line there at the first. But I was no hero when she and I broke up. You had a right to hate my dumb ass over that. It's just what it is. Crap happens. Everybody messes up. If you're lucky and you keep trying, you work it out somehow. We got through it. Over time. Me and Aly—*and* you and me."

Dante had to swallow the giant lump in his throat. "Yeah. I guess we did."

Connor reached across the table between them and clapped a hand on Dante's shoulder. "You're too hard on yourself."

"I don't think so. Not really."

"Yeah. Really. You and me, we're solid. Don't let what's over and done with eat you up, okay? Apology accepted."

"Gracie! Drink up." Carrie picked up Grace's beer and held it out to her.

"I am." Grace took the heavy glass mug and

set it down without taking a sip. It was her damn beer and she intended to drink it at her own pace—which was snail-like compared to Carrie and Erin. They'd gotten to the brew pub early and polished off a pitcher before she arrived.

Erin scoffed. "You are not keepin' up, girl-friend."

"You're not a schoolteacher yet," razzed Carrie.

Grace reminded herself that the two were half-sloshed and there was no point in taking anything they said too seriously. "Okay, you guys. I love you with all the love in the universe and beyond. But stop trying to pour beer down my throat. I can do that myself."

"You're no fun," whined Carrie.

"Yeah." Erin piled on. "It's like you don' really like us anymore."

"Not true." She had Carrie on one side and Erin on the other, so she wrapped an arm around each of them. "Love you both. Mean that."

They leaned their heads on her shoulders. Erin said kind of mournfully, "Love you, too…"

It was sad, really, when a girl and her two forever BFFs just weren't getting along.

The waitress appeared and set another pitcher on the table. "From the three hotties at the end of the bar." She tipped her head toward a trio of twentysomething guys who looked like maybe they worked in construction. They were all in worn jeans, heavy work boots and dark T-shirts, all three of them smirking, raising their beer mugs in unison.

Of course, Carrie signaled them over.

They started out on one side of the round table, with Grace and her friends on the other. Names were exchanged. Turned out one of the guys had graduated from Valentine Bay High the year Grace and her friends were freshman. One was from Astoria and the other had recently moved north from Coos Bay.

Took them about half an hour to start coupling up. The guy from Astoria, whose name was Keith, ended up focusing on Gracie. She nursed her second beer as he talked about high school, the construction company he worked for and his favorite band. It was all just a dance, everyone hooking up old-school, in a bar with alcohol, instead of on the apps. She wondered what she was doing here.

She could've had dinner with Dante and the girls.

Both Erin and Carrie got out their phones and snapped a bunch of pictures to post on Snapchat and Instagram. At seven thirty, Grace had had enough. She hooked her bag over her shoulder.

"Whoa," said Keith. "You're not leaving already?"

"Gracie, hold on." Carrie stopped whispering with the guy from Coos Bay and chimed in. "You can't go yet. It's early."

Grace dropped some bills on the table. "No, really. Gotta go."

"At least give me your number," Keith insisted.

"Sorry." She went ahead and just hit him with the truth. "I'm seeing someone."

"What?" Erin's mouth dropped open. "Who? Since when? There's a guy?"

"You never mentioned a guy," scoffed Carrie. She waved a hand. "You're lyin'."

"Yeah." Erin leaned on the local guy, who had his arm wrapped around her. "I don't know what's the matter with you lately, but you need to get over yourself."

For a moment, Grace just stood there, looking down at her best friends since childhood and three guys she didn't know. She had no idea what to say. She needed to sit down with her girls and talk about how lately they seemed to have nothing in common and she really didn't know what to do about that. Would a long talk solve anything—or just make the problem worse?

Who knew? And in any case, that talk wasn't

happening here at Beach Street Brews, with three strangers to witness it, the music too loud and everybody drinking. Nothing good was going to come from trying to face hard truths tonight.

Feeling like a stranger in her own life, she said, "I'll call you." With a quick nod to Carrie and then Erin, she turned and got out of there before someone said something they couldn't take back.

Dante heard Grace's RAV4 pull in at a little before eight. He made himself wait until Nic and Nat were settled in their room for the night before he sent Grace a text.

Meet you on the deck for a beer?

She answered right away, which eased all the annoying, formless fears that were chewing at the edges of his mind—completely unacceptable fears. That she would meet someone else and tell him it was over. That a night out with her girlfriends might remind her of all the ways she could be having a good time if only she hadn't agreed to be secretly exclusive with a divorced single dad.

They were having a fling. He shouldn't be taking this so damn seriously.

Too bad he didn't know any other way to be.

No beer for me, she wrote, but I'm on my way.

He resisted the burning need to shoot back, *You drunk already?* Because yeah, he was a jealous, controlling ass and he needed to make an effort not to show it.

A moment after he sat down at the outside table, she materialized out of the shadows. The moon made a silver halo around her pale hair. She wore a filmy top that slid off one shoulder and white shorts that clung to the perfect curves of her hips. Her smooth legs went on forever.

He rose as she came up onto the deck—that made it easier to reach for her when she got close enough to touch.

"Missed you." He kissed her. She tasted like all the best things, everything he wanted. He needed to try to remember that he didn't own her and what they had wasn't meant to last. It could never work out long-term with her for all kinds of reasons that right now seemed hazy and pretty much meaningless.

She sighed into his mouth and pulled away too soon.

"Come back here." He tried to claim her lips again.

But she put her palms against his chest, exerting a gentle but firm pressure. "If you want to keep this thing we have a secret, we can't be climbing all over each other when Natalie and Nicole are at home."

She was, unfortunately, right. If either of the girls got up and came out to the living area, they would have a clear view of whatever was happening out on the deck.

Reluctantly, he dropped back into his chair and picked up his beer.

She sat down across from him and smiled at the tall glass he'd brought out for her. "Ice water. Sometimes it's like you can read my mind." She picked it up and drank. He watched her pale, smooth throat move as she swallowed. She met his gaze when she set the glass down. "Where's Owen?"

"In with the girls." He asked, "So, good time with Erin and Carrie?"

"Not really."

He felt much too pleased to hear that. "What happened?"

"We're just not singing from the same playbook anymore. They were pushing drinks I didn't want at me and then when I got up to leave, they were pissed, said I was cutting out on them—oh, and don't believe anything you see on Snapchat or Instagram."

Wariness crawled up his spine. "Who took pictures of what?"

"These three guys bought us a pitcher. One of them ended up sitting next to me. Carrie and Erin whipped out their phones and started snapping away."

"This guy got a name?"

"Keith."

"Last name?"

"He never said." She gave him a long, steady look across the table. "He never even got that close. But social media is a swamp and you've got a jealous streak. I kind of figure full disclosure up front is the way to go with you."

He didn't even try to hide his slow smile. "How'd you get so smart about men?"

"Lots of annoying brothers and three summers in Europe."

He wanted to touch her again, to kiss her. To keep going from there. But that wasn't happening tonight. And he had a feeling she needed to talk more about her girlfriends. "So then, about Carrie and Erin…?"

Her beautiful mouth twisted down at the corners. "From their point of view, well, I used to be fun and now I'm a drag who thinks she's too good for them. We probably need a heart-to-heart, the three of us, but I'm kind of afraid that will only make the problem worse." She grinned across the table at him. "Aren't you sorry you asked?"

"Nope—and longtime friends go through changes. You can't always be on the same page. Give it time. The problem may work itself out on its own eventually."

She rubbed at the condensation on the side of her glass, her soft mouth drawn down in a thoughtful little frown. "Like you and Connor?"

"Yeah—and I had lunch with Conn today, as a matter of fact. It's all good with him and me now." *And as long as he doesn't find out about us, it's likely to remain that way.*

Gracie sat back in her chair. Gathering her hair in one hand, she slid a hair elastic off her wrist and anchored the thick, silky mass into a high ponytail. "Sometimes I see right through you, Officer. You're afraid he might find out about us and hit the roof over it. What you're forgetting is that Connor is not you and about a hundred years have passed since you two got into it because he had the balls to fall in love with Aly. Maybe he's learned something from what happened back then."

"Unlike me?"

"I didn't say you hadn't learned anything."

"Gracie. You think I'm a dinosaur."

Her ponytail bounced as she turned to face him

directly. "Don't put words in my mouth. You're definitely Homo sapiens. Or close. Neanderthal, maybe?"

Something like tenderness washed through him. She was not only gorgeous and funny and smart, she was strong. If she didn't like something he was doing, she said so. She had no qualms about giving him a bad time. Marj had been...softer, somehow. Less outgoing, less sure of herself. When they first met, at Portland State, he'd liked that she tended to defer to him, that she never really knew how to hold the line against him. He pushed. Marj gave way. It took her a year after their divorce to finally stand up to him and announce she was going to see other guys.

Gracie frowned across the table at him. "You're too quiet. What's going on?"

"I got a call from Marj today."

She watched him so closely, like she was picking up clues from his expression and body language. Gracie really cared how he was doing, what might be bothering him. "Everything okay?"

"Everything's fine. Marj always loved the Fourth of July in Valentine Bay. The parade in the Historic District, fireworks on the beach at night..."

"Wait. Your ex called to say she wants to come to town for the Fourth?"

"Yeah. And it was two calls. First, she called to feel me out about it. I said sure. She made a hotel reservation and then she called back to say that she and Roger would arrive in the afternoon on the third and go home the morning of the fifth. I invited them here for dinner on the third. She asked if they could join me and the girls for the fireworks and I said yes."

"That was nice of you."

"I'm not nice. We both know it. What else could I say but come on up and watch the fireworks with us? Marjorie is a good person and Roger is… Well, the girls really like him. Why shouldn't my ex and her new husband come into town for the holiday and watch the fireworks with Nic and Nat?"

Gracie reached across and put her hand over his. Her touch soothed and burned simultaneously. Was he in too deep with her, already? It sure felt like it. "You *are* nice, Dante. At least, on occasion. You really hate that your ex and her husband are coming, don't you?"

He wanted to drag her hand to his mouth and bite the back of it. "I don't hate it, no."

"You just *hate* it." Her white teeth flashed in a devilish smile.

"Exactly."

"It will be good, you'll see."

"I'll reserve judgment till after the fact."

She gave his hand a last, reassuring pat and pulled hers away. Somehow, he managed not to grab it back.

For a few minutes, neither of them said a word. They sipped their drinks and stared out at the night. It was a comfortable silence, the kind that happens between friends.

And they *were* friends. They had *been* friends before the night they ended up in his bed together.

The question was, would they still be friends when this crazy, hot thing between them burned itself out?

Thursday, Grace was at home in the cabin when Dante called at twenty minutes to noon.

She saw it was him and answered with one word. "Yes."

"Fifteen minutes." His voice, low and rumbly, caused every nerve in her body to snap to excited attention.

"I'll be naked."

And she was. Their second nooner was even better than the first.

Friday, Gracie picked up the girls from day

camp again. They stopped at the beach cottage on the way home for the finished Medieval Faire gowns.

Saturday, the Faire opened. Gracie wouldn't be going. She had to open at the Sea Breeze.

But early that morning she went to Dante's house for breakfast with him and the girls. Dante made them all waffles and eggs and then Gracie took Nic and Nat back to the cabin. She braided their long brown hair—French fishtail braids, woven with shiny ribbon to match the gowns that Harper had made. Since it was a costume event, Dante had grudgingly given permission for the girls to wear light makeup.

Grace supervised the application of cheek and lip color and mascara, too. They put on the gowns and the soft Mary Jane–style shoes Harper had found for them on Etsy.

"Gorgeous. Both of you," Gracie said, when they all three piled into the tiny bathroom so the girls could admire themselves in the full-length mirror that hung on the back of the door.

"Wow! These dresses turned out so good," said Natalie, her pretty face aglow. "Better even than I was hoping for."

Nicole, wide-eyed, nodded in agreement. "The braids are so beautiful."

"*You* are absolutely beautiful—both of you," Gracie said. Because they were.

She took them back out to the main room and gave her phone a workout, snapping pictures from just about every angle as they happily posed and preened.

They were the best, Nic and Nat. They brought it sharply home to Grace why people wanted kids. She could actually start to see herself with a husband and children—not now, of course. And no, not with Dante. He'd made it way clear it wasn't going to be him.

But the right guy. In time.

"Let's go show Daddy!" cried Nicole.

"Right now!" agreed Nat.

They trooped back to the main house, where Dante called them both beautiful. His voice was kind of gravelly, the way it got when something moved him. To Grace, he had that look—the look of a loving dad confronting the reality of how fast his daughters were growing up.

She took more pictures, some with her phone and some with Dante's. This time she had the girls pose on either side of their dad. All three of them were beaming, the girls out of pure happiness, Dante with such pride.

Then Natalie insisted, "Gracie, we need you in a picture, too."

"Yes!" agreed Nicole. "We need pictures with you."

Grace handed Dante back his phone and hers, too, and he did the honors.

After that, she got lots of hugs and thank-yous from both girls. She felt kind of sad to leave them, but she waved goodbye and returned to the cabin to get ready for work.

It was a gorgeous day, cool and clear with only a slight breeze. At the bar, Grace rolled up the wide garage-style door that led out to a big patio with a view of the beach and the endless blue ocean. She and Marianna, the waitress, set up the café tables and opened the umbrellas to shade them from afternoon sun.

They opened at eleven. By noon, they were packed. The Sea Breeze had a small kitchen in back. They served bar food—sliders and nachos, potato skins and hot wings. Grace called Ingrid at 12:30 and she came in at a little after 1:00 to help out. For the next three hours, Grace worked behind the bar, setting up, mixing and pouring nonstop.

When the crowd finally thinned out and she got a break, it was past four. She claimed her usual spot at the quiet end of the bar and Ingrid served her a tonic with lime and a nice big plate of nachos.

"You sharing?" asked a familiar deep voice behind her.

A thrill zinged her through her, just at the sound of his voice. She had it bad for him, no doubt about it. "Maybe."

Dante took the stool next to her and signaled Ingrid, who brought him a clean plate and his favorite pale ale. "I was kind of hoping I might catch you in a quiet moment."

"And you did." She was so glad to see him. It made the sweetest ache under her breastbone, to have him right there beside her. You'd think it had been months instead of a few hours since she'd left him and the girls that morning. He wore the same light blue T-shirt he'd had on then. The shirt showcased his big arms and ripped chest.

And she needed to quit staring at him like she'd rather have him than her nachos. She took a long sip of tonic. "What did you do with my two favorite medieval princesses?"

"One of the day camp moms took them to her house with her daughter and my niece and a couple of other girls. I got a call from my sister-in-law just before we left for the Faire, inviting them. There's a pool, evidently. They took their swimsuits and a change of clothes when we left the house. They're having a swim party and then hot dogs for dinner. I'll pick them up at eight."

And that meant he had three hours or so to himself.

Too bad she had to work until seven. "So, how was the Faire?"

"Packed with people."

"Excellent. A big success, then?"

He ate a chip, nodding. "Nat and Nic loved every minute of it. They were in the minstrel show and they demonstrated medieval dances they'd learned in day camp."

"I wish I could have been there."

"I've got pictures." He beamed a proud-father smile.

"Show me."

He got out his phone and handed it over. As she scrolled through the shots of his beautiful daughters at the Medieval Faire, he leaned close. "Come home with me."

She wanted to. So bad. "Can't. Gotta work."

"Secret flings are a pain in my ass," he muttered.

So let's just go public, she longed to suggest.

But she only went on looking at the pictures

and munching her nachos. She already wanted so much more from him than he was willing to give.

And she was far from ready to chance losing what she had of him on the off chance he might suddenly be willing to give her more.

Chapter Eight

The next day, Sunday, Dante took Nat and Nic to his parents' house for Sunday dinner. All four of his brothers were there. Pascal and Tony brought the wives and kids. Marco, at twenty, was still single. And Mac, the baby, had turned nine months old the week before. Aly, Connor and baby Emelia had gone to Daniel Bravo's this Sunday. Gracie had said she would be at Daniel's, too.

Dante sat at his mom's long dining room table and ate her amazing pot roast and fantasized about what it might be like if he had Gracie beside him. It was only a dream. He knew it. And he'd never been much for dreamy imaginings.

But lately, well, sometimes he couldn't help himself. And being dreamy about Gracie felt damn good.

He wore a smile on his face a lot more than usual lately. No, he didn't get enough time with her. But when he did, he made every minute count. And when he had to leave her, he had the next time with her to look forward to. Even when he couldn't be alone with her, he saw her coming and going along the graveled road that ran by the house, saw the lights on in the cabin and knew she was in there. At least a couple of times a week, he lured her onto his deck after dark so they could hang out together for an hour or so, talking about whatever they had on their minds while simultaneously trying to keep their hands off each other.

His brother Pascal elbowed him in the ribs and muttered out of the side of his mouth, "Mom's talking to you."

He turned his head to meet his mother's blue eyes. "What, Mom?"

"I said, you look like a man in love." Catriona O'Leary Santangelo beamed him a wide, beautiful smile. "It's a good look on you, Dante."

"No clue what you're talking about." His mother was too damn perceptive by half—not that he was in love with Gracie. He was just...

Okay, he wasn't sure what to call it. Crazy. Wild. Out of his mind for her. All those things. It was called chemistry and it felt like nothing else because the chemistry with Gracie?

Off the freaking charts. Like no chemistry he'd ever experienced before. It helped him to understand the power of the attraction between Aly and Connor—and his own mom and dad.

But, as he continually reminded himself, for him and Gracie, it wasn't the kind of thing that was meant to last. She was young with a lot to do in her life, and he was divorced and set in his ways. It was only for right now and it was amazing. And somehow, when it was over, he would find a way to keep his friendship with her.

"What's her name?" asked his mother as she picked a slice of cooked carrot out of Mac's hair and set it back on his high chair tray.

"Oooo-bah!" crowed Mac. He grabbed the bit of carrot and shoved it in his face.

And Dante's mom was still looking right at him, waiting for an answer. The whole table was a little too quiet, he thought.

His dad came to his rescue. "Leave the man alone, Cat," said Ernesto with a chuckle. "Whatever he's dreamin' about, he's not sharing it at the dinner table."

* * *

Both Tuesday and Wednesday of the following week, he joined Gracie in the cabin in the early afternoon. With Gracie, each time was better than the last.

Life was good. So good that he was much more patient when his daughters compared him negatively to the wonderful, perceptive, thoughtful, permissive Roger.

So good that when Marjorie and Roger arrived on the third of July, he happily grilled them all burgers out on the deck and felt only minimal resentment toward the stepfather his girls adored. Gracie had to work that night. She left the cabin at around five thirty, shortly after Roger and Marj arrived. They were all out on the deck and he was firing up the grill when her RAV4 emerged from the trees.

"Grace!" Marj called. She said to Roger. "I haven't seen her in years." She got up and ran down the side steps to intercept the RAV4. Marj leaned in Gracie's window. He could hear their voices faintly, though not the words they exchanged. The sound of Gracie's laughter floated on the breeze, causing a tightness under Dante's breastbone, a rising feeling full of heat and tenderness. He wished she could blow off the Sea Breeze for the night, come have burgers on the deck with him and the family.

And there was nothing out of line about wishing that. Because they were not only lovers on the down-low, they were friends.

Roger, at the table, asked, "So, new tenant?"

"Gracie? Yeah, she's using the cabin for as long as she needs it." It just felt weird, to talk about Gracie with Roger—but then, talking about anything with Roger always felt weird to him. "She's a good friend." *And so much more.* Not that Roger was ever going to know that.

Nic, who knelt on the deck boards brushing Owen with her Princess Jasmine hairbrush, started in about the Medieval Faire and the costumes Gracie had arranged for her sister to make for them.

Nat, at the table next to Roger, chimed in with praise for Gracie—and her sisters, Harper and Hailey, too.

Over in the driveway, Marj stepped back from Gracie's car. She waved and Gracie drove away. Dante felt bereft.

Was he ridiculous?

No doubt about it.

"You seem a little…pensive." Roger was still looking at him.

Marj chuckled as she dropped into the chair on

Roger's other side. "Darling, don't analyze my ex." It was a command. Marj was so perky and bossy with Roger, like a whole different woman from the one Dante had once been married to. It was kind of disorienting. He felt glad she was happy, but found it strange to see this other, more assertive side of her, nonetheless.

"Sorry, my love." Roger leaned in. They shared a quick kiss, after which Nic and Nat dragged them both into the house. A moment later, he heard Nat singing "Let It Go" at the top of her lungs.

Owen, stretched out on the deck not far from the table, lifted his head and let out a howl, just singing along.

The next day, the Fourth, Dante and the girls met Marj and Roger for a late breakfast at the Tufted Puffin Café down in the Valentine Bay Historic District. They wandered around window-shopping for a while and then watched the parade, which consisted of floats created by local organizations and businesses and various service vehicles. Once that was over, Marj and Roger went off on their own. Dante took Nic and Nat to his brother Tony's for a family barbecue.

At nine thirty that night, they arrived at Valentine Beach, where they met up with Marj and

Roger and just about everybody else in town. Dante brought a couple of blankets and his ancient boom box.

Launched from a barge offshore, the fireworks started at ten. The local radio station played music synchronized to the display. Dante turned his boom box to the right station, as did at least a hundred others up and down the beach. It was quite the extravaganza.

His daughters sat on either side of him, staring up at the night sky, transfixed. Marj leaned her head on Roger's shoulder. Kind of a perfect end to another Independence Day.

Except...

Dante's mind wouldn't stop straying to thoughts of Gracie. She had the closing shift again at the Sea Breeze. He wanted to get out his phone and send her some silly text, just to let her know he was thinking of her.

But she was working and probably wouldn't check her phone for hours yet anyway. And the girls and Marj and Roger were bound to notice if he got on his phone in the middle of the fireworks.

They weren't a couple, him and Gracie. He needed to keep that thought firmly in mind. If she was here with them right now, he would have to play it strictly friends only, because those were the rules he himself had laid down. He wouldn't even be able to put his arm around her, let alone steal a kiss as "Born in the USA" filled the air and bottle rockets exploded overhead.

And come on, even if she'd had the day off, she very well might have planned to meet up with her sisters and brothers or a couple of girlfriends. He had no real claim on her and he needed to remember that. It was only for now and that was how they both wanted it.

"Hey, guys…" As if he'd conjured her straight from his own out-of-control fantasies, there she was, wearing a Sea Breeze T-shirt, white Chucks and white jeans, that sleek waterfall of platinum hair in a high ponytail. She grinned down at them.

"Gracie!" his daughters cried in gleeful unison.

"Happy Independence Day." Marj beamed up at her, and Roger gave her a friendly nod of greeting.

"Sit with us," demanded Nat.

As a sparkly globe of purple light burst open in the night sky and Katy Perry's voice blared from the speakers up and down the beach, Nicole jumped up, grabbed Gracie's hand and pulled her down to the blanket. "Isn't it beautiful?" Nicole leaned into her.

Gracie fondly nudged Nic's shoulder with her own. "Spectacular."

It just so happened that Dante was on Gracie's other side. He almost didn't dare to look at her for fear that all his aching, confused emotions would show on his face.

Really, it wasn't supposed to be like this, not for him. He understood himself, knew too well his own hotheaded nature and had spent most of his adult life trying to keep a lid on it. Injustice and insults, bad stuff some people did to others— all that got to him more than it did to the average guy. He was one of those men who could fly off the handle, go off like a human bottle rocket if he didn't make an effort to keep his emotions under strict control. He'd learned to carefully consider just about every move he made. He tried to do the right thing, take good care of his girls and just generally lead a useful, productive life.

And until that fateful night a month ago when he'd invited Gracie over to cry on his shoulder, he thought he'd been doing a pretty good job of all that.

But now…

Well, how did she do it—give him all these damn *feelings*? He'd never trusted feelings. Too often, they made people do stupid things.

And he was being doubly ridiculous now, acting like a twelve-year-old with his first crush. He'd wanted her here with the burning fire of a thousand suns. And yet somehow, now that she was sitting right next to him, he'd yet to so much as say hi to her, let alone glance over and meet her eyes.

Carefully, he turned his head.

She was looking right at him, a slow, devilish grin curving those perfect, shell-pink lips. He got a whiff of her perfume, equal parts sweet and tart. It sent a spike of heat straight to his groin. He drew his legs up and wrapped his arms around his knees to disguise his response to the barest hint of her scent.

"Back at the Sea Breeze, everyone's out on the patio watching the fireworks," she said. "Ingrid gave me an hour-long break."

"I'm glad," he heard himself say.

One sleek eyebrow lifted. "About what?"

Holding eye contact seemed dangerous. He glanced upward as bright balls of light with thick, glittery tails shot upward from the water, fanning out as they rose. The opening strains of "The Star-Spangled Banner" swelled on the cool evening wind.

She nudged him with an elbow.

He leaned into her and whispered, "I'm glad that you're here."

She laughed, the sound filling him with equal parts joy and pain. It was like nothing he'd ever known before, to feel the way she made him feel. He hated it.

But he kind of loved it, too.

The next week, Grace and Dante stole two long lunches together, on Tuesday and Thursday. Instead of food, they had each other. Both times were the best time ever—and each encounter was much too short. Too soon, she would find herself standing in the cabin doorway, wearing nothing but panties and a tank top or a wrinkled T-shirt, her tangled hair in her eyes, feeling all kinds of lazy and sexually satisfied as she waved him goodbye.

The weekend after the Fourth, a minor miracle occurred. The girls' day camp counsellors took Nic and Nat and several other local kids on a weekend campout over Friday and Saturday night. Gracie worked both nights, but Dante was on his summer schedule, which meant the weekends were his.

When she arrived at the cabin in the very early hours of Saturday morning, he was waiting on the front step with Owen. They spent the rest of the night together and all of the next day too, making love for hours, sharing every meal, taking Owen for long walks down on the beach. Saturday night at six, she left him reluctantly to go to work.

"Be in my bed when I get home," she commanded as she kissed him goodbye.

He lifted his mouth from hers just long enough to reply, "Count on it." And then he was kissing her again, deeply. At length.

She arrived home at a quarter to three Sunday morning to find him right where she'd told him to be. He held back the covers. She stripped off her clothes and joined him.

It was so good with Dante. She never wanted it to end.

And he seemed pretty taken with her, too. More than once that magical weekend, she seriously considered broaching the subject of where they might go from here, of actual dating, doing more than each other, like maybe dinner and a show. They could take it slow, go only places where they were unlikely to run into anyone they knew.

Time in bed with him was the absolute best. But she liked him so much—as a lover, as a friend, as someone really special to her in so many ways. She just couldn't stop wishing they could be together without sneaking around.

She kept trying to come up with the right words to broach the "next level" conversation. But she was nervous to approach him about it. He'd been so firm that he didn't want anyone else to know they had a thing together.

Why didn't he, really? The more she thought about this secret they were keeping, the more she wondered why they even needed it to be a secret.

She needed to ask him about that, talk it out with him. Too bad the right words never seemed to come to her.

And then all of a sudden, it was Sunday afternoon and he had to go pick up the girls at Valentine City Park.

The next week was not so great, secret fling–wise. When Dante could get away, she couldn't. And the other way around. Twice, they met on his back deck after his daughters were in bed. They would each have a beer. Mostly, what they talked about was how not getting together was driving them both a little bit crazy. Somehow, though, they managed to keep their hands off each other. If one of them would weaken, the other would mention that they were in full view of the living area should the twins decide to leave their room.

That Saturday, it was the girls' turn to host a sleepover. Nicole and Natalie invited their cousin Heather and three more of their Valentine Bay friends. Sunday, Dante took the girls to his parents' house for dinner and Grace went to Daniel's.

By Monday, she was feeling a little depressed at how difficult having a secret fling could be. Her schedule and Dante's just weren't matching up and that made her sad.

Was she getting too attached?

Well, the guy had made it painfully clear that what they had was *all* they would have. He'd given no indication he was ready to change things up, and she'd never quite figured out how to talk to him about that.

On the plus side, when they did manage to slip off alone, it was fabulous. Mostly, she really loved it, having it be just the two of them, just for now, nobody's business. The limited time they had together kept both of them focused on making every minute count.

Still, it was starting to get old. It was starting to remind her that she'd never really had a guy who was all hers, straight up, for everyone in town to see. Niall and Keegan and Paolo were across an ocean in another world and just for the summer.

Yeah, she'd had a couple of "serious" boyfriends in high school, but she was a kid then, with a very protective big brother. Daniel used to make her leave the bedroom door open whenever a boy came over. And when she finally did have sex her senior year, it was in Randy Daughtry's ancient Ford Courier pickup.

Ugh. In some ways, all this sneaking around

with Dante made her feel like a teenager again. And just lately, not in a good way.

She needed someone to talk to about it. A little quality time with her BFFs would really help. She texted Carrie. When she didn't hear back in the next few hours, she tried Erin.

Erin's reply was not encouraging. What? U got a minute to spare 4 us now?

Well, that just made her feel worse than ever. Hurt and sad and more than a little bit angry, she stared at Erin's text and had no idea what her reply ought to be.

They needed to talk. And probably not about Dante. First and foremost, they had to deal with what had gone wrong in their friendship, the friendship that they'd always vowed would last their whole lives. Grace really didn't know what she'd done to piss them off. It was time she found out. Can we talk?

Erin wrote back, Bout what?

Are you at home? I'll come over.

Whatevs

Grace decided to consider that a yes. I'm on my way.

At the two-bedroom apartment in a ten-unit

complex on Pine Avenue, she found both Carrie and Erin at home.

Erin let her in with a sigh and a heavily ironic, "Well, look who finally showed up."

Carrie sat on the sofa drinking a canned Bloody Mary, an open pizza box on the coffee table in front of her. She raised the can. "Been a while."

"Drink?" asked Erin with zero enthusiasm.

Grace figured maybe attempting to be social would pave the way for her a little, get them off to a decent start. "Sure, thanks."

Carrie swept out a hand toward the fridge. "Help yourself." Erin plunked down beside her on the sofa.

Grace got a hard lemonade and took the chair across the coffee table from them. There was a moment. Dead silence. They stared at her and she returned the favor.

Finally, Grace waded in. "So lately, it's seemed like we're kind of drifting apart, you know?" Okay, yeah. Weak. But she had to start somewhere.

"You're always busy," Erin accused.

"Too busy for us, anyway," Carrie threw in with a toss of her head.

"You never want to chillax," said Erin. "You've always gotta be somewhere. It's no fun and it's like we don't even know you."

"And what about Keith?" demanded Carrie. It took Grace a moment to remember the guy at Beach Street Brews. And Carrie knew it, too. She scoffed. "You don't even remember Keith."

"No, I do." Grace knew she sounded superdefensive. She had no reason to be defensive. But somehow, she felt that way. "Of course, I remember Keith."

"He's a good guy and he really liked you and you just…" Shaking her head, Erin blew a raspberry.

Carrie waved her Bloody Mary. "All of a sudden, you're seeing someone—someone you so far haven't bothered to mention to your two best friends for just about your whole life?"

Grace realized that, at this point, there was no way she was talking to her supposed BFFs about Dante. Just wasn't going to happen. "Listen, who I'm seeing and whether or not I wanted to give Keith my number? Come on, you guys. This isn't about men. This is about you and me and why you're so angry at me lately."

"We told you." Erin took a long drink of her canned margarita. "You're always busy. You never want to hang with us…"

Carrie said, "It's like we don't really have much in common anymore."

Was it like that?

Yeah.

Grace sat a little straighter. "Well, so what?"

Carrie blinked at her and Erin gasped.

Grace leaned in across the coffee table. "Look. Maybe in life people don't always see things the same way. Maybe I'm all absorbed right now in stuff that bores you guys silly. So what? I love you both and I always will. You matter to me. A lot. And I really hope I still matter to you."

Another long silence crawled by.

And then Carrie said softly, "Oh," and burst into tears. Erin started crying, too. Grace felt the moisture welling in her own eyes.

They all three jumped up at the same time. Carrie and Erin darted around the coffee table for a group hug.

"Okay," Erin sniffled. "Maybe we were kind of being bitches about this."

"But we *miss* you," cried Carrie. "We need to see you more."

"You're right." Grace took the tissue Erin offered her and dabbed at her eyes. "Once every week or two, at least, we need to get together, no matter what."

And then Erin, looking thoughtful, qualified, "But then, we gotta accept that maybe sometimes that won't happen and just make it work when we can."

"And not get all judgy," Carrie added. Looking sweetly remorseful, she blew her nose.

They sat down again. Grace finished her drink and said yes to a second one and a slice of cold pizza. Carrie and Erin filled her in on what she'd been missing.

Both of her friends were still working at the same upscale restaurant in Astoria. Carrie had said yes to a second date with the guy from Coos Bay. Erin was still keeping things strictly casual on the relationship front.

Grace explained that yeah, she was seeing someone exclusively. But he wanted to keep it just between the two of them, so she was respecting his privacy.

"A secret love is kind of romantic," offered Erin in a hopeful tone.

"And fun?" Carrie put a question mark on the end of that.

Grace laughed. "Meaning, am I having a good time with him? Yeah. Super good."

Her friends said that was all that mattered and she left it at that. They set a date to get together next Monday, when all three of them were off work. Erin and Carrie would come to the cabin for dinner.

"About time we saw your new place," grumbled

Erin. And then she laughed. "Not that we're bitter or anything."

"Yeah," agreed Carrie. "Sometimes we're bitches, but we love you so much!"

There was more hugging. "Next Monday. My place. Six o'clock," Grace reminded them as she went out the door.

She got in behind the wheel of her car and paused to check her phone. There was a text from Dante. He'd sent it while she was with her friends.

God, I miss you. Come over for dinner with me and the girls? Another text came through as she was starting to reply. He wrote, So much for dinner, then. Meet me on the deck, 9:15?

She answered smiling, feeling eager and happy, just to know she would see him soon. I'll be there. Sorry about dinner. I've been at Carrie and Erin's. Just coming home now.

Be naked, he suggested—well, it was more of a command.

She laughed out loud. I'm thinking maybe we shouldn't risk scarring your daughters for life.

The sacrifices a man makes for his children, he replied.

The night was overcast, but Grace could see Dante clearly—the outline of his broad shoulders, the shine to his thick, dark hair. He was waiting for her at the table on the deck, limned by the spill of golden light from the fixture by the slider. No sign of Owen. He must be in with the girls.

Dante stood as she approached. "We haven't been alone in over a week." He was scowling.

"Wait. Is that an accusation?"

"It's a fact and I hate it." He grabbed her hand. "Come here." His warm touch sent a thrill of longing sizzling through her.

"The windows," she reminded him.

"This way." He pulled her across the deck and down the steps on the far side.

"Um, where are we going?" she asked as she trotted along behind him.

"Right here." He ducked under the canopy of a big leaf maple a few yards from the side of the house. "Nice and dark. No one will see us. And we'll hear if the girls come looking for me." He reeled her in close and put those big arms around her.

She whispered his name in eager welcome as his mouth came down on hers.

Wrapped up in Dante's arms, protected in tree shadow, Grace surrendered to the man she couldn't get enough of, to his body pressing so close to hers, to the hungry perfection of his kiss. Now and then he would lift his head—but only to slant his mouth the other way and claim her lips again.

"We're like a couple of hormonal kids," she remarked breathlessly.

"Just kiss me." And he took her mouth once more.

She felt better about this secret fling of theirs now that he was holding her, surer that this thing between them was the *right* thing. Yeah, she wanted more. But what they had in this moment was pretty darn spectacular.

And it didn't end with kissing. Eventually, his hand glided between their bodies and eased her zipper down. And then his fingers were there, working their magic.

He swallowed her moans as she went over the edge.

She returned the favor, going to her knees on the soft, mossy ground, taking charge of him in the most elemental way, reaching one hand up over his hard belly and ripped chest to cover his mouth and muffle his groans when he came.

"Come up here," he whispered roughly, taking her by the shoulders, pulling her upward until she was back in the cradle of his strong arms.

For several sweet minutes, they held each other. She tucked her head against his throat and he stroked her hair.

Then, when they were both breathing normally again, he knelt and brushed the damp moss off the knees of her jeans. Rising, cradling her face in his big hands, he kissed her once more, this time gently, with melting tenderness.

Then he led her back to the deck, where they sat together under the stars.

Again, she considered broaching the subject of changing things up a little between them, taking a step or two toward going public as a couple.

But before she could frame the words, he mentioned Nicole and Natalie. "Twelve more days and they're on their way back to Portland," he said.

"It's hard, huh, to let them go?"

"Yeah. I love it when they get here, hate it when they leave. The house always seems too big and way too quiet."

She reached across the table and took his hand in reassurance. "You're doing a great job with them—both you and Marjorie, I think. They're happy and outgoing and they have a lot of friends."

He wove his fingers with hers, but only for a moment before pulling away.

It wasn't fair that she felt hurt. They did have an agreement. But it caused an ache deep inside her, that they couldn't even hold hands for fear Nic and Nat might see and get the wrong idea.

Which really *wasn't* the wrong idea at all.

"It's after ten," she said, and stood. "I should go."

"Wait. What? You can't stay a few minutes longer?"

"No. I need to get back. I've got the day shift tomorrow."

"You go in at what, eleven?"

"Ten thirty. And I was hoping to get an hour or two before that to work on my lesson plans for the coming year." It was true, as far as it went. Her first year of teaching would be extrachallenging. She had to build her class curriculum from scratch. And she wouldn't be able to get into her classroom until right before school started. The more she had done before the mad scramble at the beginning of the term, the better.

He stared up at her, his face shadowed with the light behind him. "What'd I do?"

"Not a thing." It wasn't a lie, exactly. It was just, well, they were going nowhere and she was growing tired of standing still.

Tonight didn't feel like the right time to get into it, though. She didn't want to lose him—well, as much as she had of him.

But then, after the girls left for Portland at the end of the month, they would have more time alone together. That might be the best course for her, to wait until his daughters were with their mother and then bring up the possibility of her and Dante becoming…more to each other.

He stood. "You need to tell me what I did, so I can grovel and make it better."

She laughed. "You're not allowed to grovel on the back deck—not as long as the girls are here. They might see and then you'd have some serious explaining to do."

"You're right. Damn it." He started to reach for her—and stopped himself. His hand dropped to his side. "You're sure you're okay?"

She gave him a slow smile. "I am amazing."

"Oh, yes you are."

"Good night, Dante."

"'Night."

She turned and got out of there before she caved and hung around for another hour, longing to be closer to him, not daring to so much as reach for his hand.

Chapter Nine

That week turned out the same as the week before. Grace's schedule never meshed with Dante's.

Thursday, she went in to work at nine to help Ingrid with payroll, bills, ordering and miscellaneous other stuff. At six, she was finished for the night.

She started to head home, but then found herself turning left instead of right, headed for the cottage where Hailey and Harper lived. Both of their cars were parked in the wide space not far from the house. Grace pulled her RAV4 in beside them.

Hailey was standing in the open doorway to the screened porch, waiting for her as she came up the walk. "Want some dinner? It's Harper's awesome slow cooker burgundy beef tips with noodles. And I believe you've had my spinach strawberry salad before."

"With poppy seed dressing?" Grace asked hopefully.

"Of course."

"Yum. Suddenly, my stomach's growling."

Hailey wrapped her in a hug and then ushered her inside. "Right this way."

The food was ready, so they set another place for Grace. She poured three waters and Hailey poured the wine.

"I'm so glad I dropped by out of nowhere," Grace said. She ate another bite of beef and noodles. "Harper. This is so good."

Harper saluted with her wineglass.

They talked for a while about what was coming up for Harper and Hailey. They had their own little company, H&H Productions. Besides planning the occasional kids' party, they were working with the local arts council now, producing a series of seasonal community events—the Medieval Faire in the summer, a Fall Festival in October that culminated in a haunted house. Then over the holidays, they would put on the Christmas Extravaganza at the Valentine Bay Theater, an old movie theater down in the Historic District.

After the meal, they cleared off the table and cleaned up the kitchen together. The process kind of reminded her of the old days up at the house on Rhinehart Hill, all of them pitching in to get the household chores done.

They sat back down around the table. Harper poured them each another glass of wine.

"Okay." Hailey turned to Grace. "What's on your mind?"

Grace swirled the wine in her glass. "I'm that obvious?"

"Only to your wise and wonderful big sisters," replied Harper.

She grinned across the table at them, but the grin faded as she tried to figure out where to begin. "Well, there is something…"

"Tell all," commanded Hailey.

"It's, um, a secret thing. The deal is, I can't tell anyone."

"But you *have* to have someone to talk to," said Harper.

"And whatever you tell us," added Hailey, "we won't tell anyone else. Ever."

"Total cone of silence?" Gracie asked sheepishly.

"Total," agreed Hailey. She and Harper looked at each other, then back at Grace. The two nodded in unison. "We will tell no one," vowed Harper as Hailey nodded some more.

Grace squeezed her eyes shut and drew in a slow breath. "I'mhavingasecretflingwithDante Santangelo." The words came out in a rush as she exhaled.

Her sisters just stared.

Hailey spoke first, in an awed whisper. "Dante Santangelo. Really?"

"Yep."

Harper said, "He's so…serious."

"But hot," Hailey added.

Harper was nodding again. "Undeniably hot."

Hailey enjoyed a slow sip from her own glass. "I have to say, sexy action with a hot cop sounds like a pretty great thing to me."

Harper pushed her glass out of the way and stacked her forearms on the table. "Hasn't he been divorced forever?"

"Six years or so, yeah."

Grace's sisters shared yet another of those speaking glances and Grace felt that familiar stab of envy at their closeness. The two of them could have whole conversations just with their eyes, no actual words required.

Harper said, "Full disclosure, we did kind of wonder if there was something going on between you two when you moved into that cabin at his place, but then you did say he was just doing you a favor..."

"And he was. He *is*. He gave me the cottage for as long as I want it. Because he's a good guy and a good friend. As for our fling, we decided not to go public, to keep it just between us. Plus, well..."

"Say it," coaxed Hailey.

"He thinks he's too old for me and he has this thing about romantic love. Like he doesn't approve of it or he's just no good at it? I'm not sure exactly. His parents are happily married and so are two of his brothers. And Aly and Connor. He thinks he failed at love because it didn't work out with his ex-wife and now she's happily remarried—so it can't be *her* fault the marriage didn't work. It's like he blew it once and he won't try again."

"You think he's still in love with the ex?" asked Harper.

Did she think that? "No. No, I really don't. I think he's over Marjorie. She's a good person and they do a great job as coparents. They truly do."

Harper reached across and fondly brushed the back of Grace's hand. "For someone who's just having fun, you don't look all that happy—and if you're not happy, you should either move on or change the rules."

"Both options suck," Gracie said. "I do want more. But I don't want to lose what we have." Her sisters gazed at her with real sympathy. "And you know, I don't think changing the rules *is* an option, to be painfully honest about it. Dante was way clear that he's not up for anything more than what we have. He likes his life just the way it is. He told me he doesn't want a relationship and he's never getting married again."

Harper scoffed. "No offense, but Dante is being an idiot about this."

Gracie gave a sad little laugh. "Yeah, there's that."

Hailey said quietly, "You need to tell that man what *you* want."

"I'm afraid to," Grace admitted. "If I ask for more and he turns me down, what can I do but call it off? I mean, a girl needs to have *some* pride, right?"

"Yeah," said Hailey. "From that standpoint, you're kind of stuck."

"And if I call it off with him, it's going to hurt. Bad. And that's just more proof that I'm in deeper with him than I ever planned to get." Another forlorn chuckle escaped her. "I guess that makes me as much of an idiot as he is."

"You are *not* an idiot," Hailey said in a lecturing tone. And then she frowned. "Wait. You know what? Now and then, we're *all* idiots."

Harper suggested, "You could tell him what you *don't* want without making it an ultimatum. You could say that the way things are isn't working for you anymore. And then see where he takes it from there."

"But what if where he takes it is straight to goodbye? Uh-uh. I'm just not ready to chance that. It's not like he wasn't up front with me from the start. I believed him when he said he didn't want a real relationship..."

"You're totally gone on him, aren't you?" asked Harper gently.

"I am, yes. And the more I think it over, the more I realize that for right now, I'm still willing to go on as we have been. Rocking our fragile *non*relationship boat could be the end of what we do have. And just possibly the end of our friendship, too. I'm not ready to risk all that—not yet, anyway."

"The time is coming, though?" asked Hailey.

Grace hummed low in her throat, a sound of reluctant agreement. In response, Hailey got up and pulled her out of her chair and into a hug. Harper piled on. They stood there in the kitchen, the three of them, hugging it out.

Nothing had been resolved.

And yet, a half an hour later, when Grace climbed in her SUV, she felt better, just to have two smart, thoughtful women she trusted to talk it over with. She felt closer to her sisters than she ever had before.

Up till now, she'd kind of seen herself as a loose end among her siblings, the baby trailing after the bigger kids, a little bit left out, often left behind. To have Harper and Hailey rally around her, take her problems seriously and treat her like an equal?

It lifted her spirits and had her feeling a lot better about her place in the family.

Stolen moments with Gracie.

Dante didn't get enough of them. Friday at ten in the morning, he was just about to text her in hopes she might be home at lunchtime. But then he got a good lead on an ongoing case. He followed it and before he knew it, the day was mostly gone.

Friday night, his niece Heather slept over. He let the girls stay up late. When they finally settled down, it was almost eleven. He went outside to nurse a beer on the off chance the lights might be on at the cabin.

The porch light glowed at him through the trees, but that was it. Like a long-gone fool, with Owen at his heels, he jogged through the trees to get a closer look.

Nobody home, the windows all dark.

For a moment, he just stood there, wishing for things he was never going to have.

But then Owen whined and Dante shook himself. Not wanting to leave the girls alone for too long, he set off at a run for the main house. Dropping into a chair at the table, he took a long drink from his beer.

Owen plunked his head in Dante's lap. He gave the mutt a good scratch around the ears. "Our girl isn't home, buddy."

He got out his phone and started to text her. But then he dropped the phone on the table without finishing the text. No point. It was eleven at night and she was probably working.

And if she wasn't working, if she was out having a good time with her friends, he didn't even want to know.

What he wanted was more time with her.

And he would have it. Soon. A week from tomorrow, Nic and Nat went back to Portland. He would miss them a lot. But at least this year there was an upside to their going: more time with Gracie.

He couldn't wait for that.

And tomorrow was Aly and Connor's party at Oceanside Gardens. Gracie would be there, too. Maybe they could sneak away for a little while.

At the very least, he'd get a dance with her. Because even though this hot, perfect thing between them was a secret, why shouldn't he dance with his good friend Grace?

And why did it piss him off, that he had to make excuses for dancing with her?

Too much pissed him off lately. He wanted more of her, but he didn't want to think too hard about what that might mean.

The whole point was to have a good time, not take things too seriously, he kept reminding himself. When it ended, they would still be friends.

Not that he could imagine it ending anytime soon.

Aly and Connor's big party was an afternoon-to-evening event, with dinner and music and dancing. The weather was just about perfect, in the high seventies, a few wispy clouds drifting across the otherwise clear sky. Dante and his daughters arrived at a little after three.

Oceanside Gardens, a sprawling estate north of town surrounded by old-growth forest, lived up to its name. The garden paths seemed to go on forever, winding endlessly through thick plots of greenery and lush flowerbeds.

Aly had hired a six-piece band. Party lights were strung from every tree and post. The tables, set with fine china and white linen, were crowned with centerpieces of white pillar candles in big glass bowls of brilliant-colored dahlias.

For the kids, Aly and Connor had provided a giant ball pit shaped like a castle and filled with what looked like thousands of brightly colored balls. The pit had a slide you could ride down into the balls and a jungle gym suspended above them. Each child got a plastic jar of bubbles and a variety of wands of all sizes and shapes. Bubbles floated in the air all afternoon.

And if the little Santangelos and Bravos didn't want to blow bubbles or bounce around the ball pit, Aly had a face-painting station and a table full of art supplies set up in the garden's giant gazebo. The parents took turns supervising the fun.

Nicole and Natalie seemed to be having the best time of their lives. There was a lot of happy shouting and way too many gleeful, ear-piercing screams.

An hour or so before dinner, when Dante got a moment with his sister, he gave her the praise she deserved. "Killer party, Aly. You really out-did yourself."

She beamed him her beautiful smile. "I did, didn't I?"

"It's great. How's my baby niece?"

"She's good. Connor's got her somewhere around here…"

Aly and Connor pretty much had it all now. They were in love with each other and their baby daughter. They'd had a rough road, spent too many years apart. But in the end, here they were, surrounded by family, celebrating their second marriage to each other. They were happy and Dante was happy *for* them.

But that didn't mean he wouldn't razz his sister at least a little. "Too bad those dresses my girls are wearing will never be the same." The girls were rumpled and sweaty, their party dresses smeared with face paint and grass stains. Funny how Nic had a virtual meltdown when she accidentally spilled her soda in her lap at Camp 18—but when there was face painting and rolling on the grass involved, neither she nor her sister cared much what condition their clothes ended up in.

Aly just shrugged at his grumbling. "It's called having fun and your daughters are good at it."

"You always were a troublemaker," he grumbled some more, trying hard to look disapproving.

"Get over yourself," Aly dryly advised.

Right then, Nat shrieked with laughter as some redheaded kid Dante didn't recognize dragged her down off the jungle gym and into the ball pit. Dante shook his head. "I think I need a drink."

"Have a good time, big brother." Aly leaned in close and kissed his cheek, after which he headed for the open bar.

Dante got himself a beer and then, very casually of course, went looking for Gracie. He spotted her more than once. She wore a silky blue sundress that tied with little bows at the shoulders, her long white-gold hair like a waterfall down her back. She looked sweet and delicious and he wanted to eat her right up.

Not possible at this party, but hey, a guy could dream. He would settle for just standing close to her, breathing in the fresh, flowery scent of her skin, imagining all the things he would do to her as soon as he finally got her alone.

Unfortunately, every time he would try to work his way toward her, some relative or longtime friend would grab his arm and start talking his ear off about how his daughters were growing up so fast, and the summer had been so mild this year, hadn't it? And how were things with the Valentine Bay PD?

At dinner, Dante sat with Nicole, Natalie, his brother Pascal and Pascal's family. Percy and Daffodil Valentine claimed two other chairs at the table. Brother and sister and well into their eighties now, neither Percy nor Daffy had ever married. The last of the Valentines for which Valentine Bay had been named, they were great-aunt and great-uncle to Connor, Gracie and the rest of the Bravo siblings. Dante had always liked them. Daffy was charming and sweet. Percy could tell you way more than you ever needed to know about the history of Valentine Bay.

Once the food had been served, the speeches began. Dante's dad and mom got up and congratulated the happy couple, as did Percy and then Daffy. There was plenty of wine to toast Aly and Connor's reunion. The two had never looked happier—with each other and with their adorable baby.

Dante spotted Gracie several tables away. She sat with Harper, Hailey and their older sister, Aislinn. Aislinn's husband, Jax Winter, had the chair beside his wife. There were also three guys he didn't recognize. The sight of those guys had irritation prickling through him. Wasn't this supposed to be a family party?

Daffy Valentine, who sat on his left, said, "Dante. I understand our Gracie has moved into a little guest cabin on your property."

He turned and met her twinkly blue eyes. "She wanted to get out on her own and the cabin was empty."

The network of wrinkles on Daffy's face deepened as she smiled. "That was so kind of you."

"Gracie's a good friend."

"Oh, I have no doubt. She has such a big heart." Daffy patted his arm with her perfectly manicured, age-spotted hand. "And I am trusting you to treat her well."

What was he supposed to say to that? Had Gracie told the old woman what was going on between them?

"No," said Daffy, as though answering the question he hadn't asked aloud. "Grace has never said a word to me about you. But I have eyes, young man, and I know how to use them."

Okay, fine. The old lady had him pegged. He respected that. Enough that he refused to lie to her face. Feeling sheepish, he asked, "Am I that obvious?"

Daffy smiled wider and patted his arm again.

* * *

After dinner and dessert, there was dancing. Dante danced with Aly, with his mother, with each of his daughters and his niece Heather. Every time he looked for Gracie, she was dancing with someone else. He hesitated to cut in, mostly because he wanted her in his arms way too much and every time he spotted her with another guy, he felt like a jealous boyfriend who might just lose his cool.

And who did he think he was kidding? He *was* a jealous boyfriend—the secret kind. And being a secret boyfriend at a party like this? It seriously sucked.

After sunset, various family members gathered up groups of kids for sleepovers at predesignated houses. Natalie and Nicole, looking worn out and happy and clutching the gift bags Aly had given them, went home with Dante's brother Tony and Tony's wife, Lisa, and their boys.

Dante shouldn't be so glad to see his own children go, but he was feeling a little nuts watching all the couples looking so happy together. He wanted time with Gracie and so far, he'd gotten none.

He felt resentful that she hadn't sat with him during dinner, at the same time knowing damn well that if she sat with him, Daffy Valentine

wouldn't be the only one to put two and two together. Gracie's brothers would probably get over-
protective of her. At the very least, Dante would
never hear the end of questions about where he
and Grace were going as a couple and how serious
was it, anyway? His mom would be over the moon
with happiness, already planning the wedding.

Uh-uh. None of that, thanks.

But damn it, he wanted a dance. If he could just
keep his absurd and pointless jealousy under control, a dance was no biggie. It was totally within
the bounds of their very real friendship and family
connection that he would ask Grace for a dance—
during which he could not only hold her in his
arms, but would also pull out all the stops to get
her agreement to spending the whole night with
him. Tonight. Again. At last.

He stood on the edge of the big flagstone patio
that served as the dance floor, his eyes on the silky-
haired blonde in the blue dress as she danced with
one of those unknown interlopers who'd shared her
table at dinner. As the song ended, Dante stepped
up. He was waiting right behind the other guy
when the last guitar note faded off.

Gracie saw him—how could she help it? He
was three feet away from her and staring straight
at her. Over the other guy's shoulder, she beamed

him a smile of pure devilment. Because she knew she made him crazy and she found that humorous.

In the end, he had to tap that fool who had hold of her on the shoulder.

"Oh!" the guy said, like it had never occurred to him that at some point, he would have to let go of her. "Sure..." He gave Gracie a nod. "Thanks, Grace."

"Ray." Gracie gave him a smile as she stepped into Dante's arms. Now that he was holding her, he felt better about everything. The music started up again. It was a fast song, but Dante kept his arms around her anyway, wasting no time dancing her away from her previous partner. "Who was that guy?"

She snort-laughed, like he was just the funniest thing. "Nice to see you, too."

Was he coming on too strong? Probably. It was a problem he had. He took things way too seriously—even this damn secret fling of theirs that was supposed to be just for fun. Drawing a slow, deep breath, he toned down the attitude. "I was only, you know, wondering..."

"Ray Danvers. He works for Jax." Aislinn's husband owned a horse ranch on the Youngs River not far from Astoria. "Ray's a nice guy."

"I'll bet." He danced her out toward the perimeter of the patio.

"It's a fast song, in case you didn't notice," she razzed him. "What *are* you doing?"

Probably blowing our cover all to hell. So what? Right at this moment, he didn't even care. He pulled her closer. "I missed you. I want to talk to you alone and I want to do that now." He grabbed her hand.

She laughed again, but she didn't pull away. Instead, she let him lead her down the nearest garden path. In-ground lights led the way from one winding stone walkway to another. He followed those walkways, branching left and then right, pulling her deeper into the lush shelter of the estate's gardens.

"Where are we going?" she asked as the stone path took another turn and they entered a small pocket of shadowed greenery hemmed in by tall trees and accented in the far corner with a narrow, rustic-looking gardener's shed. The music sounded far away now.

"This'll do." He pulled her around in front of him and backed her up until she reached the shed. Her eyes burned into his and her breath came fast. Apparently, he wasn't the only one glad they were finally alone. He braced his hands on either side of her head and bent to steal a quick, hard kiss. "Nicole and Natalie went home with Tony and Lisa. Spend the night with me tonight."

She lifted those long, pale arms and rested them on his shoulders. "I was hoping you might say that."

All of a sudden, the world was a beautiful place and he was a very happy man. "That's a yes?"

"Um, yeah." She sounded a little bit breathless. He liked her breathless. He liked it a lot. "That is a yes."

"Excellent." And he could not wait another second to kiss her. He bent his head and she lifted that plump mouth at the same time as he clasped her waist and slid his hands lower, until he cradled her perfect bottom. Once he had a good grip on her, he scooped her up off the ground.

With a hot little moan, she wrapped her arms and legs around him. Carefully, he braced her against the wall of the shed and deepened the already drowning kiss as her soft, sweet, delicious mouth opened so willingly for him.

"So good," she whispered as he lifted his mouth just enough to slant it the other way.

"The best…" He sank into her kiss again, his mind spinning, his body hard and hungry—to be alone, just the two of them, to get out of all these damn clothes. "It's been too long…"

"Secret flings." She made a cute little growling sound, nipped at his lower lip and raked her fingers up the back of his neck into his hair. "So inconvenient…"

"We'll have time tonight. I don't pick Nic and Nat up from Tony's until noon tomorrow."

"Good." She kissed the word into his mouth. "Very, very good…"

And then they stopped talking. Which was more than okay with him. He kissed her for the longest time, letting himself get lost in the feel of her wrapped all around him, her breasts so soft against his chest, the core of her pressing into his hardness. It was sheer agony of the most spectacular kind.

Until a man's voice directly behind him demanded, "Just what do you think you're doing with my little sister?"

Chapter Ten

Dante muttered an oath.

Gracie buried her face in the side of his throat. "Connor," she said glumly.

Dante stroked her silky hair, wanting to soothe her even though she seemed more disappointed than upset.

She braced her chin on his shoulder and said to the man behind him, "Go away, Connor." If Connor moved, Dante didn't hear it. There was only silence. Gracie whispered in his ear, "He's still there. Your sister's with him."

"It's okay," he promised her. What else was he going to say? Slowly and carefully, he eased Gracie to the ground. She landed lightly on her feet and gazed up at him, her eyes calm as the ocean on a clear, windless day, her skin translucent in the moonlight. He touched her smooth cheek and whispered, "You good?"

"Never better." She drew back her slim shoulders and smoothed the full skirt of her dress. He offered his hand and she took it. Together, they faced her brother, his lifelong best friend—the friend he'd beaten the crap out of when he first learned that Connor had been with *his* sister.

And really, to be fair, Connor had given as good as he got that day. Dante might have fractured one of Connor's fingers, but Connor had broken Dante's nose.

Right now, Connor was giving him some serious stink-eye, but at least he was restraining himself from throwing the first punch.

For Dante, it was a moment of uncomfortable truth. He recalled his boundless fury at Connor all those years ago for daring to get something going with Aly.

And right now? He had no idea what Connor might be thinking. Probably nothing all that good.

Back at the party, the band was playing the Avett Brothers' "No Hard Feelings." Gracie's hand was cool and soft in his and he felt like crap for putting her in this position. Still, whatever happened next, he was glad for every moment he'd held her in his arms, for every night on the deck, just the two of them, under the moon, for the sweet, free sound of her laughter that always made him feel that the world was a better place than he'd ever realized before.

What happened next was that Aly snickered. "We knew there was something going on with you two. You're not fooling anyone."

Connor gazed at him steadily. "I meant what I said last month at Fisherman's Korner. We're good." At Dante's slow nod, Connor added, "But we couldn't resist giving you a little taste of your own medicine."

Aly taunted, "Tell me, big brother. How does it feel to have your best friend all up in your face because you had the nerve to get together with his sister?"

Dante considered the question and then answered it honestly. "Not so great." He was equal parts embarrassed at his own past behavior and resentful that his sister and brother-in-law had interrupted a completely amazing stolen moment with Gracie.

"Okay, you guys." Gracie waved a dismissing hand. "Whatever your point was, I'm guessing you've made it."

Connor said, "He gives you trouble, Gracie, you come to me. I'll set him straight." He was only half joking, and Dante got that message loud and clear.

"Move on," commanded Gracie.

Aly slipped her hand in Connor's. "You kids have fun, now." Together, they set off down the path.

Dante waited until they'd disappeared around the next bend before turning to the woman beside him and tipping her soft chin up with a finger. "So much for the families not finding out."

She gazed up at him with the strangest look on her beautiful face—a sad look? He wasn't sure. She shrugged. "What happened at Fisherman's Korner?"

"I apologized to your brother for being an ass way back when he and Aly first got together."

"Wow. About time, huh?"

"Past time."

She studied his face for several seconds before asking, "So, then. What now?"

He snaked an arm around her waist and pulled her up nice and tight against him. "Right now, all I want to do is get you home alone."

Dante got back to the house first, put the truck in the garage and then stood out in the driveway to wait for her, impatience thrumming through him with every eager beat of his heart.

Finally, her little SUV turned in and rolled to a stop a few feet from where he stood.

She leaned out the window with a silvery laugh. "How am I going to park if you're in the way?"

"Come to my place."

Her eyes shone so bright. "Will do."

She parked in her space by the cabin. He met her midway between his house and her car. She paused and gazed up at him through the moon-dappled shadows made by the tall trees. "You're blocking the driveway again."

He couldn't wait to kiss her. "Come here."

With a husky giggle, she swayed toward him. He took her by her silky bare shoulders and pulled her into his waiting arms.

Nothing compared to this—holding Gracie. It never got old. Every touch, every kiss, every breathless little sigh was a new revelation. Now he had her close, it kind of didn't matter what happened next. He could have stood there in the driveway beneath the giant trees, kissing her, holding her, kissing her some more.

She was the one who finally pulled away—but only far enough to ask against his parted lips, "Are we going to stand here all night, just kissing and kissing?"

"Yes." He caught her lower lip between his teeth and pulled on it gently.

She laughed and kissed him some more, turning in his arms at the same time. Still kissing, they started walking toward the house.

"You want anything?" He asked as he ushered her in through the side door.

"Just you…"

And they were kissing again. He guided her backward, his mouth fused to hers, through the mudroom, the kitchen, the living area and on down the hall to his room.

"Where's Owen?" she asked as he untied those little bows at her shoulders.

"At the dog sitter's. He's staying over—and I really like this dress. Mostly because I've been dreaming all night of getting you out of it." He peeled down the front. She was naked underneath. "No bra…"

"It's built in."

He pretended to frown. "And here I was thinking you went without one just to drive me crazy."

"*Did* I drive you crazy?"

He bent close and caught a pretty little nipple lightly between his teeth. When she moaned, he smiled against her soft, pale flesh. "You have no idea…"

* * *

Much later, satisfied and at peace with the world and everyone in it at last, holding her close, skin to skin, he couldn't help wishing they could just do this every night. Be together, in and out of bed, whenever they felt like it.

No sneaking around.

And why not, really? Why couldn't they have more?

He asked the question of himself—and automatically, the answers came to him. He'd tried having more, making a family, sticking with it no matter what. And look where that had gone. He was no good at the true-love-forever thing. He didn't want his daughters' lives disrupted, couldn't stand for them to develop a close relationship with Gracie and then have it all go to hell.

And what about Gracie? She was young and fresh and ready for anything. The last thing she needed was to tie herself down to a grumpy cop with a ready-made family...

She shifted against him, lifting her head, bracing up on an elbow to gaze down at him. "What?"

He caught a lock of that pretty pale hair and rubbed it between his fingers. "Not a thing."

She gave him that smile, the one that said he wasn't fooling her one bit. "Liar." But she said it softly, with affection, and then tucked her head beneath his chin again.

"Tired?"

She made a small, throaty sound in the affirmative.

He reached over and turned off the light.

"The guy is so hot." Erin took a contemplative sip of the white wine Grace had chosen to go with her chicken alfredo. "And those arms. Those shoulders…" Erin put down her wineglass long enough to kiss the tips of her fingers in a gesture of sheer appreciation.

Carrie tossed her head back with a moan. "Officer, cuff me now!"

No, Grace hadn't said a word to either of her girlfriends about her secret fling with Dante. But he'd been out on his deck grilling dinner when Carrie and Erin arrived. And Grace's BFFs loved nothing so much as discussing the do-ability of a good-looking man.

"I hope your secret boyfriend is something really special, because I can't believe you're not all over that." Erin sounded downright accusing. "I'm disappointed in you. I mean, you and Dante are friends and he's single. And *you're* single. He lives—what?—fifty yards from your front door?

You wouldn't even need your car to get to him. Talk about a missed opportunity."

"We are *so* disappointed in you." Carrie faked a sulky face.

"So sorry to let you down," Grace replied, sounding not the least apologetic. Really, she did feel a little bit guilty for not admitting that she was totally on top of the hot cop situation, both literally and figuratively. Because they *were* her friends and when it came to guys, the three of them had always confided in each other.

But Dante was such a private man. It seemed wrong to discuss their relationship—or whatever the heck she should call what they had—with her friends.

How had it become so complicated? She was constantly stewing over how she wanted more from Dante. And yet she still wasn't willing to take a chance and tell him how she felt.

A walking cliché. Oh, yes, she was. Friends with secret benefits! Terrific idea! What could possibly go wrong?

She just didn't want to talk about it. Not right now. There was nowhere to go with it except in a circle.

Erin leaned forward in her chair. "You're too quiet about this. And what is that look on your face?" She turned to Carrie as understanding dawned. "Do you see what I see?"

Carrie's eyes got wide. "Oh. My. God. I see it." She shifted her gaze to Grace and accused, "It is so on between you and the hot cop single dad."

Grace kept her mouth shut as she tried to decide how much to say.

"He's the one, isn't he?" demanded Erin. "He's the guy you're seeing that you're not telling us about."

"Wait," commanded Carrie.

"What?" asked Erin.

Carrie reached across the table and gave Grace's arm a squeeze. "If you don't want to talk about it, that's okay."

"Speak for yourself." Erin glared at Carrie. "Talking is *good*. She *needs* to talk about it."

Carrie held her ground. "Say the word. We'll shut up."

Erin threw up both hands. "I can't fight you both. Fine, Gracie. You don't want to talk about it, say the word and we won't."

"Much," smirked Carrie.

Grace bit her lip and shook her head. "There's not a lot to say. It's a temporary arrangement that we agreed to keep just between us."

"But now *we* know," said Carrie.

Grace blew out her cheeks with a hard breath. "You guys and Connor and Aly. And Harper and Hailey. And just possibly the rest of our families by now. Maybe others. I wouldn't be surprised."

"So as for the secret part," Carrie concluded for her. "You're saying not so much at this point."

"Essentially, yeah."

Erin said, "And *you* don't even care who knows— I mean, the secret thing is *his* deal?"

"Exactly. And even Dante's kind of accepted that the truth has gotten out."

"Is he pulling back from you, now that people know?"

"No."

"And *you* still want to be with *him*?"

"Yeah. I do. I really, really do."

"Then why are you wearing your sad face?"

"I'm not."

"You so are."

"You like him a lot?" Carrie suggested. "Maybe too much?"

Why deny it? "Yeah. And I don't think he's up for anything beyond what we have already."

"But *you* want more?" asked Erin softly.

Carrie was nodding. "Gracie. It's written all over your face."

"Yeah, well, I don't think I'm getting more."

"Oh, babes!" Erin cried as she and Carrie jumped from their chairs and surrounded her. Bending down, they hugged her from either side. Carrie stroked her hair and Erin patted her shoulder.

Carrie said, "Whatever you need, you just let us know."

"I love you guys," she whispered and hugged them back.

When they returned to their chairs, Erin announced, "Just for the record and then I'll leave it alone—he's an idiot if he walks away from you."

"I'll drink to that." Carrie emptied her glass.

The next morning at a little before eleven, Grace got a text from Dante. Want some company? The cabin? About noon?

She stared at her phone, a giant smile on her face. Her heart felt lighter as pure happiness filled her. Dante was coming over and everything was suddenly right with the world.

And that was when it hit her.

"I am in big trouble," she whispered to no one in particular. With a slow, careful sigh, she sank to the edge of the bed and set the phone on the old bureau next to it. "I've got it bad."

So bad. Worse every day. Stronger than liking

him a whole lot and longing to make it more. This was a huge deal, what she was feeling. This was...

Grace did not allow herself to think the forbidden word right then.

But it was there, nonetheless. A fiery ball of longing had tucked itself under her breastbone and become impossible to completely ignore.

This, with Dante, it was serious for her, way beyond anything she'd ever known. It wasn't going to just run its course. Dante wasn't Niall or Keegan or Paolo to her. He was her true friend and the man she wanted in her bed. The man she wanted to tell all her secrets to. The one she longed to turn to when things weren't working out, the one she wanted to be there for wherever, however, whenever he needed her.

And the girls...

Yes. Nicole and Natalie, too.

No, the girls didn't need her, exactly. Nic and Nat already had a good life. They actually seemed to enjoy both of their homes—with their mom and their stepdad in Portland *and* with Dante in Valentine Bay. They didn't *need* another parent, per se.

But they did like Grace and she liked them. A lot.

She could...add to the good they already had. She could make their time with their dad even better. She could take a little of the weight off Dante, help ferry them around, make dinner half the time. She could be there for the girly things, the hair braiding and the all-important search for just the right outfit for this or that event. She could lend an ear if either of them wanted to share a secret that only a woman might understand.

And yes, those were all things that would get handled anyway, without her. The girls had a great mom and a loving, attentive dad. They had everything they needed to get a good start in life.

All Grace could offer them was more...

More could be good for them and for her.

More could be excellent.

If Dante would only let her in.

Grace fell back across the bed and stared blindly at the rustic beam ceiling above.

So, then. The girls would be going home in less than a week. She wouldn't approach Dante about her deepening feelings until after they were gone. If he turned her down, Nicole and Natalie didn't need to be there while the breakup was happening.

On the bureau, her phone buzzed with another text.

She sat up long enough to grab it and flopped back across the mattress again.

So is that a no?

"Dante." Just saying his name out loud sent a sweet little shiver racing along the surface of her skin. She pressed the phone to her chest and reminded herself to count her blessings. However it all shook out in the end, right now was amazing. In less than an hour, she would have his arms around her—and she could not wait.

She really had it bad for him. So very bad. Noon, you said?

Yeah.

I'm here at the cabin. C U then.

He arrived right on time. They spent a perfect hour in her bed.

When he left, she stood at the door and watched him drive away in his cruiser. Her body felt relaxed, thoroughly satisfied. But her heart was a big ball of longing.

For everything. The L-word from his lips, a future to share with him.

One step at a time, though. She was fine with that, with taking it slow.

But in the end, she did want it all. With him.

She wanted all the things he'd made it painfully clear he would never give.

The next night, she joined him and the girls for dinner at his place. When Nat and Nic went to bed, Grace stayed for a couple of hours. They sat out on the deck. With Owen snoozing at their feet, they watched the wisps of clouds drifting past the moon, spoke of inconsequential things and somehow managed to keep their hands off each other.

Thursday and Friday, she worked six to closing and he couldn't get away at lunch either day.

Saturday morning, Gracie was still sound asleep when someone knocked on the door. She peeled one eye open long enough to wave her hand over her cell phone and see that it was 7:25. She'd arrived home at three this morning. Four hours and change did not add up to a good night's sleep.

She put the pillow over her head and hoped whoever it was would go away.

Another knock.

She dragged the pillow off her head. With her eyes scrunched shut, she shouted, "Come back later!"

Then she heard giggling. *Nicole and Natalie.*

A third knock, this one more tentative than the two before.

By then, she was awake enough to remember that this was the Saturday the girls returned to Portland. "Coming!" she shouted, and threw back the covers.

"We're sorry to wake you up," said Natalie when Grace opened the door.

"But we have to leave today," added Nicole.

"Come have breakfast with us," said Nat.

"Please," added Nic.

Owen, at their feet, panted eagerly up at Grace and beat his tail against the boards of the front step.

Grace felt kind of forlorn. "Can't you just stay and never go?" She made a pouty face.

"We will miss you." Nic gazed up at her through serious brown eyes a lot like her dad's. "But we live in Portland, too."

"I understand, I guess. And I will miss *you*," Grace replied. "And yes, I would love to have breakfast with you. I'll be over in ten minutes."

When she got to Dante's, the girls had already set the table and Dante had crisp bacon on a serving platter and tall stacks of pancakes ready. Grace poured herself a cup of coffee and sat down with them.

Nic and Nat talked nonstop—about how they hated to leave their Valentine Bay friends and cousins, but they needed to get back to Portland, where one of their friends was having a birthday party next weekend. And they'd been invited by another friend to the big water park an hour south of Portland in McMinnville this coming Wednesday.

Dante seemed kind of quiet. Grace sensed he was already missing them.

Too soon, breakfast was over. Grace helped clear the table and then carried a couple of suitcases out to the crew cab as they loaded up to go.

Finally, it was time for goodbyes.

Gracie hugged Nic first. "I already miss you."

"Me too." Nic's small arms squeezed her tighter.

"We'll see you in two weeks and then in September," Nat promised.

"They're here for just the weekend in mid-August," Dante explained kind of gruffly. "And then I'll go get them for Labor Day."

"I can't wait," Grace said, reaching for Nat.

Nat hugged her good and hard and then tipped her head up to meet Grace's eyes. "Be extra nice to Owen while we're gone."

"He misses us so much," Nic explained with a sad little sigh.

"I will help your dad take really good care of

him," Grace vowed. "In fact, I'll take him back to the cabin with me now. How's that?"

"That would be good." Nat nodded up at her. "He won't have to be alone."

A moment later, the girls were climbing into their booster seats and buckling up.

Dante got in behind the wheel. He leaned out the window. "I'll be back in a few hours. Any chance you'll be around?"

She ached for him. He always tried to be so tough. But really, he had a heart of pure mush and it was so painfully obvious how much he hated to see his daughters go. "I'll be here."

With Owen sitting at her feet, Grace waved them off. She felt a bit teary eyed, watching them go. It gave her a deeper sense of how hard it must be for Dante every time they returned to their other home in Portland.

Four hours later, she and Dante were in her bed wearing nothing but a matched pair of satisfied grins.

He wrapped a big arm around her and pulled her close against his side. She snuggled in with her head on his broad chest.

"I hate when they go." He idly stroked a hand down the bare skin of her arm.

"I noticed." She brushed a kiss on the hot, muscled flesh just above his left nipple.

Smoothing her hair out of the way, he trailed a finger along the side of her throat. "But I could get used to having more time like this with you, to being able to kiss you on the back deck without thinking about who might be watching."

I don't care who might be watching, she thought as frustration welled within her. *I don't care who knows about you and me. I want Nic and Nat to know that we have something good together. I really do. And we need to talk about that.*

Stacking her hands on his chest, she rested her chin on them, captured his gaze—and had absolutely no idea where to start.

I want more from you, Dante.

Ugh.

You could kiss me on the back deck whenever you wanted if we just tell the girls that we're more than friends.

No.

Where are we going, you and I, Dante?

Yuck.

It all sounded pitiful and needy and wrong inside her own head.

Clearly, more thought was required before she broached this particular subject with him.

He pressed his palm to her cheek. "What is it?"

Nope. Not going there. Not until she'd at least figured out what she wanted to say.

"This." Lifting up, she pressed her mouth to his.

He made a low, pleasured sound against her parted lips and dipped his tongue inside.

After that, they didn't need words.

A good thing, too, because she sure hadn't found the right ones yet.

With the girls gone, they did have more time alone together. In the next week, they spent two lunchtimes in her bed. And on Monday and Wednesday, when neither of them had to work at night, they shared dinner on the deck and she stayed the night at his house.

Thursday morning before she left him to get ready to open at the Sea Breeze, he asked her if maybe she could get Saturday night off. "I want to take you to dinner."

Her heart soared.

A date. An actual date. Out in public where anyone might see them.

This was progress, right?

But then he added, "I know this great seafood place on the river in Astoria."

Her soaring heart crashed and burned.

Astoria. Of course. Where the chances were pretty small they would ever run into anyone they knew.

Yeah. It was time. She needed to find the damn words, to tell him what she wanted from him.

However. An actual date was a step in the right direction. She decided to be glad about that.

"I'll check with Ingrid," she said.

Ingrid gave her the night off. She and Dante had dinner out like any regular couple. It was a good night. They laughed and talked about their families and their jobs. They shared a dessert and whispered together the way people in actual relationships do. And then they went back to his house and he gave her lots of deep kisses and more than one orgasm.

The next week, it was pretty much the same. They got together whenever both of their schedules allowed. She loved every minute she had with him. She didn't want anything to change.

She just wanted to *not* be a secret. Yeah. That would do it for her for now.

That Friday, she had the closing shift at the Sea Breeze and she slept nice and late on Saturday morning.

Nicole and Natalie arrived while she was still sleeping.

They woke her the same way they had the day they left—with giggles at her front door. She let them and Owen in. They stayed for an hour, laughing and chattering, bringing her up-to-date on their lives in Portland and their trip to Wings and Waves Waterpark, which had a giant wave pool and the coolest tube slides ever.

Then Dante appeared. He hustled them off to their grandmother's house for a barbecue.

After they left, Grace sat on the old sofa in the cabin and tried not to feel hurt that Dante hadn't invited her to go with them. Because how could he invite her? If Dante took her to a Santangelo family get-together, everyone would start wondering if the two of them were more than friends.

Well, they *were* more than friends. A lot more, at least as far as she was concerned.

And it wasn't working for her that he didn't seem willing to actually acknowledge that.

With a groan, she bent forward and put her head in her hands. Really, she had no right to go blaming Dante for not giving her what she hadn't even asked for. She needed to stop being a big baby about this, to either tell him she wanted to change the rules, or let it be and enjoy the ride for as long as it lasted.

Up until this thing with Dante, she'd always been an enjoy-the-ride kind of girl.

Not anymore, though.

She wanted to *be* with him and she wanted the world to know that she was his and he was hers.

Never, ever had she felt this way before.

And it really brought her spirits down that he seemed perfectly happy to keep things just as they were.

Sunday, the girls came over about noon. She went back to the main house with them and Dante fixed lunch for the four of them. Then she was treated to a karaoke performance that included just about every Disney song ever written.

Too soon, it was time to pack up the truck again. Dante would drive the girls to meet their mother, come back home just long enough to change clothes and then head for the station house, dropping Owen at the dog sitter's on the way.

Gracie hugged the girls goodbye and waved as they drove off. Missing them already, she decided to cheer herself up by going to dinner at Daniel's.

At the house on Rhinehart Hill, she played with her nieces and nephews, spent some time with her sisters and just generally felt better about everything with her family around her. She didn't see Dante until the next morning.

She was lying in bed, half-awake, at a little after seven, thinking of getting up and making some coffee when he tapped on her door. "Gracie?"

Of course, her hopeless heart beat faster and she couldn't stop the happy smile that spread over her face. "Coming!" She rolled out of bed and went to let him in.

"There you are." He looked at her with those melty dark eyes and suddenly nothing else in the world mattered as much as the fact that he was standing there on her front step, in jeans and a T-shirt, his hair still wet from a shower.

"Did you just get home from work?"

He nodded. "God. You look good."

"Please. I look like the bed I just rolled out of."

"You're beautiful." He stepped over the threshold, crowding her backward.

"Just come right on in, why don't you?"

"Thanks. I will." He reached for her. Wrapping a big arm around her waist, he pulled her up close. "I've been thinking all night about getting my hands on you." His mouth came down on hers before she had a chance to warn him about morning breath.

And really, morning breath? Who cares? Nothing mattered but his kiss and his arms so tight around her—that, and getting prone.

Or maybe up against the wall.

Or straddling him on the sofa...

He had her cami and sleep shorts off in seconds flat as she tore at his shirt and whipped off his belt. It took him a moment to get out of his boots and socks. And then he shoved down his jeans and boxers and he was every bit as naked as she was.

They fell on each other, moaning.

The next hour went by in a hot haze of pleasure. Even in a one-room cabin, there were so many surfaces to explore. They ended up in the bed, their arms wrapped around each other.

As her heartbeat settled into a slower rhythm, she nipped the side of his neck and whispered, "Coffee. I need it. Now."

He held her closer. "No. I want you here."

She laughed and playfully shoved at his broad, bare chest. Reluctantly, he let her go. Bracing his head on his hand, he watched, grinning, as she darted around grabbing her rumpled cami and sleep shorts off the floor and yanking them back on.

She was at the kitchen counter loading up the coffee maker when he came up behind her and eased his warm arms around her again.

Smoothing her hair back, he nuzzled her neck.

"I came by last night before I went to work, but missed you," he said in her ear.

"I went to Sunday dinner at Daniel's."

He caught her earlobe between his teeth and teased at it lightly, causing a cascade of shivers to skate down her neck and over her jaw. "Were Aly and Connor there?"

"Mmm-hmm."

"They warn you off me?"

She pushed the brew button and turned in his hold. He'd pulled on his jeans, which hung a little low without his belt, revealing V-lines a fitness model might envy. She stuck her thumbs in the belt loops on either side of his hard hips and tugged him a fraction closer. "You were not mentioned. By either your sister or my brother."

He guided a swatch of hair behind her ear, his eyes kind of guarded. "What about your aunt Daffodil?"

"What about her?"

"Was she there?"

"Yeah." She looked at him sideways. "Why?"

His shrug was too offhand. "At Aly and Connor's party three weeks ago, Daffy and Percy sat with me and the girls. Daffy mentioned you, said she was trusting me to treat you right. I got the impression she'd noticed that I couldn't keep my eyes off you."

It pleased her no end to picture him blowing his cover because he couldn't stop staring at her. "Aunt Daffy's a very perceptive woman."

"Did she say anything to you last night—about us? Give you any strange looks?"

"Nope. We shared a hug when I got there and she didn't say a word about you. As for strange looks she might have sent my way, I didn't see any." And this seemed like the perfect moment to make her position clear on this subject. "The truth is, I don't really care what anyone says about you and me, Dante. And I don't care what they know, either."

He ran a slow finger down the side of her neck and then outward to her shoulder, where he idly fiddled with the lace strap of her cami. "The way I see it, if Daffy and Aly and Connor and every-one else in town have decided to just keep their mouths shut about us, that works for me."

A sharp spike of irritation twisted in her stom-ach at his words. Okay, yeah. He was a very pri-vate man. But she was so tired of being his sexy little secret—or if not a secret, something no one was supposed to talk about.

It was way past time she made her position clear.

But she really didn't want to get into some deep discussion about where they were "going" and how she wanted "more" from him than he'd said he could give. She'd been racking her brain to come up with a light, evenhanded approach to this issue.

And then, as she stood there at the counter with him so close she could melt right into him, it came to her—the perfect way to find out what she needed to know. "So I've been thinking…"

He lowered his head a fraction. Those fine lips hovered just inches from hers. "I really love the way you think."

Maybe not about this, though. "You know, there's a family dinner at Daniel's pretty much every Sunday. We all have an open invitation."

He tipped up her chin with a finger and brushed his mouth across hers. "I'm aware." He kissed her again. "You taste so good. I can never get enough of you. Let's go back to bed."

She slipped her thumbs from his belt loops and pressed her hands against his beautiful, bare chest. "Dante, listen to me."

The sex fog in his dark eyes cleared a little and

a tiny frown drew down between his thick black eyebrows. "I'm listening."

She stared up at him, keeping her gaze steady and true. "I want you to come with me next Sunday to Daniel's for the Bravo family dinner."

He blinked, a dead giveaway. She knew she wouldn't like whatever he said next. She was right. He stepped back an inch or so. "Gracie. If I go to Daniel's with you, they're all going to think we're together."

Because we are together.

That little spike of annoyance in her belly? All at once, it was a spear shoved clean through her. "So then, that's a no?"

"I thought we had an agree—"

"Just say it, please."

"Gracie..."

"Say it."

"No. I think it's a bad idea. I think we really need to keep things—"

"Shh." She stopped his words with the gentle touch of her fingers to his lips. "I understand," she said softly. "You don't need to say another word."

"We did agree from the first—"

"Yes, we did. I get it. It's fine." Lifting on tiptoe, she replaced her fingertips with her open mouth.

It was a wet kiss, a long kiss, slow and hot and full of sexual promise, a kiss that said everything he needed to know at that moment. Everything about right now.

And nothing more.

Because right now was what they had and he didn't want more.

Okay, yeah. Maybe she ought to do the adult thing—communicate. Maybe she should talk it out with him, tell him what her sisters had said to tell him, that she needed more or she was moving on.

But ultimatums weren't her style. And it was all just too sad and depressing. Not to mention, it hurt. A lot. She'd been agonizing over this for weeks now. The longing had kind of worn her down. It just shouldn't be this hard with a guy, should it?

But it *was* hard. The hardest thing ever.

And she knew why.

She felt so much for him. More than for Joey or Randy in high school. More than for Niall or Keegan or Paolo. She might as well just admit it—to herself, at least.

She'd fallen in love with this man.

And that scared her to death. Especially now

she fully understood that her love was going no-where.

She'd fallen in love with Dante Santangelo and he didn't want anything more than great sex for as long as it lasted—oh, and her friendship. He wanted that, too.

And she wanted *his* friendship. Maybe. Eventually. If she ever got over him.

She just saw no point in humiliating herself. He'd made it way clear he wouldn't let her—or anyone—in. He was never going to the love place.

"Gracie…" He said her name with real feeling. With need and affection, with searing desire. Like she was everything to him, like she carried his heart inside her, precious, cherished. Protected. Safe.

Yeah, it was a lie, but such a perfect, beautiful lie. She needed to indulge that lie.

One last time.

Scooping her up, he took her back to the bed and laid her down on the tangled sheets.

She reached up her arms to him, twined them around his neck and pulled him down to her, so close. So tender. So exactly right.

Just the way a last time ought to be.

When he came into her, she rocked him slow and sweet, legs and arms locked around him, feeling him within her, so hot and deep, as their kiss went on and on. He tasted of wonder and pleasure and all the love he refused to give her.

But it was beautiful, anyway. He gave what he could. And as she moved with him, so tight, so close, she knew he had no idea that she was letting him go.

Afterward, she cooked him eggs with sausage. She made sourdough toast with marionberry jam. As they ate, she asked him about his work schedule.

"I'm off for the rest of the day," he said, and she knew he was filling her in on his schedule so they could figure out when and how they might next hook up. "I'm going to get some sleep. And I told my dad I would help him haul some stuff to the dump. So there goes my afternoon."

"Your mom'll want you to stay for dinner."

"Probably." His eyes made promises she wasn't going to be available to help him keep. "But I'll be home by eight, eight thirty. How 'bout you?"

She sipped her coffee and then shook her head. "I promised Cassie and Erin I'd be over for dinner. We tend to run late when we get together."

Now he was looking rueful. "Tomorrow, I'm pulling a twelve-hour shift. Six a.m. to six p.m."

"And I've got to work tomorrow night."

"That's inconvenient."

She gave him a little nod for an answer.

"I'll miss you." He said it tenderly.

She replied in kind. "I'll miss you, too." And she would.

So very much.

The next evening, Dante picked up Owen from the sitter and got home at six thirty.

He'd had an hour free at lunch and sent Gracie a text hoping maybe they could steal a little time at the cabin. She'd never texted back. And by now, she would be mixing drinks at the Sea Breeze.

Tomorrow, he didn't go in until four in the afternoon, so he had a good chance of seeing her tomorrow morning—late, so she could get enough sleep.

As he unlocked his front door, he was thinking he would send her another text just to check in, make sure everything was okay with her. There had been that rough moment yesterday, when she'd invited him to Sunday dinner at Daniel's and he'd turned her down.

She'd seemed okay afterwards, though.

More than okay. She'd kissed him and that had led to another totally satisfying interval in bed. She'd even made him breakfast after and he'd been reassured that they were back on the same page about everything.

He pushed the door inward. That was when he saw the plain white envelope on the floor. It had his name on it. He bent to pick it up as Owen went around him, headed for the kitchen.

When he peeled back the flap, he found a single folded sheet of paper and the key to the cabin.

Chapter Eleven

Dante,
When this crazy, wonderful thing started
with us, we agreed it would last until one of
us called it off. And that's what this is—me,
calling it off. Thank you for the cottage. I've
loved living there. You really came through
when I needed a hand. Take care.
Gracie

His gut twisting and his heart beating a ragged
rhythm under his breastbone, Dante stood in the
open doorway and read the note through five times.

Take care?

That was it?

That was all he got?

After everything they'd had, she thought she could just scribble a quick note and give back the key?

He stuck the key in his pocket and whipped out his phone to call her and tell her in no uncertain terms that a damn note wasn't enough. Not by a long shot. They needed to talk.

They needed to work this out. She couldn't just run away like some irresponsible kid. She couldn't just...

The indignant thought died unfinished.

Because damn it, yes. She could. Those *were* the terms. He'd set them. He'd *agreed* with them. He'd really thought the terms were a good idea at the time, reasonable and clear. So simple and forthright.

He was an idiot.

And he should have known, shouldn't he?

Yesterday morning, when she'd asked him to Daniel's, he should have recognized the invitation for what it was, should have understood that she was saying she wanted more.

Should have figured out that if he turned her down, he very well might lose her.

His hand was shaking. *Both* hands. He glanced

from one to the other, ordering the shaking to stop and the aching emptiness in his chest to fill up with acceptance.

But acceptance was not happening.

Crumpling her note into a tight little ball, he let it fall to the floor. He dropped his phone on the entry table and went to the living area, where he flopped down on the sofa and shut his eyes.

There was no point in calling her. She'd made her position crystal clear, given him exactly what they'd agreed on.

A tidy, easy ending. No drama. Quick and clean.

He should be grateful. It was just about the best end he could have hoped for.

If only he was ready for it to end.

If only he hadn't started to doubt that he'd *ever* be ready to have Gracie walk away from him.

He lay there with his eyes closed, wishing he could just fall asleep and forget everything.

Didn't happen. Several minutes crept by.

And then Owen whined and licked the back of his hand.

He got up, fed the dog, made a sandwich and ate it standing at the kitchen window, looking out at the graveled driveway that wound into the evergreens and the cabin, barely visible back in the trees.

Owen whined at him again. The dog sat by his left foot, gazing up at him hopefully.

"She's gone," he said flatly. "She moved out today—apparently."

Another whine, the sound somehow more hopeful than ever.

"What? You need to go over there and see for yourself?"

That brought a short bark in the affirmative and three hard smacks of Owen's tail against the floor.

"Okay, then. Have it your way." He turned for the slider, Owen right behind him.

When they reached the cabin, he almost changed his mind. He didn't want to go in there and see all the ways she'd left him behind.

But then Owen whined at him again and he stuck the key in the lock.

Inside, it was pretty much as he expected. Her bed was gone. So was the chest of drawers she'd brought with her. The drawers of the other bureau were empty. No sexy satin and pretty lace, no naughty pleasure toys.

She'd cleaned out the fridge and taken the food she'd bought from the cupboards. The bathroom still smelled faintly of her bodywash and shampoo, but the medicine cabinet was empty.

When he returned to the main room, Owen was

curled up in the doggy bed she'd bought for him, his long face resting on his favorite chew toy. He looked up at Dante without lifting his head, his caramel eyes glum and faintly accusing.

"I don't even know where she went," he said to the dog, who just closed his eyes and chuffed out a heavy sigh. "Maybe back to Daniel's..."

Not that it mattered. Wherever she was, she didn't want him there. She'd made her point and he needed to let her go.

And he would. He'd get on with his life and let her get on with hers.

Alternately furious and bleakly resigned, Dante somehow managed to get through that night, the next day and eight hours of work.

He got home at three in the morning and tried to sleep. Mostly, he stared at the dark ceiling overhead and punched at his pillow a lot, trying to get comfortable, trying not to think of silver-blond hair, sea-blue eyes, a wicked laugh and sweet pink lips.

There was no point in going after her. He had nothing to offer her. He was set in his ways, not going to change, didn't have whatever it took to make the love thing work. The best thing he could do for her was to leave her the hell alone.

But at nine that morning, as he stared out the window over the sink, sipping coffee without really tasting it, he finally broke.

He called her.

It went straight to voicemail.

Miserable, disbelieving and angry that she wouldn't even take his damn call, he barked out a message.

Grace sat at the kitchen table in the cottage she now shared with Harper and Hailey, who had left at a little after eight to head over to the Valentine Bay Theater where they would be staging their next theatrical extravaganza.

The phone was right there on the table beside her. She watched it light up with Dante's name and she sent it to voicemail. Maybe he would leave a message, maybe not.

When the voicemail icon appeared and the phone gave an annoying beep, she set down her coffee cup and shifted her gaze to stare blindly at the cupboards above the sink. It hurt so much, being away from him.

She missed him—missed everything about him. The cloves-and-cedar scent of his skin, his reluctant smile, the proud jut of his strong cheekbones. His touch and his voice and his kisses...

It was awful, this being in love with Dante. Leave it to her to fall for a man who claimed outright he was bad at relationships and wouldn't be having one ever again.

She didn't want to talk to him and she wasn't going to talk to him. No way. There was no point. Rising, she refilled her coffee cup. For a minute or two, she stood at the counter, glaring at her phone, waffling about whether to check that voicemail or not.

Her constant longing for the mere sound of his voice won out. She took her cup back to the table and autodialed her voicemail.

His message was short and straight to the point. "What the hell, Gracie? We need to talk." He sounded really pissed.

Which was in no way her problem.

For another three or four minutes, she sat there stewing—aching to call him back, reminding herself that she'd already decided she wouldn't.

Finally, she gave in to her own hopeless longing and texted him. I've moved in with my sisters. She typed in the address of the cottage. I'm here until 2 p.m. You're welcome to stop by.

His response was instantaneous: On my way.

"Great," she muttered angrily, her silly heart beating so fast she imagined it leaping into her throat and right out her mouth, hitting the floor with a wet slapping sound, then flopping around desperately like a landed fish.

He would be here any minute.

Jumping up, she ran to her bedroom. Stripping out of her sleep shorts and Reed College T-shirt, she ran for the bathroom, where she brushed her teeth, splashed water on her face, put on deodorant and mascara and combed her hair.

What to wear?

God. Was she pathetic or what?

She did know him, after all. This wasn't a reunion. He was going to get all up in her grill about the way she'd left him and then remind her that it was all for the frickin' best.

Really, why did she have to go and fall in love with him? There were good guys in the world who actually *wanted* someone to love and cherish and bring home to the family.

She needed…sexy underwear.

Even though there was no way he was going to see it. He could crawl on his knees across a sea of broken glass swearing to love her forever, vowing never to leave her in a million years and to accompany her to dinner at Daniel's this coming Sunday—and he still wasn't getting a look at what she had under her clothes.

Not today, anyway.

It took a good three minutes of pawing around in her lingerie suitcase to decide on the perfect pair of lace-trimmed cobalt-blue satin cheekies and the bra to match. She put on the undies and then went to the dresser to whip out her best secret weapon: the faded, tattered jean shorts that showed way more than they should every time she bent over. Paired with a too-tight T-shirt and brass-riveted flip-flops with a cute bowtie detail, she was ready to face the emotionally unavailable man of her dreams.

And pigtails. Dante couldn't get enough of her in pigtails. And he wasn't going to get enough. In fact, he was getting *nothing* of her.

Not today.

She zipped back into the bathroom and braided her hair.

The front door buzzer sounded just as she snapped the elastic around the tail of the second braid. She smoothed her too-tight T-shirt and went to let him in.

One look at him standing there outside the door of the screened porch and all her false bravado fled. He looked tired. And sad.

And that broke her heart even worse than having to leave him because she wanted more and he wouldn't go there.

She pushed open the door.

He didn't step forward, but just stood there on the step looking her up and down. When he finally met her eyes again, she felt the pull of him so strongly. Her belly hollowed out and everything inside her burned.

"Now, that's just cruel." His voice was deliciously rough and low.

She flipped one of her pigtails back over her shoulder. "Yeah. Sorry. I was feeling kind of bitter. A little sexual torture seemed like a good idea."

He almost smiled. But not quite. "Let me in so we can talk?"

She considered his request. The thing was, she wanted him so much and there were beds and a couch in the house—not to mention all manner of other possible surfaces where they might get up to stuff she wasn't going to do with him. "How about a walk on the beach?"

He stuck his hands in the pockets of his black jeans and nodded. "Yeah. That'd be good."

Much like Dante's house and the cabin she missed a lot, the cottage was perched on a hill above a section of beach. She led him along the trail that led to the edge of the cliff and then down in a series of switchbacks to the sand.

He took off his boots and socks and rolled the

cuffs of his jeans. She slipped off her sandals. They went on across the sand until they reached the shore where the cold, foamy edges of the waves lapped at their toes.

It was nice, for a minute or two, just walking together along the wet sand, a gentle wind blowing, the air misty and cool. She wished he would take her hand—and then reminded herself that if he did, she would only pull away.

Finally, stopping and turning to face her, he got down to it. "I didn't want you to go. You know that, right?"

She pressed her lips together and gave him a nod.

"You just up and left—out of nowhere. I think I deserved more than a six-sentence note. Seriously, Gracie. The least you could have done was to break the news to me in person."

She really saw no other way to answer him but with brutal honesty. He deserved that. And so did she. "Dante, I'm in love with you." There. She'd said it. Too bad he flinched at the L-word, as though she'd slapped his face. "Don't look so shocked. You're here and you wanted to know, so I'm telling you. I love your daughters and I'm crazy about Owen. And I am in love with you."

"Gracie..." He started to reach for her.

She whipped up both hands, palms out. "Don't. Please."

He sucked in a slow breath through his nose and let his arm drop back to his side.

She made herself go on. "The thing is, I've never actually been in love before and I know I've handled this badly. But, um, we had a deal and you have made it painfully clear that, when it comes to love, you don't want to go there. You don't want a relationship. You don't want *more*." She lifted her hands and stacked them over her heart. "I do. I want it all with you. But I didn't ask for it all. I just wanted a step. That first step. I thought dinner at Daniel's could be that step, but maybe that was too much for you. If not, and I misjudged you and you're actually more willing than I believed, then please. Tell me what step you're willing to take. How far you're willing to go to get closer to me. Tell me your first step and we can take it from there."

"Gracie…" He looked stunned. Stricken. Totally wrecked.

"What?" Her voice had gone pleading now. "Just tell me. Just say it."

He swallowed, hard. "Thank you, for telling me."

She waited. But he said nothing more. "That's

it? That's all I get." It hurt, stabbed her to the heart all over again, to declare her love to him and have him dish out a reluctant thank-you in response. "You know what? There's no point in this. I want more and you don't and that's kind of the end of it, wouldn't you say?"

"You're right." His voice was so low, she wouldn't have heard him if she hadn't been staring directly at him. "I'll go." And then he turned on his heel and started walking.

She stood in sea foam, watching him stride away from her across the sand.

That day, Dante did something he'd never done before, something of which he did not in any way approve.

Though there was nothing physically wrong with him, he called in sick.

He called in sick and then he sat in the house and thought about Gracie. When he started to feel like the walls were closing in, he took a beer out on the deck. He sat at the table, with Owen moping at his feet, and thought about Gracie some more.

The next day, he called in again.

That day, he did exactly what he'd done the day before. It was just him and Owen, in the house or on the deck. He stared into space with Gracie on his mind.

Saturday, he was just about to call in a third time when he somehow managed to stop himself in the act of picking up his phone.

He still had *some* self-respect, after all, a little kernel of it, deep inside. He had C Watch that night and damn it, when the time came, he was going to work.

It started raining at around ten that morning, a drizzly, gray, lackluster kind of rain. He stood at the slider and watched it dribble down from the sky and wondered what was wrong with him, really.

Something definitely was. Gracie had said she loved him and he'd said thank you and walked away.

The more he thought about that, the more he despised himself.

He'd always considered himself a good man, one who did the right thing, a guy who stepped up when action was called for, did his part no matter how tough the challenge. Not some tongue-tied idiot who turned and ran the minute shit got real.

This was so bad.

He missed Gracie so much. He couldn't stop thinking of her, of her big heart and smart mouth, of the way she'd stood there so proudly and said it right out loud: *Dante, I'm in love with you.*

It was driving him crazy. *She* was driving him crazy. He'd never felt this way before.

Yeah, it had been hard when Marjorie left. He'd missed her and the girls. He'd regretted that he'd failed so miserably at his marriage, been ashamed that he hadn't been able to make it work. But that had been nothing compared to this. He felt like Gracie had ripped his heart out, stuffed it in a suitcase and hauled it off along with her when she went.

When Marjorie left, he'd had no urge to break things.

Now? Oh, he did have that urge and it was powerful—to start grabbing random objects and throwing them at the nearest wall. The big ceramic bowl on the coffee table, for instance. It would make a very satisfying crash that would send shards flying everywhere if he hurled it at, say, the fireplace...

He was sitting on the sofa, staring at that bowl, reminding himself that breaking stuff was juvenile, messy and completely pointless, when the doorbell rang.

"Go away," he muttered to whoever was out there and continued glaring at the bowl.

The doorbell rang again. And then there was knocking.

It gave Dante a certain dark satisfaction to just sit there and contemplate that bowl.

Whoever it was went away—or so he thought until he heard knocking on the slider. Resigned, he glanced over his shoulder to see who it was: Connor, with a what-is-your-problem expression on his face. Owen was already over there, whining hopefully at the door.

Dante didn't want to talk to Connor. Or to anyone, for that matter.

But Connor had that look, the one that said he wasn't going anywhere and Dante might as well give up and open the damn door.

He dragged himself upright and went to the slider. "Yeah?" he demanded through the glass.

Connor just waited, with the rain dripping down on him.

Dante pulled the damn door open. "What's this about?"

"Let me in. We need to talk."

"What about?"

"Stop being an idiot or I'll be forced to beat some sense into you. God knows you probably deserve it."

Apprehension clutched at his gut and tightened the skin at the back of his neck. "Is Gracie okay?"

"She's fine—no thanks to you. And it's wet out here." Connor stepped forward.

Dante cleared the doorway and let him pass. "You want coffee?"

"Is it made?" Connor raked his damp hair back, swiping raindrops off his forehead in the process.

"Only takes a minute."

"Sure, whatever." Connor pulled out a chair at the table and Dante went over and brewed him a cup.

Neither of them said a word until Dante set a full mug in front of Connor and took the chair across from him.

Then Connor commanded, "Talk."

Dante eyed him warily. "There is no point in—"

"Talk."

A stare down ensued.

Dante dropped his gaze first. "How much do you know?"

Connor rubbed at the space between his eyes, like maybe Dante was giving him a headache or something. "She called Liam Monday." Liam was fourth-born in the Bravo family, a year younger than Connor. "She asked if she could borrow a truck the next day. So, Tuesday, while you were at work apparently, Liam, Harper and Hailey helped her pack up her stuff and haul it all to the cottage.

"Tuesday night, Liam called me. He explained about moving Gracie to the cottage and asked what was going on. He said it was obvious she was wrecked about something, but she wouldn't say squat about it and Hailey and Harper wouldn't talk, either. So last night, I stopped by the Sea Breeze for a beer on the way home from work—or that was the pretense, anyway. Really, I just wanted to check on Gracie, see how she was doing. She wouldn't tell me anything, either. But I'm guessing you broke my beautiful, sweet baby sister's heart and so here I am to find out what is the matter with you." He knocked back a slug of caffeine and set down the mug. "I'll say it again. Talk."

"There's nothing to say."

Connor was absorbed in an intense study of his coffee mug. "Talk."

"I'm not…what she needs. And she left. And now it's just me and the dog and both of us are miserable."

"But you sent her away, right?"

"I didn't. No. She left. She left because there were things she wanted that I couldn't give her."

"Couldn't? Or wouldn't?"

"Fine. Wouldn't. Happy now?"

"Not about this. Why?" Connor demanded.

"Why what?"

Connor shot him a glance of pure exasperation. "If you're not willing to give my sister what she needs, why are you miserable that she left?"

Dante shook his head. "There is no point in talking about this."

"Answer the question."

"Because I feel empty. I'm lonely, I'm sad and I hate it."

"You hate what?"

"Being here without her. It's bad, okay. It's no good at all. I mean, I just don't get this. I hate this. I've got all these damn *feelings* and I don't know what to do with them."

"Yeah, well. It's never a great idea to throw away what you want the most."

"I did not throw Gracie away."

"Yeah, Dante. You kind of did."

"You don't get it."

"Well, one of us is clueless. And it's not me. Dante, we've been best friends on and off for as long as I can remember. I know you better than you think. You're a good man, the best. But you've got way too much pride. You think things ought to be a certain way and you don't like feeling out of control. I remember when you got together with Marjorie. She is such a nice woman. No drama, no conflict. You said she was perfect, but what you really meant was she was *safe*. She wasn't going to make you feel the way your dad's always felt about your mom, the way I feel about your sister—all hot and bothered and out of control. You really thought you'd dodged a bullet with Marjorie, didn't you?"

Dante was thinking that punching Connor in the face just might be more satisfying than throwing a bowl at the fireplace. "What exactly are you getting at?"

Connor had the balls to chuckle. "Gracie. She's not safe and she's not always going to do things your way. But she *is* the one for you."

Dante scoffed. "The *one*?"

"That's right. Now you finally know what it's like. Welcome to the real thing, Dante. Love. It's finally happened for you."

After Connor left, Dante decided to stop moping around the house. He went out and bought groceries, took Owen for a run on the beach and then headed over to the gym for an hour. He had dinner with his parents and his second-youngest brother, Marco.

And then he went to work. It was a busy Saturday night with a couple of robberies to deal with and a nasty domestic that had almost turned tragic. He had no time for brooding on whether or not true love had finally caught up with him in the form of a gorgeous blonde with a wicked sense of humor and zero willingness to put up with his crap.

Sunday, he went through the motions of living all over again. Monday was the same. The week went on like most weeks do.

It was Friday before he began to accept that he was not going to get the woman he loved by just getting up and getting through each day like some wimpy little dweeb.

A real move would have to be made.

He spent the weekend figuring out exactly what that move should be.

Monday was Gracie's first in-service day at Valentine Bay High. School was starting the day after Labor Day and that meant she had essentially one week to get her classroom student ready. At the same time, she had to attend a raft of meetings— OSHA, first aid, departmental, new-teacher orientation. Some of those meetings seemed to drag on forever. Between the meetings, there was the mad scramble to get her room in order. There was too much to do and not enough time to do it in. The upside? The work overload kept her from dwelling on how much she missed a certain stubborn, impossible man.

Love was hard. Especially when you felt torn in two—your brain telling you it just wasn't going to work out while your heart screamed to hold on, never give up!

Her heart just wouldn't quit hoping. Every night since she left him, she would lie there in bed in the dark, her whole body aching, just kind of burning up from inside with the love that Dante wouldn't let her give him.

She needed to forget him.

But she knew that wasn't going to be happening anytime soon. Her job was to keep a reasonably good attitude, put one foot in front of the other and get through each day.

As she drove back to the cottage that Monday afternoon, she reminded herself that she needed to focus on the good things—on the sunshiny day after the gray, rainy weekend, on her first real job as a teacher at last.

"Good things," she whispered under her breath as she turned onto the tree-shaded driveway that led up to the cottage. "Good things…"

The cottage came into view—along with Dante's crew cab in the cleared space where she and her sisters parked their vehicles. The man himself, in dark-wash jeans and a crisp blue button-down, sat on the front step in the thick shade of the tall trees.

For a terrifying moment, she was certain she must be imagining him, that her hopeful, yearning heart had her seeing the impossible.

She blinked three times in rapid succession. He was still there, his expression a little apprehensive, so handsome that just looking at him twisted the knife of longing within her all over again.

Her frantic heart beating so loud she couldn't hear herself think, she realized she'd stopped breathing. "Breathe, now," she whispered, "just breathe," as she carefully guided her Toyota into the empty spot beside the pickup and turned off the engine.

She had stacks of stuff to carry in, but her hands were shaking and her body felt strangely numb. If she tried to carry her big tote and her laptop and the ream and a half of paperwork, it would probably all end up on the ground.

So, then. Later for that.

With slow deliberation, she pushed open her door and swung her rubbery legs to the ground. They wobbled a little when she stood, but it was okay. She could do this.

Dante was already on his feet. She started toward him, her eyes tracking right and left—anywhere but directly at him.

Which was cowardly. Weak.

And she was not weak.

She needed to face him, to look directly at him. Whatever she saw when she looked in his eyes would tell her everything. Maybe more than she wanted to know.

A certain calm descended.

She paused in midstep and made herself meet his eyes.

That was all it took. Just one look in those dark, hungry eyes of his.

One look, and she knew.

"Gracie." He said her name like it was everything to him, like *she* was everything.

She took three more steps and stopped maybe two feet away from him. He reached for her hand. She gave it.

Oh, that moment. She would hold it in her heart for all of her life. The moment his strong fingers wrapped around hers, the first time he touched her after she knew that he had figured it out.

He finally understood. She was his and he was hers and that was how it was going to be. Now. Tomorrow. For all the days to come.

"It's nice out here," she said, and realized her

knees were kind of wobbly all over again. "Can we sit down?"

"Sure." Keeping a firm grip on her hand, he dropped back to the step. She sat down beside him.

A lovely sense of unreality assailed her. Was this actually happening?

Fear crept in.

Did she have it all wrong? Had she totally misread the promise she'd seen in his eyes?

There was a simple way to find out.

She straightened her shoulders and made herself ask him, "So then, next Sunday? Dinner with the Bravo family up at Daniel's house?"

He leaned in until there was barely an inch between his lips and hers. "God, yes." He said it prayerfully, a sacred trust between the two of them. "I'm in."

A bolt of pure joy blasted through her. This was real. It was happening. She let out the breath she hadn't realized she was holding. "I'm so glad."

His dark gaze scanned her face slowly. With something like reverence. "I love you, Gracie. So much. All my life I've been scared of loving someone the way I love you."

She couldn't help grinning. "You're still scared."

He stared at her, his gaze steady and true. "I'll get over it. As long as you're here to help me deal with all these big emotions you somehow make me feel."

"Big emotions are good," she informed him gently. "You're going to learn to love them."

He made a low sound. It might have been agreement. With maybe just a hint of irony, too. "As long as you're with me."

"I will be. Right here beside you, no matter what. I swear it."

He closed the sliver of distance between them. Their lips met, careful. Hesitant.

At first.

And then his arms came around her. She breathed in his beloved scent of cedar and spice as they shared a kiss full of promises she knew now they were both going to keep.

A cool wind came up, stirring the trees, creating a space between the branches so the late-afternoon sun could reach them. It felt good, the breeze, the brief warmth of sunlight on her upturned face.

She opened her eyes. They shared a long glance of perfect understanding. He wrapped an arm around her and she rested her head on his shoulder.

For the longest time, they sat without speaking, just being there on the front step under the wind-ruffled trees, together.

And then he took her hand again. She straightened enough to meet his waiting eyes.

"Marry me," he said. Before she could answer, he went on, "Don't decide now. I just want you to think about it. Think about it knowing that I want to spend the rest of my life with you and whatever it takes to get there, well, that's what I'm willing to do and..." His voice trailed off. He looked terrified, suddenly. "I'm pushing too fast."

She squeezed his hand. "No, you're not."

"You sure?"

"I am. It's what I want, too. Marriage. To you, Dante. And I just might be getting that urge to do something crazy like drag you to the courthouse right now, today."

"Something crazy sounds pretty damn good to me."

"Except..."

"Except what?" he demanded gruffly.

"I'm thinking we really need to consider how Nicole and Natalie are going to feel before we go taking any major steps."

"They love you almost as much as I do."

"I love them, too. And for their sake, we can't rush things. They need time to adjust. Up till now, they've had you all to themselves. We have to show them that my being in the picture won't threaten what they have with you."

He turned her hand over, spread it open and brought her palm to his warm lips for a sweet, quick brush of a kiss. "Go on."

"I think first, Nic and Nat need to start seeing us as a couple."

"Yeah. I get that."

"They're coming to you this weekend, right?"

"Right."

"Okay, so I want to move back to the cabin before they get here. That's going to be a challenge for me. I've got a full week of meetings and classroom prep at the high school."

His thick eyebrows were suddenly scrunching together. "The moving's no problem. I'll make it happen."

"Then why are you frowning?"

"I was just thinking that what I really want is for you to move into the main house with me."

"Oh, Dante." She pressed her hand to his smooth-shaven cheek. "I want that, too."

"Well, then, why don't you just—"

She silenced him with a finger to his soft lips. "We'll get there. But for the girls' sake, I think we need to start from where we were when they came back two weeks ago. Our mission this visit is to get them to begin seeing us as a couple, while at the same time reassuring them that they are still your priority, that you're no less theirs than you ever were. That you're just...starting to be mine, too."

"Our mission," he said in dazed voice. "We have a damn mission?"

She laughed at his bewilderment. "Yes, we have a mission. And it begins with me at the cabin, everything pretty much as it was when they left two weeks ago, only this visit, we introduce a little hand-holding and some mild PDAs. See how they take it. And then at some point, you have the talk with them, explain to them that we're, um, dating."

"Dating? We're getting married, that's way beyond dating."

She tugged his hand up and over her shoulder so his arm was wrapped around her again. "It might take time, to get Natalie and Nicole comfortable with the idea that we're a couple."

He drew her in closer and dropped a kiss on the top of her head. "Okay, so I'll try to be patient. We'll see how it goes."

"Good." She tipped her head back to look at him, happiness moving through her, filling her up with all the possibilities that came with giving her heart to the right man and knowing that they had their own forever ahead of them. "One way or another, it's all going to work out."

He kissed the end of her nose. "Promise?"

"Yes, Dante." She reached up to clasp the back of his neck and pulled him down for a kiss. "I do."

Epilogue

A little while later, she led him into the cottage and down the hall to her room. She closed the door and engaged the privacy lock so they could share a more intimate celebration of their reunion.

When her sisters got home, Grace explained that she was moving back to the cabin at Dante's place.

Harper asked, "Should we be celebrating?"

Dante hooked his arm around Grace and pulled her close. "She said yes."

Hailey clapped her hands at the news.

Harper grinned. "Congratulations. You're a very lucky man."

Grace warned, "Keep it to yourselves for now.

We need to see how Nicole and Natalie feel about the situation."

Hailey vowed, "We won't tell a soul."

Harper had a bottle of prosecco in the back of the fridge. She popped the cork and they shared a toast to love and happiness. Then Grace packed a bag and followed Dante to his house.

Owen's glum mood vanished the minute Gracie walked in the door. She greeted him with hugs and enthusiastic reassurances that she was home to stay.

The next day, Dante got all of Gracie's stuff moved back to the cabin. Even with her demanding schedule at the high school, she managed to get everything put away before the girls arrived.

On Saturday morning, Dante insisted that Grace go with him to the pickup spot. The second Roger's white minivan rolled to a stop, the girls jumped out and ran back to the crew cab as Grace and Dante got out to greet them. Nobody seemed the least surprised to see her there. Not Nat or Nic— or Marjorie or Roger.

There was a barbecue at the Santangelo grandparents' house that afternoon. Dante invited Grace and she said she would love to come. Dante's mom, Catriona, hugged Grace at the door and then wore a giant smile on her face all through dinner.

As for the girls, they didn't say a word that day

or Sunday about what might be going on between their dad and Gracie. Not even when the four of them went to the Bravo house for Sunday dinner.

But then on Monday morning, Grace woke to a knock on the cabin door. She could hear the twins out there, giggling and chattering together.

She rolled out of bed and went to let them in. "Am I invited for breakfast?"

"Yes!" declared Natalie.

Nic gazed up at her with a strange expression on her face—a little shy, kind of coy. "Gracie?"

"Hmm?"

Nic's cheeks flushed the prettiest shade of red as Nat asked the question for her in a nervous little whisper. "Are you our dad's girlfriend?"

She'd imagined Dante discussing this subject with them first. But it was a direct question, so she answered honestly. "I am, yes." And before she could decide the right thing to say next, the girls started squealing in delight.

The three of them danced around the cabin, laughing and hugging. Then at breakfast, Nicole announced, "We're too old to be flower girls. So when you guys get married, can we be your bridesmaids?"

So much for taking it slow with the girls. Across the table, Dante looked a bit smug. After all, he'd told her the girls would be thrilled to see them together. She nodded at Nat and then at Nic and said she would be honored to have them as her bridesmaids.

Several hours later, at the drop-off point, the twins ran straight to Roger's minivan to inform their mother and stepfather that their dad was going to marry Gracie—and they would be bridesmaids.

Both Marjorie and Roger seemed to take the news in stride. It was almost as if they already knew that something was going on between Marjorie's ex and Grace.

That night, and for every night thereafter, Grace slept in Dante's bed.

In mid-October, he took her out to find the right ring. She chose a diamond solitaire on a platinum band.

And on the second Saturday of the following June, Gracie walked down the aisle to him. When the pastor said he could kiss his bride, Dante lifted her veil gently, reverently. He gathered her into his arms and whispered, "Forever," as he covered her eager mouth with his.

* * * * *

COMING SOON!

We really hope you enjoyed reading this book. If you're looking for more romance, be sure to head to the shops when new books are available on

Thursday 14th May

MILLS & BOON

Coming next month

MARRYING HIS RUNAWAY HEIRESS
Therese Beharrie

'It isn't a boat. It's a gondola.'

'My mistake,' she said blandly, and made him smile. She did that a lot. And he was smiling more than he ever had before. That worried him, too. But it didn't stop him from smiling at her. Or from thinking about how different she was now, when she wasn't thinking about the decision she had to make.

What if she didn't have to make it?

He couldn't pay attention to the thought when the gondolier called for them to get in. He did, using the man's help, then gently nudged him aside to help Elena. She smiled brightly, and it became obvious why he'd wanted to help her. Apparently, he would do anything to get that smile. To keep it there, too.

It stuck as they sat down and the gondola began to float down the canal. It was a bright, sunny day, and the blue green of the water around them sparkled as it stretched between buildings. A gentleman began to sing, rich and deep, and Elena sighed at his side. She snuggled closer, not intentionally, he didn't think, but it made him hold his breath.

That might not have been the right description of it. It was more like someone was squeezing his lungs, so he had less capacity to breathe. He'd felt that way the entire day. When they'd been exploring the stores around St Mark's Square. Or when Elena had insisted on feeding the pigeons, then got alarmed when more and more of them came.

'What is it with you and pigeons?' he'd asked. 'I told you this wouldn't end well.'

'I thought you were exaggerating. You exaggerate.'

'You live in Cape Town, Elena. You've been to the Waterfront. You know what pigeons are like.'

'I thought European pigeons would be different.'

He'd laughed, harder when she hid behind him. She'd ended up giving the bag of seeds to a kid before running away, causing the pigeons to scatter. They'd eaten pasta and chocolate crêpes and taken pictures. Once, Elena had photobombed another couple, then apologised profusely and taken about twenty pictures of them alone to make up for it. Now they were here, on the canal, having someone sing to them.

It was a lot to process. Not the experience, but the emotions that accompanied it. And the thoughts. Those insidious thoughts that had popped into his mind all day, then scurried away before he could put his finger on what they were suggesting. They all pooled together now though, growing into an idea that stole his breath.

It was based on never wanting to see Elena as tortured as she had been the night before. To keep her as happy as she was now, as she had been all day. It was built by the memories of how she'd elevated his business banquet that night in Rome because she fitted so perfectly into his world. She went head to head with him when he did something stupid, forced him to think about the way he treated people, and made him feel more like himself than he ever had. If he'd ever encountered his equal, she was it.

She was it.

'This is so nice,' Elena said at that moment, as if sensing his confusing thoughts. And his body, as if confused itself, responding by putting an arm around Elena's shoulders.

He froze. Until she rested her entire body against him. Then he melted.

It was like the hug from the night before. Warm and comfortable. Except there was more now. She was looking up at him, smiling, and he felt himself stumble. Whatever part of him had been standing steady in the face of the onslaught that Elena was unknowingly waging against him broke down. Whatever sanity he had left that told him not to indulge his ridiculous idea fled.

The proposal spilled out of his mouth.

'Marry me.'

Continue reading
MARRYING HIS RUNAWAY HEIRESS
Therese Beharrie

Available next month
www.millsandboon.co.uk

LET'S TALK
Romance

For exclusive extracts, competitions
and special offers, find us online:

f facebook.com/millsandboon

𝕏 @MillsandBoon

◎ @MillsandBoonUK

Get in touch on 01413 063232

For all the latest titles coming soon, visit
millsandboon.co.uk/nextmonth

MILLS & BOON

THE HEART OF ROMANCE

A ROMANCE FOR EVERY KIND OF READER

MODERN

Prepare to be swept off your feet by sophisticated, sexy and seductive heroes, in some of the world's most glamourous and romantic locations, where power and passion collide.
8 stories per month.

HISTORICAL

Escape with historical heroes from time gone by. Whether your passion is for wicked Regency Rakes, muscled Vikings or rugged Highlanders, awaken the romance of the past.
6 stories per month.

MEDICAL

Set your pulse racing with dedicated, delectable doctors in the high-pressure world of medicine, where emotions run high and passion, comfort and love are the best medicine.
6 stories per month.

True Love

Celebrate true love with tender stories of heartfelt romance, from the rush of falling in love to the joy a new baby can bring, and a focus on the emotional heart of a relationship.
8 stories per month.

Desire

Indulge in secrets and scandal, intense drama and plenty of sizzling hot action with powerful and passionate heroes who have it all: wealth, status, good looks…everything but the right woman.
6 stories per month.

HEROES

Experience all the excitement of a gripping thriller, with an intense romance at its heart. Resourceful, true-to-life women and strong, fearless men face danger and desire - a killer combination!
8 stories per month.

DARE

Sensual love stories featuring smart, sassy heroines you'd want as a best friend, and compelling intense heroes who are worthy of them.
4 stories per month.

To see which titles are coming soon, please visit

millsandboon.co.uk/nextmonth

JOIN US ON SOCIAL MEDIA!

Stay up to date with our latest releases, author
news and gossip, special offers and discounts, and
all the behind-the-scenes action
from Mills & Boon...

 millsandboon

 millsandboonuk

 millsandboon

It might just be true love...